Andrea Clinton

aka

Samirah

Life Knows No Bounds

Volume I:

"1 Who Luvs U More"

*Read a book
and free your
mind*

Ask !!!.

Andrea Clinton

AROUND-THE-WAY PUBLISHING
P.O. BOX 519
EAST ORANGE, NEW JERSEY 07018
AroundTheWaypub@aol.com

THIS BOOK IS A WORK OF FICTION. SO, NAMES, INCIDENTS, CHARACTER, PLACES AND THINGS ARE ALL FICTITIOUS.

FOR INFORMATION ON DISCOUNTS FOR BULK
PURCHASES PLEASE CONTACT US AT:
AROUNDTHEWAYPUB@AOL.COM

COVER & INTERIOR DESIGN BY: ANDREA CLINTON

MANUFACTURED IN UNITED STATES OF AMERICA

ISBN 978-0-9818376-3-5

DEDICATION

Bismillah,

Many thanks go out to my biological babies who aren't really babies any more, my two children **Tunisia-Kamillah** & **Eddie-Yasin**, who were patient with me over the years when I was held up in the writing lab pushing out the many stories that are now coming into fruition. My children are a blessing, and I can not tell you of the many times when an entire day would pass by, and I would look back and feel so guilty that another day had gotten away from us. I was merely lost somewhere out there in space generating and crafting stories to share with the world. But tell that to my conscious.

I am so very proud to have two such articulate and intellectual children. I thank **THE CREATOR** and I thank them much for being in my corner where many others had flipped me the bird for not being who they wanted me to be...

I pray Tunisia Kamillah and Eddie Yasin that you are awarded the highest level of jannah (paradise) for your patience, support and unconditional love; and please remember, when critics critique, anything that I've said and done *right* regarding these writings and other affairs is from ALLAH/GOD, and anything I've done wrong is from me, and may ALLAH, the God of Abraham/Ibrahim, Moses/Musa, Jesus/Isa and Muhammad, forgive me for it, Amin.

Mommy loves you much!!! Muuaaaah!!!

Andrea Clinton

Look for these Novels from the Author in the near future:

REALISM & NATURALISM

LIFE KNOWS NO BOUNDS SERIES
*1 Who Luvs U More
*A Blessing & A Curse
*Where Do We Go From Here
*1 Man is Smoke & The Other is Fire
*Witnesses say Sharrin Killed Slacking Mom

OTHER NOVELS:
*Notes & Messages
*SAKINAH, and her 7
*Walk On By
*Cut From A Different Cloth
*City Boy In a Country World
(Turn them jokers Out!!!)
*Dope Fein Move
*That Alien

SHORT STORY NOVELS
Mother, May I:
*Tripp'n
*Hard Knocks Life
*Bad Mother Syndrome

Men I Know:
(From out the mouths of Men)
*I Don't Like The Black Woman
*...Until The Day She Dies
(I will always love her...)
*She Got Papers on'me!!!
*Darius died, then he Died
*A Man will Adapt
*Ain't I My Brutha's Keepa

SCI-FI NOVELS
When It All Went Down
Them Things That Chase In the Night
Dreams
Maybe I'm Crazy!!!
I was in Love with Him
(Every time they came I jumped, not on the outside, but inside strong)

FANTASY BOOKS:
Reg & Kamalus

SURREAL NOVELS
Mutha Africa
Them & Men
...into The Heart of Men

AUTOBIOGRAPHY
An American Muslimah's Plight
Strange
American Muslimah: Me
Little City

BIOGRAPHY
Clinton Family Ain't No Robinsons

I've spent most of my life writing fiction to escape the harsh realities of this world. On my blog http://around-the-way.blogspot.com/ I ask, as your creative guide that you allow me to take you out of this world and into so many. At times, I write far out fantasies or genuine realities as a mental vacation away from the here and now, which is why most of us read or run out to the movies anyway. I wasn't always interested in sharing my voyages; I felt they were *mine, my* vacation away. But now, I've decided to share those journeys with you, allow you to escape right along with me. We probe these journeys through various genres in fiction. But all attack real life issues, even when they're set in far out genres as Surrealism, Sci-Fi and Fantasy. My goal is always to entertain you while sending a message, so *here's to praying I've done so.*

Andrea Clinton

In loving memory of my family:

My Grandparents
Dorothy Louise Carter
George Clinton, Sr.

My Aunt:
Robbie Montalvo

My Brother
Leeman "Salaam/Peanut" Hicks III

My Step Father:
Leeman Hicks, Jr.

My Clinton Cousins:
Darryl and Donna

My "Dancing" Cousin:
Adrien aka *Abdullah* & brother, Jeff Huggins aka *Mustafa*

My Wlliams Cousins:
Vicky, Neesy, and Sandra

My Uncle:
Roy Bonnor

Nephew
Tywon

A Young Brother I Watched Grow:
Sharuffin (Flip)

And A Brother Like No other
Jameel Swint

Friends:
Sheena & Corky Moore; Trelonda; Mook aka Tijuana Johnson;
K. Williams; Chocolate; Sugar-Bear; Cookie; Ray Davis of P/Funk;

May they all
R.I.P

ACKNOWLEDGMENTS

Many thanks are due to:
Those who supported and/or inspired
Some or any part of my writing endeavors:

Mother, **Gwendolyn Hicks** who always has my back; sister, **Karen Clinton** who was my first audience, love you truly; father, **Tommy Clinton**, and step mother, **Christine Clinton** who was there for me when I was in loss; and my uncle **George Clinton** of *"P/Funk"* for following his dreams, which inspired me to pursue mine; Sister, **Margaret** who inspired some of Alisa' character traits - I love & miss you so much; brother, **Homicide** aka **Dwayne**; Grandpa, **Rev. Irving Carter**; Grandma, **Julius Keaton**; uncle, **Rev. David Carter** who was very insightful; Agent/Author **Eugene Napoleon**; cousin, **Aaron Bonnor** (chill); ex husband, **Dawud Abu Yasin** who pushed me to finish my novels during good times and bad, together or apart, and his/our son **JJ Baskerville** (my heart) and his baby girl **Jaylin**; friend **Sean Blakemore** (from the film *Motives I & II*) who inspired the character Omar with a question he asked (and GOD willing will play him in the stage play or film); friend/sister **Anita** & Brother **Mahmood Ali-Mathis**; ex-Student **Madiyna** and *ALL* others; cousin **Mandell-Tyrone Clinton**; good friend **Safiyyah**; *my family at:* **Master Kevin Thompson's, Shakil's School of Martial Arts,** Ush!; Muslim Sisters: **Nafeesah, Amina, Eman**; Bro. **Isa & Tanya & Edwards family**; Aunt **Dorothy** & Cousin **Maurice**; friends: **Lori Farrell, Renee' Taylor, Tonia Lewis, Karla Barnett-**where are you, **Leah Perry, Faheema, Niki,** and my sister **Najibah** and the **Abdur-Rahman Family**; and Shout Out To My Family: **The Clintons, Carters, Williams, Huggins, Keatons** and **Giles**; and the special person who's given me sound advice, which I pray continues, may ALLAH bless, guide and protect him for it-ameen, **DIAZ**.

The Professors who instructed and inspired me to no end:

Montclair State University
Dr. Paul Arthur; Dr. T. E. Benediktsson; Dr. Jonathan Greenberg; and **Anthony Pemberton, M.F.A.**

Union County College:
Dr. Sondra B. Fishinger; Dr. Shorts; Dr. Maxwell; and **Dr. Hogan.**

Andrea Clinton

Note To Readers:

Bismillah,

I have to say, it took some pondering on my part regarding whether or not I would address the issue of some of the content in this novel. It is not a habit I have of using or insinuating words like: Nigga(z)/Nigger or other vulgarities to include Damn and Hell (out of context). But since my writing is never idle, meaning, its aim is to take the reader somewhere beneficial, I found it necessary to reach into the language chest and snatch out a few undesirable words in an effort to salute realism.

Considering the fragile state of us African Americans on the subject of the use of the word Nigga(z)/Nigger, and the bitterness it brings when used in-house or out, *I apologize if my using this word offends anyone.* Use of this word is to employ language as a tool or device and not to exploit the word as a trend or hidden mockery. I've done no different than authors in the past who've employed the use of the word in their novels to tell of slave times, or of prejudice people spewing hate at blacks, including blacks on blacks. It is not my intention to abuse the word to seem *street* or to be down with the prosecutor, so to speak. It is very unfortunate that this word is so heavy, it's a language of its own.

Had I not thought it would take away what I was trying to do in the story, I would've shown how each and ever time a character heard the word Nigger, they got a veiled pulsation, a hidden vibe that transcends through them just as it does most of us when we hear it. I'm sure some would disagree, especially those of latter generations who use it to no end, but that's because if one uses the word often, they learn to ignore that negative feeling and go with the flow of using it as everyone else around them does. This is something non Blacks do not realize when they attempt to throw Nigger around, and how could they— we've, well younger generations have mastered hiding the feeling the word bares, so how would *anyone* know what we feel in our chest about it?

Regarding the vulgarity I employed, although minimal and heavily inferred, understand the Realism genre is character driven. Focus is on the character and not the plot, etc. So when exhibiting *real* character traits, there are things we writers must institute to convey the character's personality, and in the case of *1 Who Luvs U More*, not including slang, bad language and other misbehaviors would never do.

Peace,

Point 2 Ponder
(Munch on this)

Life is for *living*, not for: wasting time, plotting, planning, or getting too relaxed in your condition or dull tiresome routine. Although life can be stable, *no one should get comfortable in it*. Because life is a cycle, a sequence of events, and if this is so, the seat in life that you presently reside in is a seat on a roller coaster that's always due for some turn or another; and when it makes those sharp turns, it'll drag you, heart pounding and racing, and with you screaming for the ride to stop. But it won't, at least not until life's ready, because **Life Knows No Bounds**.

Just as in real life, after settling their feet in the dirt, the characters in *Life Knows No Bounds* get a subliminal rug snatched from under their feet, and an electric shock to their nerves. It jilts and wakes them providing an un-invited invitation to remodel their lives. Without notice, they're dumbstruck, lost and need to be found, and **THAT'S LIFE**.

Claire: Sad, but that's life Urma: What's life? Claire: A magazine Urma: How much it cost? Claire: $1.00 Urma: But I don't have a $1.00 Claire: Well that's life Urma: What's life? Claire: A magazine Urma: How much it cost? Claire: $1.00 Urma: But I don't have a $1.00 Claire: Well that's life Urma: What's life? Claire: A magazine Urma: How much it cost? Claire: $1.00 Urma: But I don't have a $1.00 Claire: Well that's life Urma: What's life? Claire: A magazine Urma: How much it cost?	Claire: $1.00 Urma: But I don't have a $1.00 Claire: Well that's life Urma: What's life? Claire: A magazine Urma: How much it cost? Claire: $1.00 Urma: But I don't have a $1.00 Claire: Well that's life? Urma: What's life… **Author Unknown, or, maybe it's just** *"Life"*

Andrea Clinton

INTRODUCTION

"Keep talking smack and Imma punch you in ya muthaf—kin' mouth Penny! Keep talkin ho and I swear—I'll tear the roof off this mutha'f—ker!" I said, ironically with the DJ Pumpin', *"Atomic Dog"* in the back ground, and us two cats 'bout to fight.

My mother interrupted me, pulling me back. "Alisa! Calm down. I got this, okay. Please, just calm down."

We were minding our business, when Um Foo-Foo, aka Penny, drove up. She double parked, ignoring the valet, and sashayed into my mother's big birthday bash. My girls, Peaches and Shakirah, caught her at the door and backed her ass right outta there. I was so tired of her always poppin' up and tryin' to compete with me that I followed them out to let her have it. I walked up behind them so she couldn't see me and as soon as we were outside—

"Ummh!" I punched her in the face. But my moms was pulling me back, so I barely got in a hit. But I still knicked her nevertheless. Then Penny got tough, and it was on.

"You ain't sh—t! You ain't sh—t Alisa! You sneakin' people now! Sucka punchin' them? And you can't even land a punch right, dumb ass! **Bring it though,** *bring it!"*

I could spit fire. I was ready to stomp a mud hole in this ho for always trying to prove that she's prettier, sexier, smarter and better than me whenever she got the chance. But I quickly realized this wasn't the place for that. It was my mother's party. And we were in a sophisticated banquet hall. Chandeliers, twinkly white lights, candles, Greek ambiance with off-white drapings and all the fixins. But this hooker had to show up, as usual, just to mess with my head.

My mother kept trying to calm me down. She didn't know who the heck this girl was. I forgot I was pregnant and was ready to hook off on that ho again, until my belly got in the way, of course. I was determined to get her, even if it wasn't actually me doing the gettin'.

"Keep on! Make me tell my girls to mash you out Penny!" I shouted, knowing they would.

"F—k them dumb ass b—ches. Tell 'em to bring it—*I did.* Y'all ghetto-rat, hoochie-mommas not about nothin'! Bring it!" Penny yelled as she began to totally lose it.

"Yo Peaches, light her fire yo!" I turned to my girls, with my mother pulling me to stop. "Yo, Shakirah, bust her up!" As if I was giving the order for a hit!

I could tell Shakirah felt kinda strange about the whole thing. We were all getting too grown to be fighting. But I knew my girl was also down because it upset her that Penny would start something, seeing I was pregnant. Peaches, on the other hand, just didn't care. Her family fights breakfast, lunch and dinner. It didn't make her no difference; what the heck she care.

My moms put her hands up to stop them from lunging at Penny. "Please girls, don't. Come on, for me. Come on this is *my* day," my mother pleaded.

Moms knew that the girls from 'round my way, we don't let *nobody* come talking smack or causing chaos with folks from our hood. Because the minute you do that, them niggaz start running up in ya hood like roaches, tryin' to take over, like them 3rd Avenue jokers did the brothers on Playwright Street. You gotta be down for people from your hood, like 'em or not. Hell, back in the day, we stomped out girls for jumpin' Tara and we don't even like her stankin' ass, but she was from around the way. So my moms knew they would get down with Penny over me, and she could hold them back but for so long. The only reason Penny's chicken legs weren't stewed already was due to the respect the girls had for my mother. But if Penny stepped too far outta line, it was a wrap.

She was lucky my other ten or so friends were inside dancing and flirting and didn't have a clue as to what was happening outside.

With all the noise and nonsense, some big security guards came out. One of them pulled Penny to the side. Catching an eyeful of her in that tight outfit, he started looking her up and down, but trying to be slick about it.

Keeping my eye on Penny, I leaned toward my mother. "Ma," I whispered, "stop turning ya back on this trick. She sneaky and she like to play with razors, tryin' to be down. She'll cut *you* just to get back at *me*." But my mother has a hard head her damn self. She rolled her eyes as if to say, *Stop with all the drama.*

"Yo, Ma! You don't know his ho! I'm tellin you!" I tried to reason.

"You don't know me either b—ch!" Penny barked, with eyebrows arched, lip snarled, fury and hate in her eyes. She looked just about how I felt, "Guess I'll go take another ride in ya man's brand new gold Cadillac, show him some feel right! You know how we do!"

Penny was an evil hussy, the kind that likes to play mind games. She'll hurt you mentally when she can't whoop ya ass. So, since no one would let us get at each other, Penny looked me over, then stared at my belly and her eyes lit up. She could tell I was pregnant for sure now!

So, to push my buttons, Penny decided to use her sex appeal to rub in my face that I was pregnant, out of shape and not as sexy as her anymore. She slithered over to one of the guards. "Hey baby," she said, knowing he'd appreciate her admiration. She looked like a freakin' maniac.

"Why you out here acting like this? Come on now, you too fine for this," he replied, looking her body over once again.

She smirked, looking at me as if to say, *Yeah you wish your fat pregnant ass could look like me and please a man, don't you?* Then she softly touched his chest and said to him as if the two of them were about to get down right there in the parking lot.

"I'm just trying to max and relax. It's this pregnant ho that's mad because her man was with me 'cause she too big and fat."

Now that was her way of sucka punchin' me. I had been gone for months and had no idea anything like that had gone on. She got it off though; she gut-punched me. And I'm sure she was hoping I would explode with so much jealousy that I'd do something stupid, hurt myself by mistake and wind up losing the baby. But the thought of Penny with my ex-fiancé left me too crushed for another outburst. He may well have moved on and started sleeping with other women. I treated him really bad before we broke up; I was terrible. The thought took my breath away. But I had to keep my focus, had to put on my poker face. I couldn't let her know that she got to me.

See, Penny *thought* she had me beat because my ex, Omar, adored a woman with a college degree. And she graduated with a master's in psychology, which she always tried to use to outwit me. Like tonight for instance, she only came to show me up, and make me envious; somebody probably told her I was pregnant or either she didn't know and came for the competition of it all. But I have to admit, she was fly: short platinum blonde hairdo, not to mention her tricked-out, tight, black minidress with diamond studs. It had straps that crossed over her chest and stretched up to a choker around her neck, showing off her arms and shoulders. Plus, she had on high-heeled sandals like the ones I wore prior to pregnancy. I guess I *was* a li'l jealous 'cause that was a baaad outfit, something I would've worn going up in a club just to make the men want me, then go home knowing I was the sh—t up in that joint.

"It's okay, baby," she said to the security guard. "I'm not about to let that jealous b—ch get me to stop acting like the lady I am, just because she's mad she's all popped out of shape."

"Listen," my moms butted in. "Call my daughter another female dog and you gonna meet a real one! Now I'm trying to be a lady, little girl, so don't make me come out of a bag on you. Walk!" My mother pointed in the direction of the brand-new, black BMW Penny had double parked.

"I came here to see E-Money, and I'm not going nowhere 'til he comes out."

Andrea Clinton

"E-Money? Li'l girl, please!" My mother warned. "My brother is old enough to be yo daddy!"

"What! Git the f—k out my face b—ch, I'm grown!"

"Li'l, you know what." My mother lunged at her, but was caught by one of the guards. As they held her back, Peaches and Shakirah moved in. Peaches pulled out two razors from her purse, and tossed one to Shakirah. That ho, Penny, reached into her dress and pulled out two razors of her own. Peaches, known for her karate, stood to the side of Penny and was about to take her head off with a roundhouse kick. It surely would've knocked Penny out cold before she even had a chance to open up those razors. Dumb ass from the suburbs trying to be down.

But that trick was saved by my uncle E-Money. He came out, saw what was going on, and pushed past Shakirah and the security guards. Nobody got in his way or tried to stop him, because he had some serious respect around the hood as one of the old-heads. Just when Peaches was about to take off Penny's head, my uncle pulled that skank into his chest and kissed her. The passionate hug and kiss made security feel awkward; they totally disregarded the girls pulling out their razors, and since it was a li'l calm now, they decided to get the rest of us back into the banquet hall. One guard, who knew my moms, started to take her inside. And since she was yelling for me, her pregnant daughter, they began pulling me to the door too. My girls began backing off. Peaches put her razors away and started talking smack to vent her frustration. I felt her pain.

As the guards pulled me into the party I looked back and saw E-Money hugging Penny and tenderly caressing her back. He was so nasty, kissing her all over, and she, submitting to his embrace, gave in to his every whim. Yikes! I was disgusted by the entire display. But that wasn't the pisser. Hey, what the heck I care who my uncle mess with? No, the pisser was that in all of her so-called ecstasy, she, still in his arms with her head on his shoulder, opened her eyes and looked at me, then winked and blew a kiss. It was another *in ya face* from her to me!

When I got back into the hall, I was so pissed at that. I wanted to calm down but I just couldn't. I could live with anything that just happened, but the thing that knocked me for a loop was what she said with her eyes just before I came inside. She told me she enjoys getting under my skin and will do so whenever she could. I don't even know this trick ass ho like that. I mean, I know her, but I don't *know* her. And I just wanted to whoop her ass, get it over with, and feel good for a change. I hate that b—ch, and I hate b—ches like her. Uuuuuuuuuuuugh!

My peoples were trying to get me to calm down. They were afraid I had gotten too angry and might go into a toxemic pregnancy, as my high blood pressure had spiked a few times already. My moms had them all freaked out about me getting worked up, so they were on my case.

"Alisa, calm the f—k down! It's over and that ho ain't even worth all this. Chill out before you lose my niece or nephew and I have to f—k *you* up," Peaches said.

We talked like that when we was in hood-rat mode, gangsta hand movements and the whole nine yards. I was one of the most feminine and ladylike ones around, and even I could get like that if circumstances called for it.

I sat back in my chair, slithering down in my seat a li'l like a snake, to show them I was trying to relax. Then, after about half an hour, I took a glass of apple juice Peaches brought me and I got lost. I snuck upstairs and found a banquet room with a beautiful balcony.

I walked out onto this gorgeous balcony, with all of its Greek pillars and flowers, and I looked out at the world. This night, and in this place, we were up a steep hill on the edge of the city, just about where it starts to look country. I gazed down at the beautiful city lights and then up at the black night, and the few stars I found. Staring up in the sky, I realized I had no business bringing a baby into this crazy world of cruel and evil people. But I let it go, the thought I mean. Self-preservation made me stop sulking and take in the spectacular view of bright twinkling lights that lit up the city for miles.

After a while though, something told me to look back down. It was the devil who told me of course. He didn't want me to be that serene. He likes me to be bitter and causing drama, actin' crazy, messin' up my life. And I'm sure it was that ole devil who told me to alter my gaze because all I saw when I looked down was Penny and E-Money still in the same spot, pawin' each other like nasty lab rats high on LSD, in amazement, carrying on in public.

I got angry all over again. So I made myself look back out at the sky before any strong emotions could set in. I had to relieve myself of any thoughts of that worthless Penny. So, I stared at neon lights from different stores, and lights from cars, buildings, and street lights. I let them carry me away.

I was good for a while. Then that devil came back, told me to look down *again*. And I did. And I saw something that rattled me, set me back into this funky li'l depression. Something that shook me so bad, I stepped back from the balcony.

I turned and came over here to this lounger and sat down. As I leaned back and tried to relax, I saw you—a Greek *so-called* Goddess chipped out of the side of a beautiful pillar. I have no one to talk to about my messy life. But maybe if I could get it all out with you, someone who would just listen, and not judge me or be mad at me like everyone else, then maybe things won't seem so bad. Maybe then I won't feel like jumpin' off this damn balcony while slitting my f—kin' throat. No, I would never do that, it's just how I feel. But maybe a good listener could help me sort this damn thing out, help me feel better.

So, I'll call you Athena, she was supposed to be the Goddess of wisdom, and I'm gonna need some wisdom right now. I'll use telepathy to speak to you in my head, so no one passing by will think I'm a nutcase. Instead they'll think I'm deep in thought, right? Come on, don't look at me like I'm crazy. You're a woman, you've loved and lost. So, I know you'll feel where I'm coming from.

Now, back to my story. What did I see when I looked down at the parking lot the second time. What was it that shook me? A Cadillac.

My Plight:

Some would say I was ungrateful, and I guess to a degree I was. But more than ungrateful, I was blind, too blind to see straight. Even now I can't see what it is I should've done. I just know what I shouldn't have done. And I know I wasn't happy. I was unhappy with myself, with what was going on, and it was the unhappiness that drove me. It drove me to do things, drove me to where I am today, nowhere, with no one. Just sitting here playing, *I know how it feels to be lonely,* by Morgana King, in my head, over and over and over again.

I was a mental-mess, and I mucked things up really bad, and now they can't be fixed. Forgive me if my story's scrambled, but how else can I tell it when my mind is scrambled. So, when my story sounds twisted, shaky, and unclear at times, just know so is my mind. Why else would I be sitting here talking to a Greek statue of a white woman with cellulite thighs, barely any clothing and no pupils? Yes, I'm really messed up in the head, and my nerves are shot. But that's how it is when you see yourself as a casualty, and the world deems you the antagonist.

Andrea Clinton

What Had Happen Was—

When it all went down, I wanted so bad to be the type to turn to drugs or maybe liquor, heck cigarettes even. But that would never do. See right down to the very end, I, out of not knowing what to do acted and reacted just doing anything that came to mind.

It all goes back to my great-grandmother. See, just before she died, she turned to me, out of everyone in the room to say her last words, "Always get a man who loves you more than you love him."

I later learned that she loved my great-grandfather much more than he loved her. And let's just say he reaped all the benefits out of that marriage, not her. Her mother and grandmother told her the same old adage that she told me, and evidently she didn't listen to them, and suffered because of it. I believe she wanted to make sure someone from my generation knew the wise saying that she eventually realized was best.

I held this old wise proverb to be true, hell, a dying woman's last words? I was sure it could bring forth happiness. So did many other women in my family, although only one or two of them actually followed it and ended up satisfied and content. I was always hard-headed though, and given the opportunity, I would follow free thinking and go wherever my mind took me, much like those folks from long ago who started the Age of Reason, and later, the Enlightenment movement. Look it up Athena. You're a so called Goddess, use your powers.

Like those of both movements, I used free thinking as a tool to open up more options in life. And where they acquired atheism, I acquired misery; *same difference.* But we were all rebellious.

And my rebel streak led me to follow through with whatever seemed fit at the time. But look at where it got me—pregnant, lonely and alone.

Sure, like all other free thinkers before me, my mind was open to ideas, but this left an opening for the devil to come and play with me, with my mind. He's so sharp he's made many believe he doesn't even exist, especially us free thinkers, because our minds sit wide open to everything. But whether we believe or not, the devil, Satan, he uses this so-called free thought against us. He makes us turn on our own souls 'cause we're stuck on being individuals, and on being different.

Us free thinkers, we think we're different. We think we're gonna show the world a better way because we're blessed with individuality. We're gonna open new doors and minds to unexplored suggestion. We're Einsteins, Darwins. Well, my free thinking opened something all right; it opened my dark side, evilness and arrogance; it opened Pandora's Box.

***

How did it all happen? A li'l while ago, around 1985 or '86, I was *really* living the Jersey life, you know. Chillin! Me and my friend Shakirah had different men coming and going. When one set of dudes dropped us off at home, another would show up right after to take us back out. Some of those guys back then were around my age, 19, some were older, and others if they had bank, hey, they could be much older. And I was always ladylike in the presence of men, to sweep them off *their* feet. And they were always taken by my good looks: 5 foot 9 and some inches tall— almost 5 foot 10, long, thick, silky, jet-black hair, light-almost-caramel complexion, long legs, hourglass frame and a pretty heart-shaped face, with regular brown eyes that sparkled and sometimes lit up a li'l in the sun.

Andrea Clinton

At a minimum, the men would treat me to dinner, or take me where I wanted to go: the mall, movies, Atlantic City to gamble, beach, wherever, and they'd spend *whatever* on me. Then after falling in love with my *winning personality*, they'd buy some expensive gift or another. Oh, I knew how big spenders liked their women; they liked them to be like Marilyn Monroe, but with a smidgen of attitude and a dose of soul. Once in a while, I'd meet a guy with old money, from uptown or further out—he'd give me a credit card with a few thousand on it. That would buy him a hug and a subtle implied promise for more, or so he thought. I knew that was a dangerous game I was playing, but I was young, and the gettin' was good, very good.

What did my family have to say about it all? My brothers Man-Man and Manny didn't mind me dating businessmen because they wanted me to get with a man who made money honestly, unlike them. My stepfather minded his business about his step kids, although he would say a little something in his Virginian accent if he was in the mood. "Okay now, that's a dangerous game you playin' out there. Some men play fa keeps. I seen many womens git killed out there usin' mens fa there monies, neva mindin' his feelins," he'd warn every once in a while.

But, my mother and aunts were always on my back, especially when my Aunt Tina came over for my mom's to do her hair.

"You a money-grubbing gold digger!" my mother would say so viciously to me.

"*I* say she a money-grubbing ho myself," Aunt Tina would jump in.

"I'm for real Alisa. It don't make no sense, and it's not cute. How you think that make me look? You running 'round using these young **and** older men to buy you things? And you coming and going with 'em one after another?" my mother would ask.

"Like you don't do nothing for your daughter, so she gotta ho to get it herself," my aunt would add stirring up sh—t.

"You need to get it together, go finish college, or go to trade school."

"Get a job," my aunt continued, working my mother up.

"Aiiight, ma dag," I said, sulking. I wanted to tell Aunt Tina to mind her damn business, but I couldn't. Those two were notorious for jumping people, beatin' them down, and they jumped each other's kids all the time. As soon as one would whoop her child, the other would follow up with a hit or punch like a damn tag team; and they'd go back and forth 'til they were tired.

"Don't aiiight me Alisa! Now you gonna get yo act together or I'm gonna whoop yo' ass!"

"Or send you down south, to Georgia," my aunt threatened, as she always did.

"Ma, how you gonna whoop me and I'm grown?"

Then they'd both chime in, "**YOU AIN'T GROWN!**" Screaming at me made my moms get aggressive in doing my aunt's hair; good for her.

"Calm down in my hair; this sh—t ain't barb wire, damn!" My aunt would shout.

Grown, or not grown? That was the question. I personally didn't know what the hell I was. I was 19, so I wasn't a child or a kid. But, I wasn't grown either. This was supported by the government who at some point stated I couldn't buy cigarettes, or liquor, but who like my parents contradicted themselves because they would give me a license to kill in a war; go figure.

"She think she cute 'cause she think she light skin—don't cha?" My aunt would say.

Then they'd both look at me with their lips twisted and repeat, again, as if I didn't get it the last million times, "**YOU AIN'T LIGHT SKIN!**"

Then Aunt Tina would give me a piece of her mind, as if I wanted any of it.

"I keep telling yo' dumb ass, you ligh-*ter*, a blink away from carmel. But, *you ain't light skinned!*" She said attempting to register this crap in my head.

I didn't pay them no mind, though it got on my nerves. Now, I do believe that I'm beautiful, but it's because of my interior radiating loveliness and glamour through my exterior. But them two country-corns too hung up on skin color to get anything that deep.

Andrea Clinton

"What do light skin have to do with anything? Y'all kill me with that!"

"'Cause," my mother would yell to close the conversation, **"ever since your second grade teacher made that comment about you being cute 'cause you were light, you been in the mirror acting like you a princess!"**

Then together they'd spit at me, again, *"AND YOU AIN'T LIGHT SKIN!"*

It was always something like that, even though it was that teacher who said I was light, not me. I'd think we were finally done, but after a pause, my mother started in on me again.

"The sun smacked you over about three times since second grade girl, please! Out here going out with all these different men. You won't be satisfied 'til things blow up in ya face. You gotta learn the hard way."

And things *did* blow up in my face, a few times. One of the worst happened just after that last conversation in the kitchen. I had decided to only date this 34-year-old man named Mack. I didn't usually do the exclusive thing; once or twice maybe, but he was special, *he was fine*, **and** had money. But I guess, his wife thought he was special too. She showed up at my house with a gun, after forcing Mack to write my address down at gun point. But that wasn't my fault. The man told me he was divorced. But *things got hot with the quickness* that night she popped up over there. Both my brothers whipped out their guns on her and backed Mrs. Mack up out our building. Then my moms, who was pissed beyond control, beat me with her shoe and anything else she could get her hands on. Then she called all her sisters. They all ran over with my cousins, their wild and crazy kids, Uuuugh! And my stepfather kicked me out. But Man-Man told him I wasn't going no where, and then he yoked me up, while my brother Manny kept smacking me in the head. Again, *that one wasn't my fault*.

So, I began listening to those who came before me. Yep, I went back to the words of one of the ancestors in my family, a dead woman, my great-grandmother. I aimed to *get a man who loved me more than I loved him*—so that I could be the happiest, most ghetto-fabulous hood-rat around my way, Thus, Omar.

Ridin' in The Car Wit' the Sunroof Top... Woo-Woo

Omar was the most sweet and most desirable milk chocolate candy bar around the way. He was about 6 foot 2 inches tall. And he was muscular, not big and cakey, ooow I hate that look. He wasn't a gym rat, either. Omar was naturally fit. I mean you could tell he hit his push-ups, pull-ups, and probably some crunches daily, but he had a nice, natural build. **Ooool** *You don't even understand.* Funny thing is, he looked much older than he was, always did. At 23, he looked like he was 27, hell, 35; probably because he was so mature and serious, all about business. But that made him seem more experienced; like even the slightest touch would— *Woooooo!*

He had a low, neat hair cut, was always clean looking, had smooth clear skin and pretty white teeth. He's the type of brother a woman always wants to give a hug, just to feel his touch, just a li'l bit. I mean, I didn't see him much, and it was in passing when I did, usually when I was with and digging some other dude so, I gave half a *Oooowee!* Tryin' to stay focused.

But me and Omar's family go way back. We lived in the same hood all our lives, since we were li'l crumb snatchers. But growing up, I didn't have nothing for him, ever. I had no thoughts, no attraction, no nothing. But by the time I graduated, maybe a year after, something just clicked. It all started when he drove up one day in a shiny *brand-new,* 1986, black cherry, Fleetwood

Andrea Clinton

Brougham, with the silver whale-belly, and the hole in the head. Since I assume you know nothing of cars Goddess Athena, 'cause y'all rolled up in chariots and thangs, here's the translation for you: the bottom half of the car was a different color, silver, just like a whale's belly is a different color from the rest of its body, and the hole in the head is the sunroof top; picture a chariot that's enclosed, with a window up top for air. You follow me? I know this means nothing to you, but think chariot, *okay*. Anyway, when I saw him roll up in that beautiful Cadi, it was on!

He may have never gotten a real glance from me before, but I have to admit, *he got a glance from me then*—several. It was like the car showed his true style, his charisma, something I never noticed in him growing up; seems a lot of dudes were coming out of their shells around then though. But not many were as handsome as he. Ummmh!

"Peace Alisa. What's up Baby-Girl?" he asked as he pulled up alongside me in that beauty, leaning over to talk to me through the window. And Baby-Girl is my nickname; you'd have to go way back to know that name, as no one used it anymore.

"Peace," I replied as I immediately put on the charm. I stepped off the curb and over to the Cadi. Something about Cadillacs bring this excited, sensual tiger outta me, puts me on the prowl.

I bent down to the window, trying to act like I hadn't seen who was driving. "Hey, is that Omar?" Then, after getting a so-called good view, I came at him with, "Hey man, what's cookin' baby? How you?"

"I'm good lady—maintaining. You lookin' good these days. How are *you*?"

"I'm here, getting my eat-to-live on, ya know. But is this you? Big Cadi and thangs?" I started checkin' it out, and I gave him a wink to let him know he was on board, on point.

"Yeah, a li'l somethin'-somethin'. Can't let a car eat up all my dough ya know?"

"I hear you, gotta feed it just a li'l so you can flash some and still have some, right?"

"Naaa, you know I don't roll like that. I stay low key—quiet in the cut; nothing flashy about me."

"I know, quiet on the scene. That's why I almost didn't know who you were. I only see you every now and then. You never out here chillin' on these corners no more."

"Never really was. I was never one for the spotlight. And the older we get, the more 5-0 be squattin' in the cut; you know how cops do. They always lookin' at us, waiting for us to slip up so they can lock us up. So I come and go ya know; stay on the move."

"I can dig it. I don't be 'round here much myself. The world too big to be chillin 'round here *e' vry* day."

I stepped back and looked his car up and down, showing him I was feeling his style. Then I looked in the back seat. "What you need all this space for maaaan? What you be up to?"

He replied so smooth it was sickening; he was really killing me, ole chocolate—Uuuaaah! Anyway.

"Naaaaa, don't blow up my spot baby. It's just space."

Chocolate dog-on éclair was killing me softly.

We fell silent for a sec, then, he smoothly shifted the awkward moment.

"So look here, when you see Man-Man, tell him I said don't forget to leave my name in VIP at the spot. I'm coming through Friday."

"Wow! 'Nough respect. You changed O', all Rico-Suave and thangs," I smiled at him.

He blushed and played it off.

"Go head girl," he replied smirking. "Why you puttin' me on blast? Maybe I didn't change; maybe you just woke up and seeing me for the first time," he said then turned with a li'l blush, looking the other way to get it together.

"Whatever brutha," then I got nosey. "You live in New York? Or work there or something? I used to see you at New York Penn Station a lot."

He just laughed, "Yeah, something like that." Then he flashed another one of those sly smiles, turning his head toward the street, lookin' as if he was up to no good but was trying to hide that fact. I mean, unlike my brothers I hadn't really hung around Omar much when we were young but I did remember that sly smile when

Andrea Clinton

he was up to something, or did something wrong, and I knew that smile meant he was gettin' his hustle on.

"Aiiight, I'll give Man-Man your message," I told him, releasing him from the pressure. "You be good brutha," I threw at him, while tapping on his door.

"You too lady. Take care of yourself out here Baby-Girl."

Dang, why so final, I remember thinking. Then another thought popped into my head. *Maybe, just maybe he isn't so bad.* As I stepped back up on the curve, he drove off.

All day—all night, the picture of him driving that Cadillac stained my brain. I couldn't get that brutha out of my head. It was like he took some lessons from the older cats' book, and had come into his very own suave style or something. I mean there was truly something about him in that car all tilted with the gangsta' lean. I know you know what I'm talking about. And I could...not...get...him...out...my...head! Oh how I tried to rid my mind of him. For days and days, I told myself, *Naaaaaa! I can't mess with that boy.* But he wasn't a boy no more. Chocolate Thunder was a man now, and this *man* kept popping up in my head. So, what did *I* do? I plotted, planned and decided to make my way to my brother's club on Friday night, well his hang out spot. I had to see what was up.

***

It was the end of the fall season, but sorta nice out, Indian summer weather. So that night, I put on something nice—a patent-leather, powder pink, one-piece short set that was sleeveless with the back out, with straps that fastened around my neck. I finally got the curl over my forehead wide and perfectly flat just over my eyebrows; and I wore my hair long and silky straight, in a ponytail that curled as it dangled and draped just below the back of my neck. You know no man can resist long hair. I wore my mother's stilettos. She has a height complex. She's 5 feet, 7 inches, not as short as she thinks, but she insists on only wearing heels; I got my height from my father of course.

Anyway, that was that, I was good to go, except for the finishing touches. I attached a few pieces of gold jewelry to my neck and wrists, and then added a diamond bracelet and two small diamond rings. I had gotten the bracelet from a doctor, Kasim. He was cute, from Sri Lanka. The rings came from an intern, Greg and another guy, Kip, in law school. *Some of my best work,* I thought as I looked down at my fingers, and began on my way—I looked good.

I called Shakirah and told her to meet me outside the club around midnight. But not on the dot; be sure to come a few minutes late. I wanted to look cute outside for a while, standing around waiting for her to pop up. She knew where I was coming from because it was something we got from some of the older girls we used to look up to.

I CAN'T GET NO MAN HANGIN' OUT AT THE DISCOTHÈQUE...

When I arrived, who did I see outside waiting for Man-Man? Guess who, Omar and his posse. They'd been there for a short while waiting for my brothers and *their* posse to show up. We all knew what it would be like when they arrived; it would be like a red carpet side show. Manny would be with a Puerto Rican or dark chocolate mami, acting like they really in Hollywood with his tanned, handsome, Puerto Rican self, knowing the girls would go nuts over him. He's not that tall for a man; about 5 foot 9 inches tall, almost my height, but he and Man-Man work out so he's muscle-bound and gets even the beautiful tall women.

Man-Man would put his champagne-colored Cadillac in park and get out. He, being confident about his handsome, caramel-complexioned, 6 foot physique, would walk up very confident, shaking hands, sharing cigars, and trying to appear humble and laid back. But all the while he'll be taking pride in the fact that he came to the spot alone, but is sure to make a grand exit with some sexy female prey of his choice, on his arm.

But prior to my brother's grand entrance, I'd just come from the other direction, so I didn't go down there by all of them. I stopped right outside the entrance and tried to profile, speaking to and laughing with a few people I knew that passed by to kill the time and signify my radiance of course. The place was already hoppin'. I knew that Omar was pressed about making sure he was on the list because my brother's hang out spot was always over capacity and usually only had room in VIP. I thought if my timing was right, my brother and Shakirah would both arrive around the same time. But even if Man-Man showed up first, he would tell them to let me in, because he would not want us to turn around and head home by ourselves looking sexy like that. Oooh, I had it all mapped out, fail safe plan.

So anyway, I saw my brother pull up. I walked a few feet toward the corner and looked up the block for Shakirah. She was walking down the street wearing a nice, tight, black, spandex dress with long sleeves, showing cleavage and much leg, with no stockings, so the brothers could see her beautiful brown legs. She wore some comfortable, but pretty sandal shoes of course, because that girl hits the dance floor wherever we go. Her jet black hair was in a bob cut, slightly curled under her ear on one side and just above the ear on the other. Plus, she had on some fly, big, gold earrings and all her gold bangles and jewelry. She always busted out thicker gold chains and bigger gold medallions than what I wore. And Shakirah always looked good, and without the loud colors I liked to pump-up from time to time, or the *over sexy indulgences*, as my aunt put it when comparing us two; so, I was jealous sometimes. But I never put her down how some sisters do, nor did I tell her something was ugly when in fact it wasn't.

I waited patiently for her to get across the street, that was up until I saw how fast she was walking, cautiously glancing back at some man a few feet behind who was trying to talk to her. The dude looked kinda scruffy, like an ate-up dope fiend. I was afraid he was bothering her, so I turned to Man-Man and yelled out.

"Man? Man-Man! Hurry up. I think this dude's bothering Shakirah. Come on, hurry up!"

Man-Man ran and one of his friends, Champ, went into the glove compartment of Man-Man's car and pulled out a gun. He followed Man-Man.

"Run Shakirah! Come on!" I yelled.

She started jogging across the street with my brother crossing behind her. When the guy saw Man-Man and Champ coming at him with the gun, he started backing up.

Andrea Clinton

"No, no, brother! I don't want no trouble! I thought she was a trick man. My bad, my bad."

"Yo, that's you Fred?" Looking back at Champ, "Yo man, that's Fred," he said, then turned back to the guy on the street, "Fred, don't be out here rapin' these girls, man! Get outta here with that brah."

Fred stopped in his tracks. "Hey young blood, Li'l Man right? Don't be like that. I knew you when you was born, and when you was a li'l boy, and ya father used to walk you down the street buying you chips and juices man—them cookies from the Puerto Rican store, remember? I know you remember 'cause I used to get some for you and my son when y'all used to be outside playin'. Remember my son Vince? Y'all call him Dolla? Dolla-Bill?"

"You know I know you Fred, *and* Dolla-Bill man, he like a brother."

"You damn real he is! We raised y'all up like us, me and ya fatha; we f—ked up though didn't we?" He paused. "We shoulda been there fa y'all. Shoulda helped y'all be somethin'," he said looking sad.

Man-Man just stared for a second or two; I think he was having a moment. Champ looked Fred up and down. "Yo, that's Dolla-Bill fatha? I just got home from doing a short bid with Dolla. Damn! He right, he said you a mess out here on that diesel. Can't imagine you once being thugged out," he said, shaking his head in disgust.

Fred said in a lowered tone than he'd been using, "My son love me! I know he do. He might be ashamed, but he love me." He turned back to Man-Man.

Man-Man felt for Fred and their generation's fall to dope. He looked over at Champ, "Chill man, don't dis' him like that."

Fred wanted to do Champ harm, you saw it in his stance, his eyes, and his head nods. But it wasn't Fred's day anymore. Those brothers from back in the day had outlived their day, and most traded in their thug card for a bag of dope or the prison system. So instead, Fred jumped into kool, old school mode, "Yo Li'l Man, listen, don't do it like that though man, talkin' 'bout raping girls. Come on man; that ain't kool. I was gonna pay her; you ain't never know me to rape nobody. Come on, look at me brah, I *still* look good baby!"

"Aiiight Fred, aiight. Just go home man." Turning to Champ, "Put that gun up chief. Fred my father's old runnin' partner. He got it like that wit' me, on lock." Then he turned to Fred. "But you scared that girl Fred. You can't be doing that man. The wrong girl out here will put a cap in that ass man!"

"I know man, I know." Then clowning around, he rubbed the whiskers on his chin, and joked, "They don't make ho's the way they used to." Clowning, but kinda serious, too.

Man and Champ laughed. Then Champ put his gun away, while Fred turned to leave.

"Y'all keep kool. I'm gonna go 'round here and handle my business, ya hear? Gotta get me one of them young thangs to party wit' me tonight. Want me some company, ya heard?"

Fred started jogging away with that old-school kool run they do. You know with his arms at his sides, hands facing behind him, with the pinky out stiff like he 'bout to have a stroke or a seizure.

My brother came back across the street, but he kept looking back at Fred. And I knew the reason why. My father put us down on something long ago, before he went down, in Rahway Prison. "Don't think because you saw me with somebody that me and them are ace-deuce-trey; that don't make us kool. 'Cause I did a lot of things to a lot of people! And they ain't gon' tell you nothin'. But they might hurt *you*, to get back at me. Don't trust none of 'em!" He'd say. So, we didn't.

When Man-Man mounted the sidewalk, Champ just stopped and stared at me and Shakirah. My brother looked at him as though he wanted to go off on him. But don't get me wrong, my brother wasn't the duke of his posse or nothing. Really none of them were, because in my day letting anyone feel they were top dog over you was a sign of weakness. So it wasn't that Man-Man was in charge, he was actually just one of the boys. But *he* had the cocaine connect, and that counts. Plus, most of them were hot-headed, bull-headed and whatever else you could think of, with only one or two who were naturally calm. My brother was one of the ones in between. That was another big reason why most didn't mess with him, 'cause *He could get with this, or he could get with that.* And those type were just too unpredictable, and that, he got from our father.

Omar, as you'll find out later on, was one of the calm, kool-headed ones. The one you think is quiet 'cause he's probably a li'l scared. But in fact, *he's* the nutcase you really better watch out for. Everyone around the way knows he has a calm head, but can be quite dangerous, and is the unspoken leader of his posse.

So anyway, Man-Man saw Champ look me and Shakirah over and said, "Yo, you betta' go head brutha!"

"What man? I'm just sayin, look at'em. They look good man. Naa, naa, aiight. But I'm just saying man. Talk to 'em. Tell 'em something 'bout walkin' around lookin' like dessert man; 'cause a nigga gon' look! They can't just be out here looking good like this brah." Then he walked away to stand with the rest of their posse. Each of them nodded at Champ in agreement.

I looked over at Omar to see his response, and wouldn't you know, he was just leaning his back against the wall with a cigar in his mouth, shaking his head. He turned away as if he was ashamed. I got annoyed 'cause had I been a hoochie momma that he was diggin', it would've been a whole other kind of head shaking.

Since my brother was scolding us, I put on my crybaby act and threatened to just walk or catch a cab. He said I was coming inside until he or my brother Manny could take us home. I retorted, "Fine with me, brah."

Most of the fellas had gone inside by that point, so I started clownin' and pimp-walked to the door. Shakirah was behind me laughing. Little did I know my brother was checking her out, and so you can imagine how the two of them spent their time later that night. To this day, I don't know why that went down 'cause Man-Man had a girlfriend, and Shakirah knew all about her.

Anyway, after we entered, we went upstairs and into the VIP room. I didn't have the same privileges as my brother and his friends and couldn't just walk all over the club. The owners were especially strict since they were at capacity. Not long before, a fire burned down a club. It was a happenin' spot and was packed to the rafters. Most of the folks there died in the flames. Ever since then most club owners were trying to be more on point.

Now, they had a dance floor in VIP, but it had nothing on the thumpin' goin' down on the club's *main* dance floors. Heck, VIP was really just a place that was a little quieter, maybe for men to get their mack on with some upper class ho who ventured into town, or some ghetto-fabulous hoochie who was in the club that night.

I caught a glimpse of Omar and his posse across the room. He was sitting in one of those huge booths with a high back, where the players gather with ho's all around 'em. Man-Man and Manny dropped by to hang with them on and off.

Omar was lookin' good. He wore a burgundy dress shirt and pants. The first two buttons on his shirt were open, but it wasn't wide open like men wore back in the disco days, showing off gold medallions practically buried in a nest of nasty chest hair. No, no, Omar was different. He left something to be desired. His shirt was open just enough to see a simple half inch chain. He sported a handsome, neatly trimmed hair cut, and rocked a baaad watch, with two fly onyx rings too. Sharp and suave, Omar was a chocolate delight for sure; seemed like he'd melt in your mouth smoother than that imported Swiss chocolate. Words could do him no justice. He had come a long way, and humbly so.

I kept an eye on him all night. That was until his *girlfriend* showed up! When Omar's girl Vanessa rolled in, all heads turned. I didn't know her personally, but I'd seen her around before. They knew she was of high society. But *I* could tell *she* knew how to put on black-face; because as dark as she was on the outside, she was *all white* underneath. And every now and again she'd say something, trying to sound black, but looked uncomfortable doing it. And I guess she'd only lower her standards but so much, because she refused to look anything less than sophisticated. She was the only heffa' up in that joint wearing a red-sequined gown, or hell, a gown *period.* She showed a tidbit of cleavage, and wore a diamond necklace, with matching earrings, tennis bracelet, and a few blinding diamond rings. Vanessa sported a long, silky, straight, bronzed weave that floated over her boobs and had to have run her at least five hundred dollars. I don't wear a weave,

Andrea Clinton

my hair's already a li'l lengthy and thick, but I know a good weave when I see one.

When she and Omar made eye contact, they were all smiles.

"Heyyy baby," he said as he stood up and reached out for her embrace.

Uuugh! It bothered me to watch!

"Wassup Boo?" as she approached with a kool-Aid smile, presenting ALL whites.

What she mean *Boo*? She ain't ghetto! Ooooooh, she was getting on my nerves already. As he pulled her into him for a hug, she slowly wrapped her arms around his neck, using all her charm and poise to fold into his arms. Uuuuuuuuuugh! I was hot—red-hot mad! This threw a monkey wrench into my plans. Heck, everything I'd just seen with them, I wanted for myself, and he hasn't even acknowledged or spoken to me.

"You been waitin' on me long Boo?" she asked him.

"Naaa baby. Here, have a seat," as he pointed to the booth with his palms.

"I see y'all started gettin' ya drink on."

"Naaa baby. I was waiting on *you*. That's the fellas drinking." This was the go ahead for everyone to greet her, *and they did*, one after the other, almost drooling like dogs. Vanessa was well-educated, one of them Princeton bookworms. Omar's crew were all taken by Vanessa's sophisticated sex appeal. But I thought she was a dog, *g-r-r-r*. Not because she was brown-skinned as some would say, because Shakirah is brown-skinned and prettier than me. I'm not one of those people stupid enough to believe color makes you pretty or ugly. There were many bruthas who turned me down because I was of the *ligh-ter* persuasion. No, I thought Vanessa was a dog because she will obviously do anything for a bone.

As Omar and Vanessa chatted among themselves, I saw all the brothers at the table whispering about how good she looked, her shape, her whatever.

Man-Man, my brother Manny and the fellas at our table were even looking at her, but Manny always has to comment, "Woo-wee, see them long chocolate legs Gee? Look under the table yo.

You can't see the split in her dress when she walks, but when she sits, it goes up to her crotch," Manny said.

"Pigs!" I said, as they all elbowed or pushed me to hush while they got their look on.

I wanted in. I needed to hear some of her and Omar's conversation so that I could feel this whole thing out. In a way, I was hoping when I last saw Omar a few days ago he was flirting. *I was sure he was finding a reason to pull up and talk to me, but I guess he wasn't*, I remember thinking as I sat there. I listened. I did my best to shut out all the chatter between Man-Man and his crew so I could eavesdrop on Omar.

"So did you get a cab like I told you or did you drive that new Mercedes you keep talking about?" he asked her, looking into her eyes.

"You know I obey. Well, maybe I shouldn't have, and then you'd have had to punish me later."

He blushed and tried to play it off. And I felt like someone shot an arrow through my heart. Not one of love, but one of disgust, 'cause that line was **whack as hell!** I remember thinking *I should run over and smack her in her neck for that dumb sh—t. Uuuuuuugh!!!* But instead, I continued listening.

"Boo, what do they serve here because, I'm famished?" She asked, mixing uppity and hip-hop jargon. *Who says 'I'm famished?' Just say I'm freakin' hungry!* I thought.

Omar called the waitress over. "Excuse me, Kathy, the young lady would like to order." Then he sat back so Vanessa could take over.

"Omar, I don't know. I'm not in the mood for this black, down and dirty soul food," she sighed, dropping the menu.

Offended, two of Omar's people, Pep and muscle-bound Sampson up and left the table, "Maaan!" Pep said. Shocked, the others looked at one another, picked up their glasses and drank in chorus. They did that to clown about it. They immediately waived to another waitress to order more drinks, being silly. I don't know why Omar wasn't insulted, they knew to be. It was clear she looked down on our, "*lower class.*" You had to see her facial expression Goddess Athena. She was snooty and reserved about *everything*, even though she tried to play it off each and every time, or make up for it by faking her blackness.

"Kool-out, kool-out. If you're famished, *something* gotta look good," Omar said real smooth to her, holding up the menu.

"Okay, hmmm," as she looked on with him. She was clearly trying not to piss him off so she could get her freak on later with her ghetto thug, hmp! Oh, I knew what she was doing! Girl ordered cheese sticks, plus buffalo wings, and ate them up as if those wings were the most tender cut of filet mignon.

But, my, how disillusional I was though. It didn't show that he had a girlfriend. Whenever I did see him I always saw him alone. So, I pulled Manny aside to get the 411. He told me that Vanessa was an uptown girl and that she and Omar had been on and off for a few years, usually off though. This explained why I was the last to know.

But, the night wasn't a total loss. All the brothers from both posses treated me like royalty, like a little sister, all with the exception of Omar, and R.I.P., another guy from Man-Man's crew. But R.I.P. didn't speak to anyone; he'd just always walk in a place looking crazy. So I didn't want that crazy mug to speak to me anyway. Best he stayed quiet in his little freakin' corner, 'cause he could get off the hook-crazy when he was ready, and he didn't drink *or* light-up.

So, I gave up on Omar. But I looked good and it was good hanging out with my big brothers and their friends. The DJ was playing **a baaad club beat**, mixing it with old disco. Like, *"Run away, you better not hesitate,"* and then, *"Young hearts, run free, don't ever be hung up, hung up like my man and meee,"* **then my favorite part of the song,** *"It's high time now, just one crack at life, who wants to live it in trouble and strife. My mind must be free to learn all I can about me, um-hmm. I'm gonna love me for the rest of my days, encourage the babies every time they say, self preservation is what's really going on today...young hearts."* Then he played some thumpin' beat that sounded almost like a bass guitar string/bed spring pluckin', like somethin' off the Flintstones. It was funky though, just plucking away. Had us hopping in our seat, throwing our hands up and bopping for about a minute or so.

Then the DJ kicked the door down with some Sylvester, *"You make me feel, miiighty real."* Ooooow that beat mixed with Sylvester wailing from the speakers made us all lose our minds.

Oooh, it was knocking. I danced in my seat through most of it, until the DJ lost his darn mind. "Okay people, before we come back to the '80s, back to today's club, I'm about to hit you with something you'll appreciate. I'm about to get all y'all out on the floor. Oooh, you don't think I can do it? Okay, GET OFF!"

Then that mo' joker put on *Get Off,* by Foxy and the whole club flew onto the dance floor, including myself.

"Aaaaaaaaah! Remember that people? Ha haaaaaaaa! Told you I'd get you up!"

As corny as it may sound with me tellin' it, it wasn't at the time. He was a baaad DJ and by him playing those old cuts, I'd almost forgotten about Omar with that heffa'. Then the DJ paused to a knockin' sound that had everybody movin'. No guitar, drums, piano, it was just a funky knockin' but with a hump to it. I can't explain it. But it was that club beat that you love to hear just because. It by itself can keep you on the dance floor, and you pray the DJ don't mess it up, or stop it; think safari.

I looked up and swore I saw Omar looking over at me. But trying not to be obvious and glance over to find out for sure, I just did my thing. 'Cause I figured, if he did see me, it was money in the bank.

The knock of that beat was so fierce, nobody dared leave the floor. And I wasn't about to let my stilettos stop me from dancing. So, I stayed out there through that song and the next, *Let's All Chant* by Michael Zager Band. The DJ rocked the heck outta that joint for like seven minutes. He mixed it to a REAL fat club beat that took you back to Africa. I was out there with him, doing my thing. You couldn't tell me I wasn't taking it back to the motherland out that mug, and everyone else was too. The beat was so hot and he timed it all so tight, that he got you thinking about some deep stuff, like *maybe what we think was stripped from us as slaves was here in us all along.* Because we tore it up out there, jungle style!

Andrea Clinton

Then I guess to clear the dance floor, he paused, then threw on *Caribbean Queen* by Billy Ocean. But the switch to a slower pace was so sudden, it made me dizzy. So I made my way back to the table, playing if off by throwing my hands up and dancing all the way off the floor. Shakirah, who thumps hard on the dance floor followed me. We always did that, just to make sure the other person was okay. Heck, you could always go back out there. For the moment, Shakirah had forgotten about that jive Man-Man was talking, and I wasn't worryin' about Omar. After all that dancing though, we were hungry. So, my brother bought food and drinks for me and Shakirah. Of course regarding liquor, he would only bring me what my mother drank, a White Russian, and only two at that. But I ate like a Hollywood star who was visiting back home in the hood: steak, fried whiting fish, a few BBQ ribs, mac & cheese, yams, collards mixed with cabbage and cornbread. Later, he even sent one of the waitresses to the restaurant downstairs, which was just about to close for the night, to buy a fifty dollar pan of peach cobbler. Please, I know how to enjoy myself when I eat! I was humming and the whole nine eatin' that pie.

While waiting at the bar for a nightcap, another White Russian, I turned to Shakirah. "At least I'm gettin' something out of tonight! Hell, I'm not gonna be able to run up on Omar, so at least I got something." Standing on her other side, Man-Man was whispering sweet nothin's in Shakirah's ear. Payin' him no mind, she picked up her Canadian Mist and soda and we toasted. You'd think Man-Man would've eased up, seeing as me and my girl were having a moment. But he kept on, kept badgering her. I hate men.

We went back to the table and sat. My brother Manny came over and sat by me. He always checks up on me.

"You good sis?" He asked, with a Bud in one hand and a cigar in the other.

"I'm straight," I replied as I lifted my drink to my face, wiggling my body as the DJ mixed and faded in Colonel Abrams, *"Trapped."* I sang along, *"Ooh oh I'm trapped, like a fool I'm in a cage. I can't get out, see I'm trapped—"*

***

People started leaving around 2:00 a.m., even though the club didn't close til 4. I said to Manny, "Dang, in New York the party just gettin' started," while dancing in my seat.

"Everybody got their rap on, and making their way to a hotel or something," Manny said.

Man-Man and Shakirah disappeared, not for long, but they were gone when I turned to look for her. I found out later he was trying to get her to agree to dump me at home and go with him. I hate a man like that, dang! But she said no, because she was my cut-buddy. I mean, he knew how we would cut the streets together, stuck like glue. Although, she *was* starting to slip a little; she was starting to like him and consider his offer. I saw it in her eyes, ain't nobody no fool. After they returned, Man-Man made a run saying he'd be back for us; Manny followed him.

Uuuugh! This would've been the perfect opportunity to put some time in with Omar, dammit! I thought.

"Dang! He is romancing the heck out of me with how he's treating her," I told Shakirah.

She smirked because she knew exactly what I was saying. "Yo, if I'd have known he was gonna turn out lookin' like that, I'd've pushed up on him a long time ago. Ya just don't think living how they did that they'd turn out so okay."

I nodded in agreement, 'cause I was falling for his mannerisms, care and concern over Vanessa. "I'd give him a 7 on a scale of 1 to 10."

"Stop lyin'! You crazy! You know he a straight 9, with all that chocolate and that body, a 9 and them some. You need to quit."

"No, for real. I know I said he's fine earlier, but, I think it was the Cadillac. I mean, I am attracted to him, but...." I snarled at the subject.

"I think you buggin' because Omar is fine! *Fine, fine, fine!* You just mad 'cause he here with somebody else and deep down

Andrea Clinton

inside you really feelin' him; *ya jealous*. And since he was doing all that talkin' the other day, he probably ain't speakin' to you all night 'cause he feelin' you too. But you don't wanna believe this so you talkin' 'bout he a 7. *You* buggin', not me. I *know* he's a good 9. I got 20-20 vision and my view tells me he is finger lickin' good. As usual when it comes down to a possible real relationship, *you* buggin'."

Maybe I am bugging, I thought, because both of the waitresses up in that joint couldn't take their eyes off him and this was *after* Shakirah pointed him out asking them to rate him; they also gave him a 9, and then some.

I believe I couldn't admit he was fine at the time because I knew him back in the day when he and his brother used to have snotty noses and dress like bums after their father got locked up and their mother fell to liquor and drugs. Yeah, I think it was the ugly picture of his past as a boy that was coloring my view of him as a man. Somewhere in the back of my mind I probably assumed he'd wind up a *nobody* after going through all he went through. If so, that wasn't nice. I dunno, or maybe Shakirah was right and I was just running scared, as usual.

And there was something about the way Omar *was* with Vanessa. Like, he wasn't clingy, but he was far from distant. He was kool. He'd get up and get them a Hennessy whenever the waitresses were M.I.A. When they were eating, he got up to get her more napkins and packages of some of those moist towel, wipe thingys. He wasn't a dancer either, so when she wanted to dance, he'd stand up all kool and sharp, put his hand out for hers, walk her to the dance floor. Vanessa was so perfect at obliging him, gracefully allowing her hands to fall into his, and letting him lead her to the dance floor, and looking and winking at him while she danced. He smiled at her as she danced, sometimes bopping his head as if he was proud of her getting her groove on. She continued dancing and when a brother would get up on her she'd simply point to Omar. And the brother would look, put up his hands as if to say, *Oh hey wasssup Omar? My bad,* and then he'd back the heck up out of there. Oh, the whole scene was sickening, and yes I say this out of jealousy. It was just too perfect a date. *And should've been mine*, I thought. Damn!

No, that's not all of what made me so attracted to him that night. *The way he ate was sensual!* Sounds crazy but, I'm telling you, even Shakirah said she was starting to catch feelings. We watched everything Omar did. He didn't eat much, but when he did, he'd perfectly place a big succulent piece of juicy steak in his mouth, not looking greedy or savage like, like the rest of his posse. His lips, when he chewed, aaah. He'd lift a napkin with those strong hands of his and wipe his perfect lips, only to run his tongue across them again. Then he'd toss that napkin, and get another, a clean one. Oh it's not what he did, but the smooth, sensuous way he did it.

There was something especially erotic about almost everything Omar did. Like, he had both a shot of Hennessy and a Bud. And when he'd require one of his many shots of Henny, he'd gracefully dump it back with his pinky out. Then, he'd lick his lips, get a napkin and slowly wipe that mouth of his again. Other times, he'd pick up his bottle of Bud, you know how bud drinkers do, gripping the top with those few fingers? He'd be sitting up with good posture, one arm just behind Vanessa then he'd take a swig, never a gulp. His lips would be ever so slightly wet from the beer. He'd lick them, so as not to lose any of the Bud, and when he did, I'd like to die in my seat, with Shakirah and the waitress by my side melting as I narrated his every charismatic and silky movement that captivated our insides.

His whole everything was way too suave for me, including his body movements in between, and how he sat, spoke, smiled, and acted so laid back. I was as messed up in the head as a man watching a woman eating a banana. I *NEVER* saw a man eat and behave in such a way that gets a woman so worked up, made you squirm in your seat. I began to see him in a whole new light. *Yeah, he's fine,* I caught myself thinking.

***

Andrea Clinton

Anyway, when the clock struck 10 to 4, it was time to go. Omar got Vanessa's mink coat, put it on her, and then his own, a nice simple leather joint. He opened the doors for her then held her hand as they passed through, blah, blah, blah. I almost felt awkward being on, *"his jock the whole time"*, as Shakirah put it. But heck, he didn't know I was studying him all night. As far as he knew, I didn't think much about him.

My brother came back, true to his word, after checking in on his pregnant girlfriend who he denied even having when he was pushing up on Shakirah, and she fell for the lie. I pulled her coattail, but only one time, 'cause I'm not no damn babysitter, and she not no fool. "I'm telling you one time because you my people, after that, it's ya ass—*HE GOT A GIRL!*" And that was all I had to say about that. Then Man-Man dropped me off and took Shakirah to a hotel where they stayed the entire weekend.

But, but wait. Let me back up. How can I not tell you the kicker of the night? Okay, as we went downstairs, leaving the club, my brother was trying to hug up on Shakirah. I was freezin' in my pink outfit, after all, the back was out, and the freakin' temperature dropped. I remember thinking, *I'm gonna be sick as hell, out here trying to impress this man,* **and he already got a woman!**

While I was standing there shivering, with my arms crossed, not even trying to maintain cuteness, I saw Omar and his girlfriend out the corner of my eye. They made a left around the club, going into the parking lot. Still in front of the building, waiting for Manny to drive up with the car, I tried to ask Man-Man for his sheepskin coat. But he was pulling and hugging Shakirah, ignoring me. I could tell he was trying to punish me for what he called dressing like a hoochie. But he was *very* pleased with Shakirah's tight, short dress though. Men!

Suddenly, out the corners of my eyes I saw something coming at me and before I could jump, scream or panic, Omar had approached with his arm extended, leather trenchcoat in hand, offering it to me.

"You want my trench?" he paused, looking me in my eyes. I was so startled and surprised, I just looked at him. He *was fine*, and I was caught off guard with his Billy Dee Williams tone of voice. "You don't wanna freeze to death out here do you?" he asked, with his gorgeous eyelashes. I was hit, hit by the bomb. *Dang him!* I thought. But I tried to play off the fact that I was taken by his thoughtfulness, as well as his good looks.

"No, that's okay. I don't wanna 'cause trouble."

"You aren't. Take it; got insulation inside," he said as he put it on my shoulders. And boy did it have insulation; it began to warm my insides immediately. It was one of those MCM Gucci leather trenchcoats. It had fur inside, and was double-breasted, with a belt. I saw my brother from the corner of my eye looking at us, and I heard Shakirah's laugh come to a halt. I silently accepted the coat, looking into Omar's eyes, and he in mine.

I decided to seize the moment by nodding my thanks in the most sensuous way, giving him a sly, sexy look. He paused for a moment then nodded back with a kool, collected wink. Then he turned to Man-Man and threw him the peace sign, and a fist. Man-Man did the same.

"Aaiiight brutha," Man said as he reached his hand out to Omar. "Aaiight player, rock on wit'cha bad self! Ha haaaaaaaaaaaaaaa!"

They shook hands and gave that half a hug, pat on the back thing that men do. Omar blushed, and humbled himself, playing it all off, "Go head man, you shot out," as he pushed off their manly clutch.

Man-Man was so ignorant about it, such a bus-head. As they stepped back, he continued. "Haaaaaaaaaa! Do you, baby. Do *ya* thang man. I approve, I approve," while putting his cigar in his mouth.

I had to shake my head. *Does Man-Man know I can hear him?* I asked myself.

The trenchcoat was right on time. It comforted me, kept me warm and gave me a sense of security. It was Gucci!

After the quick handshake and hug, Omar took one of the cigars Man-Man held out to him. "Hoooooe! Good looking out. Aaaiiight man, peace," he said to Man-Man.

"No problem brutha; you know you my peoples."

Andrea Clinton

Omar turned to jog back toward the parking lot. As he reached the end of the club, just before turning the corner of the building to continue to his car, he began walking slow. He looked back at me and our eyes met. For five seconds, we had a moment. Then, he turned into the parking lot out of my view. I was touched; I was taken. I swear, I'm telling you, that slick, sly sucker knocked me out without even throwing a punch!

Wanna Be Where You Are

After that enchanted evening, ghetto-chic enchantment of course, I didn't see Omar for almost two weeks. I was wondering what that whole thing was all about. I began to lose faith in it. People, mainly men, say we women always look too much into things. But eyes don't lie.

I was tired of waiting, and I wanted in. I wanted to know what the deal was with him. But I didn't even know how to track him down. Who could I ask? I couldn't ask my brother Man-Man. He'd tease me and I didn't want him to think I fell into his friend's smooth trap. I thought about asking Manny, but I was worried that he'd tell Man-Man. And forget about Shakirah. That dumb girl, she can't get right. She was now so into Man-Man, she was blind.

After thinking on it a moment, I realized I had no choice, Manny was my only real option. After all, he was always going behind Man Man himself, trying to sneak and do stuff.

There were many Puerto Ricans in our hood. But most of them were born here. Only Manny and his cut-buddy Geronimo came straight from the island. Geronimo moved here at age 10. Manny been here since he was four or five.

Both Manny and Geronimo's fathers had grown up in the same spot in Puerto Rico, although you can tell Manny's father got black in him. Manny and Geronimo formed a tight bond because of this. Every time Manny got into trouble, it was because he was

Andrea Clinton

hanging out with Geronimo and his crew. Heck, when he was with Jose and Jewels, two other Puerto Ricans in Man-Man's posse, he never got into trouble. But Geronimo, he was a whole other story. Imagine, the older cats in the hood gave him this nickname when he was only 11 years old because he fought all the time. And he was a wild, crazy fighter at that. Cutting someone meant nothing to him. But that didn't bother Manny none. He thought that crazy look was kool.

Man-Man was always getting on Manny's case about following Geronimo and doin' dirt, because Geronimo was a so-called semi-pro boxing hitman who worked with more than his hands. But I knew Manny couldn't help but gravitate toward his Hispanic brother. Didn't bother him that he might end up in jail for doing dirt with Geronimo. But it *did* bother him that Man-Man would really go off if he ever found out.

So I decided to turn to Manny. But, I had to be slick about it. I knew what to do. I had to blackmail him.

"Manny, I know you was with Geronimo and them when they robbed that gas station, and almost beat that attendant to death."

"Shut up! Why you all loud! You don't know nothing, girl."

"Yes I do. Why you was with them that night then? Huh? And if you don't do me a favor, I'm gonna tell Man-Man!" I gave him a look that let him know I was playing, but serious.

"What? Why? I always got ya back and you gonna blackmail me? That ain't even kool! And I ain't even touch that dude, I was just there."

"An accessory—shut up! Shut up and do what I say or else I'm tellin'."

"What? What you want money—I know you loaded all them dudes you been stickin'."

"No, I need you to tell me where Omar be. I need to give him back his coat. But don't tell nobody, especially Man-Man. I don't want him thinking nothing."

"*You stupid!* You blackmail me and that's the best you can do? Hell, he play pool over on Orange Street every Thursday. But if you don't know nobody, you can't get in, 'cause you a girl. Now, leave me alone."

"Who hang out in there?" I asked as if I was the one ruling things.

"All the old heads. The old-time pimps, thugs, players, all of 'em. And why you want to return his coat all of a sudden?"

"Because it's good manners," I tried to play it off.

"My ass nigga! Ha haaaaaaa! You wanna give 'em back his coat 'cause you like him!"

"Noooo, noooo."

Manny started laughing, and I was ready to choke him. "Haaaaah, you like *Player-Player*. Girl, you know he the player of the year? That's why we call him Player-Player; it's our nickname for him."

"What? He really is a player? He wasn't no player in grammar school with that snotty nose and bummy clothes. You know, y'all use to hang together back then with him and his brother. And he wasn't no player in high school either. Where all this player-player stuff come from?"

"He a smooth operator now. That man so smooth, them girls go nuts over him. Fightin' and the whole nine. Uptown and downtown girls; New York and Jersey girls; the plain Janes and the Jayne Kennedys; the dark and the—"

"ALL RIGHT—I get it!" I yelled, "Well, I don't fight over no man."

"Yeah, but them girls will whoop yo ass. The only thing save you from catchin' a beat down is *our* reputation, and maybe not even then, haaa. You betta' listen up girl! Plus, before you go with him, I gotta interview him, make sure he not coming with no game. You can't be just another ho on his belt."

I know that was him being concerned, because Manny is my brother, blood or not. I just couldn't help but get angry at the words, *another ho on his belt.*

"Manny, I just wanna give the man his damn coat!" I marched off with an attitude because he began to smirk, and then started laughing at me. But when I spun around to wave my hand at him and roll my eyes, I saw in his eyes a bit of worry. See, we ALL took him in with open arms, my mother, father, and then stepfather when he came on board with us. My mother helped raise him from like six years old. He was back and forth living with his real mother, Lady. But my moms was always taking him back in, because Manny was subjected to all kinds of crap at Lady's house and it pissed my mother off. She had a pretty good idea of what went down there. After all, Lady's house was where she bought *her* weed. That is until Lady fell off the scene, acting crazy in them streets. And that's when my moms told Lady to give Manny to her before the state took him.

By the time the state *did* come to see about Manny, he'd been with us for about three years. They said it was no sense in taking him out of my mother's care. So, they left him there and came back to check on him from time to time for six months or so. And from then on, they just started cuttin' checks, hardly ever comin' around. Yeah, we were a real family.

Man–Man is a few years older than me, and one year older than Manny. He was our saving grace most times, keeping us out of trouble. I had it worse than Manny though, because I had both Manny and Man-Man watching over me. Manny fought for me more times than I could count. He even got jumped in high school, trying to protect me.

With all this love we had for each other, the last thing he wanted to see was me become a statistic, *just another ho,* as he'd put it, or get hurt, even though they all said one day I'd get mine. Manny believed Omar had a whole other side to him than being a player, he just didn't know if he'd give that side to me. He was more suspicious than Man-Man, who kinda saw himself in Omar. But, I had my own agenda. I didn't know how this would tie into my great-grandmother's saying, *get a man who loves you more than you love him.* But, if what other brothers have told me over the years is true, I was too irresistible to any man. I was banking on that; most girls who are good-looking, pretty or sexy bank on the compliments they often hear. I just hoped he wasn't one of those men who only go for women who are brains or bookworms like that Vanessa seemed. Because I was smart, but I was no bookworm. And yes, I am one of those spoiled women who like a man to pay my bills, dag-on-it! So what? My stepfather pays all of the bills, and the money my mother makes is her's. She's not selfish though; she buys him things and makes sure he has.

So anyway, I was hoping whatever made him give me that coat was a sign that I made some headway with him, but I wasn't sure. So I figured I'd see how he'd react when I showed up at the pool hall. So it was a go. That Thursday, me and Shakirah went down to the pool hall.

***

We took a cab there. I had the trenchcoat in a Gucci suit bag I had, trying to impress Omar. As I began to walk inside, Slug, an older gentleman of about 66, walked up and put his arm in front of me. "Where you think you going Alisa?"

See, you never know who knows you, a lesson I was always learning, which took me back to my father telling us, "Don't think because you saw me with somebody that me and them are ace-duce-trey…I did a lot of things to a lot of people!" Although we knew a lot of the old heads by name and reputation, we never really paid them much mind. But Slug knew me by name because, as I found out later, he knew my father, and of course my brother who is now in his prime and comes to the pool hall. And them 66 years of age didn't fool me. I knew he was a killer, known for poisoning, stabbing, shooting, and beatin' dudes to death.

I heard a voice calling out, "It's okay Slug. She's with me." It was Omar. I smirked to myself thinking it was on. I just knew he was about to come over to get something goin'. But nooooo, he was sly. He was nothing like he was with li'l missy at the club.

Omar stood over a pool table, looking down at the balls on the green felt table. He chalked his, what do you call that stick? Whatever it is, he chalked it. Then, he hit a ball or two. I walked over, Shakirah following, with a smile on my face. He was serious, but you could see a hidden smile.

Just as I approached he said, "Hey lady. How you doing?"

Andrea Clinton

I was stunned that with all the mannerisms he showed Vanessa, I got that limp greeting. "Fine, how are you?" I replied.

"You know, I'm good. Gettin' a few games in with my people here. Is that my coat?" He nodded at the suit bag slung over my arm.

"Yeah, I had to do some investigatin' to figure out how to find you. I ain't want you to think I was tryin' to beat you for ya coat or nuttin," I said as I was so ghetto speaking back then. I've grown since then though, but I still pour on the slang and other crap, mostly when I'm pissed off at somebody.

"Naaa, come on. I don't think you'd go out like that." He took the bag from me as I handed it over. Then he walked to a coat rack and hung it up over in the corner.

"So, did it do the trick? Did it keep you warm?"

"Oh yeah. Gucci has that affect on me."

He smiled, but he never smiled like this before. Not even with Vanessa at the club. Yet there he was, smiling at me with those big, pretty, white teeth. And that made me feel good. I made him smile, standing there in a white tank tee shirt with his strong arms showing, and a diamond watch on his wrist.

"If I see a Gucci coat, I'll be sure to pick you up one."

I laughed a cute li'l giggle to play it off, but I was dead serious about that coat. "Aiiight, you do that."

After the laugh, there was a little silence. I was glad Shakirah saw her uncle Slim, and started talking to him. Because then I appeared as if I was ready to go, but it was she who was holding me up.

"Do you want a drink?" he asked me.

Now you know I wish I was 21. Don't get me wrong, I'd have taken it if it was another bar or something. But this pool hall was in the hood, and I didn't want to put them in jeopardy with me being only 19.

"Naaa, it's early. What is it like five o'clock?"

"Well, for some people that's happy hour."

Then the comedian came out of me. "Well happy hour's for folk who work. I'm joblesssssss."

He laughed with me and then shot a ball on the table. Standing there watching, I said to myself, *I like him.*

"Well, what you doing with yourself? I know a pretty young lady like yourself ain't hanging around out here living off ya good looks."

Little did he know that was EXACTLY what I was doing, as well as loafing off my mother, stepfather and brothers. Heck, anything I had or owned was what I got from some sucker across town. I had listened to my mother about one thing and opened up a bank account to save every penny I got. I was up to almost $7,500. And aaaalll of it was from some clown or another who was smitten with my pretty face or fine body. Oh, it would've been more, much more, but I love clothes and shoes; I have a horrible shoe obsession.

But I couldn't fess up to any of that, you know, not working but loafing, so instead I lied. "I applied to Montclair State University and Rutger's University, waiting to see if I'm accepted. Hoping to transfer from junior college."

"Oh, that's good. What you thinking about majoring in?"

I remember thinking, *Dang why he going down that road?* That's why I only did two semesters and stopped at junior college. It was just too many decisions to make: what classes, what days of the week do I work, what days do I study, and what do I wanna major in. *DANG!* I thought. It was just too much to think about.

But out of my mouth I said, "I dunno, medicine, business, I'm undecided."

"Well, once you get in there the world is your oyster, right?" he replied, trying to be positive.

"Yeah, yeah, that's what they say." I dreaded this whole conversation; he knew it too. So instead, he invited me to a game of pool. But as we played, he kept talking about my career, and what I wanted to do. I felt like I was in a meeting with my parents, my grandparents, and the high school counselors all rolled into one. He didn't know this was a sore spot of mine, a really sore spot. I was already aggravated and pissed off with everybody telling me to reach for the stars, when I'd already decided to take these few years to chill that eventually I blasted out, zipping straight to the point so he could get off my back.

Andrea Clinton

"On the real—I just wanna chill! I wanna just find somebody who's about something, who wanna be something, and let him love me and take care of me. I wanna chill! Take care of our home while he takes care of me. Then one day, maybe we can think family. But, much later cause I wanna be selfish for a few years." I paused, so did he. "I just want somebody who wanna chill out a few years just loving me, going places and seeing things, doing things, having things, ya know?" I meant it Athena; I wanted to chill out like you so-called Goddesses do, ya know? Coming and going and just chillin'.

Without a blink, and with an attitude, I chalked my stick and hit the balls on the table, his, mine, and the eight ball. Heck, he pushed me to share my true goals. So there, he had it.

In no time at all, he had turned into my dang father, preaching from the jailhouse. I looked up at him, and he was looking at me. But he was kinda looking past me too. It seemed as if he was fixated on a thought, something that had me and my ranting in mind. I didn't know what it meant at the time, but I was sure to find out.

And what I later learned was that his fascination, his admiration, and his intrigue over me, wasn't actually about who I was, but who I could be. I didn't see this as a positive thing. I felt he wanted to make me over, change me and groom me. *He wanna change me like a pimp does a hooker,* was what I thought. Except, he wanted to trick or prostitute me into **being somebody**. *Ego tripping at the least,* I thought. Because the only time we heard sh—t poured on that thick around the way was in community centers, or from teachers in school. Other than that, you turn out, how you turn out. Choose your own route or your poison! And *no man* **EVER** pushes a woman to be somebody, unless he is a control freak, or a **pimp**.

But wait, wait, let me back up! I'm getting emotional and when I do, I jump the gun. Okay, let me get a grip, let me back it up.

Okay, basically what I'm saying is, from the very beginning I felt he just wanted to play dress up dolls with me, except for real. He'd be my black Ken, and I his black Barbie, and *he'd* be the li'l girl controlling me, us. But, turns out my free thinking is my worst enemy.

But gettin' back to the pool hall, he downplayed his feelings after what I just spit at him, while I continued to hit balls on the table. Afterwards, we stood there exchanging short words, supposedly engrossed in the other men who started playing pool. They were both famous and great pool players, and one was even from out of town. So, when they played, everyone watched. We backed up a little still looking on, and made time for short chatter, basically with Omar explaining things about the game, the men and their reputation. This changed the sullen mood I almost fell in.

Suddenly, just as he talked me into going with him to the bar, both of our pagers went off—*his first*. He was about to apologize, feeling embarrassed as having a pager meant one of two things, he was a doctor, of which he was not, or a drug dealer, which put him on blast.

I looked at him in dismay just as mine went off, because if a woman had a pager, it was understood to mean **one** thing, something totally different, I had a jealous man who kept track of me. Forget being a doctor or a drug dealer, it meant that some man was head over heels for me, and wanted to be able to contact me *whenever* possible. Okay, well that was sorta true. Ramaad, an ex boyfriend, gave me the pager, and I never returned it because I liked the way it looked on me. But I always hid it from other guys because I knew what they would think; I just forgot to hide it this time. And whether a guy or a girl, a pager is embarrassing unless you're the bragging, showboating type. Sure enough though, I had to hear it.

"Oooooow, okay. Well, you need some change to make that call sista?" He started digging in his pocket, as if he was really trying to get me some change, trying to be funny.

I just had to grin and bear it because *I bought that* even *wearing* a man's pager.

"No—no—no, I don't need no change, this is my ex boyfriend's pager. We actually broke up a li'l while ago because I wouldn't wear it for him." This was a true statement.

Andrea Clinton

"Wait, **HAAA!**" he bellowed. "Wait, but *now* that he's out the picture you wear *his* pager? But you couldn't wear it when he wanted you to?" As he fell over the bar stool laughing.

I was a little miffed at him laughing at me, but I wore a li'l smirk and tried to play it off.

"Why you laughin'?" I asked in a cute but ghetto tone us females use to flaunt.

"Because you're funny. When he wants you to wear it, for him, your man, you won't. But when y'all—" He broke up laughing all over again.

He had a point. I knew it. But I had one too. *I'm not no damn dog*, and that's how a pager from a boyfriend made a woman feel. Like he paged and we barked—it was like a damn tracking device!

As Omar laughed on and on, my smile loosened and fell from my face. With a smirk, I picked up a soda I ordered and drank. Then I helped him get over his li'l laughter, by hitting *him* up. "So what's up with your pa—" But he cut me right off, probably afraid of what I'd say next.

"Naa, naa, naa. Come on, come on. Don't worry about mine, mine is for surgery. I'm due at the hospital." And we both just burst out laughing.

I wanted to say, *Let's see how hard you laugh when they cart your butt off to jail for hustling*, but I just let it alone. He was smart, so I think that went without saying.

Just then, Shakirah came over and leaned on my shoulder. Why would she do that?

"You ready to go?"

I was pissed at her for putting me on the spot. Of course I'd have to say yes, I didn't want to look like I was on his jock, or sweatin' him.

"Yeah, I guess I'd better go now." Lookin' at Shakirah as if to say, *Jackasssssss!*

"Okay lady. It was nice to see you again. I guess I'll see you around," he said with a cute, handsome smirk on his face.

Then Shakirah seeing my face and realizing she busted up my rap, chimed in. "You and ya posse going to see Doug E. Fresh and Slick Rick at the spot tomorrow? We going. Maybe y'all can hook up then."

He started smiling at me, as I stared at her for being so rude; he saw straight through me.

"Aiiight. Me and the fellas talkin' 'bout checkin' it out. So I'll see y'all there."

I was still staring at her in disbelief then I turned to him to play it off.

"Okay, will do." And just as I was fixing to stand up from the bar stool, he had the nerve to shoot an adrenaline rush straight thru me. He, as a gentleman, gracefully took my hand as I stood, and said in a low enticing tone, "Aiight baby."

I thought, *Mmm. There go those manners, where they been hidin'?*

"Don't bring no sand to the beach now precious," he continued in a tone with more volume and a hint of swagger, while tucking his lips in.

"Wooooow!" Shakirah said as she spun around and headed out laughing. "No he didn't!"

I couldn't believe my ears; he's the one with the girlfriend all up in the club, after a li'l flirtation with me in the street. I spun my neck around like that little girl in *The Exorcist* and got real indignant, but playfully of course.

"No, don't *you* bring no sand to the beach brutha."

Men really have nerve.

He smiled as he let my hand go. And with me standing only a shake away, he turned his smile into a smirk.

"I don't have no more sand," he said while looking into my eyes. "I put my sand back out on the beach the other night, the night I left you at the club, and I haven't been back to that beach since."

He picked up his drink and gave me a slick smile before taking a sip. He's so sly. He knows he has a silky, smooth way about him.

I squinted at him and his slickness. But, he just held his drink, with his other hand pressed on the counter, looking into my eyes to show me *something*, again. I turned my head away. It was time to pour it on—make a much needed and arousing exit. I began

Andrea Clinton

to walk away and decided to look back at him while grazing my hand past his.

Not expecting such an action, after my somewhat delicate visit, he looked down at my fingers slipping through his and back up at my face. With my hair bouncing, I let the distance that grew between us pull me away from him, as there's something about a woman being pulled away from a man that makes him want her more, and ever so impatient to have her. And I know it affected him, because he clutched his fingers to catch mine as they slipped away. Then he looked in my face, and I in his, as our souls filled with an untimely and arousing rush. That moment was dangerous; it was mutual enchantment at its peak; it was overwhelming.

Neither of us wanted to part, not even for a moment, yet it is those parting moments that steal a place in the heart. I turned with poise and continued out, and I believe he watched me.

Bad Timing All Around...

The next night, the big night, when two of the hottest rappers were gonna be at the spot, I had the most *horrific stomach virus known to man*. I think I got it from this old lady I saw in the street the day before who was barking up phlegm, and was all germy-looking. But wherever it came from, *I was sick as a dog*.

Earlier that morning, my grandfather came over to visit us and saw me sick. He ran right out and got some blackberry brandy to put me to sleep, and Old Johnny Walker to get rid of the sickness. **WHAT THE—!** Who in **HELL** made that stuff? The taste of JW can bring a rock to life—DAMN! But I'll tell ya, he gave me a shot of JW and blackberry brandy to chase it, and *it was over;* a fat lady sang that morning.

Shakirah was there, trying to comfort me before she went with Man-Man to the spot. She was seriously on Man-Man's jock, *knowing he had a girlfriend*, although not about the baby on the way. I couldn't have cared less about any of it, which goes to show just how sick I was. I was trying to tell her to tell Omar I was sorry I couldn't make it, but the words just wouldn't come out my mouth. Shakirah kinda figured it out, half catching the words I was spewing. And when she later went to the spot, she waited for Man-Man to disappear then found Omar to tell him how sick I was.

Andrea Clinton

Would you believe he later asked my brother for permission to stop by and see me? After getting the okay, brutha left the spot after the first performance, went to the store to buy a bunch of stuff, then came to my house. Evidently, he asked Shakirah or Man-Man what was wrong with me, because he showed up with the ingredients to some concoction, made nice-nice with my mother, then went into the kitchen to mix it all up.

Not like my moms didn't know who he was. After all, she grew up around the same neighborhood with his parents. But it was a little awkward, because she hadn't had any dealings with him since he was grown. There were just greetings in the street and her asking how he was doing, his family and so on.

My mother left him in the kitchen, came into my room, sprayed the room with Lysol, and me with Fendi darn near making me sicker, threw my unmentionables in the drawer and opened up the window. After all that was done, she called him in the room.

Oh, and did I mention I was a mess? I mean, thank the Lord I took a bath midday, because no man should smell a woman when she's deathly sick *and* in the raw zone. I'm not talking about body funk, but a bad virus can give off a smell of sickness that is appalling. But, my hair was messy, kinky-wavy and all over the place, that's the bad thing about lengthy, thick hair, my mother brushed it in a ponytail for me. And I had on a yellow pajama tank top, and yellow Big Bird pajama pants. He kept saying I looked cute, like a little girl, but I could care less. *I was as sick as a dog.*

After drinking his concoction, I was good for about fifteen minutes. We talked, or rather he talked, don't ask what about, I could barely stay with him. I had the chills and was shivering as if I had bags of ice strapped to my back and chest. Omar kept putting blankets on me, then he said, "Is it all right if I hold you? You think your mother would mind? I don't want her to come in here and black out on me. You look too cute sittin' over there between them big pillows. Look like you need a hug."

I lifted my head and said, "I would mind. I don't know you like that." He smiled, even chuckled a little. I guess he saw I wanted to smile myself at the little funny I'd made, but I couldn't because my bones ached too much. Then I drifted off to sleep. Later on, I awakened to he and my mother's voice, talking about some show, with my head was on his chest. I remember thinking, *What the heck is this? I'm sick. You crazy? Get off me. I'm not even feeling right, and I probably look crazy.* But I was too tired, so I slept on his chest. I hated I was too sick to enjoy that. Because as I said before, he had natural and desirable muscles.

All that night, I tossed and turned. I pushed covers off me, and then pulled them back on. I moaned. I shook. I shivered. And each time I would go through a change, I saw him beside me, either sleep, nodding, or awake and looking at me go through my tantrum, sometimes feeling sorry for me, and sometimes laughing at me when I'd toss the covers or have a li'l fit. A few times, he was laughing with Shakirah and Man-Man who'd come in from the spot and were checking up on me. I once turned over and saw them on the fire escape smoking cigars and drinking something, probably that JW.

Man-Man must've really been kool with Omar diggin' me, because he gave him some sweatshorts and one of his tee shirts to sleep in. It was one of those *Malcom El Hajj Malik, Marley, Mandela, Martin L. King, and Marcus Garvey* tee shirts, the good ones.

Finally, I woke up at seven the next morning. I was feeling better. I didn't know what did the trick, the JW or Omar's concoction, but I was glad to be coming around. I ran to the bathroom and showered, changed even. I did my hair as best I could, putting it in a ponytail with a li'l part on the right side of my head. I threw my gold earrings on to have some kinda prettiness going on after all of that virus mess.

Just to back up a li'l, I couldn't believe my mother let him stay and be all hugged up on me like that. He must've bought her some good wine or something, I dunno. But that sucka made nice with Moms because he had a plan. My mother said every smart man will get in good with a woman's mother and never mess it up, and I guess he was smart. But that also told me something, just like it told my moms—he wants in, into my life.

When he woke up, I gave him a washcloth and towel. Then I went and started to fix some eggs and sausage. But I wasn't well at all, it just seemed like I might be coming around at first. But I

Andrea Clinton

figured it was the least I could do, even though I started feeling miserable again. Omar came into the kitchen and saw me cooking.

"Oh nooo, that's how you'll get me sick too. I'll do it." I obliged and sat down to let him fix breakfast instead.

Without even knowing it, I fell back asleep at the kitchen table. When I woke back up, he'd made a huge meal. There were two kinds of eggs, scrambled and fried, grits, sausage, a pile of toast, and coffee simmerin' in a pot. He said it would be rude to come into my mother's house and not make food for her. But it could've also been that my stepfather came in from his haul 'cross country and saw some young man in a muscle tee shirt at his stove, because he had enough for everybody in the house to eat.

I found myself feeling down all of a sudden, thinking, *This man is moving way too fast, he better have some damn money.* I figured, worst case, I'd enjoy all I could while the gettin' was good. Best case, he may grow to love me more than I love him, and then—but that wasn't a good time to make a judgment call. *I was sick as a dog.*

So, I ate a bite of eggs and a piece of sausage and then returned to my room. My mother, liking him for her daughter no doubt, was in my room cleaning, and spraying more Lysol. I wished like you-know-what that she would just move and let me lay down; I was whining and tossing all around on the chair outside my room. But then he came and convinced me to lay on the couch in the TV room.

"A different environment would be better for you anyway, plus let the room air out," he said.

He don't know I was 'bout to cuss him out. For what? *I just wanted to sleep Athena.* But as soon as we got all settled in the TV room, I fell asleep and when I woke up, he was gone. But it didn't matter because I went to the bathroom, tore it up with sickness, then came back and went to sleep again. I was definitely not better, that virus thing was still in the raw.

Later though, I heard Omar knocking on the door to my room. He'd brought me some soup. He opened the window to give me fresh air, stayed 'til I fell asleep, then left again. And this continued, with him checking in on me for a few more days. Each day I was awake a little longer, until his concoction would knock me out again. During that time, my family opened up to Omar coming over, taking care of me, and having interest in me. And he and my mother bonded. They even went back in his past where she gave him some advice on coping with it. She felt comfortable in doing so because she was around back at the time of his youth, and she saw it all go down when his family lost their religion.

"It's a new day Omar, and you as a grown man now control your own destiny. You have say now. If you feel your life changed drastically for the worse since your family stopped practicing Islam, return back to that path of praising God. Your mother went back to Islam and she been doing good staying off drugs, *and look at what she had to overcome.* Join her, help her. Y'all ain't the only Muslim family who fell off of what they supposed to be on," my mother advised, "I know plenty."

Omar confided in my mother, telling her of his deep feelings. She having some knowledge of his past could only look on feeling for him and his pain, as it's one thing to see a person go through it, but it's another when that person explains it in a way that makes you experience it.

"It's just been so long since things been right, Islamically. And now I'm used to a whole other way of life, hustling to survive. When my father was in jail and my mother on drugs, I even got a whole new family in the streets who helped me and my brother feed ourselves and my sister. Hell, we were paying the rent, and buying and hiding the food when my mother would mess up the money and food stamps, and look for more stuff to take; and I was only ten years old! That wasn't right for me to have to go through that, none of us."

"But it makes you the strong responsible man you are today *Omar.*"

"I guess. I remember that life though, the Muslim life; peace and harmony. *Remember how peaceful and safe it was around here?* Before crack? And Muslims were a family; when my father was short on rent, all the brothers gave him ten or twenty dollars and we made rent, $600. We were always going to the mosque, reading the Qur'an, Islamic school, Islamic picnics, keeping our hair cut tight, and being around all my Muslim friends everyday,

Andrea Clinton

no stealing, no robbing, no drugs. I remember, and I want it back badly. But something is holding me back from it, keeping me away from it." He started looking curious and concerned.

"I dunno what it is, but it's strong. It won't let me loose, and won't let me back in. It's like a damn oversized demon that has control over my free will. I don't even tell my father how I feel when he gives me Islamic Studies lessons Sundays at the prison, when I visit him. He got enough worries, hoping I don't get killed out here, or my brother wherever he is. He just thinks I'm hard-headed and won't visit the mosque, or *masjid*, which is what we call it now; that's Arabic for place of worship. It would be nice to have that peace we used to have. Peace in your mind, your chest and in your house." He touched each part of his body that he mentioned.

"Maybe that peace of mind just ain't for me no more," as he looked out the window with what looked like tears building in his eyes.

I caught the tail end of that conversation, and with all that talk of peace, my mother looked like she was considering Islam. She remembered seeing the Muslim's closeness, and peace, but I don't think she *ever* felt it on the inside until she listened to Omar ache to have it again.

She even shed a few tears talking to him because as she told me several times, "I witnessed the rise and fall of the black Muslims, it was good while it lasted, and although we didn't always agree with them, we saw a need for their presence, and the fight they had in 'em; seemed like it was what had been missing among the blacks since *Nat Turner.* But then, the Muslims died out, like everything else that comes along to help blacks. And like those of us who were Black Panthers, a lot of the Muslims were exposed to drugs and jail, followed by self-destruction *and a lot of death.* I experienced it and saw it with my own eyes; I don't need no textbook to tell me about it. Wanna know how they knocked us off this time?" my mother would ask. "*THE MAN* used chemical warfare to take us *back* down a few notches; they threw heroin and liquor stores in the ghettos; took our asses *out* before we even knew the new type of war they waged on us. Then, they boxed us in hell so we could take one another out." When she'd depressed herself enough, she'd stare off into the sky leaving me there, all alone.

Yeah, he and my moms bonded, but as for the rest of the family, Omar and my brother Man-Man were already close friends, they were as we used to call it, **ace-boon-coons**. Man-Man used to share his food with Omar and his brother, and sometimes his clothes too when their family was down and out. So, he didn't mind Omar coming over to the house now. In the past Omar, I guess out of embarrassment of his poverty due to his moms on drugs, wouldn't go to anyone's house. He'd just wait outside the building or on the corner in front of the bodega waitin' for them. It wasn't a talked about thing, I just noticed it many times.

Manny didn't mind Omar coming over now, but he felt his behavior with me was strange, so he started conducting an interview with Omar about his intentions. And basically Omar passed the interview.

My stepfather obviously grew to like Omar because he finally started answering to Omar's, *Hello, sir.* He even sat one day and played spades with them, and he rarely comes out of his room except to walk around and see if everything is kosher with us.

As for me, I could care less how much he came over, not like I was well to enjoy it. He watched me toss and turn, and laughed with my family who said I looked like an ate-up, sweaty Pocahontas-wannabe.

Andrea Clinton

Tag—You're It!

By the end of the week, I was finally fully awake and feeling great. Once I showered and did my hair, I grabbed the telephone and gave Omar a call. He'd left his number with my mother. I got no answer, so I kept calling all day to say thank you, but still no answer. Ironically, I didn't feel funny 'bout calling him so much.

Later that evening, my brother Man-Man came in.

"Guess who's sick?"

"Who?" I answered.

"Omar. He went to the emergency room this morning. Now he's in the hospital. Room 414. And I'm startin' to feel sick too." Holding his stomach, he headed to his room. "You gettin' everybody sick!"

It was around nine o'clock at night, but I wanted to see Omar. So I paid Jerry, this lady next door, to take me. She was on crack and would do anything for a few dollars. I was just happy to be bringing him the concoction he'd made for me, and of course to see him, return the favor.

But when I got up there and walked in the room, Omar was on the bed, tilted upward, looking feverish, with guess who? *VANESSA.* She was standing over him, kissing him on his cheek, rubbing his face and chest. I was crushed. It was like someone wearing a cast-iron shoe just kicked in my chest, smashed my heart, and made my stomach drop to my feet. What a letdown!

And yes, this made me want him more, but now for yet a different reason. Before I wanted him because he looked sexy in his

Cadillac and because of his hustling financial status. Then because he was much more suave and sophisticated than guys we grew up with. But at that moment, it was because he seemed unattainable, not available, not for sale; he was *someone else's man.*

I was pissed and felt empty inside. I mean, she was with him how I saw *me* being with him, caring for him. And her touching and kissing on him made him so desirable, and all women like a man who's desirable. I wanted him. But he was hers.

As sick as he was, he saw me step into the room, but was too messed up to react one way or another. She was so engrossed with hugging and kissing him that she didn't see me. So I placed the jar of concoction on the table by the door, and slipped out the room with my head hung low.

I called Jerry on a pay phone and left a message with her son saying I was walking down the main strip and to come get me. Before I knew it, I was back home. I sat alone in my room, with tears rolling down my cheeks, feeling very sad. What's a sista to do? My mother came in and saw the tears. She asked what was wrong, so, I told her what happened. She liked him for me, so she tried to mellow me out.

"You two only recently started liking one another," she told me. "You can't expect so much so soon. Give the man a break, he been through a lot, and he trying to find his way. He's made it more than clear he wants to be with you, relax and let him get well, then talk about it."

I felt I owed it to Omar to try to see him, so I brought him flowers. I took them up there *twice* but made an about face each time after seeing *Vanessa*, leaving the flowers with the nurse. After the second time, I stopped going. I knew it was more than *a player playing* with how he treated me. But I didn't have time to be sitting around trying to figure things out, or to be waiting on no man who got a woman *all over him*. And her being there with him was killing me. I didn't know why it bothered me that much, but it did. I was really starting to stress; I couldn't eat, was always thinking about him; I was going nuts. And I wasn't going to just run up in there and get my feelings hurt. And *I don't have patience*, so I backed off, all the way off. I let him go.

Andrea Clinton

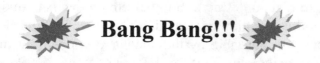

Bang Bang!!!

Omar was in the hospital for about a week, beating my sick record. But I gotta tell ya that week felt like a month with time ticking very slow. As soon as he started feeling a li'l better, he called my house from the hospital. But both times, I wasn't there. I never called him back because I was starting to catch feelings for him, and I couldn't afford to do that and get hurt. So, after I dropped him those flowers the last time I went up there, I decided to forget about him. Remember the plan, what great-grandma said, *he's* supposed to *love me more than I love him*, and if not him, hell somebody was supposed to.

After a few days, he was discharged. And before he did anything else, he wanted to see me. It was seven o'clock at night by the time he got settled in his place. His sister and that girl brought him home. He called me and asked if I could come over, but I was on my way out.

"On your way out—where? With who?" he said getting jealous, knowing how I run with guys.

He sounded angry as if even he thought we were starting something; but now here I was going out with a brutha. The same way I felt when I saw *Trixie*, that's right, ole Vanessa, at the hospital smooching all over him.

He was just coming home and I didn't want to get him all stressed out, especially after being there for me when I was sick, so I just said, "Out. I'm going out." I was stuck on protecting my feelings and not falling for the okie-doke, but was trying to be mindful of his feelings.

" *With some dude?* Who? Tell me so I can rearrange that date right quick!" In a firm tone.

I felt for him, but who felt for me while he was resting and getting well, and I was the one rolling around in bed and couldn't sleep all day and all night? Listening to Teena Marie's *Portuguese Love,* and *Out On A Limb* and Phyllis Hyman's *Living All Alone,* which was killing me, and her, *Can We Fall In Love Again,* which finished me off. I was a mess. So I put up my defenses and I stood firm; self preservation, I ran it in the hole.

"Look, I'm glad you good now, and you and your girl good, and I hope you got my flowers. But right now, I gotta bounce. Take care." Then I hung up the phone.

Now why did I do that? Here's where you find out a nuckaz true colors. Now see, as I explained earlier, I knew his family's issues: the fights in his house when he was young; his father coming home from jail and beating up his mother and her new boyfriends; father beating mother for doing drugs, and bringing them in front of the kids; father beating mother for being wild in the streets; hell, his father even beat up drug dealers, even shot and tried to kill one for selling her drugs, and letting her build up credit with them; and finally police kicking in the doors to get the father for attempted murder, which is why he's there now. I mean, I remember all that action with their family; crap was happening every few days with them. When you are walking down the street, or playing outside as a kid, and you see all this crazy negativity, it stays with you. And somewhere in my head, I knew it had to affect him somehow. But, I never, ever thought about seeing the effects of his past. *That Negro can get **Psycho** when he ready.*

After what came next, I had to rethink this whole *Omar* thing. Because I was my mother's child: spoiled, sometimes selfish. And, at times I liked to play games with a man. You know, to keep him on his toes, get him jealous, or just get him back on top of his game. But if ya man is Norman Bates, you can't bug-out like that. All kinda crazy sh—t can happen to you if you try them games with him. They'll find ya ass sixty years later, buried

Andrea Clinton

between two slabs of cement, with a king-size knot on ya forehead and a <u>giant bone</u> stickin' out ya neck 'cause that muthaf—ker done broke it. I'm tellin' you, them Psycho—Norman Bates nuckaz get crazy! Deranged!

I mean, I know I shouldn't compare him with his father, but the first time I saw Omar witness drama with his parents will forever stain my brain: when neighbors said he and his father found his mother shootin' up in a locked room in the house with some guy, and his father dragged the guy out, beat him up and left him bloody, broke her drug needles in the streets, and then dragged her out the house, down the stairs, and slapped her around; *NUTTY!* Then he went and got drunk for the first time, and sat on the porch all night long. ***That type of nuttiness has an effect on the kids.*** I mean, I know Omar's mom bought that on herself but, dang—you gotta have the psychiatrist on speed dial messing with them type niggaz, or a straight jacket that straps on by remote.

Anyway, the night Omar came home from the hospital, I had a date with Qydeer, someone who used to live around here, but moved away when he was in junior high school.

One of those days when I was sad over Omar, he came by to visit the old neighborhood and saw me in the laundromat looking sad. He asked why I looked so down and before I knew it I said, "I just lost a good friend." Then I gave him a hug and asked how he was doing.

We talked for a while, and then he gave me his number and said he wanted to take me out to dinner one night. I considered it, but for all the wrong reasons. I wanted to get Omar out of my mind. Had I been thinking, I wouldn't have even bothered, because Qydeer and Omar had history, baaaaad history.

They used to go to the Muslim school, back in the day, and didn't quite get along *then.* This was before all the activity at Omar's house, when things were kosher at their home and they were down with and living properly like all the Muslim families 'round the way.

But when some of the Muslims split up due to differences of opinion, around the late '70s, ***this is when*** you saw many of the Muslim's conduct change; and the kids followed their parent's behavior. Some of my Muslim friends suddenly weren't so tight anymore, and were told to stop speaking to the others of them. They would even fight, calling each other names like *Two-faced Uncle Tom*. Some said the white man is the devil and the others said Allah loves us all, and, *"Devils come in many forms!"* I was confused like, *Dang! Why y'all gotta fight? Can't y'all just get along? You're confusing the order of things."*

I never fully understood it. Omar and Qydeer were two of the worst Muslims acting out, because this issue gave them more of an excuse to hate one another. They were always at it.

So anyway, I decided to call Qydeer. When he picked up, I simply said, "Come get me." He said okay, remembering where I lived. As he drove up that night, the night Omar had gotten home from the hospital and called me, I heard some arguing outside. I looked out the window and saw Qydeer's car, so I ran downstairs hoping to be gone before crazy Omar hit the scene.

As we drove away, I saw my brother come out the corner store, glaring after us. I'm like, *What's his problem?* So I asked Qydeer what was going on and he said, "Nothing. Ya brother just has a problem with me taking you out. Do you?"

Thinking my brother was just being over protective I said, "No. If I did, I wouldn't have agreed to go out with you. Anyway, let's hit a movie or something."

See as far as I remembered, Qydeer was quiet. He wasn't a hell-raiser like some turned out to be. How it was, if those Muslims let the disagreements between them stop them from practicing, like Omar's mother, then their households usually became chaotic, and that made their kids turned out to be a hot mess, *one way or the other*. Believe me, I've seen enough to have plenty examples. But if their parents were still on point, survived the trials and tribulations, including the death of Malcom X or the breakup of their Muslim group with this one or that one, then the kids were still on point. And this you loved to see, it gave hope to the community. And from what I could see, Qydeer's mother was still on point. I saw her downtown, from time to time, covered up and the whole nine. So I felt safe that she was keeping her son on point.

We went to the movies and saw *The Color Purple*. I should've known this night would become emotional because that movie set the tone. It really affected me and I could not rise above everything it made me feel.

"You wanna go to dinner, get some grub? Maybe that will take your mind off of it," Qydeer suggested.

"Yeah, I guess. I guess I'm just so emotional because my family is from Georgia."

"Yeah, I hear you. It touched me too. Especially that whole father thing, having a baby by him, and then it wasn't her father. I'm like dang."

"I know. I gotta see that again, though."

"Well, I'm sorry. Once was enough for me. I can't get emotional like that. Too girly."

I found that so funny, so I grabbed his arm. I don't think I grabbed it to flirt or because I was touched by him getting in touch with his feminine side. It was more because I just needed a man to replace the one I lost, the one I never had.

While we were havin' dinner, my pager started going off. I know I wore it around a guy again, whatever though. I ignored it for a while, but it kept saying 9-1-1. So when I got up to go to the bathroom, I asked Qydeer for some change for the pay phone. You didn't think I'd spend my own when I was out on a date, did you? Get serious! Anyway, I took the change and went to the phone booth to call Shakirah, who was blowin' up my pager by now. She said Man-Man and Manny were going off, riding around looking for me and Qydeer. She was both excited and afraid as she told me what was happening.

"*GIRL!* Omar came by your house and he was mad! R.I.P. was there and told him your brothers were out looking for you and Qydeer. I was watching all this from my window and saw Omar get *even more* pissed than he already was when he heard you were with Qydeer. Like after waiting about ten or fifteen minutes, Omar and R.I.P. were talking, one of Qydeer's boys pulled up in his Honda and was like, 'Yo, yo, you seen my boy, Qydeer?' Girl, *Omar lost his damn mind!* The guy's car window was halfway down, Omar walked in front of the guy and kicked the window in. Then the guy tried to pull out a gun, but Omar smashed his arm against the car door, banging it 'til the guy dropped his piece. He snatched the guy and dragged him out of the car window and started beating him bloody. Girl, every time he hit him, you heard it. **BOW! BOW!**

"Before all that went down, your moms had managed to calm Omar down, tellin' him that he didn't want to scare you off with a temper, and to just give you a day to think, because right after she spoke to him she called me and told me to page you. But then this guy pulled up and being one of Qydeer's boys, it was just the excuse Omar needed to let lose. Girl, people started coming over to watch. I'm looking down from my window, seeing it all! He beat him senseless!

"Man-Man pulled up, mad, but he calmed down a little, laughing at Omar beating this guy up. He was like, 'Yo, this nigga crazy, haahaaaaaaaaaaa! That's Qydeer boy O' whoopin' right? He putin' a hurtin' on that boy! He *really is* nuts. My boy!' Putting a cigar in his mouth. Then he was like, 'Damn he 'bout to kill this nigga, yo haaaaaaaaaaaaaaaaa!' with that loud laugh he do.

"Man-Man being sarcastic yelled to Omar, 'Ay, O'? Omar? Yo, you wanna get a body man? 'Cause you 'bout to get one you hit that nigga one mo' time,' then Omar bust 'em a hard heavy one across the face. **BOW!** Man-Man was like, 'Haaa.'"

Man-Man was tellin' Omar in his own way to stop and think. I guess the way he'd have wanted someone to break it up if it were him fighting 'cause nobody likes a person to grab on 'em.

"Girl, Man-Man was like, 'Hey, if you don't care, I don't care man.' Then he turned to Omar's partner, you know, Pep; Pep followed Omar to ya house. So, he turns to Pep, 'Yo, you not gonna get ya boy?' Man-Man asked while lighting his cigar. 'I figure he won't mind one of his boys calming him down.'

"But Pep stayed right where he was, smoking his cigarette, and shrugged his shoulders talkin' 'bout, 'Unn unnh! Psssh! That nigga be done when he done!' Man-Man just shook his head at how Omar had everyone cautious of him; then he smirked."

Shakirah went on to tell me that Manny the class clown said, "Yo, I never saw nobody beat somebody to death before, this will be my first–**hoooooo, yo** you see that hit? He bustin' that big dude up!"

Andrea Clinton

She said Man-Man turned around and smirked at him, puffing on his cigar, "You stupid. You saw people get beat to death before, plenty of times."

"Nope. I saw a nigga get shot, stabbed, hell, even beat with a tree branch to death, but never death by hand. *Poppy this gives you a rush,"* he said in a Spanish accent, putting one hand on his chest and the other up by his shoulder doing the Salsa dance. Then he made a horse sound, "Hhuhhuuuuuuuuhhhh!" And they laughed.

Shakirah continued telling me what had happened. "Girl, Omar kept beating him, I dunno, maybe because the guy was so damn big. It wasn't 'til ya mother yelled to Omar to stop before he killed him that Omar finally quit beatin' that dude. Man-Man just puffed his cigar. Omar paced around a little, and then went into the corner store and came out with a paper towel wiping his hands, which were filled with blood from busting that dude up.

"Man-Man told Omar to go upstairs and change, to look in his closet and get something to wear, and Omar ran up inside ya building. Then Man-Man paced around and was starting to get revved up again. Because even though *that* was over with Omar, he still didn't know where you were or if you were safe. He was starting to yell. 'Yo where the hell is Alisa? Sh—t!' Then Manny didn't find nothing funny no more and was sitting tense and quiet, waiting to bust a cap in Qydeer.

"When Omar came back downstairs, seeing them two worried, he got stirred up again and started pacing, with his hands on his hips. He saw me in the window and told me to page you."

"Who, Man-Man?"

"No! Omar told me to."

She went on, telling me about all their pacing and worrying. She said Omar's whole crew showed up; they were nervous, which was unusual. But remember Omar was their unspoken leader and it was unusual for him to display his anger. I *never* saw him angry like that, not in all my years of knowing him. I mean when we were younger, when he fought, he just fought, win or lose and that was that. Just a few rages here and there. But this time, Omar had gotten so vexed and worked up such a rage, they figured he was about to land himself in jail.

Don't get me wrong, he was jealous over me. But I'm not that vain or slow, most of his anger was due to his beef with Qydeer; they hated each other.

Shakirah started filling me in on the rest, "I'm not sure what they were saying about Qydeer or what he did that's so bad, but Manny yelled, 'Yeah man, ev'rybody know that nigga did that sh—t! It was on the news and the whole nine!' Then Omar chimed in with, 'And this nigga out with Alisa! Damn!' Then he turned to Pep and screamed, 'How he wiggle back into town man! *How? How this nigga get this sh—t off!*' Then Pep just turned his head afraid or as if he was ashamed. I dunno girl, maybe Pep is in charge of things like that, like security. I missed what it was they said Qydeer did, but it made your moms nervous, so she went back in the window and called ya crazy family; then, called me again to see if you answered my page."

I was listening on the phone to Shakirah like, okay calm down! Chill! I didn't know where my head was, but I was not feeling this whole thing. I wasn't afraid, nervous, concerned or anything. I guess my head was still probing the friendly skies over Omar and that girl. I know it sounds nuts Athena, but, I couldn't concentrate or pull it together; it was like a dream turning into a nightmare. It never even dawned on me to think, *What are they all so mad over? Did Qydeer do something foul before he came here? Is my life in danger?* I was too focused on, *I'm having a nice time, a nice date.*

So I hung up, went to the bathroom, then sat back down at the table. I noticed Qydeer kept looking at me as if he was trying to read me, but I ignored it and just smiled.

"So who keeps beeping you all night, some nigga?"

"No, Shakirah, you remember Shakirah?"

"Yeah, I remember her, I saw her the other day. She looks different, put on a few pounds. I remember she used to be so skinny, we called her Skinny Minny."

"Well, she's still skinny."

"Yeah but not like before." Then we both laughed.

Everything was going fine. We were eating. I had fried chicken with hot sauce, yams, mac and cheese; he had beef ribs. I mean, it was all good in the hood. He even introduced me to a slow gin fizz. It was a very sexy tasting drink. But that should've been a clue. If he's still on *the truth*, as they called it when Muslim folk practiced Islam properly, then why would he know this drink? *Muslims don't drink!* And why would he be introducing it to me? But I was so freakin' slow this night; sue me.

So anyway, I asked him for a few quarters to put some music in the jukebox. As I went down by the bar area, all of a sudden I hear: Pow! Pow! Pow!

I dropped down, looking for cover. As I hit the floor, I glanced over to Qydeer to see if he was okay? This man falls to the floor, pulls a gun from the back of his pants, aims at the window and starts bucking back. No one was shooting anywhere near me, so I jumped up to run out the front door. But other folks started running also, crowding the entrance, Qydeer too. So I backed up to get out the way. My mother always told me, don't run in crowds, stop, think.

Qydeer grabbed me by my hand.

"No! I'm not going out there! I don't know who's out there! And why niggaz shootin' at you?" He didn't say anything, just watched his back, and quickly tipped out. He must've thought I was joking because he came back for me.

"Nigga please! You def'? I ain't goin' nowhere wit' you! I'll get a cab." He just waved his hand at me and ran out to his car. I peeked out the window and watched him get in and drive off.

As things started to calm down, I went over to the bartender, asking for change. He tried to get funky on me. So I told him I was Man-Man's sister, "Man-Man fool! From the spot!" Then he not only got me the phone, he dialed the number himself.

He was about to hand me the phone when the police came barging in, so he just said, "Yo Man, this Keith at Soul Spoon. Ya sista down here and some fools was just shootin' at her and her date, some dude. He left her though."

After he hung up, I just sat while I waited. When the cops showed up, I started moving around from seat to seat, avoiding the cops asking me anything. When they did come to me, I tried to act as if I was too shaken to speak, and kept my eyes open for my brothers.

After awhile, Man pulled up driving Omar's car, they both got out the car. This was a rare thing. You never saw them two together in a car like that. They didn't roll together, ever. Oh, they'd have each other's back. But with common enemies, they'd get knocked off easily if they rolled up side-by-side. So they NEVER rolled together, period.

I should've felt special, having them show up together to pick me up, but I didn't. I felt like a troublemaker. I kept thinking, *I hope nothing else jumps off, 'cause they'll always remember it as my fault. And here we go again with me going on a date that causes serious drama—gun drama no less. And Mommy always sayin' it's gonna blow up in my face one day. Damn! Please not tonight!*

I was scared when they showed up, not of them, but from what happened; it finally hit me. Omar got out the car first, 'cause Man-Man was driving. By the time I saw them, the police were already waiting. As soon as Man got out, they put him up against the car door and patted him down. Omar looked back at him, and Man-Man yelled, "No, no, just go make sure my sister's all right."

I couldn't go out, the owner was blocking the doorway, but he stepped to the side, letting Omar in. "What's shakin', O'?" he said, as Omar shook his hand while still making his way to me.

I couldn't help but be happy to see him; it just hit me all of a sudden. Before I knew it he was lunging at me, grabbing and hugging me. I could tell he saw the fear written all over my face. I was receptive and hugged him back ever so tight.

Omar asked what happened, but then put his hand on my mouth not to speak, 'cause there was a cop just behind us. The cop asked him to spread 'em, he wanted to check him. Omar went up against the counter and did what he was told. I got nervous.

"What are you doing? He just came to pick me up!"

"It's aiiight baby. They gotta check everybody until they catch them fools." Hearing this, the cop figured Omar was good, so he backed off.

Just then, Man-Man walked in and hugged me. **Please note:** my brother *NEVER* hugs me. I mean, unless it's graduation, or something like that. Or like when one of my favorite uncles was shot dead in the streets in front of me, while taking me to the corner store, which is another story. I was his pest of a sister, and we were kool with that. But he was worrying, and now he could put his mind at ease. But both he and Omar wouldn't rest until they got me out of there and questioned me about Qydeer.

We got in the car. We were about six corners away when we met up with fifteen or so vehicles, SUVs and the whole nine, and Manny was riding shotgun in one of them, toting a gun of some sort no doubt. I didn't like this business of a posse. It was too much like in the Old West, which is why bruthas in the hood changed from calling themselves gangs and crews to sayin' **'My posse.'** I guess to seem more cowboy like, considering way back in the wild west days more men died than in many wars, so they say. That thought had never occurred to me before, but it sure did make sense when seeing all the boys round up like herds. Together, both Man-Man and Omar's posse's looked like a huge goon squad of thugged out cowboys on a gun slinging trail.

We drove to The White Castle in the next town over to avoid heat from the police. And I called my mother to tell her I was safe. She asked for my brother and told him that Qydeer had called for me. I dunno why she didn't' tell *me*. So anyway, R.I.P. went inside and ordered like 100 burgers and 100 fish, and whatever else them goons wanted.

While they ate, I sat outside talking to Omar and Man-Man, leaning on Omar's car. I didn't have much to tell them. I mean me and Qydeer only went to the movies, had dinner, talked and that was it. But a few things I told them had them concerned. I told them, "Qydeer said Man-Man didn't want him taking me out; and when I came from the phone booth, Qydeer looked at me funny, asking who was I speaking with. I told him Shakirah, then I got up and went to the jukebox to put a song on, and that's when some dudes did a drive-by."

Then Man-Man said what he and Omar were both thinking,

"This nigga gonna think you dropped a dime on 'em."

I was like, "Drop a dime on him for what? Why would I do that?"

Man started pacing, while Omar explained, "I was already pissed 'cause you was out with another nigga." He raised his eyebrows as if he wanted me to know he didn't appreciate that. "But then I'm told you out with *this nigga* and I'm like damn! This fool got an S.O.S. out on him for raping his girl's 15 year old daughter and beating the son damn near death."

Man-Man jumped in, "You know what a S.O.S. is, *right?*" He was getting annoyed at me now.

"Yes I know. But, who the heck gets a **Shoot-On-Sight** put on them nowadays besides a crackhead? *He gettin' high?*"

Man continued, "They don't know if he really raped the daughter. They said his girl could've made it up because she caught him cheating on her with her sister. But, this nigga put cigarettes out on the little boy, beat him so bad he broke his leg; he beat him almost to death and the li'l boy was only four years old."

Then Omar hit me with, "Remember Base, Geronimo's half brother?" I shook my head to say no. "The one who doing time in Trenton prison?" he continued. I still wasn't sure who he was talking about. "Well, Qydeer started going with Base baby mother a couple of months ago on some payback mess, not long after he got home from prison. Those were Base's kids Qydeer did that to, on some old Ra-Ra sh—t 'cause Base didn't help him when some niggaz did him dirty when they were in prison two years ago.

Man chimed in, "Base said he remembered Qydeer when he was young, you know a young Muslim around the way. So he tried to look out for him and told him to get with the Muslims up there. But Qydeer didn't listen, talkin' 'bout the Muslims up there were on some new stuff. Base said Qydeer tried to amp on him to show them other bruthas he was tough, 'cause Base had already made a name for himself. Qydeer swung on him and yelled he was gonna kill Base and all this crazy stuff, tryin' to impress or make a name for *himself.* Base got tired of Qydeer smackin' his hand when he was only trying to look out for him. So Base washed his hands of him and them big dudes got together and stuck 'em."

"They raped *Qydeer?*" I shouted.

"*Yeah, Qydeer,*" Omar said calm and firm, looking like he was debating on whether he should get jealous over my outburst about Qydeer's rape. But he continued, "And now Base got every body on the street lookin' for this nigga, because when Qydeer came home, he came with a vengeance. He been on the run for like three weeks now."

I sat watching and listening to this stuff in amazement as Man-Man continued, "I'm mad 'cause this *Chester the Child Molester* came into town, and asked my sister out and put *her* in jeopardy! He betta' hope I don't get to him first. *I don't want no reward money*! I'm taking his ass *OUT!*" My brother looked like he could spit fire, he was so mad.

"Man, I been wantin' this nigga from way back," Omar said feeling frustrated also.

"Yeah I remember, on that move right?" my brother said, sharing some secret between them. I don't think it had nothing to do with anything I knew of, just some other street stuff I didn't know about. And I didn't want to know. I was disgusted and it showed.

"You okay baby?" Omar asked me. Then my brother rolled his eyes and stepped away. I think if I read him correctly, he was thinking, *Man, I'm too aggravated to hear him talk this mushy sh—t to my sister.*

I just nodded yes. I was too mind-boggled to feed into what was happening that night. My mother used to always threaten me with going to Georgia. Now here I was, ready to go. I'd even pay for the ticket. I might not have been ready to do something positive or meaningful with my life like school, or Peace Corps or nothing, but I surely didn't want no parts in this sh—t.

"Look at me," Omar said, lifting my head up with his hand ever so sensitively. "You okay?" I guess he wanted to make sure by looking into my eyes, as I was staring at the ground.

"Yeah, I'm kool." But even a fool could see this was just too much drama for me. I'm used to catfights, things I can control. I mean if this was a war between girls I would've been kool. But this was a man thing, and all that testosterone was making my nerves jump. Because if there's one thing I learned early on, you can't control no man, unless he wants you to control him. I don't care what you think, and these bruthas had their mind set on a gunfight at the O.K. Corral.

Omar was good at acknowledging my feelings, even from the beginning, and before I could put a finger on them myself.

"I wanna go home. This is too much for me. I don't belong in all this."

My eyes started to water so he drew me toward him, placing my head on his shoulders, and holding me with care. I knew I was safe, and I felt that this little nook, this corner upon him that I was drawn into was a safe one. But I also knew I'd mess it up, I just knew it. As I lay in his nook, I knew then that someday I would mess up this comfort zone, as I am who I am, and I do what I do; me, the f—kup, who's always lost and need to be found.

He felt me tremble in his arms, "You're not still sick are you?"

"No, I'm fine, been for a while. What about you?" I said, looking into his face, his eyes.

"I'm good. No fever, no chills. I *been* feeling better though, they made me stay another day because my sister and them were so worried."

"Them, huh?" I said with a li'l witticism. I felt the pit of my stomach **drop** when he said, '*them*' so I had to let that out; I just had to say something.

Then we fell into a dead silence, both afraid to think about me walking into his hospital room seeing Vanessa all over him. I was afraid to discuss it; I didn't know how the discussion might end. I mean, I could tell by the way he was holding me that he didn't want us to part, and I took comfort in that. But, it had to be dealt with, and I was never one for good timing, but was always one for botching a good thing up.

So, I dove in, "Look—" as I began to move back and get things started, but he did something that scared the pants off me. My great-grandmother once told my mother, "A good man is a man who will stop you from sticking your foot in your mouth or doing the wrong thing at the wrong time." I think she'd charge O' as being a good one.

Omar stopped me in my tracks, "Not here, not now. If we gotta do this, let's go inside where we can be alone."

I should've known better, he's a very private person, and his peoples were already talkin' no doubt.

Andrea Clinton

But you know what really got me spinnin' my wheels? As I walked to the door, he opened it for me. *Those darn manners are gonna make it hard for me to be strong in my spot if he tries to pour it on thick,* I thought.

So we went inside, but I didn't want to sit at a booth, too paranoid about getting caught up if bullets started flying. So I went to the far corner, sat at a table, and just looked at him as he sat across from me. But then I felt weak staring at him, trying to be strong; so I turned away, and he got it started.

"You know, I saw you that day when you came to see me at the hospital. I'm sorry I was too sick to go after you."

"It's fine. I mean, what can I say, that's your lady right? And her job is to be by your side," I said with one eye brow raised, *'cause he told me he left that sand at the BEACH!*

Hey, that was how I felt. He says one thing, but girlfriend felt that was her man. And it didn't seem like he told her nothing different, 'cause hell, she was still there, always popping up.

He looked away as if he was holding back or trying to find a way to speak his mind tactfully, "It's not like that baby, she just showed up by the house one day when I was sick, called my sister and they took me to the hospital. Me and her got—" He paused then said, "we *had* this on-and-off type relationship. One minute we're on, and a month or two later we're off for like seven or eight months. I never minded it because it was something to do, I mean, she was kool."

"You don't have to explain yourself to me. It works for you two, so—"

Then he cut me off, I just turned my head a li'l and dropped it.

"I know I don't have to, but I want to. I don't want you thinking that's my lady. I mean, she's nice and thoughtful and all that good stuff, but she's not my lady."

I looked at him, eyebrows raised, as if to let him know I refused to fall into the okie-doke; then I spit some reality at 'em,

"JUST A SPECIAL F—KIN' FRIEND WHO KEEPS POPPIN' UP!" I sighed, and turned my head away from him, then said, "You don't have to tell me this stuff. You don't owe me nothin'."

"*I do owe you,* I owe you an explanation because…." He paused. "Because I dig you *baby,* and I been showing you that. And I know you feel it. But I need you to *know* it. Look at me."

My punk ass looked at him.

"When you ever know me to be fake or phony? I don't have to lie to you, and I couldn't if I wanted to. How I feel about you is written all over me." He opened his arms wide as if to say, *Look at me, see, all of me wants all of you.* "I want to see what's up with us."

Like the punk I am, I gave in to his sweet talk. *He broke down,* so I had to.

"You don't know what I went through these past days," I said as I shed a tear or three. "I was, I was feeling played out. My feelings were hurt. I felt like a sucka, like you played me out big time, 'cause you know your reputation of being a player, and I didn't like that sh—t at all. But I knew I had to pull it together, so I figured I needed to go out, let somebody make me feel wanted, appreciated, not play me and other girls against each other. I started thinking, I'd probably end up sad or in tears behind some other woman all the time anyway, with you being this player."

He sat back and turned away from me, rubbing his head, like I was a handful. Then he spun around like in *The Exorcist* looking angered. "**What I gotta do?** Huh? Tell me what I gotta do to get you to see ain't nothing out here, no girl, no anything or anybody that I'd put before you. God-Allah, and my mother aside, *there's, no one.*

"I mean, I know things with me and you kinda took off from outta nowhere Alisa, but it wasn't no mistake. Baby seriously, think about it. You think I rode around the corner and saw you when I was in my car by mistake? I made it my *business* to ride by and signify. I mean, no harm intended baby, but everybody know you materialistic. So, I drove past in my Cadillac to get your attention. I know you, we grew up together. You don't think I see the niggaz you be ridin' with? Jags, Benzs, BMWs at the least. I know you don't like no bum nigga; you like a man who doing things and have things. So I flossed, and you went for it, like I knew you would. *Like I hoped you would.*"

Andrea Clinton

Then he paused, not sure what else to say. I realized this was the best he could do to make me understand that he wanted me in his life. He knew I was in no way offended at the materialistic comment, as I am who I am, and *no* woman want a broke ass, non havin' man.

"Listen, it's hard right now, and I can't really say everything I wanna say—"

I just looked at him because he was being silly and quoting Teddy Pendergrass from the *Bluenotes.*

"Don't be trying to copy Teddy Pendergrass." And we laughed. "Get ya own words man." I kept laughing at him. It was just like me to put a man on the spot like that. So I made it better by getting up and moving in for a hug. He tried to act like he was pushing me back.

"Ha-ha-ha, you got jokes, but now you ain't gettin' no hug, laugh at that." But he quickly let me in, then hugged me and kissed me on my cheek.

We sat like that for a few minutes just enjoying the hump we'd gotten over. I wish it could've stayed like that forever, cheek to cheek, just chilling.

Then I noticed his tight grip on my back lightened, so I backed up a hint and looked at him. He was staring at Man-Man and Manny, arguing and yelling in the parking lot. I turned and looked, then ran outside with Omar following.

"Why y'all arguing? What's wrong?"
Neither would answer me, so I just listened.

"Man, how was I supposed to know he was gonna bust off like that? I wasn't with him. I was with y'all riding around looking fa her ass!"

"Call that nigga and tell him don't come here Manny. I'm serious 'cause me and him gon' throw some blows if he show up here, man. He could've killed her ass! Then what? Would you still protect his ass if she was dead? Huh? And what was you gonna tell Mommy after that!"

I knew then what had happened. Evidently Geronimo and his boys were the ones who were shooting up the restaurant. They must've just found out. Man-Man was mad because I could've gotten shot, killed even. He didn't care much about that cowboy look in Manny's eyes that he gets. It's like one of those crackhead looks. Like you're trying to talk him down from his high, and he wants you to, because even he knows he too strung at the moment for his own good. But if you don't and he geeses himself up too much, it's a wrap. He will light the town up like fireworks and rockets going off on the 4th of July.

I also knew why Man-Man threw that *Mommy* bit in there. We all get out of hand, the three of us. But when you say "Mommy," we calm down. Not that we're afraid of doing whatever, we just don't wanna break her heart 'cause she been begging us since we were young not to go to jail or get in any bigtime trouble that could put us away.

Manny started pacing around like a mad man because he had to face the fact that Geronimo was careless and nearly got me killed. And he didn't want to face that fact, because if he did, he'd kill Geronimo. And that would feel just as two-faced as killing Man-Man. So instead, he paced, back and forth, back and forth. And both posses migrated to the other side of the parking lot because he looked crazy as hell.

I wanted to talk to Manny, but I first asked Man-Man if Manny had been drinking. When Man-Man said no, I turned to walk over to Manny, but Omar stopped me.

"Do you think you should mess with him when he's like that? He been drinking, *I know when somebody been drinking.*"

I wasn't afraid, so I downplayed it. "He aiight, Man said he ain't been drinkin'. He more mad 'cause he feel his back is up against the wall." Then I walked over to Manny, "Yo Manny, you aaiiight?"

He turned around, pissed. I dunno if I've said this or not Goddess, but Manny is a little more emotional than Man-Man. He takes things personally, and gets his feelings hurt. He stopped and looked at me kinda crazy.

"Yeah! I'm aaiiight."

"You know Manny, Man-Man was just—"

Then he cut me off, "You know I would never let nobody hurt you! I don't play that sh—t! *I would never let nobody hurt*

Andrea Clinton

you! You family, girl!" He almost knocked me down running up on me, hugging me.

Somebody didn't know what they were talking about because Manny did have a drink. I smelled the beer on his breath. He wasn't drunk though, because he, like Man-Man always kept his wits about him, especially when in the streets. But, Manny will pass out drunk in the house, and forget who you are, or that y'all kool when drinking a lot, which is why Omar was being cautious.

"Manny, chill man. I'm good. I never even thought you'd do something like that. Man-Man knows you wouldn't either."

"No, he thinks I'd let Geronimo hurt you on some old dumb sh—t! And I wouldn't do that! Family is family!"

I backed up from Manny, "Listen, you know the deal with Man-Man and Geronimo. Man-Man just a li'l jealous, 'cause you and Geronimo got something in common that you and Man-Man don't. He jealous 'cause y'all both Puerto Rican. He just working on emotions Manny-baby. He know you wouldn't turn on me for nobody, not even Geronimo."

"Well he betta' know," he said, looking over at Man-Man, squinting his eyes and pacing, doing the two-step. Then Manny looked at me and suddenly seemed to feel a li'l better. He reached out and gave me another hug.

Now, no one could've predicted this, but while he was holding me, while I was in my brother's arms assuring him that I KNOW he had my back and loved me like a blood sister, out of nowhere, and like crazy, loud blasts of wild gunfire went off everywhere, and cars were going into skids and crashing. Manny pushed me down so hard I heard my knuckles bang against the cement as I hit the ground. He whipped out a gun and started shooting at some cars. While he was shooting, he bent over me and grabbed hold of my pants by the waist and dragged me behind a car a few steps away. The whole time, I made sure to keep my head down. *People began shooting like crazy all around.* Bang! Bang! Bang! Bang! Here, there, all over, every-dag-on-where.

Something told me to peek around the car to see what was going on, and to see if anyone was hit. And when I did, Manny got shot. I saw it out the corners of my eyes. I saw him take a bullet in his stomach. I tried to grab hold of his leg to pull him down behind the car. But he wouldn't budge, he saw too much Al Pacino in *Scarface*. He kept shooting like a madman, and screaming all this stuff in Spanish, until he took another bullet in the side of his neck.

How that happen was, okay, rewind: I reached up for him, again, thinking he was gonna fall weak from that shot in the stomach and get shot again. When I looked up to grab him, I saw another bullet pierce his neck, and his body went limp. So, I grabbed his leather jacket and snatched him toward me with everything I was worth, with the jaws of life, and he fell on his back.

Just then, all HELL broke loose; a loud shotgun blast knocked out the window where Manny was just standing. That blast would've blew his entire stomach out had I not snatched him down; they were aiming to kill him.

As Manny lay on the ground behind the car, I tried to look him over to see how bad off he really was. He was a bloody mess. Out of the corner of my eye, I saw Omar and Man-Man, squatting on the ground, shooting. Suddenly, their bodies jerked as if they might've been hit. But, they kept on shooting, so I figured they must be okay, right? Wrong!

I stayed with Manny and tended to him as best I could, talking to him through my crying, "Sssssh Manny, you gonna be all right." Every so often, I'd have to drop my head as a bullet hit something near me. I, in a millisecond thought about people in Africa and the Middle East who go through this on a daily basis; I wept for them because that type of crap ain't right for innocent people to have to go through. I became so messed up waiting for it to be over. I didn't care much about anything anymore, and I think I was starting to lose it.

The gunman's car that was closest to us started driving off, but those in it were still shooting back. Two other cars stayed behind, keeping up the fight. But I was so worried about Manny, I couldn't think on it. I had on a shirt and a sleeveless white tee under it, so I snatched off my shirt and wrapped it around his neck to stop the bleeding. I didn't know what to do about his stomach, and I'd just spotted a wound in his chest. *And blood was everywhere.*

Andrea Clinton

Then a thought popped into my head, *Man-Man.* I looked over and saw him and Omar lying on the ground. It looked like a bullet struck them while they were lying there 'cause their bodies jerked.

Omar was trying to reach out to me. "Nooooo! Stay! Stay down! I'm good!" I said as I looked at him struggling with his gunshot wounds. A man to the core he was trying to be strong even in his looking helpless.

Bullets were still flying and hitting everything in sight. Those guys really wanted them dead. Had it not been for Man-Man and Omar's posse's scattering when Manny was acting crazy prior, firing back at those cars from different directions, we all would've been killed instantly; because of the way those guys just came out of no where, and we would've been all clustered together.

Finally, a second car drove off and there was only one left. *I had had it.* It was like the firing was never gonna stop. I lost it. I just up and ran over to where Manny's gun dropped a few steps away, not even realizing what I was doing, and picked up Manny's gun. I had to be runnin' on instinct because I don't like guns and never had nothin' to do with 'em. Even after my father showed us kids how to shoot, I still didn't mess around with guns.

But at that moment, I didn't hesitate. I grabbed that 9mm and started in on that third car, along with both Omar and Man-Man's people who had scattered even more, which probably drove off the second car. We all just let in on them, banging back. The first shot threw me, like when you're learning to drive and press your foot down hard on the gas and the car jerks because you're not used to the pedal and the movement. But after that, it's all gravy. This was no different. And I had instantly remembered everything my father had taught me. So, I just banged out, but never hitting anyone.

I had gotten tired, and didn't want to shoot senselessly, so I paused. I saw the third car try to speed off. When I realized they were getting away, I aimed for one of their tires and shot it out, just like they do in the movies. The car swerved, slid into a parked car, and then slammed into a pole.

By then, cops were coming from different directions, sirens and the whole nine. R.I.P. came from behind me and took the gun out my hands, then ran behind The White Castle. He already had a lot of guns on him, but was rubbing mine on his leg as he ran. I knew what he was doing, but I was a mental mess.

I turned and stepped toward Man-Man, who was quiet and stone-cold still on the ground. I crouched down and kneeled beside him. Then I looked to the right of him and saw Omar, who had stopped moving, and his eyes were shut. I knew the cops would get to us in any moment, so I searched both of their pockets but neither had any weapons. I wasn't worried about drugs because they had runners for that. Pep, who was shot in the arm, ran over to us, took off his jacket and laid it across Omar's chest and held it.

"Look in the back of that car Alisa and get one of those jackets and put it on Man-Man, hold it down to stop the bleeding."

Just as I was getting the two jackets out the car, I heard some lady who'd just come out the store scream, "Omar and Man-Man dead!"

All the composure I had was lost. I looked at their still bodies and screamed, and I cried. I lost it. Manny who was shot *more times* was still alive, twitching and all, but alive. I went back over to Man-Man and Omar and I couldn't move. I just stood over their lifeless bodies, helplessly squealing gibberish sounds of loss, with anxious yells in between. It was a nightmare. Then I saw Manny twitch again and I ran to him, crying and screaming, "You better live Manny! You better live!"

He, lying on his back, looked over at Man-Man, with tears rolling out his eyes. And I couldn't tell, but it seemed like Manny didn't care if he lived or not. Seeing Man-Man dead on the ground, I think he felt it was only a matter of time 'til he'd be dead anyway. Man-Man was the glue that held us together, kept us in line no matter what. Even though my stepfather was there, although on the road 60% of the time, Man-Man was the real man of the house, advising and being there for *everyone*.

By the time the ambulance arrived, I was hysterical, crying, shaking, chirping weak, helpless cries. Four ambulances arrived on the set, one after another. The EMTs rushed over and were working on Manny. He was very strong. I'd have thought he'd be dead, but he was still breathing.

Andrea Clinton

Meanwhile, the police caught the guys in the last car, and packed them into a cop car. When I saw they were about to be hauled off, I was so furious I walked over to see who was inside. Crying and pissed, I wanted to know if it was Geronimo who killed my man, my brother and probably my other brother. I was cursing him to no end. But when I got there, it was three young black boys in the back seat, around 15 or 16 years old. I started yelling that they were gonna pay for what they did, and one of them shouted, "F—k you, b—ch! That's what you get for setting a nigga up!"

My eyes grew big and my mouth dropped opened. It wasn't Geronimo who did this. Some part of me had already figured that out. Heck, we gotta live around each other, and the crap Man-Man was talkin' wasn't worth no beef, no matter what threats might've gotten back to Geronimo.

But now I knew, it was Qydeer. This might've come to me later because each person who was drawn down on was someone that Qydeer wanted to get at. Man-Man for arguing with him about going out with me; me, thinking I, or we set him up; Manny because as the saying goes, *If you get one brother, you better get the other;* and Omar, who Qydeer was beefing with *anyway.*

God forbid if he passed by and saw us all in there, all his marks in the same spot, you can't ask for nuthin' betta'.

But now I knew who did what, I hoped that at least Manny lived so I could tell him and he could get Qydeer back.

I felt my free thinking on Qydeer was null and void, hell Qydeer's mother living right had nothing to do with him living right; no such thing as a full proof theory. But I was going through so many thoughts and emotions at that point, *I just fainted.*

Life's a Itch and Then You Die
Should Stick a Needle in My Eye

I woke up to my mother and stepfather in the emergency room. I couldn't speak to them; I couldn't even face them. I turned my head to the other side of the bed and saw Shakirah sitting there, eyes bloodshot-red, crying. I couldn't face her either. So I just shut my eyes and I guess my brain needed the rest because I soon fell asleep. A few hours later, they admitted me. I couldn't understand why, but they said I'd had a seizure and that my blood pressure was high. I was like, "What?" I got disgusted over that, and was still sad at the death of my brother, and the death of the man I didn't even get a real chance to love. So I went back to sleep again.

It wasn't until the next day that I finally got it together to wake up for good. But, as soon as I got up, I heard my mother in the hallway crying like crazy. I figured out what'd happened, and said, "Manny died too." So I turned my head, with tears rolling, and shut her out; I went back to sleep. Believe me, I am good for that. If I don't like something, I'll tune it out. If I can't handle something, life, anything, I'll go to sleep. And I don't feel no way about it. I'll pass out to sleep now if this story gets too deep!

Anyway, that evening, there was no one in my room. My butt was hurting from constantly laying in the same position so I tried to sit up. I couldn't with the pounding headache so I pushed

Andrea Clinton

the buttons on my bed for the nurse. She came in and helped me up. I asked for something for a headache and she bought me Tylenol, my best friend. Then she bought me juice, and water, etc., checked my pressure and all that kind of stuff.

She was Korean and hard to understand. But I asked her who else was in the hospital from the incident or was shot. She said, "Thwee die las-nigh. I ony know two otha shot alibe, Sanson and Pete. Aaah, one nex-door an one in surgwee I tink. I no reaw show," she said.

I really couldn't make out all she was saying. But I knew those were my brothers and Omar who died. Heck Omar and Man-Man had to have been D.O.A., dead on arrival. And I knew Manny died when my mother was hollering in the hallway, I know that cry.

Also, I figured the Sanson she mentioned was really Sampson, and Pete is Pep's real name. That nurse was killing the English language, but she was nice.

Pointing to the room next door, she said, "He jus-woe-up." Sampson is also from Omar's crew. Anyone would assume he'd survived, 'cause he built like a brick sh—t house, thus the name Sampson. I figured it was probably him next door, and I'd go pay him a visit, maybe we could cheer each other up.

I got up, went to the bathroom, then I put on a robe that my mother had left for me and walked with my IV pole to the room next door. I hoped which ever one of them was in there, wasn't a hot mess, shot all up, because if he was, I was gonna turn myself right around and go back to sleep.

When I walked toward the room, I peeked inside, scared to death. I thought I'd see Sampson bandaged from head to toe; with arms and legs in a sling. I realized that I hadn't seen Sampson at all after the shoot-out, only shootin' a shotgun off a few times in the beginning, but then no more. Maybe he was muffed up; *I didn't know.* So I crept into the room, again, scared to death, eyes half-shut. And when I dared to get the courage to fully open my eyes, I saw, to my very own surprise, a tall, muscular, milk chocolate, very handsome, beautiful, brown-skinned *Omar*, sitting in the bed, reaching for a cup on the rollaway table. I ran into the room at warp speed. He didn't even see me until I was two shakes away.

"Aaaaaaah baby," he said, "I was so worried about you. They made it seem like you was in critical condition; you wouldn't wake up. They said a girl was shot up six times and then they wouldn't let me in to see you. I thought it was you and they were hiding it from me or something. Girl you had me causing chaos up in this joint."

I loosened my vice grip from around his neck, and looked into his face.

"That's because I wasn't in critical condition, I was next door taking a long nap. I guess that shows just how long I was out," I said as tears began to fall down my face.

He beat me to the punch though. He started shedding tears immediately.

I was so, so happy to see him. "I thought you were dead," I whispered. "They said you were dead when you were on the ground outside of The White Castle."

"I know. I could hear, but I was hurt, and I tried to pull yo' cowgirl butt down before you got shot but I didn't have the strength, so I just closed my eyes and made *duaa*."

"Made what?"

"A personal prayer. I asked Allah to aid us, all of us. And he did. Cause you alive, and I'm alive."

A smile broke across my face, but disappeared just as quick when I started to cry again. I couldn't bring myself to tell him that Man-Man didn't make it. And I hadn't heard about Manny yet, but I knew he was dead. No one could survive that many shots in those places. I stood there now with my head hung low. But Omar could see I had something to tell him.

"Who else got hit? My sister and them wouldn't tell me anything," he said.

I looked at him and the tears began to fall. "Man-Man didn't make it."

Omar just let loose on me with a whoppin' wail, "Oooooo-noooooo! Nooooooooo!" He punched his leg and began to crying.

He didn't cry silently like I did while watching him. Omar bellowed. He tightened his fist with every vein bulging to the top of his skin. He was killing me, stifling me, snatching whatever was

Andrea Clinton

left, right out of my chest; *that wail.* I can still hear it, feel it too.

Then, after letting loose on me with that slave-cry, Omar, I guess realizing how worked up he was getting, turned his head to the window to keep some dignity.

I'd hugged him immediately, from the initial bawl, so he didn't have to live with me seeing his face, with him crying like that. But I knew the extent of their relationship. Man-Man and Omar didn't have to be together daily or in the same circle to be best friends. Man-Man was always there for him; he fed him when O' didn't have anything; he shared all he had with him; he even snuck him into his room sometimes when it was chaos at Omar's house back in the day. They didn't know I knew all that though.

Hell, Man-Man had been a damn good friend and brother to Omar, *and Omar was to Man-Man also.* O' always had Man's back, and even gave him a connect one time when Man was in some kind of trouble. Their two posse's were really more like one, but it worked best for them to do their individual thing because they were both leaders and didn't always see things the same way; Man-Man was a li'l more aggressive, where Omar was sly. Even so, they were brothers to the bone, and that's why this hurt Omar so much.

With Omar crying in my arms, I didn't know how much more I could take. I'd cried myself to sleep; that's how I dealt with it, with things. But I knew *my hell* was coming; Man-Man was *my brother*, and the funeral was to come next.

Finally, Omar calmed down, got quiet but was still thrown. Then he asked about Manny. "How is he?"

"I dunno. I been sleep. I don't know what's up with anyone, *but I'm sure he died too;* he was shot in the neck, chest by his heart *and* stomach." I told him as I began to sob a li'l. "My mother woke me up with this crazy cry last night, like she just got some bad news; that funeral cry." I paused 'cause I got an immediate visual of Manny lying there in the parking lot, full of bullets. "He was still jerking out there; he had blood everywhere."

He shed tears again, this time for Manny, and we cried together for a minute. Then, to stop me from crying, he started to speak of others. "Sampson was shot twice. Pep was shot too, but Pep got discharged a li'l while ago, his brother stopped by and told me they waitin' on a ride." As he looked down, we went into another one of our silences again.

Then he got started again. "Man-Man, *AND* Manny! *DAMN*!" He started to cry again, not as bad as before though. I guess he couldn't fight not crying anymore though.

I got him tissues, and fiddled around, cleaning around his bed, so he could get himself together. Then, when he was settled and cleaned up, I kissed him. I got tired of waiting around for a rhyme or a reason, thinking about right or wrong with his religion.

So much had happened, I questioned if I was being silly. But without waiting for an answer, I went ahead and kissed him. He kissed me back. It was involved, not just a quick peck. But it was nothing like we would want our first to be. We were two suffering souls, and the kiss felt just like that. It shouldn't even be considered a sin, if that's what it's considered Islamically, because there was nothing sensual, no adrenaline flow, nothing sweet about it. It was pure emotional tragedy. Then we pressed our foreheads against each other and were still.

I looked down to see blood seeping from a wrapping around his chest. "What's this? Oh my God! Where were you shot?"

"In the chest, arm, and leg. Tiki-Boon shot me. I saw when he rose out the window and aimed his piece up at me. He hesitated at first, but shot me anyway."

"Tiki who? Tiki Jones? Louis!"

"Yep."

"Noooooooooooooo!" I said. I was shocked, he was only like fifteen. That punk ass boy. He moved away years ago, like Qydeer. His parents pulled a *Jefferson's move*; they moved on up and out, into a big mansion somewhere, made it rich.

"Yep, looked me dead in my eyes, and put one in me." The look on Omar's face was one of stillness, but also anger. It was a look I *NEVER* wished to invoke. It was calm and laid-back on the surface but was lifeless, yet calculating beneath.

We spoke a little longer about fiddle this, and faddle that. We had a good two to three hours together just chilling. I fed him, and ate myself. I got him juice, and lay in his arms what little I

Andrea Clinton

could without causin' him pain or startin' any bleeding. We even played tic-tac-toe. Then lo and behold, who should enter but his sister **KA'REEMA**, miserable heffa'.

As she came into the room, his sister spoke with a smirk on her face, in a way that said drama. "*Hey Alisa.*"

"Hey," I cautiously replied. Ka'reema had never done anything to me, because I always ignored her, and didn't mess with her. That's how I do with people who are quick to fight. Plus she was much older than me, like four or five years older, so there was never a reason to mess with her except for a, *Who got weed?* moment she may have had.

Ka'reema's about 5 foot 7 inches tall, shapely, but thick legs from running track, and definition in her arms. She was chocolate like Omar, but maybe a hint lighter than he. She had long hair, just below her shoulders I mean, and usually wore it in cornrows, a ponytail or pushed back with a hair band and bangs. I noticed whenever she sported those boring styles because I figured it was probably to keep the hair out of her face while running track.

Around the time of the shooting though, she was sporting a bob cut like Shakirah's. And she always had on earrings, not the small hoops she used to wear back in the day, but the big joints all of a sudden. I guess she was getting more feminine with age. But, she had a walk that was like a woman switching, you know that cocky-sexy switching that female athletes do; like a sexy walk with a li'l pimp in it. She was nice lookin' but she wasn't the most feminine joker in the world. And she had such a harsh attitude, sheesh.

"What you doing up here youngen? I heard you was out there in the line of fire too."

I just turned my head, because older or not, I wasn't gonna take none of her sh—t! I *knew* all the drama up in that household had an effect on *her*, 'cause she crazy, from the rip, with everybody. Heffa' fight like we eat. See, she was the person in the neighborhood who gave all the girls a beatdown at some point and time. She rarely met her match either. So girls my age ignored or avoided her and her two friends. Not out of fear, but because she was a rough number. You wasn't gonna beat her easily, if at all. Heck, if you did manage to get in your licks and give *her* a beatdown, you'd have to watch your back 24/7, either that or go through her two friends. *And she looked rough,* older than she was. All of Omar's siblings did, as I said before, *even Omar,* he looked like a grown man of thirty something; handsomely mature.

"What's new Alisa? You can talk. You and my li'l brother kickin' it?"

He was hugging me by my waist, so I just looked at him as if to say, *Is this girl about to start with me?*

"Ka'reema stop! Where's Ma?" he said.

Ka'reema in a sly voice said, "She's in the hallway, with *Vanessa,* talkin' to the nurse."

Vanessa was the one person I did not want to see, so I tried to stand up. But after the three inches I pulled up, he pulled me back in place. Now, not that I minded. Heck, we'd gotten quite comfortable with one another. But, I don't know that heffa'! She could've come in and cut me or something. And he couldn't help all banged up. And Ka'reema probably woulda been over in a chair, feet propped up enjoying the drama. I was no fool. I knew even though they had a *see you when I see you* relationship, it was *still* a relationship. And it was a tight one where neither allowed others to interfere with them hooking up. But now here I was. And even that type of relationship they had would drive a woman to wanna strike.

Even though there was no real commitment between them, I knew there was still a sense of possession. That's how it always is with females; you see how the female sheep follows the male sheep around after mating, we're possessive by nature, and I was stepping on her turf; hell, wallowing in it.

Ka'reema, with her fickle behavior and attitude came out of nowhere, "So Alisa, your brother out of surgery yet?"

I was happy to hear Manny was in surgery; that meant he was still alive.

"Manny in surgery?" I asked.

Staring at me in shock, Ka'reema went into a ghetto moment, where a sista does these hand movements and swings her head to the side, with her whole body tagging along after. "What? Manny ya brutha? Puerto Rican Manny?" she said smiling.

Andrea Clinton

Did Manny bump uglies with this girl 'cause she is way too happy, I thought to myself.

"Yeah, well, adopted brother, whatever, but he's in surgery?"

I know our hood is big, I mean huge, but how could she not know Manny was my brother? I thought everyone knew. Most people knew everything about each other, granted she was heavily into sports until a few years ago, but dang.

"Oh, I never knew he was your brutha. Uuumn," she said with this plottin' and schemin' look on her face. "I shoulda guessed it. He always at ya house and with ya brutha. But no, I was talkin' about Man-Man."

Me and Omar both shouted, "***WHAT?***"

"What you mean Man-Man?" I asked.

"He in surgery. That's what the nurse told my mother earlier."

Oh boy, I was so happy! I was starting to shed tears all over again.

"Don't get too excited. They said he might not make it, 70-30 chance they say," like she was merely gossiping with her girlfriends.

Omar got angry. "What you mean don't get excited! That's her brutha!" Then he and I hugged and he said what sounded like, *alhamdu-dee-lah*, and some other stuff in Arabic. Stuff his father taught him before and while in prison over the years.

"What about Manny?" I asked.

She got that stupid look again. "Manny been back from surgery for a while now; he came back before Omar did. I sat with him a bit, while my mother was here with big head O'."

I was so happy, I held on tight to Omar and he hugged me too, until he pulled something in his chest. We let go, but not a moment before *it* walked in. That's right, his ex-girlfriend Vanessa from the club, Ms. High-Society aka *Trixie*, my name for her.

"Omar, who is this?" She paced in slowly, looking serious and concerned like she was gonna have an upper crust fit. Until I stood up that is. Did I mention I was almost 5 foot 10, Goddess? And like Ka'reema, I ain't nothing to play with either. I just *choose* to be ladylike. Lady *like*, not a lady.

Then a moment or so after, his mother, Ms. Sista came in. Big bad momma from back in the day, 'til she started them drugs. She drug free now and real humble, but she still no joke, even though her health is no where near what it used to be thanks to drugs. "Peace Ms. Sista," as I nodded to Omar's mother, not paying Vanessa no mind. I wasn't afraid of that heffa'. I was just excited about my brother. I turned to Ka'reema. "What room is Manny in?"

"I dunno the number, but three doors down, and make a left. That room right there."

I began to dash out, but Omar called out to me, saying, "Aaye-aye-aye." I spun back and gave him a quick peck. I started to pull away, but he grabbed me back for another, hurting his chest. He knew I had to jet and see my brother Manny. But he wanted to assure me, tell me in his own way that it's all about us. He didn't want no kind of mix-up like before when he was sick and couldn't pull my coattail to the deal.

So after that lovely peck, I grabbed my IV pole and headed to Manny's room. I don't know why, but I felt sexy and self confident, even in my yellow tank tee shirt and matching pajama pants and slippers, dragging an IV pole. Maybe it was because *he* made me feel confident.

As the door closed behind me, I heard the skinny heffa' Vanessa yell. "When my mother wanted to marry a man from the ghetto, *the hood*, my grandfather told her, 'You can take a man out of the hood, but you can't take the nigger mentality out of that hood-rat.' I now see exactly what he meant. I try to introduce you to new things and this is—so this is why your ghetto ass been acting funny? Because of this ghetto, fake Pochohantas b—ch?"

I remember thinking, *why I always gotta be a fake Pochohantas b—ch? Because I'm ligh-ter with lengthy thick hair? Sheesh!* Why not Jane Kennedy, it'd be a li'l more accurate.

"Vanessa, watch ya mouth," Omar's mother said sternly.

"That's right! Watch ya damn mouth in front of my mutha!" Ka'reema said loudly.

I didn't mean to listen but, I'm just sayin'.

Omar in his deep tone said, "It's a wrap baby."

Andrea Clinton

"What?" She replied, getting annoyed. "Speak English to me Omar, not that ghetto slang, please! I'm really not in the mood to decode your language. I've been up for hours worrying about if you were going to live or die."

"See, that's what I'm talking about. How long you think it was gonna go on? Running in the hood for ya ghetto-loving, ya ghetto-chocolate-brutha fix? Ain't that what you called it? Huh? I don't hear you bragging on the phone to ya girlfriends now 'bout ya chocolate hood-rat, or ya blacker-the-berry thug and all that other geeky crap y'all laugh about!" He was gettin' worked up.

Ka'reema burst out laughing. I told you that girl love drama. Omar, ignoring her I guess, continued.

"Go back to the suburbs; tired you looking down on people. You gets no more here baby! No more ghetto-Hershey-kiss and all that other crap you callin' me to them stuck-up skanky women who like to run to the hood, slummin'. Tell ya prissy friends *your* well ran dry. Go see Sampson; you was always eyeing him, sayin' he look like a fine wrestler. Go!" He paused, then said, "Get out before I say something disrespectful."

I started to take off before she could leave Omar's room, because I didn't want to be seen eavesdropping and I did want to get to my brother. As I turned away, I heard a li'l bit of the tail end of their drama.

"You'll call me again Omar! You know you will. *You know I was the best thing that ever happened to you*. These ghetto girls can't show you a good time. *I was your ticket* out the hood."

"What do you uptown girls be thinkin' 'bout? *Oh Allah.* That's what I get for stepping out of pocket! *BYE! Get Out! Please!*" he shouted.

I didn't stay to see her leave. Boy was I tempted to eavesdrop a bit longer, but I wanted to see my brother even more.

***

When I walked into Manny' room, he was out of it. He was chillin' on his pain meds and the TV was a little loud, so I turned it down so it wouldn't disturb him. I sat there with him for a while, looking at him, and then the TV, and hoping he'd eventually wake up. The nurse came in and I asked how he was doing.

"The bullet just missed his lungs, and he may need a blood transfusion. I'm not sure; I don't wanna quote his chart wrong. But he was shot four times."

"I thought it was three? I pulled him down before that shotgun..." I described the whole event to her.

The nurse looked distressed at the ordeal that she'd obviously only heard bits and pieces about. "You are a young lady. You shouldn't be caught up in that kind of thing."

"I know, and I *don't* roll like that. I don't even know how I got caught up in all that."

The nurse left, shaking her head. I know hearing it, most people, even you, would assume I'm used to this type of activity. But, I may live ghetto-fabulous, and I may have survived the hood so far, but not everyone here is involved in the street drama that happens. Can you imagine what kind of city it would be if *EVERYBODY* was involved? The Wild, Wild East.

Anyway, I was sitting with Manny for about 10 minutes or so when that Vanessa girl came standing inside the door. "Can I speak to you out here for a minute?" she asked in an angry voice.

I stood up, ready to jerk out my IV to whoop this girl's tail right quick; because she was not gonna disturb my brutha. Or worse, make him have a heart attack or something, just 'cause she wanna argue over a nigga! Her li'l play toy.

She stepped out into the hallway and I began to follow. But just then, Omar's mother walked up and took Vanessa's arm.

"Sista dig ya self, dig ya self. This is a hospital." I stepped in the doorway as Ms. Sista continued, "You can't approach that woman with this, plus she a patient in the hospital. Sista on the issue of men, you gotta deal with the man. That's how women end up in jail over these men out here. You gotta deal with him on this. And he done told you, whether you like it or not, where he is with this."

Andrea Clinton

She politely tried to lead Vanessa away, rubbing her arm so Vanessa would feel her good intentions. Vanessa, disrespecting Omar's mother, pulled away and took a step toward me. I snatched my IV out and blood started spilling down my arm. But I didn't care, because that heffa' couldn't dis Ms. Sista like that. Around the way, *everybody* listened to and respected Ms. Sista **and** all those older Muslims when they tried to talk sense to us, whether they was still 100% religious, covered up or not. Even if you decided to do your own thing anyway, you still showed them respect when they tried to help you or give you advice. It's things like this that tell you if someone is from the ghetto or not. 'Cause if you are, you know the do's and don'ts. For example, it really don't matter which type of Muslim: the type of Muslims from the '60s who wear the scarves behind their necks like the nuns do, which Ms. Sista used to cover like. Or the ones with the coverings like in the Middle East, which is what she covers like now. Both get mad respect in the hood; and so do the Muslim men who always giving the guys in the hood advice, be it the ones who wear the beanie they call a koofee or the ones with the bow tie. Just like the Ministers or Deacons of the churches; *you wouldn't disrespect them.* These things were just common knowledge. Who you think have ya back when something big hits the ghetto communities? All them religious people. And who will fight and march for you? Again, it's just common knowledge. Vanessa had no clue about any of this, and those things that happen or go without saying. But, trying to dibble and dabble, messing with Ms. Sista, she was 'bout to find out, for real.

I decided to back up and keep my distance from Vanessa, so it wouldn't look like I was trying to run up on her. But even so, she still started shouting, "I need to talk! No need to run, we need to talk!" I looked at her as if she was crazy, and even Ms. Sista looked at her strangely.

"Run? Nigga I ain't 'bout to run from *you*. **Who you?** What you need to talk to me about?" And she looked like me coming out the room was just the invite she needed to get something started. Ms. Sista saw it coming, even when this yuppie didn't. Ms. Sista put her hands on her head and said, *"Oh Allah, please."*

Vanessa asked, "Did you know he had a woman? I'm his lady. You need to back off."

I looked up at the ceiling like, *Here we go! She says yeah, and he say nay.* I got so aggravated I said, "Look, take that up with him. Don't bring that drama to me." I could feel she didn't know not to walk up on me too close, and I didn't have time to wonder how much to take from this rich nigga, 'cause a girl in love *or* like *will fight you.*

"He only with you because you a cute little hooch from the ghetto! Probably wanna screw like a bunny, a little whore."

Hooch, I thought. *Ain't that a dog? Did this ho just call me a b—ch?* I wondered.

"He'll leave you for somebody like me, who'll help him get out the ghetto, pull him out of the slums! Because he knows he'll never amount on his own or with a ghetto girl like you."

That angered Ms. Sista because Vanessa called her son a user, an opportunist, and said he'd never amount to anything. Even I knew Omar better. She just kept on.

"A nigga will lie to get some. What? You think you Ms. 5000? He just lying to get in ya draws!"

Ms Sista held up her hand to the ho. "You gonna stop right there! Now I don't know what kind of relationship you and he got, but you don't stand here and disrespect my son to my face! I'm surprised at you Vanessa. And I knew this girl since she was young. She do her thing and mind her business! And she's right. Talk to him, and if you can't straighten it out with him, then leave him alone. And I'm his mother telling you this!"

Do you know this hooker still didn't want to listen? Omar sent Ka'reema to see what was happening. And just as she turned the corner, Vanessa dropped her pocketbook and lunged at my face. Before she could get a hit in, I threw a quick jab and knocked her into the wall. Then she tried to run up on me again, so I hooked her in the eye twice, with my left and my right. She flew back into the wall, but didn't fall. And I was content with sending her back uptown, with a black eye.

Watching the whole thing, Ms. Sista clutched her chest in disbelief. Ka'reema finally caught up to us, pissed as hell, pulled

Andrea Clinton

Vanessa and slung her. "Yo Vanessa go 'head girl; stop disrespectin' my mutha. She told you not to start nothin'," Kareema warned her.

"*Your mother?* You see what Omar's slut did?"
Vanessa had my blood all over her face from the punches. The IV had left blood dripping down my arm, and my arm and hand looked like something out of a scary movie.

Vanessa kept yelling at Ka'reema. *She must not have known where that train was headin'.* "That b—ch's blood is on my face, near my mouth and you wanna talk about ya damn mutha!"

Wow! Why did she say that? *What in hell was she thinking?* Wooooooooooooow!

From outta nowhere, Ka'reema smacked the sh—t outta Trixie, *BANG—ZOOM!* Her smack made my punches look like baby slaps; he-he-he-he! That girl slid down the hall a li'l bit and rolled on the walls, no lie. It *was funny as hell.* I didn't laugh then, I got a kick out of it later though; still do.

Ms. Sista reached out for Ka'reema and said something I always hear my Muslim neighbor say, *I-oo-thoo-be la* or something like that. My neighbor said it's seeking refuge in God. I stood there smiling like Ka'reema was when she watched us go at it. She loved to see a good fight, but she hated stressing her moms, a sickly, recovering addict who'd done a lot of damage to her body.

By now, security had come down the hall, saw me bleeding, and saw Vanessa crying and cursing. Spoiled rich brat couldn't get her way now, and she couldn't handle it. They walked over to her, got her pocketbook and escorted her out. Another guard approached me and walked me to my room. I didn't want to seem like a hood-rat or uncaring so I turned back to Ms. Sista, to show that around-the-way respect, "Ms. Sista, you okay? I'm sorry 'bout that. You know I'd never disrespect you."

Then, of course, Ka'reema put her two cents in. "But you did it nevertheless," she butted in, rolling her eyes, and starting to pull her mother away.

But Ms. Sista knew my caliber, and said, "It's not ya fault. You was minding ya business. You told her to walk."

"Are you okay though?"

"I'm fine Alisa, praise Allah." I guess the whole deal was just a bit much for her, the shooting, and now this. She was probably thinking, *Omar's coffee just keep brewing!* That's how men do, especially when they're young and got that negative run in 'em. They keep stuff going.

When I walked past Omar's room, I couldn't even bear to look in. Plus, I was bleeding a mile a minute. And since Ka'reema and Ms. Sista had already gotten back and were sitting with him, I just went into my room. He saw me pass by though.

"Baby come here; Oooooh! What the he—" He saw the blood on my arm and even on my gown now. "What the heck happen? Y'all said she was aaiight? Alisa, baby come here."

A nurse, who was following me and the guard leaned her head into his room, "She's okay, somehow her IV was pulled out, but she's fine. I've gotta go get her cleaned up."

I heard him with a surprised squeal, *"WHAT THE HECK HAPPENED?"*

We entered the room and the nurse cleaned my arm and put my IV back in. Afterwards, I lay in the bed and looked at TV. And of course you know what else I did. Yep, I went to sleep.

***

While I was falling asleep, I heard Omar's voice calling me. But I wasn't sure if his family had left, and I didn't want to be bothered. So I lay there thinking. I kept thinking why would uptown girl put up such a fight for a man she's always on and off with anyway? Then I thought about how good he treated her, made her feel special in the club. I thought about how they talked, ate and mingled with others, and all the while it was really all about one another. And judging by that night I imagined how good he must be to her when they hit the sheets. Then I knew. He turned

Andrea Clinton

her out, and this was why she put up a fight; it was why she always came back to him.

His way with women is what every woman wants from a man but rarely get. She had it in him, and being the spoiled, uppity, rich girl she was, she had it on *her* terms. And now she felt I was stealing it away, and nobody likes to be robbed. But I wasn't stealing her man, right? Every eight or nine months? Is that a real relationship?

On the flipside, considering what he said to her in his room, she could've probably just felt he was a good ghetto screw. Her walk on the wild side. Hell, he should've taken *her* to The White Castle that night. She woulda seen some *real* wild ghetto sh—t.

But fighting over a man? I thought. *That ain't my stick.* I needed time to think, and he wasn't going nowhere. So I lay there and fell into a long, deep sleep.

Later, I felt someone over me. I jumped up, going for the person's throat. I thought it was Vanessa, but it was Omar. He tried to block me and hurt his chest. But I was so hurt behind fighting over a man, that I had no pity for him. Yeah I'm a piece of work—whatever!

"Why you trying to kill me? I thought you were glad I lived," he said, joking with me.

I turned my head toward the window to ignore him.

"You mad at me?" He tried to get my attention at first, then took a moment to think about it. "Alisa, I told you the deal with me and her. I'm not hangin' out with her no more. She heard I was shot and came. Don't do it like that baby."

"She seem to always know when you in the hospital."

"Oh what you think I called her and told her to come up here?"

"Funny that she came."

"Alisa please! It's all over the news. Anybody could've told her. Hell, everybody know I'm here!"

I knew he was telling the truth. She's one of those women who would come no matter how long she stayed away from her ghetto boy-toy, just to keep things kool for whenever she wanted his company.

They both got a kick out of each other though, I was no fool. And what if the kick he got out of me wasn't as stimulatin' as the one he got from her? Heck, I'm ghetto, *ghetto-fabulous*, but I'm ghetto. And she *is* what I *appear* to and *pretend* to be when I sport my few diamonds, and designer clothes. She's the real deal, *Ms.- Rich-Ms.,* born into and showers with money.

"I don't like the fact that I fought no woman behind no man! That ain't me!"

"But you did it nonetheless. And you shouldn't have been fightin', you're a lady."

I rolled my eyes 'cause I ain't no lady. I'm a woman! But that wasn't the point. I had no choice but to fight.

"And what, let Ms. Preppy hit me? You stupid!"

"She wouldn't have hit you. If anything she would've gotten in ya face, and you'd have hit her."

I couldn't believe my ears. He actually thought that tramp was *that* damn ladylike.

"For your information, she dropped her pocketbook and was going for my face, nails ready. But her preppy ass was too slow!"

He laughed. Can you believe he laughed! I'm already jealous and then he laughed 'cause he feel his preppy girlfriend is too good to fight, would never do it. I lost it.

"Whatever, get out!"

He tried to kiss me, but I stopped him. Me pulling away made him hurt his chest and arm again, so he stopped. Then the nurse came in and saved the day. She had heard all the laughing. When she saw us two together, she told him to go back to his room. Omar tried to be stubborn. But a security guard showed up and said, "*Work with me man.* The nurse got the last say brah."

So Omar went back to his bed, and I to sleep.

Andrea Clinton

Knock Knock,

"Who's There?"

"The Anti-Christ, no wait, The Devil"

The next morning, the nurse came in to take my temperature. She said that Omar asked me to come to his room. But the thought of giving in and going to him hurt my insides. So I got up and headed for Manny's room instead. As I walked past Omar's he called out to me. When I didn't answer, he did a little laugh that just angered me more.

When I got to Manny's room, he was sitting up with my mother and stepfather. I didn't even know they were there. My mother said they were about to come see me. She said Man-Man made it through surgery and they were watching him in ICU. I was angered to see them all there. Why didn't they come and see me and how I was doing? I felt like I just didn't matter anywhere.

Manny knows how I get about things like this because he gets like that when it comes to his mother and her family. He has one aunt he can count on, until it comes to her husband of course.

He was awake now, and lookin' good considering. Seeing what I was going through, he held his arm out to me and I bent down to hug him. He didn't have a lot of strength but said, "Thank you!" Then tears rolled down his eyes, and that made them roll down mine. We had history now, tragic history, that Vietnam-type history that seems to thicken relationships; God bless their souls.

We sat there for a while with Manny, and then we went to go see Man-Man, just me and my mother. This was good because it gave my stepfather and Manny a chance to talk, as they often do their little whisperings. My mother didn't say much to me; in fact, she was kinda angry the whole time. She felt the whole shootin' was my fault. And I didn't ask her why she wasn't speaking much to me because I knew what she would say, "You always causing some kind of problem to somebody." I didn't want my feelings hurt with her cussin' me out. *God forbid,* I thought, *if she finds out I fought in the hospital.*

When we got to Man-Man's bed in ICU, we just stood there watching him, not being able to say anything much as he couldn't hear us. He looked a mess with a breathing tube in his mouth and wires going up and down his bed, and in and out of him. I couldn't believe this was actually Man! I felt so horrible; I felt so bad for him. Damn! Got me shedding tears just talking about it. So anyway, I leaned over and gently kissed him on the forehead and heard my mother whisper under her breath, *"The kiss of death."*

I stopped, not believing my ears. I know she's always thinking something negative about me. But she usually tries to hide her thoughts because if she says them, "She can't erase them," as my stepfather used to tell her.

I shed my tears and she was none the wiser. She thought I was crying because of my brother. All she did on that note was to say that he'd be okay, unconvincingly. Then we walked out together.

But when we were a little ways beyond the door, and she could see there was no one around to disturb us, she let me have it. "So you were fighting in the hospital last night?" I was 19, but no matter how old I got my mother still spoke to me like I was a child; *I was waitin' for her to spank me.*

I didn't say a word. I knew I had no win. The only way my mother would understand is if she had been there. And unlike Ms. Sista, my mother woulda been throwing down. I mean don't get me wrong, Ms. Sista can fight and she used to be quick to do it too. I've seen Ms. Sista beat her sister up in the middle of the street over some liquor. But that was before she cleaned up her act and went back to Islam. But my mother was always a fighter, and if provoked, she would jump into the battle. And as much as she be on my case about things, can't nobody touch me.

The quieter I stayed while she kept at me with her ghetto head, neck and hand movements, the more my mother kept riffin' *at* me. She got so annoyed that I wouldn't explain myself that she began hitting below the belt. "You don't wanna answer me huh? Why? Because you fighting over a man? He nice and I like him, but I don't know if I like *you* for him. What he coming with, you ain't ready for, and you gonna mess it up. Knowing you, you'll probably mess around and turn *him* out."

Now this got me. This pissed me off. Because see the black baby boom generation used the term *turn you out* in one way, negatively. Like in the '60s and '70s when a man got hooked on dope and wanted to get his woman hooked, or if a pimp wanted to prostitute a good girl, they'd say, *"I'm gonna turn this b—ch out."* It meant you would rearrange the person's whole state of being; flip 'em. Like, you'd change them beyond repair; mess them up in the head so they can't get right; you'd be able to let 'em go when you accomplished this deed because like a yo-yo they'll be back, turned out. And based on the way she was putting it to me, I would do this to Omar; I'd be his kryptonite. We *were* walking together, but I stopped and looked at her and she continued past me.

Then before I knew it, my mind and spirit took off on a journey of their own. "I don't believe you! You act like I'm the Anti-Christ. You make mistakes when you're young, they're considered *mistakes!* But when I make them, I'm just *like* the Anti-Christ!"

She was a li'l ahead of me and spun around and shrieked, "No, not *like* the Anti-Christ. Thee Anti-Christ! No, the Devil!"

I couldn't believe her. She was my moms. Why would she speak to me so foul? I mean, I knew she thought I may have almost gotten her son killed. **But damn!** And it wasn't even my fault. *I didn't know what was going on with Qydeer*, and I sure enough didn't know what beefs he had with this one and that one. She kept at me.

"You're just selfish. You're out to get what you think will keep you comfortable in life. You wanna have things and you don't care who you use to get them. But this time..." She just stopped speaking, shaking her head.

"This time what? *WHAT!*"

"This time you may have killed my son for it you stupid b—ch!" Then she spun around and walked off. If I didn't know any better, I'd think she wished something awful on me.

I stood there staring for a long time. I didn't know I was so close to the rooms until I looked around, wiping my eyes which were blurred. Not far from Man-Man's room, I thought I saw a shadow, but then I thought, *Naaa.* I turned and went the other way. I looped all the way around so as not to walk by Omar's room or see anyone I knew. As I turned the last corner, which was on the way to my room, I picked up my speed because I didn't want to see or hear from anyone.

I went into my room and sat in a chair. I looked down at a tray, sitting near the bed, holding a cold breakfast. There was some cereal and some other crap they'd brought. I dropped my head in my hands and cried hard. I thought, *Maybe it is my fault.* I couldn't see how, but I was feeling, "mighty low," as Sophia said in *The Color Purple.* Just then, I heard someone come into my room. I lifted my head and saw that it was Ka'reema. I remember thinking, *Dang! Where is this going? Is she gonna blame me too, wanna fight because I fought in front of her mother?* You just never knew with this crazy ho.

But, she wasn't negative at all; she was coming in on some old other stuff, a side you figured must exist somewhere in her, because they use to be so religious, but *never* actually see.

"Hold ya head up girl. That wasn't ya fault. That b—ch just strung out on him." Then she nodded toward the hallway. "I overheard you and ya mother. She ain't the quietest woman when she mad."

I couldn't believe she was talking so calm. *My God,* I thought, *she can take human bites...outta life.* I felt like what some of my associates said they felt when they got locked up at the women's prison, and the toughest girl came in talking calm, just before they all jump you. So, I was on the look out for a butt whooping or *something*.

She sat on my bed, and since I was just sitting, looking at her all stiff, she said, "Don't be so quiet. I come *fee-sa-bee-lee-la*."

I made the most scrunched up face. "What?" I wasn't used to them bustin' out in Arabic back then; I thought she was havin' a seizure or somethin'.

"That means I come for the pleasure of God; to be nice, silly girl."

I calmed down a little. "I don't know what y'all be talking about sometimes; thought you were speakin' in tongues."

She laughed and I giggled a time or two.

"You still silly. You stayed laughin' when you were young. Anyway, mothers can be like that though Alisa. You can't be letting nothing they say get you uptight. Especially when you not even as bad as I was out there in them streets. I mean, my mother used to curse me out when she was on that stuff, and it hurt 'cause there was a time *she didn't even curse!*"

I wanted to say, "I remember." But instead I replied, "For real?" Hell, our hood echoed from the empty parking lots after the '60s riots where a lot of houses were burned down, so I heard it all; all the shoutin', fightin' everything from up their end of the block. How could she not think anyone would know about her mother cussing *EVERYBODY* out? Anyway, she continued talking.

"Girl please, I was messing with Danny, and I got pregnant. I'm not proud of it, especially because I got an abortion so I wouldn't be ashamed in front of my mother. But then a call came to the house asking if I was fine from the surgery and she found out. It took Omar, my other brother and our older sister to pull her off me. Turned out, she wasn't even mad that I got pregnant. I mean she was, but she could've gotten over that. She was mad because I sinned, killed my baby. I know where she's coming from now. But then, I kept thinking, *All the crap she and my father did, and what she did when he was gone, how she gonna judge me?* But they don't judge you, they just feel sorry for you, especially because they'll be the ones sitting around watching you suffer. And it hurt even worse because ya big mess up takes place after all they've invested in you, time, money, talks, you know?"

I instantly had a whole new respect for Ka'reema. I had heard her put it down to people before. But this time, she truly was telling it like it was. Because my mother always said, "I don't like seeing my kids suffer."

I thanked her and she said, "Ain't nothin'." I tell you that girl is made out of stone. I was ready to start feelin' kinda comfy and cozy toward her, but she clearly wasn't having it. She stood up, pulled my tray over to me, and told me to eat, otherwise I'd end up stuck in the hospital a lot longer.

After seeing Ka'reemas' split personality, just like my mother's new feelings regarding the Muslims, *I began to fee sorry for them*, those affected by the division I mean. All that good inside them, lost, 'cause the older ones lost focus. And it seems the younger one's will to survive has shielded or blocked them from showing their true peaceful nature to the cruel world; now they seem selective of who they'll show it to, when and if.

As she was walking out, Omar came walking in. But he was movin' sort of slow as he was in a lot of pain. The doctors told him he needed to start walkin', get himself some exercise. So, he convinced the nurse to let him walk himself into my room.

"What-up girl?" he asked sounding like a cowboy. I said nothin', just shook my head. "I heard ya mom-dukes." He finally made it over to me and sat on my bed. "You know not to pay that sh—t no mind right?" I guessed he must've been right, as he rarely curses, only when he's mad. He paused and waited for an answer. "I mean, Moms gonna always talk turkey 'til you get it right. She just scared—"

I cut him off with, "I know."

Then he bent down and flicked my chin with his index finger.

"Then why you in here looking all down and out?"

I looked away and answered, "I'm just tired, too much going on."

He just stared at me, and I hated it because it was that same look he gave when it seemed like he had me and some plan in mind.

"I know. Just hang in there; all this will blow over. And Man-Man made it this far, he gonna take it to the end zone, like we

Andrea Clinton

used to do in little league football, remember? He know where he come from. He tough like ya father. And ya crazy father lived through six gunshots right?"

I turned my head around 'cause I never knew that.

"Who? What?"

"Ya fatha! What he got arrested for."

I shrugged my shoulders.

"My bad. I thought you knew. I just remember him going after that man. I got the man's face, but I forget his name."

"Bones," I interrupted.

"Yeah, Mr. Bones. When ya pops took some bullets to the body and one to the face?"

Then I remembered that scar on my father's face, and I just nodded which told him I was putting things together, and remembering. He didn't feel comfortable and tried to change the subject, but he knew he'd opened up Pandora's Box.

"Anyway, you still mad at me?" he asked.

"No, I really don't care."

"You don't care about what? The subject or me?" He said with all kind of bass in his voice.

"Whatever. I don't wanna talk about nothing right now." I stood up and started toward the window. He grabbed my wrist and I snatched it away. He tried to go after me, but hurt his chest in the process. I almost said, "Good for you." But he acted like he was in horrible pain, so I stopped. *See, I know boundaries.*

"You okay?"

He paused a minute, "Yeah. I'm straight. I just didn't take my pain meds."

"That was smart. Why?"

"Because I wanted to come in here and see you without my head spinning. I'm not no junky; I can't think off that sh—t!"

"So why you yellin at me?"

He looked angrily in annoyance over his pain, and at me for picking at him while he was hurtin'. "I'm not yelling. You just trying to be difficult." Then he sighed in pain. "You know I'm digging you, and you know I'm 'bout it, but you keep wanting to give me a hard time."

I quickly walked away so I'd be out of his reach. Standing at the window, I thought of something, "You know, if I wasn't trying to get you out my system by dating the first clown that asked me to go out, I probably wouldn't even be in this situation."

But he got me back.

"*We* wouldn't be in this situation."

I wasn't expecting that. I thought he would be all defensive. But he could care less. Little did I know then that he knew me better than I thought. It was one of those things where you live around a person, could even be outside playing kickball with 20 other friends, and you may not even be paying attention to that person, but they watching you like a hawk, for whatever reason. This is what I came to learn was the situation with him and me. Omar had had a crush on me for some time, but never showed it. And because he had the crush, he was always watching me, so he knew my antics. So, I turned it up.

"Don't get cocky! This could've all happened 'cause you beat that guy up outside my house, damn near killed him."

Do you know saying that to him was like no skin off his back? It surprised me a bit.

"You shouldn't have went out with his boy, Qydeer, and maybe he'd have met up with him and not been riding around looking for him," he said trying to outwit me.

I walked back a few steps to look him in his face, and in shock said, "You mean to tell me, you beat up his boy because *I* went out with *him*?"

"What you think?" he asked, in a sarcastic, arrogant, wicked way.

"I think you nuts! *Helloooo!* You can't just go around beatin' people up like that! 'Cause you jealous!"

"Well I did!" He said, starting to fix the wrapping on his chest. "Look I'm a man, I'm not no girl. I do things like a man do things. If a nigga cross me, he git got! You know how it go. *I'm not gonna jump rope with him*, or have a dance contest. Come on now; who you think you dealing with? And if he'd have been with Qydeer walking down the street and they saw me, they'd have both got me, hell I'm gonna feel sorry for him for?"

Andrea Clinton

I just stared at him in disbelief, 'cause heck, he's the one that got-got, in the end it wasn't them. And where was all that Islam? And what was that look he had on his face while he was fixing the wrapping on his chest? And how did the dude cross him when he just asked about Qydeer?

Suddenly in my mind, I saw, *I saw his father*, drunk, and falling down his front steps, angry, yelling at Ms. Sista who was high on something. That night, they were both looking *crazy*, with his father not able to hide his shame or loathing for their situation. Then the next day, he'd wear a mean, disgusted look because of how far he'd fallen; like, he was disgusted over their condition. *That* was the look Omar had when he fixed his chest wrapping, like he and Qydeer's beef disgusted him, and on many levels.

Funny the things you remember, and how you apply them. Reminds me of when this girl once said to me, "Alisa, I remember when I was little and ya mother pulled a gun out on ya fatha in the hallway." Heck, I didn't even remember that, not 'til she said it. It's like, you can't help what you remember. And I couldn't help remembering his father's temperament when I looked at him, and I wondered if this man might one day **kill me**, 'cause I'm not easy.

Anyway, I stood there staring and he must've noticed while he was fixing his wrapping because all of a sudden, the beat down he gave wasn't totally about me. "Look, come down off ya high horse, that whoopin' I gave that man wasn't *all* about you. It was some other stuff too, some old stuff."

I stood there still staring in shock to his mode of thinking, and his change in direction. He continued because he saw in my eyes a serious second-guessing of me asking myself if he was the kind of man I wanted to be bothered with.

"Baby look, it was just happening so fast. I came over there pissed, ready to stop you from going out with who ever you was with cause that sh—t didn't rub me right. It was really pissing me off. Ya moms calmed me down. But then R.I.P. tells me you with that fool, and now I'm mad for three more reasons. And then that fool came drivin' up!" Then after a short pause and contemplation, Omar spoke even more indignant and ghetto, **"And I ain't never like that nigga no way."** Staring at the wrapping around his chest as he fiddled with it, knowing he should be ashamed, but not really caring after all he'd been through. "Then…" He paused for a moment, then started up again, "Manny and Man came and they was all hyped, worrying 'bout you. It was just too much going on, just like you said!

"Then they started yelling 'bout some dudes were shooting at the restaurant where you were and you might be hit. And *that* made me calm all the way down, 'cause it was getting real now. I needed my wits. But I messed up, got emotional, praying you wasn't hit, which was good, but *I didn't stop to think*. We shoulda got you and stepped; we were all out in the open!

"Messin' 'round here liking you so much, not thinking, I made us all a damn mark; hangin' outside The White Castle. I know better than that, and with this nigga out on the loose with a S.O.S. out on him, and after what I did to his boy. What the—" He took a pause and stood up from the bed. "See baby, it ain't all good on this part of town either. I'm so busy trying to get wit' you, I ain't looking out *for you*, or my people, and damn near got us all killed. You in here so busy feeling half sorry and half grand about ya-self. You don't even stop to think that maybe some of us trippin' over what went down too."

As he headed toward the doorway, I was about to walk up and hug him from behind. But the nurse came in and said, "There you are, I was looking for you. We gotta put that IV line back in your arm. The doctor ordered more antibiotics for you and said you have to take the pain pills at least twice a day. Come on."

So I couldn't follow him to his room just yet. I had to wait. I tried to see him again a little later, but his mother and sisters were there. Uuuugh! So I went to see Manny. I walked the long way to avoid Omar's room, and I stopped off to see Man-Man who was still touch and go; he was hangin' on by a thread.

Later that afternoon, the doctor came by and said I would be released the next day. But Omar had a few more days to go. He kept drawing a fever, which I guess was in part due to the fact that he'd just had the flu or whatever that was, and his body hadn't fully recovered from that.

And Manny and Man weren't even a question. It would be awhile before either of them got out.

Andrea Clinton

Once Upon A Time In The Hood,
The Sun Shined In The Hospital···

I got tired of waiting to see Omar. By now I'd bathed twice, brushed my teeth twice, changed my hair I dunno how many times. Shakirah came and was back and forth between me and Man-Man's room. My mother talked to Man's baby mother, *Ms. Ronny*, and tried to convince her to only coming up to the hospital once, and to wait at home the rest of the time so she didn't disturb her pregnancy. She was only six months along and had high blood pressure the entire time. But Ronny refused to leave Man's side. So Moms asked Shakirah to do this, that or the other so she wouldn't go to Man's room and run into Ronny when she came and refused to leave.

Taking a break from Man-Man, Ronny came by to see me once. But when she poked her head in, I played tired because I hate being phony and I wanted her to go ASAP. It was horrible for me to be kool or normal with her, knowing my best friend was sleeping with her man.

After Shakirah left, that was it. I needed to see Omar. You'd think with my brothers in such a condition that would take my mind off of him. But, he was still there.

Since my mother had wrote me off, Shakirah was nice enough to buy me a yellow Tweety Bird tank and pajama pants. So I freshened up, then slipped my IV bag through the pajama top, put on the pants and went to see Omar. He threw in my face how I came in the room toting a IV pole, not like his didn't sit by his side with all them antibiotics and fluid bags draping from it.

When I walked in, Pep and R.I.P. were there. Sampson the big bull was there too. He'd come in from his room around the corner. His big body ate them bullets for breakfast. But anyway, Ka'reema and Ms. Sista were also there.

I said hello to everyone and walked over to Omar, but assumed he didn't really want to see me after what happened between us that morning. They all kept talking. But I could feel the fellas thinking, *Wow, them two really doing this. Man-Man little sista and Omar?* I knew what was on their mind, because heck I would've said the same thing. For one, me and Omar had merely greeted each other when we ran into one another over the years. And two, Man-Man was crazy over who I went with around the way, especially his friends. Manny never got too bad, but Man always went overboard.

Well I walked over to Omar, he was sitting with his feet propped up and the back of the bed tilted upward. I was a little nervous about what to say because they may not have known what we went through that morning. But he and I did, and I didn't know if he would be receptive to my company or be like, "What? What you want?" I kinda knew he wouldn't, but it doesn't pay to be cocky.

As I got close to him I said a little nervously, "So how you feelin'?" And before I could fully finish the sentence, he took me by the wrist and pulled me down to him and kissed me; a sweet peck, nothing fresh. He knew I wasn't coming in before because of all those people, and what happened earlier. He realized I got up the guts to just come; I told you he always seemed to know me, even before I knew myself, which is why he was always so pissed when I did something he didn't figure on.

It was both a relief and a discomfort though that he just pecked me, you know with all those people there that we grew up around.

Ka'reema was sitting directly on his right side and used our kiss as a reason to weasel her way out, and in there with Manny, "Illllk! I'm getting outta here, I'll be back." Then she left.

Omar couldn't help himself, "Aaaw girl, you just want that plantain over there in the other room." And they all laughed. Seems everybody either knew her and Manny had something going on, or was realizing it.

Ms. Sista laughed too, "Leave that girl alone. And y'all stop that kissin' stuff. Y'all not married **Omar**. That's not proper for a Muslim. Fear your lord."

"Aaiiight *Ummi*," then he turned to me, "before you ask, *Ummi* means my mother."

"Let me guess, in Arabic."

Then we laughed, and he tapped me as if to say good girl, 'cause I was catching on. Still don't know why they just don't speak ALL English.

"So what's up girl? You all right?" he continued.

I squeezed in his bed with him and asked, "Are *you* all right?"

He turned his head away and then looked back at me, "Hey, you know, I'm kool."

I kissed my hand and then patted him on the forehead and said, "Yeah you aiiight."

He smiled at me, then I continued to cheer him up. "You ain't do nothing wrong O'. What we talked about earlier, let that go; no need to be so hard on yourself. You human."

He just looked at me and turned away again. He knew I was right, but the man in him felt there was no room for that line of thinking because regardless to whatever pep talk he received, he had to be on point.

"They releasing me tomorrow," I said.

"Oh yeah? Tomorrow when?"

"I dunno."

"So you leaving me?"

"*No I'm not leaving you.* I'll spend some time up here with you."

"Naaa, you should go home, get some rest."

"I don't wanna get no rest."

But then I saw something in his eyes, like he didn't want me to be up there. And suddenly it hit me during the short silence between us. They still hadn't caught Qydeer and his boys. That whole time I was still in danger, and it hadn't dawned on me.

"They still haven't caught him, have they?"

"Not that I know of. Why? You worried?" he asked.

"No, not about me, and not you, but Manny and Man-Man are helpless."

"Girl, as many guards and cops they got on this floor, nothin' gonna happen to them."

I hadn't noticed, I guess I was sort of narcissistic, living in my own world. But since there were warrants out on Qydeer, and he had hits on him as well, they decided to put a lot of officers on the floor figuring he may feel he has nothin' to lose and set it off up there.

We visited a while longer before I went back to my room and fell asleep. By the time I woke up later, Omar was out for the count, doped up on the pain meds and everybody had gone. I pulled the blankets up on him. The guards and cops weren't sure about me walking around, but they were kool. So, I looked in on Manny and talked to him for a while, looked in on Man who was doing better, but still not himself. Then went back to my room, and went to sleep.

Andrea Clinton

They are Good,
But Ain't I A Stinka?

The next day, the doctor released me around noon; I dunno what good it did because I still hung around the hospital, getting juices, water and so on. Each day, I went from one room to another, talking, and laughing and playing cards. And since Omar was in less pain, he went with me to see my brothers. He was happy to see Man alert and looking a li'l better. When he first saw him, he shed tears for old boy. We all knew Man wasn't out of the woods yet, so he didn't feel ashamed about crying. His eyes watered with Manny a little, but since Manny was almost as good as him at that point, he had more kick to him than Man-Man.

After a week, Omar was released. Some days after that Manny was too. And then two weeks later, Man-Man came home. All this in a few weeks time. Omar was confined to the house, except for the times he went out for physical therapy.

After a while though, my stepfather sent Man-Man and Manny to Virginia, so they could heal properly and wouldn't be trying to get back in the streets. The only reason he didn't send me was because I hadn't gone home yet.

I was staying with Shakirah in their new apartment. Man tried to mend fences between me and my mother. So did Manny, Omar, everybody. But she said she didn't care if I came home or stayed away, and I resented that and didn't want to go home. I was tired of her feeling negatively about me.

Since she and I were not getting along, Omar felt he and I would only make it so far. He had a superstition that when a person isn't right with their family, they can't be right with their mate. "And keep the family ties, that's what we Muslims say. I can't remember if it is Qur'an or Sunnah, but," he kept saying. Whatever! I thought. I had no clue as to what he was talking about half the time. He'd have me, then he'd lose me. So I took from what he would teach me that I could, and get sleepy off the rest.

He invited us out to dinner, but Moms came late, and I never showed up. Well I did, but I stayed at the other side of the restaurant until she left, forty minutes later. After she drove off, I went over to Omar's table. He saw me walking toward his table in a mirror on the wall. He shook his head in disbelief and rubbed his head. I pulled a chair out and sat down.

"You are bad. And this is a bad sign for us. My mother always said, what ever a person will do to their mother or father, you can assure they'll do to you, especially their mother. And look at you—"

I smiled, getting a kick out of my misbehavior, "Ain't I a Stinka," I said. I always did funky things like that, but usually to men, not my mother. I couldn't help it this time though. I was mad at my mother. Where was the motherly love when I was in the hospital? On the real tip, she hurt me, and that cut like a knife.

He was miffed, but calm because of his disbelief in my deeds.

"Girl, are you serious? *Do you know that is your mother?* Allah says in the Qur'an the way to paradise lies at your mother's feet. *Are you crazy?*"

"Did you order yet?" I asked as I waved to the waitress to come so I could place my order.

He just stared at me, probably wondering what he was really in for, acting all superstitious. Not that he wasn't making sense but for one, that's *his* religion, and two, although it scared the pants off me, I didn't want to hear *that*. She should love her only daughter just as much as she loves and cares for her drug dealing son. Not that Omar wasn't right, because he was, but I am a very sensitive

Andrea Clinton

person, and she hurt my feelings. She said I was the devil's li'l helper—the Anti-Christ; *the Devil*. And she never came and apologized for it. I felt she didn't care and she didn't really miss me, or feel bad about disregarding me.

***

For the rest of that evening, I started feeling bad about what I did, 'cause he kept looking at me in disbelief, shaking his head, like God was gonna strike me dead or something. Then, I didn't even know why I did it. God forgive me.

Is Um Is, or Is Um Ain't Yo Baby?

As time went on, Omar and I did a lot of talking. And we found out more and more about each other. One day, I learned what I'd already figured; he'd been with Vanessa on and off because he could handle that type of relationship better. It was easy to just give her affection and attention every now and again and leave her good to go. Of course, he wasn't gonna tell me he stayed with her so long in that situation because it made him feel like a man to have someone to treat like a queen. Instead he told me it was because the women were sticking their chest out just like the fellas. And in his mind, there wasn't a whole lot a females out there who weren't either on crack, getting drunk or had their hands out talking about their bills all the time. I dunno, whatever.

What he disliked, and what kept him backing up from her from time to time was that she was always talking to him about his dreams, and what he wanted to do or be. He said he didn't like her being uppity and talking down to him and usually had to put her in check. He also said she was trying to groom him and push him to obtain status in her class, the upper class, so she wouldn't be on the arm of an uneducated hoot-rat.

"I was already off doing things she didn't even know about, and I already had plans, and things were going according to my plans with exception to a few bumps in the road," he said.

Andrea Clinton

I had a feelin' he was talking about me and my bull crap was the bump in the road, and this Qydeer thing. But Omar said what he really wanted was to open a few businesses, like corner stores, and a deli. He had a lot of money saved, but just needed a little more time hustling to get his nest egg or safety net, *which is typical of many drug dealers to say, but then they get that hustler's addiction.*

"So I do have goals, they just weren't along the lines of what she was on."

Then he blew my mind.

"I rolled past you in my Cadillac that day because you were the only thing on my list that I hadn't put my foot forward on. And if driving past you didn't work, if superficial things like nice cars and a pocket full of money wasn't your thing anymore, **all of a sudden,** I was going to approach you straight up. But I thought, *what are the chances Alisa isn't still a gold digger?"* Then he laughed.

You know me by now Goddess. I set the record straight in case he didn't understand. "Well, you need to know I don't have no problem with a man paying my bills."

He laughed and threw a sly remark right back at me, "Baby you don't have no bills." He continued laughing at me.

Oooooow, that got me mad, we laughed it off though. But I said to myself that I was gonna go make some, huh.

But one thing that lingered on my mind was, why? Why did he put so much effort into capturing my heart? Because as time went on, I felt like he was doing the very thing to me that he didn't like comin' from Vanessa. He was always pushing me to be bigger, better. You'll see what I mean, keep listening.

He was real special in the beginning and made me VERY happy: he bought me what I wanted even though he felt he shouldn't; he did it just because I desired it. But that didn't come as easy as he made it seem. He always pecked me on the cheek, mouth, or hand for no reason; he always made me feel secure, wanted and needed; he always opened doors for me or pulled out chairs; and he was always overprotective of me. He'd be like, "Was that nigga disrespecting you!" Or, "Where are you! You aiiight?" He'd say when I'd call him while I was out. He was very protective though. Like once, this guy got mad because I didn't give in to his weak rap. I walked away rolling my eyes and he called me a b—ch. But when he saw Omar, he started backing off saying, "My bad man, I didn't know she was with nobody. I thought she was being stuck up."

Omar stormed after him. "What the f—k you say to her man? What?" But the guy was already in his car, driving off. Please, as soon as he saw Omar, he got his car keys out. Omar turned around red-hot mad, and then I had to calm him down by holding his hand.

Funny though, I often had to do little things to get him off his *angry horse*, as I liked to call it. Like I'd put my head on his arm then maybe rub his back. And what man can resist giving in when you kiss him on his cheek? Continuously? I never understood why that calmed him down so much, but it did. I guess he knew with the way he'd get angry, it was the only thing I really could do to keep him from getting too worked up, so he obliged.

Basically, in the beginning, we couldn't stop talking. We shared thoughts, memories, feelings, plans, likes and dislikes for a few months. We got especially friendly, but we never got *intimate*. He said we shouldn't have been doing what little we did because it was still a form of fornication, and in Islam, fornication is *haram*, prohibited. **That used to get on my nerves**. His father was telling him all that crap, getting' on my nerves! He said he wanted to try something new, or turn a new leaf or something like that.

But hey, I was feeling him out anyway, because with all the hanging out and spending time together, he never asked me to be his lady, and I ain't no ho, I only grind with my man. But hey, ain't nobody no fool either, I was down to sample them goods. What's one sin? But he wasn't having it; his father was working overtime calling and talking to him about Islam from the prison.

But regarding being a man's lady, you don't assume you are 'cause you'll get ya feelings hurt. As far as I am concerned, if you don't ask me to be your lady, *we ain't exclusive brah!* Don't take me for granted; I don't know your intentions unless you speak them. I mean, a man kinda leaves you out there in the open to other

Andrea Clinton

brothers when he says to someone, "Yeah, we seeing each other." Seeing? What the heck is seeing each other? I *see* niggaz everyday.

Now I know what you're thinking, *Dang, she know how he acted the last time he got jealous.* But he bought this crap on himself. And I told you before, I like to play my little games every now and again. I don't play them to hurt him, but eeeevery now and again, a man needs a little wake up call. We spoke on him claimin' me, but he downplayed it and was truly being stubborn about it.

Long story short, I went out on a date, he-he-heeee! Oh Athena, I wanted to see what would happen. Omar dropped me off at Shakirah's and another dude picked me up. His sister Ka'reema saw me in a Spanish restaurant with this dude. She came over to our table trying to be funny talkin' 'bout, "Hey Alisa."

I said, "Hey."

She was like, "Where's Omar?"

I shrugged my shoulders and in a way that said, *why you asking me.* But I said "I dunno. I saw him earlier but I have no clue."

She looked at me like, *Girl, you know I will rag yo ass messin' with my brother.*

But I looked at her like, *Aaanhun, I know you will, but hey, I'm here now. Busted or not, I gotta hold my composure.* Heck, I know she'd have whoopped my tail, but not easily. Well she might've had a 65% chance, but I was gonna be going for mine too. I didn't say I was no punk. I wasn't 'bout to make it easy for her, she was gonna earn this butt whoopin'.

When she turned to walk away, she nodded at me to come join her. So I excused myself, went over and simply told her, "Look, no disrespect but ya brother into women like Vanessa who want to hang out, then keep truckin'. I might not be the best of women. But hey girl, if he not gonna claim me as his, then what am I sticking around only him for? I ain't his groupie; at least gimme something to go on. And heck, Vanessa was at least *getting' some.* Me, my sh—t dry like the Sahara. I gotta get this whole '*in Islam we try to avoid sex before marriage; work with me, I'm trying to be on the truth—marriage one day this and that crap.*"

She was with me until that last bit. "Don't disrespect the deen," she said.

"The what?" I asked.

"*Never mind.* I feel you though. I guess he gotta wear this one. He gotta make up his mind about if he's gonna be on the *haqq* or not, not half-step."

"On the what?"

"**On the truth!** He gotta decide if he gonna follow the religion right," she said with impatience, "bye," walking away.

I never, ever heard about me being out with another dude. But he must've overheard a li'l something about it because he started giving me the raised eyebrow, like I was caught with my hand in the cookie jar.

But men have to understand, when you don't make a little, minor commitment like asking a woman to be your lady and then carry it through to the best of your ability by being faithful, or at least trying hard to be, then you're saying, "You just like any other ho." And even if you aren't saying that, that's how it feels! Because marriage is the big commitment, *but brutha you won't even take the minor*, I thought.

I understand Muslims do the whole, *engagement thing*, and not the *girlfriend thing*. But then, he shouldn't even be chillin' with me right? See, that's what I said. And my gut feeling told me, *he just doesn't want to commit.* After all, how much of a Muslim could he be? He hustles drugs, right?

He would say to me, "Muslims fall astray all the time, just like Christians. But that doesn't mean they're not Muslim, just like a Christian or a Jew sinning doesn't make them other than the religion of their choice because they fall off their path."

Poppy-cock, I thought to myself.

"It just means they're acting and living in a state of *kuf,* a state of disbelief."

But I didn't understand that back then, probably because I thought the Muslims were supposed to be people who were trying HARDER to do right, and mostly were, and if they weren't at least trying to do right then they would abandoned ship. But in between?

Andrea Clinton

"It sounds like an excuse to keep doing wrong and making yourself think you have time to get to paradise to me," I replied to give him something to think about.

He didn't say much after that, just turned his head and daydreamed. But I'm sorry; I am just sworn to not listening to hypocrites or religious half-breeds.

Another time we got into it because of the no sex thing I said, "Why do you follow some things, and do what you want on others? What kind of Muslim does that? Just act like a Muslim."

"Alisa, if I did, I wouldn't be with you." Then he walked off, leaving me standing there, hurt.

Next time I just stuck to the subject and said, "With no commitment at all, you don't owe me nothing, so no telling what you'll do. But hey, do what you want, half-stepping in Islam, whatever." Okay, so I didn't quite stick to the subject of him not making me his lady. But the Islam thing was really all I had. I wasn't trying to break him, I wanted in. Hell, *I let him in.*

He didn't like me saying that about half steppin' in Islam, and it got him pissed, "Watch how you talk to me."

Boy I bit my tongue, I just said, "Hey it is what it is yo."

He walked into another room, said he didn't want to discuss it, but I saw he did. But he'd gotten so used to trying to make me happy, with exception to the issue at hand that he didn't want to make me angry with his reply. So instead, he left the subject alone. But the tension between us continued. It got so bad that folks around us could feel it too, and their actions finally pushed us to get down to the nitty-gritty.

I never flirted with guys in front of him Athena, and I never dated anyone else during this period, with exception to that one time. I also never got angry when he spoke to other women, not even Vanessa's friends who'd be at the spot pulling him to the side to patch those two up. Penny, the skank I was arguing with in the parking lot here at my mother's party, well, she's Vanessa's cousin. Yeah, some people do it like that, passing their man around the family. Anyway, she saw me walk in the spot with Omar. But she was still determined to play me out and arrange a meeting with him and Vanessa.

Now let me stop for a moment, to fill you in on something long overdue. I know Penny, the upper-class *slut,* from back in the day. Our drill team used to go up against each other when we were in junior high *and* high school. She, like Vanessa, came into the hood slumming with our men, only to run back uptown and look down their noses at us. I didn't make the connection that they were cousins for awhile, especially because Penny *isn't* as upper crust as Vanessa. She's almost upper middle class.

Oh and forgot to mention at this point, Man-Man and Manny had come home from down South. I told you, my mind slips, so you gotta work with me 'cause I start buggin', talkin' 'bout this stuff. Anyway Man-Man was a new daddy, Ronny had a preemie, but all of us, Man, Manny, Omar, me and Shakirah went out to celebrate. Man was able to keep his two women from finding out about each other, and Shakirah thought he and the baby's momma had broken up—whatever!

Anyway, Penny was on the side kickin' it to Omar. And he looked annoyed at her, but not enough for me. I got pissed after a minute or two.

"Okay, she doing it like that." I started walking toward her and Man-Man tried to pull me back. I said, "Have my back, but don't stop me from getting at a b—ch who disrespecting me."

I calmly, yet angrily, walked over to where they were. Omar met me part of the way. "Baby, hold up. Wait. Be a lady," he said, trying to grab hold of my side.

I shook my head at him. Mistake number one is, and I sing it from the mountaintop, *I'm not a lady! I'm a woman!* Being a woman means I can get with this, or I can get with that. Unlike a lady who is taught, made, bred; trained! And she won't knock ya freakin' teeth in.

But there, at that moment I just looked at him as if to say, *Don't! Don't, cause then I'm gonna think you was being foul just like this here ho!*

He stopped in his tracks, and put his hands up as if to say, *I don't want no trouble.*

I respected that because it showed he respected how I felt. I wasn't a woman shielding my turf, 'cause he didn't supply me with such. I was simply not letting her disrespect me. And like Drew Barrymore in the movie *Firestarter*, when she was throwing them balls of fire, my warning to Penny was, **"BACK OFF! BACK OFF!"** I mean this had happened more than once with her calling or pullin' him on the side, how long was I supposed to let it go on?

"Why the hell y'all keep tryin' to disrespect me?" I said pokin' at her face.

Penny knew me well. She and I often battled center stage in drill team competitions. And she knew when my anger reached a certain point, it was on, 'cause them huzzies used to pick and pick even during school days when you ran into them 'til you popped one in the eye. She jumped back with, "That brutha don't belong to you. He a player and he doing what players do; you think you special?"

"I don't know about all this playing you talkin about, but you 'bout to catch a beat down!" I said with my eyebrows raised. "You see him here with me, and you gonna keep disrespecting me? You and ya cousin gonna have to put ya li'l temper tantrum on hold, and deal with him on somebody else's dime, 'cause you ain't dealing with him on mine."

I could see Omar bite down on his jawbone out the corner of my eye; the li'l sign he was mad. He was angry because he felt I shouldn't have spoken about him like he was just another nigga. And I believe he was mad because it threw a monkey wrench in his li'l player status. But like Penny said, he don't belong to nobody. It seemed everybody knew this about him.

"You know what Alisa? Don't walk up on me like that. I was talking to Omar, and if he felt I was disrespecting you, and you supposed to be his girl, he should've said something."

I just looked at him as if to say, *See what ya neglectful ass causing? Ya ain't claiming me verbally or in action. Even she see it! Got people addressin' me on it!*

"No, he don't have to say nothing because I speak for myself. You disrespect me, *I* deal with you!"

Then I put my finger in her face. This ticked her off, and she tried to jump bad, popping garbage now, but again, she was on my stompin' grounds. A few girls I knew walked up on her, so she dug herself, starting to take steps back as she mouthed off less and less.

I wouldn't pop her in her mouth in the club and have people think I was fightin' over a man, but I wanted to put her in check and let her know that crap wasn't gonna keep happening.

Ooooow! Omar was heated. He took me by the hand, and we started out of the club. As we passed my brother, which wasn't far at all, he shook Man-Man's hand, who giggled and said, "What's it gonna be man? You gonna have to handle this. I can't have my sista out here constantly fighting over you. You know I don't have that."

Man-Man was always on some Billy The Kid thing. He was a fan of his and studied his life. Like The Kid, Man-Man would often laugh when he was dead serious. He did this no matter what the situation, and would still buck-shot after your butt if need be, laughing all the while. This is what happens when you buy your sons cowboy hats, toy guns, books and movies.

Everybody knew Man-Man was like that. Omar knew it, not that he was afraid of him. But he knew he'd have to take Man's words seriously; it showed on his face. And that made him even more mad at me for not being a lady. *Poop on being a lady!* I thought to myself. **I'M A WOMAN.**

As soon as we got outside, Omar got all puffy in the chest. "What's up with that? Huh! **Why you have to put her in check by disrespecting me?**"

I was just as pissed because I figured he must think I'm some kinda joke. *I'm not gonna claim you if you not committin', and if I bring it up to you, and you still don't commit, then kaput!*

This is how I felt and still feel 'til this day. But I finally stopped hen pecking and set it off on him. "I'm not playing no games with you Omar! You don't wanna commit, **DON'T**. I'm not in the business of begging a man to wanna be with me! And I don't pretend a relationship is what it isn't! You can't commit? Fine, but **SUCK IT UP!** 'Cause I'm not gonna beg you to make me yours."

I paused turning my back to him, but ended up spinning full circle. Then I ripped into him again, *"DON'T!* Don't ever think I'm stupid enough to run around claiming you, acting like you my man or anything like it when you don't even have enough feelings for me to make me the real McCoy, 'cause I'm not ya li'l chicken-

Andrea Clinton

head, runnin' 'round here peckin' afta you! You wanna be a player, play on wit'cha bad self! *You may not love me*, fine, *but I love me!*"

Then I turned from him and saw a cab squattin' down the street. I started going for it. But why did I do that? Why did that man snatch me back and commence to pull me to his car saying, "I bought you here; **I'm taking you home! Stop all that soap opera drama. Running to jump in a damn cab!**"

I was pissed, don't get me wrong. But when I thought he wasn't looking, I smirked at his anger and obvious feelings for me, standing up there letting me be bratty telling him off for *his* neglect. He was mad though. You could tell he was twisted with anger. Yep, he was biting down hard on that jawbone, poppin' veins. I remember him doing that since we were kids, did I say that already? Anyway, now, he was angry because his back was up against the wall and he'd have to eventually let whatever his reason for not committing go, or let me go, and I could feel he didn't want to let me go. But he was holding on to his stubbornness and it was eating away at his insides, probably giving him an ulcer.

We went to his house, both angry at one another. I dunno if I said it, but he has his own place outside of town. And only a few people know where it is. He's paranoid like that. When we settled in, we just sat there for a while, and then he blurted out, "I'm sorry!"

You know what I wanted to say to him, right? Say it with me, ***Damn right you're sorry!*** But I had to give in. He was so respectful, and had impeccable patience with me and corrects his wrong in a heartbeat. Well, with most things. But I had to gratify his feelings also. So I simply said, "I'm sorry too."

But for the rest of the night we didn't say much else. We just watched *Yo' MTV Raps* with Ed Lover and Dr. Dre., then fell asleep. Oh you didn't think I was gonna put-out to this Negro who couldn't even make me his lady did you? Don't get me wrong, I'm always the one trying, and he was always doing the good Muslim thing, bless his heart, but I didn't do anything that could even remotely contribute toward us having sex, and decided not to until this whole, "*is-you-is or is-you-ain't my baby*" thing was resolved.

I mean dang, we women have given up the hopes of marriage before sex, and what good it does, men just abuse and misuse that. But now I can't even get a stupid girlfriend title first? Please! I love me more than that. My momma ain't raise no fools! He lucky I didn't take it waaay back, make him court me first. Whatever that involves, ha!

We still didn't talk about commitment, but I'm stubborn with mine. *He can play if he wants, but he'll see,* is what I thought. But after the way we were that night, down and out like never before, I felt things would change and he would make a move toward something more concrete. I didn't know when, but I just knew it wouldn't be far off, or so I thought.

I cared for him, but Great-Grandma's words kept running through my mind like a stream of lava, "Get a man who loves you more than you love him." I know now she meant so he would treat me right. 'Cause a man *you* love more will abuse that love, right? But a man who loves you more will move clouds for you. So, I wasn't gonna let myself love him yet, not until I knew he loved me more. But that's beside the point right now. Am I your girl or what? You know—

***

When I ran into Ka'reema one day, she told me to understand that Omar never really loved another woman before, other than his mother and sisters. I mean, I knew of eight girlfriends he had in high school, but that doesn't mean he loved any of them. And she meant *being in love*, in a serious relationship as an adult. So he was afraid to open up and let me in is what she felt. I was glad to know this. It helped me to not start being a bastard out that mug. But I felt although he might be afraid to open up, he was *more* afraid to lose me.

Andrea Clinton

So when he went on, with us hangin', chillin', whatever, never mentioning us, I showed my tail. I had told him before, "Don't mess with me! I'm not the one." But he took a chance and moved too slow, or either he didn't get it, so I had to show his hard-head.

One afternoon, we were on our way to his niece's birthday party. I had bought her earrings, and this cute little dress with a matching pocketbook. I was so proud of the gifts, and looked forward to getting to be as close with his family as he was with mine. I mean we all grew up in the same neighborhood. I knew them, and they knew me and my family, but that was the extent of it; our families merely crossed paths.

When I picked up the dress, the manager of the store asked me if I wanted to see some shoes to go with the dress. And this was after he'd already over extended himself by showing me all the dresses and the matching purse. *Oh you know I was working it and playing on his obvious attraction to me.* I'd caress my stomach at times, and let my hand travel to my thigh so he'd look me up and down. I played with my earring and tilting my head as if I were sneaking to look him over, which worked him up to being bold. I winked when he showed me something nice as if I shared the attraction.

Omar, who couldn't take more than five minutes of shopping, was outside, smoking a cigar. Because I was inside with a man though, he watched us on and off through the store window, I timed it, every three puffs. It didn't matter to me though, you get what you ask for, and Omar was asking for it. So anyway, he saw the man helping me out a lot. So, it was then time to cash out. I headed to the register with two arms full of stuff to choose from. It wasn't a whole lot, but I had to make it look like a bunch of stuff so the manager would help me over to the counter and piss Omar off. But even when he saw the manager reach toward me, he still didn't barge in. And what was worse, he didn't bother to come in to pay for the stuff. I guess he felt as much as he threw money my way, I'd better have something. But I only had $400 on me and this stuff cost $157. I twisted my mouth thinking, *He shoulda bought his black behind in here.* Yeah I was spoiled but, I was on some old *gimme mine* stuff.

So, I paid for the stuff, and started making my way out. Omar looking in the window, plucked his cigar and headed inside to get the bags from me, our ritual. I wasn't far from the front doors, the guy, walking just behind me, caressed my arm. He held out his business card and said, "Call me sometime, I'd like for us to get to know one another." I took my time looking down at the card, then up at the man while taking the business card so Omar would see. And it didn't take long. He had barely walked into the store before he started flipping out. Ya know that look I gave him that night in the spot? The look that said, *Don't, cause then I'm gonna think you're just as wrong.* Well, he shot me that same look and I backed *UP!* My hands flew up like I was in a bank robbery and I dropped my head down.

"You out yo muthaf—kin' mind man!" he yelled at the manager. But the man just backed himself up and called for the security guard who was already watching us.

Omar lunged after the manager, but the manager ducked and went under the clothing rack, "Hold up man! I didn't know she was with you, hold up!"

Omar kicked the clothing rack over, with the man caught in it. He was stuck and couldn't get up. I think Omar was about to stomp him but the security guard rushed to the rescue by jumping between him and Omar, so we'll never know.

Thank God Omar knew the security guard; he was an off-duty cop from around the way. He told Omar to walk, putting his hands up in the air as if to say, *Please man, walk.* He asked the manager to walk too as he helped him get from under the clothing rack, all twisted up.

The funny thing is, the manager said, "I want him arrested! You saw what he just did?"

The guard turned to him and said, "You don't wanna do that. It would be worse for you; let him walk; he didn't touch you."

The manager looked at the guard, then at Omar who raised one of his eyebrows. Feeling a sort of enlightenment to Omar's possible importance, he took the off duty cop's word for it, and straightened up the clothing rack, with an embarrassed look. Then, he turned to help a customer at the far end of the store. As he

Andrea Clinton

walked away, he looked back, angry at me for starting the mess knowing I was there with a crazy man. I just smirked and shrugged my shoulders, 'cause I felt, *Hell, you saw me when I came in with Norman Bates, you just got too excited and took a chance nucka.*

Omar shot me this fierce look holding out his hand. "Give it to me!" I tried to look confused as if I didn't know what he was talking about. But he wasn't going for it. He just gave me one of those *warning* looks, squinting his eyes and biting his jawbone again and I forked over the manager's card, with a mocking look on my face, of course. He snatched it from my hands and ripped it up.

I opened and held the door for him as he stormed out to his car, looking back at me angrily. I walked behind him, smirking. I'd never seen a tantrum like that. Hahahaaaa, even now it's kinda funny.

We arrived at the birthday party and he never said a word to me, the whole time. I was fine though. I talked with his aunts, cousins, everyone else.

Ms. Sista seized the opportunity to talk with me, "Baby-Girl, you gonna have to have patience with Omar. Things don't always sit well with him. He stuck in his ways. And sometimes, it ain't even for the reason you think. He got this struggle going on inside. In Arabic, it's called *jihad*. I know some think that means holy war but it doesn't. It means struggle, and Omar got a serious struggle going on.

"He's been out here living without his father and getting caught up in a lot of negative things. But because he's Muslim, he can't let go of other things, Islamic values. Not to mention, he just don't trust people's intentions, and is used to playing it safe when it comes to people, women especially.

"I guess I did that to him," she said. "I guess he remembers all the games I used to play when I went through my thing in them streets, ya know. I had them backing me up on all kind of flimflams. Damn near got us killed. But anyway, if you have patience, you'll be fine with him 'cause he care for you. You just gotta gain his trust. Yeah, I made it hard for him to just get a woman, the right way *or the wrong.*"

That shed new light for me, as I always blamed Vanessa for their null relationship, and it may have in turn just been that he can't trust women. Maybe this was the second verse to what Ka'reema said about him never having loved a woman before.

Omar happened to be walking into the room and looked over at me as if to say, *What are you up to?* I waved my hand at him and murmured, "Boy please!" Trying to look at somebody, standing in the doorway like he's Freddy Krueger from *Nightmare on Elm Street*, ear hustlin'. If someone saw that look, they'd think he couldn't wait to knock my head off. But I knew what it was. He was digging me getting closer to his mother, but was still mad so this was his display. I say closer because me and Ms. Sista were always kool, short chats here and there I mean.

And although I appreciated Ms. Sista giving me the 411 on her complicated son, I had to turn toward her and let her know right quick, "Well Ms. Sista, I'm being overly patient with Omar. He wants a woman all for himself but won't commit to calling her his own. I'm not in that mess. I mean I'm not asking him to give me the ring in the Cracker Jack box, but he could at least read me the cartoon on the bubble gum wrapper."

She moved in closer and whispered, "Girl what the heck are you talking about?"

"I dunno, see what I'm saying. He got my head all messed up and I can't even throw analogies out there right." Then we laughed. Omar started to drift out the room, so I leaned toward her and whispered, "Do you know it's been around three months and we still haven't had sex?"

"Well I hope you haven't. Remember sister, we're Muslim. We ain't supposed to be physical unless we married. I mean the flesh is weak, and it is odd you two being around each other so much that you haven't fallen weak, but you'll get no sympathy from me. At least you got him, many of them girls out here would love to have him, be thankful. And he a handsome chocolate bar too." She laughed. "Hang in there, y'all may marry if you kool out."

"Ms Sista please, I can't even get the man to halfway commit, and you talking about marriage?" We both laughed at that.

Andrea Clinton

Then she chimed in, "You still don't get it baby. *You will though.*"

She wasn't lying. I eventually did get it. Almost too late though, and there wasn't much to it. Basically, he was battling with what he knew to be right with the Muslims, against what was the norm out there among all of us. That was all it was. And with that kinda conflict, he couldn't move in either direction.

Ka'reema later asked me to come outside with her. We walked up in front of the tall bushes in the neighbor's yard. She looked around to make sure we were alone, then lit a joint. Since I hadn't seen Freddy Krueger for a bit, I decided to go ahead and hit it. But I had to make sure not to smoke so much that he noticed. I shouldn't have done it; it's not really my thing. I knew Omar was against me or anyone he cared about doing any of that stuff, but that was even more reason for me to do it. Besides, people were busting out new bottles of liquor everywhere back inside the house, what's the difference?

But anyway, Ka'reema decided she wanted to give me a talking to as well. "So you and Omar still having commitment issues—" she started, as she passed the joint to me.

I stopped her in her tracks. "No, he having commitment issues. But if he keeps it up, he won't for long. I don't know what his problem is," I said, then hit that spliff with a deep lung and passed it back.

"I don't know what either one of y'alls problem is. He crazy 'cause he act like being ya man whether through Islamic marriage or otherwise is gonna come back to haunt him. And you acting up, in restaurants with niggaz and thangs," she replied as she gave me this half angry look, and hit the joint again. "I know how you roll Alisa, I've seen you out there on the set before you started messin' with Omar; I know how you get down. Every man you ever dated was either a drug dealer, a baller or from old money." She passed me the joint again.

"Omar ain't 'bout to let me be all up on him for no dough. If I'm not coming correct, he'd rather be alone." I hit the joint with a deep lung again. I don't even know why I smoked at all. It was giving me such an offbeat feeling, felt dopey, probably because I felt like I was gonna be in trouble, and have to face the warden.

"I personally don't know how y'all gonna turn out. Y'all both nuts because y'all do things together like y'all a couple, and beefing because y'all not, but then y'all still chillin' out like a couple! Y'all nuts! Do you know if I got a guy's number, or did some of the things he said you do to pluck his nerves, Manny would snap." Then she clammed up quick, grabbing her mouth with one hand, and the joint with the other.

"Manny? Manny who? My brother Manny? Haaaaaaa!" I started running in place, "Ooooh snap! Ooooh snap!" Being silly in my disbelief that them two *really* doing things. I'd forgotten about them in all this time.

She got excited, "Girl, don't say nothing, sssssh! Shut up— please, 'cause we don't want people to know we kickin' it; that's why we don't come around y'all." She yanked me to stop running in place, but being silly with her big, hefty, manly hands. Dang she heavy-handed.

"Damn girl," I said trying to pull myself together. "When this start? At the hospital?"

"No, me and Manny used to kick it before on and off. It started because I used to ignore him 'cause he younger than me. But that was about two years ago. He kept pushing up with *how much he liked me*, and *'Why you doing me like this?'* Eventually, I gave in and we bumped uglies. That turned to every now and again, and sometimes a few times each month, then we stopped. But then at the hospital, we just decided to see what's up, for real this time though. But keep that to yourself!"

I was in shock; as many other women as Manny had been with in that year, who'd have thought she was one? But then Manny liked those hardcore street broads. He was always hollering, "Hurt me, hurt me mamacita," when he flirted with them. I mean, she pretty and many would say has a nice shape, but she a li'l rough; and she can thump with the best of them. He better not raise them hands to her, or they will rumble up in that joint.

We'd gone back and forth with that joint, and it wasn't skinny either. She started to pass it to me again, but at that point I said, "No that's all right. I don't want to start no mess with ya brother. Especially since y'all think I be messing with his nerves."

Andrea Clinton

"No, *I know you do;* you like that mess Alisa. Some men like that mess. But I guess he deserve you acting up, since he won't commit. I've done it before." With this, she put the joint out and we started walking slowly to the house.

We took our time so we could air out, but by the time we were approaching the steps Freddy was at *this* doorway now. He came to the door looking at Ka'reema and me, biting down on his jawbone, which I gotta say, I find so dang attractive. I dropped my head, half smirking. He could tell I was ashamed and trying to hide that I was high.

I thought Ka'reema would stand in front of me when we went up the stairs so I could squeeze by, behind her and go in the house. But she was high now and didn't care about her brother and what he was thinkin' or gonna say.

"Move nigga! I'm grown. Don't be looking at me like I'm a kid," she said as she brushed past him and went on in the house, leaving me. Why couldn't she play it off and act like we sistas do when we cover each other in a jam like that? Why she had to blow up *my* spot?

I looked at her cussin' him out and walking past him, and saw him look past her and onto me. He was biting down on his jawbone, and his veins were moving on the side of his temples, on that handsome face. I couldn't keep standing there so I drifted up the stairs and toward the doorway, head still hung low, high as hell, which I tried to avoid showing him. I had no choice but to walk past him. After all, I couldn't just stop and stand right there, 'cause that was room for conversation, and I already felt ashamed because I passed the level of high that I could play off or have full control over. Plus, my eyes were bloodshot-red, and barely open from being high, I could barely see.

But he knew all this, so he stood there, in the way, giving me this look. Uuuuugh! The closer I got to him, the more I felt like a kid. You know how some people can just blow ya high, or mess it up. Well this was what he was doing, messin' up my high. I squeezed past him so uncomfortably stiff and slow, turning to the side to slither through the tight space he provided me. Oh, he was very successful at completing his mission of making me feel uncomfortable. Although he killed a li'l of my high, I was still messed up.

Once I passed him, I just hurried on and went to sit in the backyard with the drinking folks. When he saw where I was headed, he said loudly, "You ain't high enough." I was so embarrassed. I just stopped, paused with my head half dropped once again, then, I picked up my head and my step and continued to the yard. I could've went off on him, but I was taught better than to disrespect someone else's house. So I just took satisfaction in the fact that he was *PISSED* that I went and got high.

***

Ry'eema is Omar's older sister, six years older. She escaped the ghetto a long time ago, lived with a well-to-do aunt during their down and out years. It was her daughter's birthday party we were attending. Her and her husband took turns talking to Omar while we were there. No one told me, but I'm not stupid. I know he was taking that opportunity to discuss us and the manager of that store.

Ry'eema is a wise and laid back type of a person, like Omar. She is good at reasoning with people, although looking at the birthday party, and people outside drinking liquor when she's supposed to be Muslim, I guess she didn't have it all reasoned out for herself. But, she and her husband must've told Omar he really had nothing to say about a man giving me his number because we hadn't etched a real relationship in stone. I say that because at first I could hear bits and pieces of their conversation, and it seemed like he was in denial of their point, but then his actions changed.

Eventually, after about three and a half hours of hardly speaking to me, where he only asked if I wanted anything, then brought it, only to leave again, he came over and sat down next to me on the long, sturdy lounge chair I was sitting on. He had that

Andrea Clinton

look like he had a hard day at the office, mixed with guilt, and anger. But he simply said, "What's up? You all right?" in a laid back tone, but as if even that took a lot out of him.

"Yep, I'm fine thank you. Or else I wouldn't have been able to sit over here with ya aunts and cousins, and everybody else but you all this time."

He turned his head for a moment, then came back with, "I know you can hang, so I wasn't worried about that. I just needed to kool my head, rationalize with some of these older cats a bit."

So of course you know I had to inquire, "And?"

"I came up with the rationale that I need a drink."

"You don't drink, you stopped." I looked at him in shock.

"Nothing hard, wine, to chill me out. But all they have is hard stuff. Need it to relax my mind; go chill out by myself somewhere; if not wine, then, herbal tea or something."

I was offended! He'd been by himself all night; well without me. So you know I acted out. "Well just drop me off at Shakirah's, and you can go do ya thing! I'm ready when you are." I was tired of him. Clutching my purse, I stood up. He dropped his head, and put his hands on his head like I took it all wrong. But heck no! I took it the way he said it.

Then he dropped his hands, looking at the ground, and then at my stilettos as I leaned on one foot, and had the other out showing off my pretty feet as if I was profiling or modeling shoes. He stood up and looked me in the face, reaching in his pockets for his keys.

"Let's go." He was tired of me too.

Now yes, I was getting angry, but something about seeing *him* angry calmed me down a li'l, just a pinch. I guess it's that something in me that Ka'reema said she knew 'bout me—that something that gives you the thrill of having caused drama, especially when someone crosses you. Because I was truly starting to get a kick out of him being mad now.

"You mad?" I said with no sign of feeling sorry, mad or bad about what I'd said.

But he didn't pay me any mind. He just kept walking. "Let's go."

Omar walked by his sisters and brother-in-law, looking annoyed, and waved. "Good night y'all, *salaam-a-laikum.*"

"*Walaikum salaam,*" they all said.

Ry'eema told me to come give her a hug, and so I did. She was always nice as far as I could tell. Then Ka'reema followed, I guess the weed helped us bond. Or was she acting like that because of Manny, hmmm.

"Come here sister-in-law, give me a hug girl," Ka'reema called out.

While hugging her, I replied, "Girl please, I'm standing outside knocking, waitin' for him to let me in and you talkin' 'bout sister-in-law." Her mother and sister laughed so hard they made me laugh a little.

Omar stopped in his tracks, turned around and looked back at us in anger. At that moment he hated to see his family bonding with me, *the enemy.* Not to mention, he probably thought, *How the heck you gonna be laughin' after you just pissed* **me** *off?* Omar turned away from us annoyed.

Ms. Sista hated seeing her baby like that. "Omar, calm down brutha. You gone get high blood pressure." He looked at her, then me and shook his head as if to say, *Ma this dang girl gonna give me a heart attack!* Then he got in the car.

I took those few steps to the car and I got in, waving to everyone. Then, he drove off. He took me to Shakirah's house never saying a word. But when we got there, he turned to me and angrily said, "Why you always gotta get in one of your nasty moods and get funky with me? I say I wanna go to a quiet spot and chill and you gotta throw some bullsh—t in the game!"

"First off, don't pull over yelling at me like you some madman and I'm ya b—ch! Second, you said you wanted to be alone, which is obviously the case, 'cause I went to ya niece birthday party and spent 'bout three hours with ya family! Not you, *but ya family!* So don't flip the script like I'm buggin!"

I stopped looking at him for all of four seconds, then I asked myself, *What are you doing?* I got out the car, slammed the crap out the door thinking, *This nigga must've lost his got-damn mind.*

Andrea Clinton

"Women Are Scandalous!"

Two days after our big fight at his niece's birthday party, I was beginning to lose faith in Omar's feelings for me. I knew that was the spoiled woman in me, and the devil trying to make me go out with another guy, so I chilled out. When I'm there, I usually hang with Shakirah's mother playin' backgammon, spades or dirty hearts. But since Shakirah and Man-Man been hittin' it off, and they practically a couple now, her moms always hittin' him up for dough, and driving to Atlantic City to party days at a time. But I found stuff to do. I chilled and hung out laughing with people who came to visit Shakirah, her cousins, aunts and so on. I had a few drinks with friends who came to see me at Shakirah's house. I visited a few people, associates I used to hang with on and off, you know.

But by the fourth day, that was it. I had had it. It was bad enough that everybody who knew I was looking for Omar's call, or his car to pull up, was saying things like, "What you expect, he got player status." What made it worse was I was sitting around with nowhere else to go. I'd visited all the people I could; and I had nothing to do.

So I went to the mall with my friend Tracey. Omar had given me a roll, $2,500, one day. I banked half, and spent most of the rest on the birthday gifts, eating out, ordering in, liquor store and treatin' folks those four days after the argument while at

Shakirah's. All I had on me at that point was $500, and I wasn't going to spend that. So I just ate and walked around the mall.

I happened to pass by this guy who smiled and said hi. He was tall, probably around 6 foot, 3 inches. He was a handsome, well dressed, professional; I believe he said he was a financial advisor. He was a light brown-skinned brother with a cute smile and had the most appealing facial features, strong cheekbones.

Before I knew it, we had run into each other at least three more times. His pitch for me to hang out with him was that running into each other so much was a sign we should chill together. So we decided to grab some ice cream and chill around the mall. My food had digested and I felt like havin' a banana split. Tracey had gone into a shoe store when I started talking to the guy. So I told Tracey I'd catch up with her and he and I walked down a ways, and into the ice cream store. We decided to sit and eat our ice cream.

I don't even remember this dude's name, which goes to show how much I cared about the whole thing. But he asked the famous question soon after we sat and had a few laughs.

"So Alisa, you have a man?"

"Not really." He asked me what I meant. So I explained and he replied that Omar was playing me. He said Omar sounded like a player because he would not snatch up a fine sister like me and make me his own. I knew what he knew not; there were some underlying issues and circumstances goin' on. Lots of times people give advice off the top of their heads like that without knowing the whole story. But I didn't bother to worry over what he said. I just enjoyed another man's company, along with the $7 banana split he bought me.

We didn't talk about anything heated, just what he did for a living, and my so-called goals. He, unlike Omar, understood that I wanted to just chill, take care of my man and live life to the fullest. He said a man like Omar wants a woman to be more independent to relieve the pressure off himself. I disagreed. I knew it wasn't about the money. Heck, *Omar was a drug dealer.* I felt Omar thought it would be a challenge to change a girl like me, because I'm stubborn, set in my ways and used to men hooking me up and taking care of me. I felt it was about the male dominating thing.

Andrea Clinton

You know, the Frankenstein Syndrome. Where a man feels complete when he *makes* a woman. Then takes much pride in the finished product when she turns out to be *the model woman*. A lot of men get like that, especially over a girl with a reputation like mine, who only date men rolling in the dollars. They try to turn us out, and when they do, they walk around with us, their trophy, like show dogs; b—ches. How many men have you seen, no matter where they come from, get a ghetto girl and dress her up, clothes, personality, education, everything, then take her around their peers to show her off—I've seen plenty.

But his take on the issue was interesting and just what I was looking for. He said he'd love to have a woman take care of home, treat herself daily to keep herself up, shopping, hair and nails, massages, etc. I liked what he was about, but he was like a hollow log with no interior. He was so mechanical; it felt like I was speaking to a robot. It seemed that he memorized the things he knew women like me wanted to hear, and spit it at me so I could be so excited to have struck gold.

We were done when Tracey came over and said she was ready to go. He said he'd drop me off, so I figured what the heck, Omar ain't been around. So we went, and I thought that if that Negro did pop up, it would serve him right to get jealous. He had no business going all those days without calling or coming to see me. What'd he think I'd do? I'm me. This was gonna happen sooner or later, right?

We pulled up in front of the apartment building, with Tracey following in her car. She got out and waved to us, and went inside Shakirah's. He and I sat and spoke for about 10 minutes more. Until of course, ole Freddy Krueger came storming out of the building, fangs out and all, crazed with anger like he came back to Elm Street to set it off with napalm or something. I immediately knew I'd better get out of that dude's car. So I did, yelling, "GO, GO, GO! That's him and he pissed; you better go." The guy started the car up quick.

Tracey, Shakirah and Man-Man rushed out just after. Shakirah was yelling, "Omar stop! Don't do it like that Omar! O'! O'!"

My brother was pulling his white tank tee shirt down over his chest and running to catch up with Omar at the same time. "O'! O'! O' man, calm down! Omar, don't do it man!" I could see my brother was trying to show some restraint because he didn't know how far Omar would go because affairs of the heart can be fatal, *but* I was still his sister.

Then the stupid guy stuck his head out the car window and tried to rationalize, "Yo chief, she said she don't belong to no one aaaiiight? So don't come over here with all that Ra-Ra sh—t."

I yelled at this fool, "Drive maaan! Go-Go-Go!" By then Omar was stepping off the curb heading toward the car, with his hand reaching behind his back to pull out his gun. When the dude saw the look on Omar's face and that hand disappear, he pulled off like he was in a drag race. I think the tire burnout noise drawing so much attention is the only reason Omar didn't pull out that gun and shoot after the car. He instead after watching dude speed off, dropped his hands by his side, turned and focused on me.

Omar headed for me. *Sh—t!* I thought. His face was filled with *FIRE!* I stumbled as I saw this Negro fuming as he approached me. I didn't know how big this was gonna blow up but I felt for sure it was gonna **BLOW UP!** *And now he was there, in my face.*

"Why you always gotta play me huh! Why you always gotta play me!" He said facing me and grabbing my arms, squeezing the life outta them. But before I could say anything, my brother dashed over and from behind wrapped his arms around Omar, bear hugging him and swinging him away from me. When he was a few steps away, Man-Man yelled at me, "Git in the house! Now! *LET ME TALK TO HIM!"*

So I just walked, quickly. A part of me wanted to smile, as the devil in some of us women like to see a man's feelings for us exhibited. But then I got a li'l worried. I never thought of Omar hitting me before then. I still wasn't sure if he ever would, but I knew that day I was close to gettin' hit, slammed or snatched up and shook the hell out of if nothing else. So I was happy to head inside. I didn't want to be out in the street with all that bull crap any way. I hated seeing it with my parents once or twice when I

Andrea Clinton

was a kid, and I hated it when I saw his parents in the streets carrying on, so I picked up my step to avoid a curbside performance.

But Omar had started yelling after me, and from the top of his lungs with that strong bass in his voice, while my brother had his arms around Omar, holding him back.

"Why you always gotta try and play me out! I'm not no sucka! *I'M NOT NO SUCKA!* AND YOU NOT GONNA KEEP PLAYING ME LIKE ONE! I'M A MUTHAF—KIN' MAN! *I'M A MUTHAF— KIN' MAN!* STOP TRYING TO PLAY ME OUT!"**

When I got up to the entrance of Shakirah's building, I found her waiting for me, pacing and pushing her hair back with both hands as if she was worried. Tracey seemed pretty worked up too. And Tracey had the same kind of attitude and disposition as Ka'reema when she was pissed off; you know, sexy mean. Don't get me wrong, she was pretty and pink, but she could get **RAW** when angered. And she was very outspoken and real with hers, so she gave me a piece of her mind while getting out her keys to leave, "I'm out girl. Omar being mad *like that* is trouble. You slippin' trying to run with that nigga *and* playing games? Girl please! You not thinkin' straight. If he feel you playin' him out, it's gonna get bad, real bad. And that ain't fair to ya brutha 'cause they kool." Then she stopped and got real serious before proceeding to leave, "You can't do like you do with **every** man Alisa. You gotta know who to f—k wit', and how to f—k wit' 'em." She waved goodbye as she walked off, "peace."

And she should know. I learned a lot of my game from her crew, even though most of them have grown up and moved on with their life. Me and Shakirah used to see them gettin' men for their dough when we were in junior high, and they were in high school. We felt our paths were already written for us, seeing them with their gold, and diamonds and knots of money. So if Tracey said I was barking up the wrong tree, I had to reconsider how I was rolling, and if I was ready to be serious with a man, or if I still wanted to run game on nuckaz.

As we headed into the building I asked Shakirah when Omar showed up, how long was he there, and how'd he know I was downstairs, outside with another guy.

"He asked what you were up to and I said you and Trace went to the mall. When she came in two hours later, he asked her where you were. Tracey kept trying to play off where you were. Then she started getting nervous and he asked her if you were out with another nigga. She said no, but he looked in her eyes and said, '*WOMEN ARE SCANDALOUS!*' Then he headed out the door, got something from behind my stairwell and ran down the stairs. We yelled for Man-Man and he came out the bedroom. Girl it happened so fast. Me and Man-Man trying to put our sneakers and stuff on to stop him. Y'all need to get it together. You and him stress *everybody else* out!"

I felt for Shakirah because I knew it was awkward for her. Heck, it was awkward for me. She never said nothin' 'bout it though, because she knew I'd never had a relationship so sidestepped. She put her arm around my neck and we continued into her apartment. I began to shed tears because I was really scared. Although it may not have seemed like it, I literally almost crapped my pants when Omar headed for me. And I didn't want to leave Omar and Man-Man alone because they were both two birds of the same feather, *nutty.*

I was upstairs for all of twenty minutes while they talked. Man-Man said he held on to Omar until we entered the building. Omar just looked down at the ground, staring, pissed. This was what Man-Man said took place between them:

"Git off me man. Let me go," Omar said to Man-Man, tryin' to calm down.

"You all right man? You sure I can let you go brah?" Man asked him.

"Yeah man, let me go," grumpy.

Man let him go and stepped to the side while Omar stepped forward a few steps, then turned around and faced him.

"What you think I was gonna hit 'er?" Omar asked, shaking his head. "I wasn't gonna *hit* 'er."

"Good to hear."

"I was gonna shake the sh—t outta her though!"

"Aiight man chill," Man smirked, understanding how Omar felt, but feeling awkard as it was his sister Omar was talking about.

Andrea Clinton

"I'm kool man," while Omar looked off down the street, trying not to show his pain.

"Talk to me man," Man-Man said to Omar.

Omar started pacing in a circle. "I can't disappear, get my head straight for a few days without her being in some man's face? I just needed to deal with some things, wrap my head around what was going on with us. And when I come here to talk it out, let her know *I do* love her and wanna be her man, she out with some other nigga? Is this how it's gonna be? Anything go wrong and before the sun sets she out with somebody else?"

"Omar, brutha, *you knew how Alisa was when you asked me if you could push up on her like a month before you gave her your coat at the spot.* You knew she had a lot of game with her, and you knew she liked money and loved to feel wanted, one way or another. If not with you, somebody. I asked *you* if *you* were ready to deal with all that, and *you* said you were."

"Maaaaan! But this is different, them niggaz didn't care about her! When she kept it movin' so did they."

"What! Who told you them niggaz didn't care 'bout her?"

He said Omar looked at him surprised because he had it fixed in his head that I was looking for dough, and the men were hoping for sex. It never dawned on him that some of them, most of them truly wanted me or grew feelings for me.

"O' some of them dudes have cried to *me, personally,* asking me to talk to her and make her understand that they would take care of her and she'd want for nothing if she opened her heart to them. But she did what she did, and they got hurt. *They wasn't no androids or robots without feelings brah!* Even the ones coming with game got hurt 'cause *she got game,* and they wasn't prepared for that."

"So I mean nothing to her, like them, that's what you telling me? She can skip out on me just as quick as she did them."

"You a smart man O', you know that girl got feelings for you. All she talkin' 'bout is you makin' her ya lady. And she didn't dis' all of them bruthas. She was in the girlfriend, boyfriend thing with a few of them. But I guess they just couldn't keep up, or you know, things happened."

"Aiiight Man," Omar stopped him, 'cause he was startin' to get jealous and didn't want to hear of my feelings for another man. "But a few days man? She can't chill a few days?"

"Omar, did you tell her you were going to take a few days to yourself to think about y'all? Did you ask her if she could hold out and give you that time?"

"Damn I gotta ask her to hold out? I said I needed some time to think, but that led to a situation with her barkin' in my ear about some mess, then she jumped out the car. But I never called and said I'm takin' a few days to myself. *She would flip on me about that.* And I didn't think I had to call her to take a few days anyway. I'm not worth more than that?"

Man replied, "*I think her man* would've been worth more than that, but then, *you ain't her man remember?* And how was she supposed to know that wasn't the end of y'all chillin' anyway? You didn't call her, and she didn't call you. Maybe she thought y'all was moving on."

Man-Man told me that his frustration behind me and Omar started to come out. He knew Omar usually kept a level head and was always on point, especially with women, so he couldn't understand how his boy Omar was lettin' me, a woman, get him all botched up in the head. So he let Omar have it. "Yo, brah, I gotta keep it real with you yo. How you lettin' a woman make you lose your kool? I don't care if she is my sister! **That ain't *you* man!** You *always* on top of things. Omar man, *you can't love her without hurtin' you?* You runnin' out here packin' ya pistol to burn some nigga who don't really even have a clue what's going on with y'all; and he don't even matter on the scale of things; you know where you stand with her! That ain't right O'." Then he put more emphasis in his words as he was getting emotional about his brother, "What if the police rolled up O'? Decided to check you or saw you 'bout to whip out on that pretty boy? Knowing how they probably on us as it is with all these crackhead snitches. That would leave you in either of two places—jail or six feet under. Maaan, if you being with her is gonna make you slip like this, don't git wit' 'er! And I'm telling you that for you, for your sake."

Andrea Clinton

"I can't *not* be with her man. Been wantin' to be with her too long Gee. *You know this.*"

"Brutha, I know you been diggin' her for a long time, years. And you my brutha so I never made it no problem, especially 'cause you always showed me respect on that tip, and didn't run behind my back. But you gotta remember, *she 19*. She still in her prime man, fresh, still got a lot of run in 'er; and you never know what kind of woman a female gonna turn out to be at no *19*. *That's my sister and I'm tellin' you this.* For all we know, she could be another money grubber like Tracey, or end up dead like Lona, dead or some sh—t 'cause she f—kin' 'round wit' the wrong nigga. Or she could turn out fine. You don't ever know with these women, man. They look up to the wrong sh—t. And what's the sense in being with her, if it will cause you to one day be without her, 'cause something went wrong? Then *you all hurt up.*"

Man paused then said, "One of y'all have to be mature, on point, and take the relationship by the handle. And today, it wasn't you. And it ain't ever gon' be her, *no time soon anyway.* If you gonna do this, it gotta be you who run the relationship. Plus, how close you think this temper gonna get you back to Islam? I know that's your goal, but *you ain't gonna get it like this man,* **come on now.** I'm tryin' to keep us all outta jail; ain't that what we been sayin? Jump on somethin' new one day? Something Legit? I can't do it alone O' and can't count on Manny, he simple like Alisa. But you—"

"Aiight! Aiight Gee. I hear you. I'm slippin' just like in front of The White Castle, chillin' when we should've been movin' out. I just, I just gotta get my head back."

"That's old sh—t man. Let that go. *We here ain't we*?" He paused and looked him straight in the eyes, **"And I'm a grown man; you wasn't slippin', *we was slippin'*. You ain't responsible for me, or the world Gee. Let's just make sure we on point and in place from now on. We gotta be on point at all times Gee.**

"And, on the subject of a woman hanging out with you? You know women. They get hooked easily and want you to be their man," Man-Man continued, shaking his head while talking about me, "not all women, but when they do, man! Heck, I would've been fine with my baby mother and just kickin' it with Shakirah on the side every now and then, a few times a month. But, once they get a taste, if they like the seasoning, they want *more and more and more*. Then they get possessive. And if they grow a likin' for you as a man, they ain't tryin' to let you go. I don't know what I did to Shakirah to make her cling like a can of peaches." They laughed. "Maybe I shouldn't have knocked her back out like I did, or shoudn't have taught her them tricks, or *some 'em. But she was fine man.* She came right up out that skinny stage and *POW!* I didn't even notice 'til that night at the spot when them two came down there." Then they laughed again.

"Yeah, I remember. You was on it; laughin' at me but you was fishing ya self."

"Yeah, but, I just wanted to hit it a few times. I gotta admit it though man, she grew on me. Sometimes I question who I like more, her or Ronny. But, I should've stopped after once or twice. Because now, I got two girls, and they both think *they* my lady. I know that's gonna blow up in my face one day, and probably soon. But O', at least I knew I had to make Shakirah my girl or else she was gonna give me trouble, or jet. *And* I got to a point man where I couldn't see her with *no* other man, just like you troop, *I was out here in my boxers ready to chase one of them niggaz from picking her up on a date;* you saw me, psssh! But how long I think she was gonna squat waitin' to find out what's up? So, I knew I had to make her mine, before I kill somebody."

"Yeah? I think you may like her even more than you know Man. You talk different about her than you did Ronny or Malikah. And you was in love with Malikah."

"Yeah, you right. But back to you O', *eventually*, my sister gonna give up and move on for real-for real. So you have to establish what it is you want with her. Do you want her to be your lady, or not? If you do, you better go and get your girl man. If she still there for the gettin', after you reachin' for guns and thangs."

They both gave half a laugh. "If you don't want to let go of that player status, then apologize to her and be her friend. But you gotta make a choice man."

Man-Man said he looked at Omar as serious as hell. He told me that Omar just turned to him and apologized because he knew it was hard for Man, being both my brother and one of his close partners. My brother said that by then Omar had calmed down and reached out to shake his hand. Man-Man shook it and then they started walking across the street back to Shakirah's.

But he said when they got inside the building Omar stopped walking. "Since it's ya sista man, and I feel like I owe you for being in the middle of this, I just wanna put you down on something. I didn't commit to Alisa not because I wanted to play her out or on that player status, because you know all that player stuff is talk and jokes, I don't care about that mess man. That ain't really me. I just let people say all that player crap because it's better than them knowing, *I don't trust women*. But I got it bad man! I mean, Man, think about it, *how can I trust women after my mother?"*

"But O' who does trust women 100%?"

"Yeah, Man, but you know how it was for me comin' up. I watched my moms closely and you know how *I* analyze things. Women have a way of getting into ya heart, and gaining ya trust just to end up breaking you down man. You can lose it all messin' with them. Sometimes they worse than us. They lie, cheat, and get into sh—t they ain't got no business in. They'll break you down to nothing. I know. I watched my father get drunk and cry everyday because he couldn't keep my moms out them streets and off that dope. Then when he got locked up for that attempted murder, all he did was worry about us because he said he knows how a woman on dope is, and he was right. She put us through HELL! **You** *know Man*. He said he cried for the first five years, until we were able to start fending for ourselves. I don't wanna be him. *That can't be me Man; that can't be me*. I don't wanna be sitting in nobody's jail because my lady got me killing somebody because she snatched my heart out my chest and threw it at me," Omar said as they walked up to Shakirah's apartment.

"Well you got the wrong woman man, because Alisa jet away from men as a hobby. I can tell she all in now, but the minute you look like you showin' ya ass, or like you feelin' some type of way about her, **SHE OUT!** No questions asked. Running away, it's her mechanism, her self defense or preservation."

"Unh, Islamically, it's said if something is not good for you, your soul, your religion, you should shun it, flee from it."

"Well, she should be Muslim because she flee with the quickness."

"Well, now you know why I never made none of those women my own; just got the panties and stepped; but that's how I was back then. The other thing is, in Islam, we don't do the girlfriend thing. We marry. And that's eatin' away at my conscience, bad enough what I *been* doing these past years."

And with that, they came in the apartment door and Man walked to the bedroom, calling for Shakirah to follow him. I had been sitting on the couch, so I got up. I didn't like the feeling of someone mad standing over me. I went to the window and looked out hoping to get into a mode that would help me have the strength to say what I needed to say. I didn't have it though, and he wasn't in no rush to start a conversation. So I, like a fool, rushed in.

"I can't do this no more." Then the tears began to roll down my face. "It's just not worth the trouble I'm putting you through when I start acting up. Or the anxiety I'm going through wondering, being patient, and waiting for you to resolve ya issues." I turned toward him. "Besides, you blame me for my actions and say it's my fault. Yet our problems are on the strength of your problems. So, let's just nice it up and go back to being friends," I said as I stared at him to get some sense of how he felt.

Omar started shaking his head as if that was unacceptable. "No," he said beginning to take steps toward me. I turned back toward the window, and looked out as more tears flowed. It was a relief to hear him say it, but this wasn't going to be a smooth transition.

"Baby look, I bungled aiight," he said. "I had some things I was going through. All this was a huge step for me, so I just needed to take my time and sort through everything. But then I couldn't because I was too busy missin' you."

I just didn't feel like hearing all the *oow baby-baby* schmoozing that the players do. So I walked away. He called after me, but I kept walking. When I reached the hallway, he was behind me, pulling my hand. I stopped and turned to him.

Andrea Clinton

"What Omar?"

"Baby I'm sorry! I didn't go about it right, but I been through a lot, and I just have a hard time trusting people; especially women. And you running with Tracey these few years, following in her footsteps don't make it easy on me to trust you from the door! I just, baby look—"

I felt like I was making him beg, and I didn't like this. So I turned to walk away. But he flipped the script on me. Wound up with frustration, he grabbed both my arms, turned me back around, and shook me as if he was trying to shake some sense into me.

"I love you all right! And *I don't like* how much I love you! That's why I never asked you to be my lady, because when you love someone how I love you, you shouldn't have problems with trusting their intentions, or where their coming from! And I already had trust issues with women. And knowing you how I know you to be, all about the Benjamin's, it isn't easy, especially because I feel for you so much. And I hoped you being my lady was something that would just go without saying in time, **but you gotta be so damn official!**"

"If we're not official who's gonna respect us as a couple? *I couldn't even respect us,* because all you do is give me the cold shoulder like you dislike me because you feel for me so much!" Then I put on that soft, pouting face we females wear when we're hurtin' for sympathy.

He growled with hostility, "Shut up! Just shut up! *Damn!*" Pausing as he was fighting whether he should kiss me or not, but he lost the fight; he was defeated by his want. As he looked into my eyes, finally giving in to love; he slowly drew his face into mine, steadily, gracefully stealing my breath with his, intimately engaging. Then he shifted to the side of my face, pulling us cheek to cheek; and he hugged me tight, delicately whispering in my ear, "I love you. Be my lady, my soon-to-be-wife?"

I was stubborn, so I counted to six. Then I gave in and hugged him back. I rubbed his back, which went against every fiber of my being. I hated to give in so easily. But, I just had to hold him. Then I answered yes, and we stood there holding each other for a good few minutes. Then I realized, what I so impatiently waited for, I was now afraid of; **I was his woman.**

WHAT–UP DOC?

I was comfortable with our new status, but sorry that we had to go through all we went through to get there. But then I realized he had to go through it in order to move on. That came to me when we went to see his father. I didn't want to go; it was the prison my father was incarcerated in. But it seemed Omar needed to go see his father because although they spoke on the phone, Omar hadn't seen his father since he was shot and he missed him a lot. He was concerned that his father was worried about him. So I went with him, *for him*, and moved my own ghostly past to the side. I should've known that that was the beginning of me doing things to make him happy even though it wasn't exactly what I was up for.

When we signed in, I let them run that metal detector thing up and down my body, emptied my pockets, and had to let this lady correction officer run her fingers up through my hair. The whole thing made me so pissed. Girl, I spend $125 on my hair! And here was this heffa', running her hands with them nasty gloves through it, the same gloves that had combed through every other woman's hair, some men too. Not to mention, my hair was up in a bun. So I had to go the restroom after she was done playin' in it and groom it back into shape.

When I came out, Omar could tell I was angry and asked if I wanted to leave. He didn't want me to feel even more humiliated

Andrea Clinton

once we got inside. Not truly knowing what I was in for, I replied, "No baby. Come on let's do it."

Lo and behold, when we walked through the doors, I found myself staring in the pits of hell; hell on earth. There was a big gymnasium type of room with a gazillion chairs filled with people.

To the left, there were women and kids with inmates sitting across from them. Some were just playing with their kids and some were sexually slobbin' down their mate. And wait, if you think that's bad, stay tuned. To the right, there was the other half of a gazillion seats. But what was happening over there was sooooo impure. My God! It reminded me of a movie I saw once where the people of Moses's time were having orgies and all that stuff in a cave when he showed up with the Ten Commandments, and even upon seeing him they didn't stop, they just kept on screwing, like animals. Or all those other stories in the bible about that kind of orgy stuff. I mean, in this jail, men had women sitting on their laps, humping, boppin' up and down like it was nothing. And all else around were acting like they didn't' see, ignoring them, or too busy doing their own thing. It was like a real orgy. Some were playing with themselves or others, you know, while in their seats. And as I looked around, shocked, I was even more crazed when I saw some of those loose women were men, drag queens—I got dizzy.

I saw girls I knew to be tricks who were most likely prostituting, and I later found out a lot of the drag queens were there making money too. I swear it was like a whole other world; **HELL**. I felt so weakly uncomfortable. I felt for the first time that I really understood when people would say, "Oh you ain't been no where and you ain't seen sh—t." I mean, in short, it was as if each of these individuals had lost all their sense of right and wrong, morals and principals, and were turned into untamed animals, sitting up there horny as dogs, screwing in front of everyone, *with no care*— I saw for the first time that the system is geared to strip folks of sense and sensibility, and to make them into unconditioned animals. And the prisoners were giving in to it.

It was too much. I felt like running to church, even if just to get away from this place. Omar was looking for a place for us to sit, so he didn't catch my stunned expression at first. When he saw two seats, he tapped my shoulder tellin' me to follow him. He saw my face and then it clicked that I was bewildered. He pulled me to him, hugging me, putting his arm around me and walking us over to the two seats where we sat down.

"I'm sorry baby, I forgot about all this. I see that crap so much; I learned how to tune it out."

"Men? With other men?

"Yeah, the day of the closet case is gone. This stuff use to make me not wanna visit."

I was still looking around, "Yeah, I can see why. I don't ever want to come back."

It occurred to me that my father might very well be one of those guys walking around in that gym. Before I knew it, I was hoping I would spot him. I didn't know where he was, but all of a sudden I wanted to see him, badly. I hadn't seen him since I was 14, a few years after he got locked up for the murder he committed. He made my mother and aunt stop bringing me.

I told Omar that when his father came out for his visit, at some point I'd leave them alone and go the snack machine. He understood, and nodded okay.

About fifteen minutes later, I saw the **biggest, most BUCK, built, muscle-bound, shiniest chocolate man I ever saw in my damn life**. He came walking toward us. It was Omar's pops, Brother Abdul-Malik. Dag-on-it! Wow! He was big as hell! Don't get me wrong, he was handsome too, with his white ass teeth, just like Omar. I'd forgotten his name until I saw him. I wanted to forget it too. I knew him as Maleek; they now called him Abdul-Malik. I dunno how they got from eek to ik, but anyway. Damn he was big! He was so huge, his muscles were about to split his tee shirt right up the sleeves. I mean this guy was cockier than Mean Joe Green back in the day, and bigger than Tony Atlas, the wrestler, he was thick with his. I muttered to myself, "Let Ms. Sista slip up now. He'll blow at her and knock her head off!" Please, I'd be a good girl if I was messin' with him. Hell, *I wouldn't mess with him*, although I dunno, he *was* fine.

Anway, Omar was like a li'l kid. He jumped up and grabbed his father's hand, shaking it and saying, "*As salaamu alaikum, rahmantullahi wa barakatuhu!*" His father pulled him in for a hug and Omar hugged him back with everything he was worth.

Brother Abdul-Malik had tears rolling down his eyes from the word go and replied, "*Wa laikum salaam, rahmantullahi wa barakatuhu,* son!" They hugged so long I thought maybe I should go get some coffee or something, give them a moment. I noticed a few other big Muslim men standing up and looking at them, pointing Abdul-Malik out to one another, and saying, "*Allah-hoo-ahbar,*" over and over again. Evidently Abdul-Malik must've been talking about missing his son a lot and what had happened to him in front of The White Castle.

Finally they parted. "Let me look at you man," Abdul-Malik backed up and stared his son up and down, "You looking strong Omar. You lookin' like you good to go man."

I don't know where it came from, but all of a sudden I pictured Brother Abdul-Malik, a smaller Maleek, falling down the stairs. I pictured myself as a little girl, watching him walking down the street drunk, crying about his life, wife and kids, because the cops took Ms. Sista's word for it and shoed him off, away from the house; I could see his face clear and everything. I pictured Omar trying to push past his mother to go after his father, to be with him, and Ms. Sista blocking his way. Then I came back to the present and saw them there, at the prison, after all those years. I was so moved, moved to sadness. I wiped the few tears from my face.

I, like Omar, would never hold the things that happened back then against Ms. Sista. But—that was some real f—ked up sh—t! But it felt good to see life bring them together again.

As I stood there, with tears in my eyes, sad about their history, their circumstance, missing each other, I turned and wiped my eyes, trying not to be obvious. I looked up to see Omar pointing at me and saying, "This is my lady Alisa, my soon-to-be-wife."

I thought his father would be like slow down, or take it slow. But, Muslims marry to save from sin, so, he was just happy to see his son avoid fornication, a grave sin.

"How ya doing sis.?" Brother Abdul-Malik asked.

I was glad he didn't try to hug me because I think I would've died.

"I'm okay. How you doin'?" The ghettoness flew out before I could control it.

"I'm good-I'm good." Then he turned to Omar. "Look like you doing good for ya self son. *Ya lady looking admirable*," he said in the most player-player slang I've heard since Bootsy Collins. He threw in a li'l of that street hand movement, you know how they used to do, just before he and his son shook hands about me, smiling and grinning. I felt like a trophy, again. And standing there, I guessed the Muslims had graduated from emulatin' scholars, trying to use big words no one understood, to just being the kool, down-to-earth old G's from around the way, but religiously bound now; it's kool though. We appreciate them for keepin' it real on the religious and street tip; it makes you *want* their advice.

But honestly, Muslim men confused me sometimes. They were trying to be so righteous. I mean, I knew it was a good thing. I admired it but I didn't understand it sometimes. Some of them would backslide into the same state they were in before Islam, but when they got knocked off and were back in jail, they'd go back into Islam, deep, strong. Like the only time they could put God first was when they had nothing else, or were forced; maybe that's why they keep gettin' locked up, maybe God makes them worship. I just didn't get it though. But then again, it was like my mother going to church when she had big problems, after not being there for years. Then when things were good she stopped. And when they got bad again, she was back in church with bells on. I dunno, I guess we all get two-faced on God huh? But, he brings us running back to him, saying, *"Oh God please help!"* Hard heads.

Anyway, I sat there and let them chit-chat for about fifteen minutes. When I figured they were warmed up and ready to get into it for real, I went to the bathroom so they could talk-talk. I told Omar I was gonna take my time, because I knew after ten minutes he'd worry.

I hung out in the ladies' room for awhile, reading stuff on the walls. And boy was there some stuff up there. Like, a picture of a woman's private parts and the words, *I ran up in it, like Mr. Bennett,* and I can't repeat the rest. There were hooker phone numbers too, and all kinds of other stuff. Anyway, I got tired of reading that crap quickly. So I went to the vending machine, which was right outside the ladies room, in an area that looked like a locker room with benches. I got some chips, juice and a cake. I sat, took my time, and ate.

There were a few other people around me, doin' the same. Like mothers who wanted the father who was locked up to speak to their sons. Boy that seemed like an epidemic.

Before I knew it, me and some other young girl got to talking. Please, if you think you got drama. I was so amazed at her life. Her man and her stepfather bumped uglies. After that, the boyfriend darn near killed her and her mother 'cause he missed and was crying over her stepfather who wouldn't leave her mother for him. Now he's locked up and has no family. But she feels sorry for him, so she comes to see him and brings him money and food. All I could think was, *What! Not after steppin' out on me for my stepfather, and then trying to kill me and my mother!* People boy, I dunno. I told her if she doesn't start loving herself enough to walk when a man gets funky on her, she'll be unhappy for the rest of her life. She understood, but regarding her taking heed to it, as Omar used to say, *God knew best.*

After hearing her drama for a good 25 minutes, I went back into the gym, carrying a few sodas, chips, cakes and ice cream bars for Omar and his father.

...Women Are Poison

When I got back into the gym, Omar said, "It took you long enough. I was like, *I know she said she was gonna take her time, but man.* What took you so long?"

"I wanted y'all to catch up." He just shook his head and let me into the aisle to sit down.

The correction officers opened the door to the yard, and decided it was time for folks to sit outside. "Ain't none of that mess they doin' allowed outside," Abdul-Malik told us, nodding to those kissing and slobbering over one another. "So let's go out."

So out we went and found a seat in the shade. I sat on an angle to give them privacy, not like I knew much about anything they were discussing. Omar and Abdul-Malik finished up some business talk, it sounded like business anyway. And then they began to talk about who was where and how and why. His father told him about his side of the family, said they wanted to see Omar, make sure he was really okay. And I remember thinking, *Damn! Now we'll have to go visit them.* Whatever! I know I'm a stinker.

Andrea Clinton

I'd gotten to the point to where I wanted *my daddy*, and I asked Abdul-Malik, "You know Grip?"

He looked at me, sort of caught off guard. "Grip who? Big Money Grip?"

"Oh yeah," Omar said, "you don't remember her? That's Money Grip's daughter. Ms. Jerry's daughter."

"What? For real? Yeah okay, I remember now. Man you grew up. And I saw Grip when I came in just now. He might still be inside. *Big Money Grip!*" he said in a street, '70s tone as he stood up. I think he got a flashback because it *was* out of character. "Wait; let me go get Grip for you, *Baby-Girl* right?" He looked surprised that he remembered my nickname.

"Yeah, that's my nickname," I said sorta happy he remembered me, and even my nickname, but shy and afraid. It dawned on me, I remember him because I watched him often, but *did he notice me watching him?* Is that how he remembered me? That scared me.

As we waited, Omar reached to hold my hand but then pulled back. "Remember what I told you. If I don't touch you and stuff, I just want my father to see me on my best behavior, Islamically."

"I remember."

Abdul-Malik returned alone and sat down. "Grip just went back up. He said come see him next week, family day. Sorry 'bout that Baby-Girl."

Why did I feel so out of it? I felt like he still didn't want to see me. I knew my mother was still mad at me over the shooting, but I didn't think he was. But I guess I was wrong. I began to shed tears. But I turned away so they wouldn't see me. When I cleared my eyes, I told them I was going to the bathroom and left.

While I was in the bathroom, I made up my mind that I was gonna see my father and ask him if he hated me for what happened. When I came out, I looked around, and saw Omar and his father standing up and staring at me. Omar came over quickly, and I felt something was wrong. I could feel it had to do with me and my father. I swept the room looking for my father again, and I spotted him. I saw my daddy. I started over to him, but Omar caught up with me, saying, "Baby no, don't."

"You saw your father, I wanna see mine," I said.

"It's not like he don't wanna see you, but he taking care of business baby. You 'bout to get him in trouble."

I looked over and saw him there with a woman. And the lady who was kissin' him wasn't that much older than me. "How is he taking care of business over there Omar?"

Omar whispered in my ear, "Ya father running coke up here. Everything ain't what it seems! He can't see you now! Act like you know how this drug thang go baby! Come on! Walk! Now ain't the time. The correction officers who down with him will get nervous and the ones who ain't will fry him; come on!"

I turned around, feeling beatin' and walked back outside where his father was, and I sat back down, but angrily, tears and all. Omar didn't touch me to comfort me, nor did I expect him to. I guess he loved and respected his father's gangster just like I did mine when I left him to his business just now.

He'd already told me that his father scolded him about having a female friend and not a wife when he told him over the phone we were coming. Said something about it being *haram*, prohibited. So, I sat there uncomforted, with him at most handing me a hard-ass paper towel from the sergeant's desk that his father got for me. Then after about 10 minutes, it was finally time to go.

I turned and said goodbye to Omar's father and started stepping away. He replied, "Okay sista, I'm expecting y'all will be handling business soon." He was talking about marriage but I didn't have no time for that garbage. I had seen ghosts of old, stared at my father who I couldn't even touch, unlike him who got to hang with his son. And with all that emotion, them ghosts were haunting me and tempting my mind. So I just walked over to the door where everyone was standing on line to go back inside. I heard his father say while I was walking, "She got a killer-con attitude just like her father. See how she arched her eyebrow with that wicked facial expression." In my head I said, *See, this like a game to them. They reunited, but I'm not and I want my father!*

Omar and his father hugged and then Abdul-Malik went back inside where he and what looked like hundreds of others had to line up. My father made his way over to Abdul-Malik. Abdul-

Andrea Clinton

Malik and my father shook hands, and my father pulled him in close. Abdul-Malik whispered in his ear then my father walked off, disappeared.

Out of nowhere, a correction officer walked over and asked me to come with him. I was so pissed, I told him, "Hell no!"

Omar asked what was the problem and the correction officer said "Nothing." We looked over at Abdul-Malik who had signaled us. He shook his head at Omar and nodded toward the correction officer, telling me to follow.

Omar whispered, "Baby go head, just go." I was leery but I smelled something brewing. I followed the correction officer to the area we just left, saw my father come over, and realized they were giving us a few minutes.

I ran to hug him and he stopped me putting his hands up. "Don't. I don't want them to think you giving me nothing. Abdul-Malik talked to one of the correction officers to give us a few minutes. I just wanted to say hi. I wish I knew you were coming."

"Well it just happened. And when I got here, I couldn't take it no more. I wanted to see you *Daddy*."

He looked me up and down, and then rubbed his head. Looking in my eyes, he said, "Damn Baby-Girl, you still got my mother's eyes." He hadn't called me that in five years, not since my visit in the other prison.

Realizing how much I missed hearing him call my name, I started to cry, "Daddy why you stop me from coming to see you? You don't love me no more? What I do wrong?"

"Baby-Girl damn! Please! Don't start hittin' me with all this. Not when I gotta go back into hell with all these niggaz. Daddy gotta keep his head tight." Then he felt he had to say something sweeter, missing me and all. "Look—you didn't do nothing wrong. I did; *he* did. That's why I did what I did to him; that's why I'm in here. But this place ain't no place for a lady." He spit the same sh—t at me that he spit when he told my mother to stop bringing me to see him in the prison system.

"I ain't no lady!" I murmured in a mean tone under my breath.

He got indignant and began clenching his fist tightly. He didn't know what I meant by that. I could tell he thought I meant I'm buck wild out there in the streets; a ho.

"Don't ever say that! You are a lady! I raised a lady and I came to jail because I wasn't gonna let nobody take that from my little girl! Ever! So don't you tell me you ain't no lady! You don't let nobody take that away from you."

Then he sighed and calmed down, lookin' almost like a little boy, helpless. "I did what I did for my little lady. So Baby-Girl, don't ever say that again, please."

"I'm a woman Daddy, a woman. A lady isn't born, she's trained. People teach her to be the way she is. She's often lost without a man or somebody making her feel all soft and pink. But a woman is born a woman, it's her natural makeup. She can hold the fort for herself or her family, whether there's a man around or not. I'm a woman Daddy. That's all I meant."

To this, he let it go, realizing I'd thought about it and weighed in on determining which path to follow, ladyship or womanhood.

"Okay, okay, I can be proud of that too, even more proud. Well listen, if you want to see me Baby-Girl, you gotta come here on Wednesdays. That's family night. I'll make sure your name is on the list. But it gotta be Wednesdays. The weekend is for business and a whole lot of other mess. I don't want you around that." He paused. "Damn, you grew up. I had so much to warn you about."

And looking at his muscles I had to tell him, "You grew up too Daddy. Why you and Brother Abdul-Malik so big?"

"Starches and weights. Not from meat though, believe that." We laughed, I with tears, happy to see my Daddy. But then he glanced away, trying not to look in my eyes. I guess it hurt too much. Then his personality changed and he got mean lookin' as he pointed to Omar. "Who that nigga there? The one you came in here with?" I swear my Daddy looked like he could've done Omar dirty just then and felt no way about it.

"That's Omar Daddy, calm down. That's Brother Abdul-Malik's son. Remember, Ms. Sista's son Omar?"

Andrea Clinton

"Sista? Oh yeah? Yeah-yeah, how she doing? I heard she left that sh—t alone."

"Yeah she good. She been good for some years now."

"That's good. So how her son? He treatin' you right? You ain't takin' no sh—t off him are you? You remember how Abdul-Malik used to be back in the day when we called him Idi-Amin, crazy mo'joker. You was young, no, you wasn't born. That nigga was crazy as hell, shankin' niggaz up in the streets and sh—t. Maaan, that was when we were teens, before he joined Malcom X and whatever, way before now on this Sunnah stuff he on. This muthaf—ker up in here like Gandhi; but don't nobody f—k wit' 'em. Excuse my mouth Baby-Girl. Been around *these* niggaz too long."

He paused, then said, "I don't speak idly. I'm saying all this to say, often times, *like father, like son.*" He dropped his head to my eye level to look into my eyes then he stood and looked back over at Omar. "Yeah, I heard of Omar, but haven't seen him since he's been an adult. Seem like he like his father used to be?"

"He mostly good to me. But he can get crazy though. Beat a nigga' almost to death though 'cause he was worried 'bout me. And almost beat up a store manager for flirting with me," I giggled remembering it. "But he good to me. Man-Man like him for me and *he's* over protective."

"Yeah? That's good. I'll see Man-Man for keeping me out the loop on this here."

"I'm the one causing him drama though. Seem like I can't help it sometimes. Just gotta be bad, poke at 'em, or work his nerves."

"Don't be like that Baby-Girl. Don't be that kind of woman. Them women end up abused or found dead somewhere. It might not seem like it, but men got feelin's, and we safeguard them. And it take a woman to have you come out swingin' trying not to let ya feelin's get hurt. Don't do it like that. Another piece of advice before you continue in ya ways. Know a man's people, and his background, because he ain't gonna flee too far from it; very few people can be individuals. And even if he do, it only takes circumstances to make him return back to what he know. So watch what circumstance you put him in.

"Baby Girl, I could avenge ya life, but I can't bring you back." He was now staring at Omar. "If you like drama and games *that* much, like most pretty girls do, you need to cut this nigga here loose. Play games with a mutt, but not this fool. I can see crazy in his eyes. He humble like his father, but them the main ones that get crazy. And crazy know crazy. And he know you a li'l off too, I can tell. He peeped ya troublesome ways already. That's why he keep looking back, checkin' on you, to see if you done started somethin' wit' me."

"Yep Daddy, that's Omar. He always think I'm up to something; usually am."

As Omar looked back at us, I replied, "He not crazy, Daddy. I'm a good judge of character, he's quiet and laid back. Now, when somebody do him dirty, *he can **get** crazy*. But if nobody bother him, he don't bother nobody."

"Same difference, same difference Baby-Girl," he replied while staring at Omar.

"*I ain't cutting him loose, Daddy*," I wanted to make that clear.

"Look, I love Abdul-Malik like a brother. Even with him being Muslim, we still got each other back up in here. Baby-Girl we go back to grammar school." He paused and looked into my eyes. "I don't wanna have to kill his son for killin' you, 'cause you gettin' a kick outta playin' wit' his feelings. Deal straight up, or leave him alone, please. You'll be hurtin' more than you. You'll be ruining a brotherhood. Women!"

"I got feelings for that man Daddy. I'm not gonna do nothing to **hurt-hurt** him."

He smirked although serious. "***Hurt-hurt?*** How 'bout, don't hurt him on purpose at all? *Y'all women are poison*," he said in his kool, old-school, '70s gangsta way.

We laughed, but then he started up again. I don't know why he couldn't stop repeating himself. I guess that's how they do in jail, "Yeah, Baby-Girl. I'm gonna have to go soon, but please, cut him loose. Or drop the drama. " He sat looking at me for a moment, trying to read me. Then he turned his head and smiled. "Yep, you gonna get somebody killed. I can smell it."

Andrea Clinton

"I'm a good girl, Daddy."

He just turned from me with this smug look on his face, putting a half a cigar in his mouth, having a chuckle or two at my expense. I almost got offended because I knew I was a good girl, right? Or maybe he saw me as what some deem as a pretty girl and felt I was no good, just like most pretty girls.

Before I knew it, the correction officer came over and waved to him. My father flipped from one mode to another, getting a hard look on his face because we had to part.

"Daddy can you call me sometimes?"

"Yeah, I can do that," he said as he put his cigar back in his mouth and started stepping back away from me. "Aiiight, time to man up Baby-Girl. Kiss-kiss."

He started walking away just like that, no hug, no goodbye. His sudden coldness made me sad. Walking over to Omar, I kept looking back at my father and noticed he wouldn't look back at me. All of a sudden, I began to cry. Omar pulled me into the nook of his arm and held me. I kept looking back hoping my father would look at me, but he never turned around again. Then before I knew it, my father, Brother Abdul-Malik and some other big guys, skipped the line and were taken in ahead of all the others. It was very clear that it was a clout thing. The thing that threw me the most is that my father didn't seem to give me another thought. I'd have expected him to stare at me for as long as he could. But he just went on about his business.

***

When we got back into town, I was quiet for most of the night. Omar must've called Man-Man because he and Shakirah came over to Omar's place. Omar and Man-Man went into the bedroom. Although Shakirah and I sat in the living room together, I didn't say anything to her either except "Wassup," when they came in. I just sat with my head down on the arm of the couch, crawled up in a ball. When my brother came out of the bedroom, he looked a li'l down and out. He called me out into the hallway outside Omar's apartment and we talked. Well, mostly I just cried. I cried because my Daddy didn't look back at me, and initially wouldn't even see me. In the car on the way back, my free thinking kicked in and I resolved to thinking my father just pacified me so I wouldn't draw attention to whatever he had going on. I shared that with Man-Man and then some.

"How could he keep dismissing me like that and still say he love me or miss me?"

"Even though our father has calmed down big-time, he's still criminal minded and will probably always be. And you, his only daughter, his Baby-Girl, are a threat to that, and vice versa. He didn't want you messin' his head up 'cause those minutes y'all had don't compare to the millions of minutes he gotta be in there. And, he has to stay focused, because in there, if you show emotions or seem human, people will take it for weakness, and come after you. Plus, in his business, they'll go after your loved ones, so chill and stop that. He ain't mad at you or blaming you for nothing, and he can't help but love you. You his *Baby-Girl* remember? He just in a circumstance he can't control, so he gotta go with the flow; and you did just pop up there.

"But, Daddy didn't even ask how you were doing," I said, saddened by it.

"That's 'cause he know how I'm doing. I see him a few times a month. Alisa, you think I'm the one running this sh—t out here? *This here is Daddy!* I'm just keeping my eyes on it. Why you think them old-school cats coming home ain't try to do me dirty by now? Or other fools in the hood?" He stopped and looked at the wall as if what he was about to say weighed heavy on his chest. "A while ago, I was stupid enough to go out there in them streets trying to be Big Money Grip, Jr., got caught up in some mess, back when I was like 19. Went to see Daddy 'cause I was in real deep. And to save my butt from jail or being killed, Daddy took it over. He incurred my debt, and been advising me from the inside ever since. I'm just his eyes, ears and muscle in these streets. But because Daddy got involved, I got a better connect, pull, muscle,

Andrea Clinton

everything I wasn't even bargaining for, 'cause nowadays, this crack thing real big. And believe me, it's a tall price to pay for a mistake *I* made. Like Mommy, I put Daddy in harm's way."

I began to see things so differently. I even began to see my brother differently because he wasn't proud; he wasn't a big-time, no good, drug dealer. Man-Man was helping to fix up a mistake and was being dutiful to my father who's wearing that mistake like a winter coat.

Holding my brother's arm I said, "When you make a mistake, you fix it, then leave it. Don't continue the mistake. I think either you paid up your mistake or are close to it. So when you're done, walk away from it."

"Easy to say, my debt been paid. All this is something else. What if Daddy's grown to love this sh—t? What if he won't let me leave on some Michael Corleone sh—t, where the son gotta take over for the father?" He looked saddened.

"Vito Corleone didn't want Michael in that business, he wanted better for him. Michael flipped and rose to the occasion on some dutiful mission, 'cause his father was outta commission, remember the movie? You want out, into a normal life without green tops, and all them other color crack bottles and the weekly drive-by with your associates."

"Michael didn't want it either at one point, but duty called, like a mu' f—ker."

"Man, if it means walking away from Daddy, strap ya boots on and step. *Anybody who don't want what's good for you, ain't good for you*, especially coming from where he coming from." Then I turned to go back inside. I looked back at him, his eyes were drifting up the staircase slightly shaking his head as if he was thinking about how one mistake could have such a continuous price to pay. I was straight, but now he was upset due to Pops.

I walked into Omar's apartment and sat down, but still didn't talk. Omar came out of his room looked around, and went outside with Man. It seemed my brother was getting conflicting feelings about his life: overseeing drug deals, Shakirah on his back about him trying to play her out and stay with Ronny, him trying to be a daddy while Ronny always on his case 'cause she was hearing rumors about Shakirah, he was worryin' 'bout me and Manny; life.

Shakirah eventually told me that when Man-Man tried to talk about his problems while visiting Daddy, all he got was, "**MAN UP!** You ain't got no damn problems! Have it all, or pick and choose. But stop whining!"

I actually agreed with my father. I mean, was it really that deep? Stop what you don't want to do, and start doing what you want to do. It's your life. You only have one, right?

But evidently Omar sympathized with Man-Man needing to hear more than some short, jailhouse scripture about being a man, from a man who didn't even know how to be a father and empathize with his son. I could hear the two guys talking through the open door.

"Yo brah, guess what I got my hands on today doing business with the Cuban bruthas? Cubana cigars baby," Omar said as he handed Man a few cigars. "Make sure you give Manny a few."

Man took them and said, "Maaaaan, I haven't had one of these in over a year. They smooth?"

"They like butter baby," Omar said.

Then I heard a lighter flick, twice.

"Huuh? Huh? That is *sweeeet*, smoothe like butter baby," Omar said stomping his foot.

"Sweet as candy baby. I remember," Man-Man said then puffed his own cigar. "Aaaah yeah, you right, smooth like butter, *and* sweet. Dang man, right on time." He paused. "This was right on time. Good lookin out brutha. Good lookin', for real."

"It's all love baby; it's all love." They stayed out there puffing their hearts out.

Although I loved the smell of the cigars they smoked, as it did have a sort of sweet aroma, I couldn't understand all that humming and commenting on a cigar, *THAT DON'T HAVE NO WEED IN IT!*

Omar stayed out there and in their cigar ecstasy, he cheered Man-Man up. I guess he figured I didn't need cheering up anymore. Or maybe he thought I was a lost cause.

Andrea Clinton

When Crap Hits The Fan:
It Smacks the Face of the Man who Threw it, or the Woman in This Case!!!

Over the next few weeks later, we fell into a routine. Omar and his father read the Qur'an for sometimes thirty minutes over the phone. True to his word, my father started calling me and I started having weekly visits with him.

But when Omar wasn't checkin' up on things in the streets, we were always home, at his apartment, twisted up in some feisty pretzel or another, sharing vivacious and pulsating feelings. *And true to form,* when he thought I fell asleep, after we were done gratifying one another, he'd always be sitting up looking out the window or laying there looking at the ceiling feeling guilty as sin. That came from all them discussions with his father about us and our circumstance, messin' his head up. I learned to ignore him though. Hell, I didn't know what that guilty feeling was and I didn't need *that* monkey on my back. I enjoyed being with Omar more than any other man I'd been with in that way, and I was so satisfied I couldn't imagine feeling bad about it. But then, I wasn't religious or even trying to be, but he was. I just knew there was a God.

Because we were beginning to be housebound all the time, we decided to try and get out more. So, one night we headed out around ten o'clock. We were starving, so Omar suggested we go to this excellent steak place and split a $40 porterhouse. "It's almost two inches thick, juicy and is so big, it sits on a big round plate of its own," he said. I was feeling down, so I said fine. Maybe a good meal would cheer me up. When we sat down at our table, we were overlooking New York and the docks with boats going by. Buildings stood tall on the other side of the water, with their lights gleaming against the night sky. It was beautiful.

We decided not to rush through dinner, and to just sit and talk a little bit. But we couldn't have a simple night out. Oh no, not us. He started with that college talk again! I forgot to mention that crap was coming up in conversations from time to time.

"Why the hell you always gotta bring that sh—t up when we having a good time?" I snapped at him and left the table. Yep, I was spoiled already, but *he* spoiled the mood.

He went looking for me and did something corny. Even though it was corny, it was the kinda thing that always moves us women. He told me to close my eyes, and hold out my hand. He'd done this to me several times before, giving me a diamond tennis bracelet, or diamond earrings to replace the li'l ones I used to wear. Other times, he'd give me either a 22k gold bangle or necklace or a diamond necklace. So, this time, I guessed he was about to hand over the emerald earrings with the crushed diamonds he knew I wanted. But when I opened my eyes, he'd set a ring box on my hand. A crushed velour, green ring box with silver trimming.

I stared at it for all of 10 seconds then I slowly opened it. Inside, was my favorite gem, a marquise-shaped emerald ring with three diamonds on each side. Then he said, "It's a pre-engagement ring."

I know you may say this was a cop-out, my "statuesque" friend. But see, you don't know him like I do. I knew his history, and I knew his heart. He wasn't copping out. He was ensuring I'd be in his life the best way he could at the time. He was afraid to commit to marriage just yet. Those Islamic lessons were grooming him, but he'd fallen into the westernized gap of things, and was afraid of marriage.

And it wasn't unheard of, although rare, to be pre-engaged. It was a happy medium to what Muslims believe in and what I believe in, which is traditional marriage. That's what I thought

Andrea Clinton

anyway. Well, anyway, I answered yes. We went back to the table and I sat on his lap. I couldn't stop hugging him and kissing him. He was embarrassed, because as a Muslim he tried to practice good behavior, especially when in public. I got a kick out of making it difficult, but I was breaking out of that habit because he would start reciting the kinds of punishments women got for actin' like this and that. Let me tell ya, that wasn't fun for me; some of those punishments are serious, raw. And I knew it was real because the Christians punishment in the bible was similar and just as raw. They both couldn't be wrong I figured.

So, I behaved; well I caught myself and then behaved. I went back to my seat, sliding my chair closer to him. I fiddled over my ring, gave him kisses, leaned on him a li'l bit while we looked at New York and the pretty lights, and before we knew it, we had our steak. It turned out to be a great evening after all, in the restaurant, and *especially* later that night. Oooooooo-Weee! Those were the early days of our lives. We were in love; well I tried to make myself be *in love. What the hell did I know about being in love,* is what I thought. But we were pre-engaged and this showed us that marriage might not be that deep, just dedication. He learned he could rely on me and trust me. And well, *I learned that I wanted a lot out of life.* A whole lot! I already knew he had my back.

***

But not everything was Kool and the Gang, or even Peaches and Herb. My mother called and asked me to come over, and against my desires I went. Heck, it'd been a long time since she'd disowned me in that hospital, a long time for us.

I went. I felt awkward going in. But, I went and sat down to listen to what the woman had to say, and was shocked to hear her ask me to come home, back home to live. She said it bothered her that I was out there in the world, and she knew nothing of what was going on with me. She had to wait to hear about it from Man, Manny or Omar. Yes, evidently Omar felt compelled to call Ms. Jerry, my mother, and tell her how I was doing from time to time, which I guess he felt he *should* do since he couldn't get me to call her.

I told her I didn't know if I wanted to come home because I was still angry at her making me out to be a bad demon seed and blamin' me for everything that went wrong in our life. Then she told me a few stories from the past, to explain where she was comin' from. She explained that while she was pregnant with me, she almost had a miscarriage.

"The whole family, including Grip, ya father, was so worried about you, thinking you wouldn't make it. Even after you were born, they kept worrying about you, afraid something bad would happen because of all I went through in the pregnancy. When you were just a toddler, you gave us more reason for concern. You drank my liquor, a lot of it and almost died. They had to pump your stomach to keep you alive. Because of that, your father smacked me around for getting so drunk I didn't keep an eye on you. I don't blame him. I shouldn't have been partying with my friends, drinking. And, another time, when you were older, I let you go with your friends to see a movie. You were supposed to come home right after, but time ticked, and we didn't hear from you for over eight hours."

"It was me, Shakirah, Peaches, and Mutha. We were just hangin' out."

"But they all called their mothers, and although they got home late, they were in by ten o'clock. You didn't get in 'til two in the morning."

I felt bad for her just then, a little bit I guess. She had a right to be worried. I was hangin' out with Tracey, my mentor, trying to be grown hangin' with her 'cause she was older than me. I was learning the ways of men, how to treat'em, milk 'em for their dough, etc., and listening to Tracey gossip on the phone.

"Anyway, I got real worked up. Alisa, there were a host of things that always left me and ya father worrying over you, since you were born. I was frustrated that this formed the fiber of our

Andrea Clinton

relationship, instead of us just being close, doing the girly, mother-daughter thing. You was out with others having fun and I was worrying over you all the time."

I listened. I waited. I wanted to see if she would bring *it* up, but she didn't. So I did. "You blame me for what happened to Daddy?"

She shook her head, suddenly getting sickeningly emotional and nervous like she was a dope fiend and I was threatening not to supply her dope. "No, no, I don't blame you. You can't help what happened to Daddy. You were young. You didn't know no better."

I just stared at her and realized she did, because she couldn't bring herself to even discuss it. The thought looked like it was making her sick to her stomach.

"You do blame me. You've talked yourself into believing that I'm to blame. You were always drinking, and smoking and then gettin' us to hide it from Daddy. And whenever something went wrong you'd get us to stick up for you, so you wouldn't get a beatin,' remember that? You telling us to do that for you so you wouldn't get in trouble?"

As I spoke, my mother started to breathe hard. She looked as if she was starting to either hyperventilate or choke off her cigarette smoke. But I couldn't stop. There was too much to say still. "When you left me in the house alone, after Daddy, Man and Manny went downtown, and that man came in here and tried to rape me, you barely getting back here in time to save me. You tried to get me to hide that too, but Daddy had already caught on to your games, and he told me to promise I'd never keep anything away from him. So I told him and he killed that man and went to jail for it. But you blame me! It'd kill you to face it was ya fault wouldn't it?"

By now, she was really entering hyperventilation. "You—you were supposed—to stay in ya room with—with the door locked—"

I cut her off. "I had to go to the bathroom! I didn't wanna go in no pee-pee-can you left in the room for me! And I didn't let him in. He came in when I was in the bathroom."

Then I paused, because it dawned on me for the first time since it happened, *he must've had a key. Where'd he get it? And why was he walking in, looking around, taking his time, reaaal comfortable-like? Not looking to steal nothing; not worried about my father coming home. Just chillin'.* Being older, wiser, without a child's mind, it was becoming clear.

Things were popping in my head, like, the fact that I'd never seen him before, only heard his voice when she'd lock me in my room from time to time. It didn't make any sense when I was a child, but being older, it hit me. "You were cheating on Daddy. That man came up here to be with you, so you could cheat. All this time, you made it seem like it was my fault because I opened the door, and you knew you gave him a key, so y'all could cheat!"

I was amazed at how certain things had begun to come back to me. Then she caught wind from out of no where and crazily *blacked-out* on me.

"I was mad because, I told ya muthaf—kin' ass to stay in the room! With the door locked, and you didn't listen!" Breathing harshly, she screamed, "Yeah I was doing wrong, and I knew it. But you supposed to do what I tell you to do! I'm ya mother! And you never do what I tell you! And look what happened! My husband went to jail fa life in prison! Fa life!" She cried hysterically. "He's gone fa life!"

Thank God my stepfather was on one of his long hauls to Alabama. She seemed to forget she had a second husband. I knew she always saw my father as her true mate. But I didn't know it was to this extreme 'til now. She sounded like a witch, kept screaming, "Fa-life! Fa-life!" She was pointing at me like she wanted her finger to zap me into something. It was starting to scare the piss outta me.

But her tears couldn't wash away my anger. "Ma, you talkin' 'bout ya husband, but when it was all going down, you stuck up for your lover? Over ya daughter? Blaming me? Shifting the blame on me!"

"He wasn't my lover."

"He was Ma!"

"He wasn't my lover."

Andrea Clinton

"He was!"

"He was **NOT** my lover!" She was getting louder and more agitated.

"Why else would you be defending him over me? Why?" When she didn't say anything I shouted, "Because he was your lover!"

Then she blasted out, **"BECAUSE HE WAS MY COKE DEALER!"**

"What?" *Threw me all off course.* That's the kinda crap happening in Omar's family, not mine. *My family is busted up over coke? Drugs? What kinda monkey-dog sh—t is this,* I thought.

"He was my coke dealer—I was a basehead! Way back before all this crack sh—t! I freebased!" She was crying and ashamed for a good fifteen seconds, but then continued, "I was hangin' with Cousin Jackie at a concert in the '70s, and some of the singers let us party with them backstage and at the hotel afterwards. The lead singer Allen introduced me to base. After that night, I didn't see him for almost a year, when he was in town and looked me up, and we started meeting once a week, having an affair, and getting based. Then he went on tour and left me with a coke habit I couldn't afford!" She started crying harder between sentences, "So I started seeing his dealer on my own. But in no time, I owed him a lot, and he threatened to tell ya father. And you know Grip woulda killed me, not beat me, but killed me. So when ya father would go hustle downtown, take you kids shopping, or go out of town, I'd let that dealer come bag up, up here. Then, that led to sneaking him in the basement.

"By then I was f—kin' up bad, and that's why ya father used to whoop my ass *all* the time. I was stealing his coke, and money. Me and Sista, Omar's mother, after years of hatin' each other, started covering each other, her with her dope habit, me with my coke."

My mother was talking, but I was in wonderland; I was Alice, not Alisa; this wasn't real. I was staring at her the whole time, mouth wide open, immobile, flabbergasted like a mug. *Yo, I come from a Fiend family,* I thought. **N***ooooo!*

"I stole. After the riots nobody was hiring and times were hard. Ya father started hustling and I stole from him, had him thinking the people he bought it from beat him for dope but it was me going in his stash. I started stealing from him, and sold it across town to buy coke. Me and Sista. And when Maleek was hustling coke, I would give her some of ya father's dope, and she would give me some of Maleek's coke. But one day, the dealer was in the basement and saw that ya father left out with ya brothers. He came up and told me to make a run for him. I did, but I locked you in the room before I left, and when I came back, he was getting ready to rape you. You know what happened after that. I threw something at him, we fought. Neighbors called the police but he ran out. Grip and them came home later while the police were still there and then, he just left out. Next thing you know they said Grip found him and killed him, but not before he shot Grip in the face, skinned him. Then he came home and whooped my ass."

She paused for a moment, as if reliving a nightmare. "Not long after, Grip got locked up for shooting the dealer. And one day you copied me and sniffed some coke and overdosed, almost died. Your heart rate was over the top." She was trying to speak without crying, but couldn't. "I could never get right with you; I was always messing you up!" She paused for a moment to get it together then said, "You looked so weak and sick in the hospital.

"Ya father had his sister, ya aunt Reeda come get Man-Man and Manny away from me. Fred bailed Grip outta jail and when he came home, he beat me almost to death! But I didn't care because I had already almost killed myself overdosing on pills. But after he beat me, he took me to the hospital, and when you were well he dropped y'all off at his mother's."

She stopped crying and continued speaking, "A few days later, he called Fred in my room when I was almost well and said he was putting me in a rehab. And he told Fred to let everybody know that there was an S.O.S. out on me if anyone ever saw me cop coke or anything else again. And when Fred left the room he told me he'd put a professional hit out on me if I tried to move away, take y'all away, or didn't come see him every week at the prison when I got out of rehab. By this time I'd already detoxed; it was coke so it wasn't long. But he found a *long-term* drug rehabilitation program for rich white people with counseling and

Andrea Clinton

all that stuff. That nigga had me boxed in; I couldn't get high again even if I wanted. I feared him more than I loved the high. But, after rehab I joined a trade program and got my beautician license, *scared to death* of ya father and what I was in for!" She started to cry all over again. "I came home, got a job in a beauty parlor. Asked ya father for permission to get y'all from ya grandmother. He said I could after six months. And so, after six months it was finally over. I moved on with my life. I couldn't hurt you anymore. I had to get well for you."

Moms broke down and cried hard like an abused child. She saw I wanted answers, but knew that was much more than I was looking for. I guess she felt it was time she reconciled her memories of the past, her problems with me and her feelings of shame and displaced guilt.

All I could do was watch her cry. I wanted to feel sorry for her, but then I wanted to whoop her ass too. Heck, my Daddy was in jail because of her. I saw now why my father used to beat her so much. I mean, sometimes he'd come in the house and beat her, and we'd be like, "She came in just before him. What could she have done so soon?" But I realize now she snuck out in them streets when she should've been home caring for us.

As an adult, hearing she was a basehead, I looked back and realized she was always up to no good. And I remembered him always fussing about her leaving us in the house alone, and not coming home sometimes.

But I was stuck because *I should've* held a lot of stuff against *her*. Like, had she not ever tried drugs she wouldn't have been doing all that cheating and other stuff with that singer. And Daddy wouldn't have killed that guy or whatever happened to him, and I might have my father in my life. And I wouldn't have messed up so many relationships, taking ill advice on how to deal with men from Tracey!

But as much as I wanted to blame her, and leave her there feeling bad, leave her there feeling *like sh—t*, knowing how it felt to be kicked when you're down, like she did me in the hospital, I just couldn't do it to her. So after watching her indulge in her pity party for one for a few minutes, I walked over to her and I hugged my mommy.

"I really need you back home Baby-Girl. I'm so sorry for the mess I made of our family," she said toning down her cry.

I was sorry too. But, I forgave her. I don't know why forgiveness came so easy, but it did. She was so helpless and pitiful lookin'; as if it were terrifyingly sad that she couldn't get a do-over for that part of her life. She was feelin' how so many parents seem to feel after their dumb youthful days. And I couldn't leave her alone like that. I'm sure she didn't do that first line of coke *knowing the outcome*. And she had too much time alone to think about all of this stuff. So, I had to look out for her. And there's no way my brothers knew the extent of what she told me; if anything maybe they knew a mere shell of her nightmare. Because if they knew, especially Man-Man, he wouldn't be all up on her like, *oh my mommy, blah, blah, blah*. Instead, he'd hold some resentment due to my father, and me. She was all alone with her thoughts of all this. She was about to drive herself crazy, and she was crying out for help. So I, in just thirty minutes, got my things from Shakirah's and Omar's, then I went back home to Mommy.

Andrea Clinton

With Every Box You Get a Surprise Trinket Inside

Days, weeks and many months went by. Nothing big happened, except they finally found Qydeer, dead as a doorknob. Seems he was strangled, which was kinda ironic 'cause the drug dealer who tried to rape me was strangled, by my father. That is, after he and the dealer pulled guns on each other, shooting at each other 'til they ran out of bullets. Then my father jumped on the guy and choked him 'til he died; that face shot my pops had musta only been a nick or went through, I dunno. But I recently hear all this.

I didn't dare ask Omar or Man-Man more about Qydeer's death, because the few times I did they always seemed to want to change the subject, which was telling me something without telling me.

Aside from that though, everything was everything. Up until Omar started talking that, "*So what you gonna do with ya life,*" stuff again, and to an annoying degree. Oh that pissed me off! I told this Negro ahead of the game that I wanted to chill. But he was pushing me more than ever to do something with my life, *be somebody.* So to get him out my face, I promised him I'd take a class to get back into the groove of things. He was happy, and I was conceding to his wishes thinking, *Here we go....*

When the new semester started, I went to class, annoyed. It was an English class with a lot of writing which I hated, as I was never any good at it. The highest grade I ever got was a B- because the teachers all said I could never stick to any one subject. I always tried to include the world in my papers. You're probably saying I do the same in telling this story too, but shut up.

I complained to Omar all the way through the semester. At first telling him I couldn't do it, that school wasn't for me. I started carrying on, having tantrums with tears, and he got angry.

"You not tryin' to understand how hard it is for me," I told him. "I can't concentrate; college ain't me."

"You think I want a dodo for a wife? I want a wife with an education and some know-how. So if something happens to me, she'll be able to teach my kids, feed them, clothe them, and put them in good schools!" He said to me, making a great point.

So, he won that round, and on many occasions. What I really wanted to tell him was that should anything happen to him, I'd just remarry. But that would've sent him over the roof. Not much gets him angry, but anything dealing with me and another man, jealousy, *sets him off.*

***

At the beginning of the next semester, I began to fuss that taking three classes was unheard of. How do you go from one class to three? He was asking too much of me.

"This is crazy. All I do is study and research! What I care about plant cells, and how they have sex or reproduce or whatever they're talking about! And what am I gonna use Algebra for? **AND WHAT THE HELL IS WESTERN CIVILIZATION**? *Ain't it just history*? And how civilized could the western region have been, all the western countries tried to conquer every part of the world in the name of religion for riches and power!" Boy it was making me sick.

He just looked at me, turned and walked out leaving me to study. I sat and pouted. I was more pissed because I felt he was

Andrea Clinton

pimpin' me. I know you probably think that sounds ridiculous, Goddess. But I know how men do. Why you think they all look up to pimps or players? It didn't matter that he was trying to get me to do something positive. It felt like he just wanted to control my mind; get me to do what he wanted me to do; break my stubbornness and turn me into what he wanted me to be as if it were his world, all about him. Because when he talked to me on mellow occasions, he spoke just like a pimp, telling me all the good things that could come out of me getting my degree. Telling me to picture what it would be like.

"Life with a degree is much easier than life without one. It's easier to get big money, higher positions, respect, no low-end job, not to mention all those designer things you like," he said with confidence. *Grrrrrr!* I felt, as who wouldn't want to give in to this?

He was trying to influence me like a pimp does a ho he wants to turn tricks for him. He was trying to show me that there were no limitations with a degree. Oooooow I was mad! I only stepped back from those arguments because my mother, Shakirah, Manny and Man told me I sounded stupid saying he was trying to pimp me. They used to laugh about it, thinking I was joking. But I was as serious as cancer.

I tried complaining to my father about it, but at this point he and Omar had been speaking on the phone and were kool. The only gripe he had was the mismatch of an educated woman trying to make it with a drug-dealing husband, if Omar was successful in helping me get my degree. He knew Omar was still hustling. It was Abdul-Malik who was in denial my father said. He said Abdul-Malik wanted to believe the lessons he had with his son had penetrated his heart, and with sex aside, Omar was sinless. I guess we all felt sorry for Abdul-Malik on that one. But my father was my father, and his worry wasn't about Omar going ape on me anymore, or whether or not he was sinning in bed, or hustling drugs. He was concerned with the possibility of Omar's street crap following him home and harming me.

"I didn't come to jail to protect my daughter only to turn around and see her killed behind some bullsh—t!" Was what he told Omar.

Omar didn't know that *I knew* my father made that comment to him. He respected what my father said, but stagnated doing anything about it. I had the same complaint as well, but I guess I got so self-absorbed that I didn't voice it, just looked Omar up and down like the hypocrite he was. Actually, I was too busy scheming on how I could get out of school and keep my man, 'cause it seemed like that was a package deal. And I had to make him accept I wasn't college material, even if I did get passing grades, which made that plan not fly too well.

By the end of that second semester, I was starting to have panic attacks. I was getting C's and with tutoring, promising my professors to move it up to B's. But the stress of it was holding me back. I was so messed up in the head I stopped having general conversations with Omar. I wanted him to feel my anguish. But he ignored me, giving me pecks on my forehead, saying he was proud of me.

One day, he topped himself and did something that was even sweeter than all the other stuff he tried to do to cheer me up. A few days before my final exams, he took me and my book bag on a ride to the beach. I guess he felt I'd had one panic attack too many. He was never there during the onslaught of an attack; he always came or called just after one though.

I broke down and stopped being so mad at him, college, everything. That was big-time nice of him to think to do something like that for me. It made me feel guilty because I had some *serious* plots going through my head.

But, we sat on the beach, on a huge blanket, in a li'l tent he bought to block some of the wind. We studied a bit of math, which he was great at, and then we did science, which he was so-so in, and finally western civ., where he told me the flipside to the Crusades. Who'd have guessed how much dirt or wrong they slandered the Muslims with doing, leaving out their own sin and damages. He told me both sides though, as if he'd read the books before. I listened, and then he suggested out of nowhere that I check out a certain chapter he said was composed of some engaging history. I was tired, but he'd gotten me interested in history, well western civilization. So I flipped the pages to see what else there was to learn about Islam.

The chapter was about Mecca and the Kaba. Mecca is the famous city in Saudi Arabia where Muslims make some sort of pilgrimage. They have to do it at least once in their lives. The Kaba is the building I guess you could call it, where they pray while circling. It was built by Abraham and his son Ishmail, the son he had by his servant or co-wife Hajar, depending on whose view you're taking, Muslim who say co-wife or Christian who say servant. I know this because Omar was teaching me stuff all along, so to read it in the book was easy for me.

So I quickly turned to the chapter he told me about, as I felt with an exam coming, I needed all the help he could give me; one less subject to fret over. But when I turned to the pages to the introduction for Islamic Studies, lying there on the book before me, in all its sparkling luster and magnificence, was an extraordinarily beautiful diamond ring, pear-shaped in a platinum setting.

I picked it up after staring at it for several seconds to marvel over its beauty and luster. I couldn't believe I was actually looking at that dazzling ring. And looking wasn't enough. I had to become almost comatose to even begin to settle my mind to believe that I found what was before me, this exquisite, exotic piece of breathtaking jewelry. It was unbelievably majestic in appearance, and glittering all over. I know I sound like something from a storybook, but, this was how it hit me. I shook my head to unrattle the sudden impact of emotions that had overtaken me.

Not being able to put up a front, I shed tears, and I knew, I felt it, he was my prince. The one I dreamed of for many years when my father was taken away from me, when my mother struck me for no reason, and when she went missing from our lives for a long time. *He* was the prince, the man I always wanted to save me. He was the one I prayed for long before my Great-Grandma killed my dream of loving a man in such a unique way, because she wanted me to assure getting a man who'd love me more.

But look how love persevered. Love was born again, but real this time. He came to save me from the world and the people in it, including myself and my selfish materialistic ways that could've landed me who knows where.

As I sat there, I couldn't fight such an enchanted moment. So I raised my head, and with what I imagined were storybook tears falling like crystals along my face, down onto my hand and over my ring, I answered, "Yes, I will marry you." I for once didn't play games with him, and such a ring needed no explanation; he wanted me to be his wife. He made me so very, very happy, fairy-tale happy.

My bittersweet emotions drove me to tears as our cheeks brushed against each other, and paused with my face close to his. Then I slithered into my little nook, and shed tears as we sat there embracing, thinking about what we both hoped would be everlasting love, with no interruptions.

Andrea Clinton

The More Things Change...

When love throws us a bone,
We get caught up in the moan,
Of that comfort zone;
Then, 'cause of rude acts and tones,
We find ourselves, **ALONE.**

Here Lies Alisa,

FREE SCHOOL
DUMB NIGGAZ

You *did not* think it would go over that smooth did you? If you did, you must've forgotten what I said in the beginning. Have you not learned anything about me yet? Make no mistake, I tried to keep positive as I lay there cradled in Omar's protective nook, but thinking positive doesn't come easy for me.

When we were home, over the next few days, I had time to ponder, and my free thinking got a grip on my mind, and the entire picture. I found myself thinking, *Girl please! Rationalize the situation. What is this all about?* And I'd come to the conclusion the ring was a huge gesture of love and support from him to me, but had a dual measure. What measures? One was a big leap on his behalf to express his love for me. It was also a push to help me make it *through school,* a sort of inspirational piece if you will. Hell, and even if you won't, that's what *I* felt it was.

But on the other hand, *he's dangling the ring, his money and all I want out of life over my head like a prankster does a juicy steak over the mouth of a fat woman on some funky ass diet!* I thought. And yes he would benefit, because he'd get the perfect, obedient, educated wife and mother of his kids, and someday-Muslim wife.

But then I felt, one really good thing came out of this old-fashioned gesture. I finally received something promising and

Andrea Clinton

sweet from him without having to initiate it with my bad behavior or ways. He did this on his own. I'd finally arrived, *he loved me more than I loved him.* My great-grandma would be proud. But now that I arrived, I didn't know what to do. *What now?* I wondered. What did she tell me to do this for? I'd only guessed what it was about in the past. But did she want me to dog him, get mine? Get all I could while the getting was good? Or did she want me to maneuver him to be *all I wanted him to be*? What? Do I keep my guard up? Can I ever put it down? What? I didn't get it. It's like trying to find a place, getting there and not knowing why you were even trying to find the place, or what to do when you arrived, and I had arrived.

To figure this out, I knew I needed to sit back and think of her life. The more I did, the more I thought that she'd want me to train him to be what *I* wanted him to be, or what I needed. Right? Wouldn't you think that? I was almost sure that this is what she would've wanted. So, I went for it. I flipped the script, again.

***

Omar and I had been engaged for six months, when we had one of the most horrific fights. It wasn't physical, but my mental is just as equivalent to any physical you could think of. Omar kept doing his street hustle, and I being forced you may as well say, kept doing the school thing. No doubt, I complained, but he smoothed things over either at bedtime, with my ring, or talk of our future marriage and all that other good stuff. But that of course wasn't my beef. It wasn't why I acted up. I wasn't so stupid that I didn't know what all we could have someday. I'll tell you what made me act up: HIPOCRACY!

One day when my car broke down—oh did I mention Omar said in Islam a woman gets a dowry, a gift, when she's marrying? Anyway, for my dowry I wanted a new blue BMW, and I got it. But one day the dang thang broke down on me. And I had to get my hair done, so I took the bus and figured I'd let him pick me up. I didn't like this idea of taking the bus though since I was used to being chauffeured, and had recently gotten used to my new car. Hell, we're going through a crack crisis and an epidemic where people had lost their minds to the pipe. See, with all the zombie crackheads around now, me wearing my jewelry and expensive clothes and shoes, and taking the bus was dangerous. But, a sista had to get her hair done.

Okay, back to what made me start acting up. On the bus, I overheard these two women talking. One was an ex-street hustler. I used to see her around, but didn't know her. The other lady I didn't know at all. Well, the street hustler was explaining to the other lady how she needed to get on her man because if he was out there hustling, what did she think would happen besides him going to jail, leaving her with kids eventually broke.

"Listen girl, I lived in that world. Ain't nothing but short-term money, and long-term jail time, and worse if you get into a drug war."

What that lady said stuck in my head like glue, especially when she said, "My husband got locked up and all me and my kids were left with was a little cash that we zoomed right through. Most of it was used up on lawyers to get him a reduced sentence, and that was a wrap. After that it was hard living, and I could've stood it *myself,* but me **and** my kids—it was hard."

From that moment on, I decided to use the fact that he loved me more to save him from the thing that could cause his demise; and no I'm not talking about me.

But time went on, and so did school and him pushing me to finish or do this or that regarding my education. I was so busy I lost sight or partial sight of my wanting to save him from himself. Only at times did I remember, inconvenient times. I told you I was messed up in the head. And please, he had big money and I had old ways, selfishness and greed. And I wanted things, diamonds and minks and pearls too. So, I got caught up in pampering myself as a means and inspiration to continue school. It didn't help that I was caught up in wondering, *Why would someone put so much effort in wanting their woman to go to school?* I mean, I understood why

Andrea Clinton

he'd try to promote it, but he was being a tyrant about it. I kept seeing his eyes back in the pool hall when he asked me about my future and my first thought was that he had some sort of challenge in mind concerning me, to pimp me or something, and this was the force behind my rebellion of college, acting up, and my loss of memory in saving Omar from himself.

Finally though, I'd had enough. I was trying so hard not to hurt him that I was hurting myself. I was sad, miserable and withdrawn. Heck, all I could think of at the time was, *He's trying to pimp me.* I mean, I was driving myself nuts about it. Yeah, I know what **you** probably say, "How could he be pimping you?" But screw you! There's more than one way to pimp a woman. You can get her all educated, have her run out and get a good job, and either live off the fruits of her labor, and/or have her available for bail money if you get knocked off.

I believed I was a challenge for him, or a project. Men do have different projects you know. For some it's a new motorcycle or car, or jazzin' up an older one they have. For other men, it's a pit bull they can raise and toughen up to fight so they can make money off of it. But for Omar I felt it was, *Break dis ho, she too high strung.* My feeling was that for Omar, breaking me was like breaking a wild horse or even worse, like trying to get one of them fast-moving Amtrak trains to pull back and immediately race in the opposite direction, because he was so adamant about it; **he wanted me upright and now**. And my thought to this was, *Well, guess what, it's not happening.*

Then, the devil started talkin' to me, **he visits me all the time. And the Devil said:** "You know Omar got his clique and the whole neighborhood thinking he gonna turn you out, bring you down a few pegs," the devil said. "He's gonna make you do a 360-degree turn. Get you educated, respectable, humble, putting up with whatever he puts out and people will laugh at you, say you met your match, a true player. Remember what he was trying to do to Vanessa? Trying to bring her uppity black ass down to earth? It was for his player status; act like you know. *If you listen to him, they'll call you an amateur gold digger.* They'll see you wasn't all that thorough at 'gettin' yours,' as you been making it seem. And that you wasn't no real playerette, using bruthas for their money to get yours like Tracey and her crew. They'll say you were an imitation, and a bad one at that. And the whole neighborhood will remember you in your dog-eat-dog status, **and talk about you**," Satan whispered, as I listened.

Now, I'm not *as* stubborn as a mule, *I am a mule*. Yeah, I guess in this case I was a jackass too, but it didn't feel that way at the time. All that whispering Satan was doing in my ear got me revved up; I couldn't stop myself. And when it was stuck in my head that that's what all Omar's pushing was all about regarding college, I smirked and thought to myself, *Let the games begin.* But remembering what the old-head lady said on the bus, I was determined to incorporate saving him from himself; I had to. Regardless to whatever, I owed him at least that.

In those next months, **I LIKED TO HAVE TURNED THAT NUCKA OUT!** Almost made him lose it. I was ugly, and it only got worse as the weeks went on. How? I started talking mean and nasty to him at every turn, "Black muthaf—ka," this, and "F—k you nigga," that. He was gonna relieve me of the stress of school one way or another I thought.

When I was chillin', studying or whatever and Omar tried to sit by me, I'd snap at him, "Don't f—kin' sit by me! Get the f—k outta here!" When he'd go to kiss me, I snarled at him, "Yo back up! Did you brush ya teeth, NIGGA?" I believe what Satan said had me going mad; I was losing control. How? Check these situations out. I'm on the couch studying, aggravated because the classes got harder each semester. When along comes Omar:

"Baby you see my leather jacket?" He was darn near tiptoeing around the apartment, carefully speaking to me, not knowing what the stress of studying might make fly outta my mouth.

"**I dunno, IS IT MY TURN TO WATCH IT—ALREADY!**" Yelling sarcastically, "Git the f—k outta my face!" I said in the most spiteful and nasty tone.

"Alisa, I'm trying *hard,* real hard to be patient, and overlook ya trench mouth, but dig ya'self, *please.*" He snatched another jacket and headed out the door, slammin' it.

Andrea Clinton

I waited until he had enough distance where he might not want to turn around and I yelled, "**I DON'T HAVE TO WATCH SH—T; STOP STRESSIN' ME OUT! STOP BEING A TYRANT, TRYIN' TO MAKE SOMEBODY OUT TO BE WHO THEY NOT NIGGA!**"

Another time, we were out having dinner and we ran into some people he knew from somewhere, Joe and Layla. They invited themselves over to our table. Now I was trying to be halfway decent that day, as being a b—ch took a lot of energy, which made me chill out from time to time. I was saving the bastard in me for later, when we got home to relax. But these two came over uninvited. Omar stood and shook the guy's hand and threw the girl the peace sign, then tried to introduce them to me. I turned my head. The girl was black and looking all hippie-ish and the guy, a white guy, was a cornball, like a computer geek or something. I couldn't imagine where Omar knew them from. I figured they were customers or old ones.

"So, Omar, long time no see. Who's your friend?" Layla asked.

"Excuse me?" I said, giving her the look of death. "Do I look like a got-damn friend?" I turned my hand over and showed her my lovely diamond and emerald engagement ring, my lip curled with anger and eyebrows arched to let her know I'd go ghetto-mode on her if she pushed it.

"Oh, I'm sorry. My—that's a beautiful ring, but I think your pretty hands bring it out," she replied as she took my hand and admired the ring, not allowing me to be the bastard I was at that time. You know those hippies, with that hippie happiness that keeps even the darkest rooms lit.

"Yeah man! Omar congrats dude. That's excellent, wow," Joe said as he shook his hand.

Then I noticed they were going to start talking and I was so blaaah, I just stood up and left, and rudely I might add. I went to the bathroom, and then came out and sat at the bar on the other side, out of view, and I tied on a few Long Island Ice Teas. Then when I was lit up enough, almost an hour later, I came back demanding to leave.

"Okay, enough of this bullsh—t, let's f—kin' go." I grabbed my jacket and looked at him as if to say, *You don't wanna make me go off up in this joint and embarrass ya ass.*

He stood up, embarrassed already I guess, because the girl, Layla opened her arms to give me a hug, and I turned and started walking away from all that hippie stuff. They said their goodbyes and when we got in the car he showed his anger, somewhat.

"Why do you always have to act like that? Alisa, I understand this college thing is on ya back, but it ain't all that baby. I'm trying to deal with ya stress and tantrums but, dig ya self…" he tried to preach to me. But I cut him off by blasting the music and looking out the window. He just continued driving shaking his head at me, mostly wondering how much more of my crap he could tolerate or excuse.

***

As time went on, word of my bull crap and behavior was being spread all over; everyone was hearing about my mess. I was hearing funky advice from my family, and feeling funky ass vibes from his family and mine because of my ranting and raving.

Then one night, me and Omar went out to dinner with Man-Man and Shakirah. I didn't want to go, but he'd talked me into it, "Come on baby, go, so you don't always look like the bad guy." But, still on my mission, as the evening progressed, I got drunk and crossed the line.

I turned to Omar, whom I had ignored the entire night and dodged whenever he tried to touch me, and asked, "Why you wear that faggot shirt? What real man wears purple?" When I saw he was ignoring me with that *I know what you doing* look, sippin' his soda as he didn't drink anymore, I just kept pushing, hard too. "Have you ever had a male experience or something? Anybody

Andrea Clinton

ever *tap that ass?*" I said with my nose scrunched up, looking him up and down.

To that Omar bit down on his jawbone so hard I thought he'd cracked some teeth, but he just stood up and left out of the restaurant. Man-Man was **HOT!** He just sat there staring at me like he was a demon filled with rage because the rumors of my rude deeds were true.

"Why the hell you treatin' him like that Alisa? Keep it up and I'm gonna give him permission to run up in ya mouth! Stupid, you so stupid! He give you everything, he treat you good, he proud of you in school—what's ya f—kin' problem? And what's got into you? You act like you losing ya mind! Damn you foolish; you don't make no sense."

"F—k 'em!" I said while picking up my drink and gulping more. "I got dis." I wanted to say, "I didn't ask for none of this, I just wanted my man, not this full load he imposin' on me." But I was so drunk at that point, I could only be rude and nasty, "F—k 'em."

"No, you know what," Man said jumping up, "keep it up and *I'm* gonna run up in ya mouth. Curse again! Curse one mo' time tough ass! Go 'head." He balled up his fist, standing over me, hoping I would say something sarcastic in my drunkenness so he could punch me in the mouth.

Then he bent down over me snatching me by my blouse and pulling me up to his face, "Why you not talkin' smack *now* Alisa?" he grunted at me. "Why you stop talkin' sh—t now! Huh! Punk-ass b—ch!" With his knuckles pressed hard in my chest imprinting their very own black and purple bruises. "*Do him right or let him go! Let me hear something else you did to that man and I swear fo' God I'm gon' whoop that ass—try me! Go head; try me like you try him! I'll wear that ass out!*" He pushed me back with a look of disgust then walked out pissed.

Shakirah sat there looking down her nose at my drunkenness like she had no remorse for me. And we were supposed to be ace-boon-coons. I guess I was just that ugly, because the most she could do was give me tough love, almost like I gave her when she was messing with someone else's man, my brother.

"Alisa," Shakirah said, "why you bugging yo? I know you tryin' not to let him pimp you but dang! Just stop going to school. It ain't *that* deep. *And I know Omar just like you know Omar.* That man ain't a bit more tryin' to pimp you than the man on the moon. You gonna mess up bad girl, and you gonna end up lonely and all alone, watch. You wrong Alisa; you wrong." Then she up and left, leaving me at the table alone, with the $235 bill. I finished my drink. Oh yeah, I had another one, left the cash and caught a cab home to my moms' and passed out drunk.

Other times I wasn't as pissed off as much as I was pathetic. Like one day, I got so drunk trying to have wine while I studied to take off the edge that I barfed in the living room all over one of his favorite rugs. When Omar came home and saw barf on his rug, and me with a tiny buzz after throwing up the wine, he got mad and threw me and the rug out, putting me in a cab and the rug on the curb.

***

I was quiet for a while. But then, like a nutcase, I said and did anything that would make him feel like crap for putting me in such a position. Because that was what school was making me feel like, crap, although I behaved decently when I was in school.

Omar, after more talks with his father, started praying like the Muslims pray with their head to the floor and stuff. I mean, he had always done that off and on, but then all of a sudden it was more than ever, like, a few times a day.

He also talked to my father about *us* when my Pops would call. But I wouldn't come to the phone afterward to hear the lecture, so I made another enemy. One time though, Man-Man dragged me down there to the prison and I just stared off like a dust-head, *that's a person who smokes angel dust or embalming fluid Athena.* I just nodded and answered yes to, "ALISA, ARE

Andrea Clinton

YOU LISTENING TO ME GIRL?" When my father yelled at me for looking away from him and Man-Man. But I said whatever when pressured, just to make it through the visit, 'cause they weren't living in the hell I was living in, so I didn't care.

Manny tried to ask me why I was bugging. He was so cute with his crazy self. "What's wrong with you? Are you depressed? What the hell? I saw that commercial and the woman was acting like you. A-yo, they got medicine for that yo," he said thinking maybe I was having a nervous breakdown or entering some mental state and needed help.

But Manny at least still hugged me, watched a movie with me, or sat and had a drink with me at my mother's when I'd leave Omar's on some okie-doke I was trying to pull being spoiled. Manny knew what it was like to feel like you had no one, or to be confused and not know what to do, so he didn't impose ill feelings on me.

Meanwhile, my mother was scared to death to say anything because she felt she'd wronged me too bad to place blame on me for anything. She probably blamed herself for my bad behavior and thinking. And either she would call Omar over to the house when I'd pop up or he would just come over to talk to her about us. But often times I would just leave. A few times though, I went in the kitchen, their meeting spot. I was tired of waiting on him to leave, so I'd go and get me a glass and a bottle of wine, and I'd ignore him. But then he'd say, "See Ma? And she don't have no shame in her game with that drinking." Then he'd shake his head or drop it into his hands.

A couple of times when that happened I said something smart back to him. "And you still don't let it stop you from being selfish and gettin' what you want from me." Then I'd headed into my room in my cute Sesame Street or Tweetie Bird pajamas pants and tank top, leaving them at a loss.

"Alisa," my mother would say later, "stop being spiteful. You only hurtin' ya self."

Shakirah, my girl, she started acting strange, and I started thinking she was on drugs. But that's a whole other thing I'll come back to.

Me, myself, well, I think I lost my mind, had a nervous breakdown like Manny said. I couldn't even plot and plan out stopping him from hustling. Plus my classes were hard and messing up my thinking. It was crazy, I mean, nonsense seemed to make sense, and wrong often seemed fair. Everything was truly intense for me back then, and I wasn't understood.

Anyway, the uglier I behaved, the more Omar would just sigh, or grunt and walk away. My mother and Ms. Sista talked him into having patience with me. His father kept after him to rush to marry and to recognize the woman as an emotional creature, etc.

Listening to all of them basically say the same thing, he was really trying to make it work with me.

I mean, in past years, I'd seen Omar half kill dudes for doing less to him than I was. My mouth became more wretched, believe it or not, but he became more tolerant. He was actually starting to wear me out. I found sometimes we were chatting here and there, smiling and laughing a li'l more. It could've been due to the way he-do-that-thing-he-do, I dunno.

But of course, the devil stay busy, so in no time I began to wonder if his rejuvenated patience was really him using college to keep me busy so he could mess around with other women, and maybe this was why he was so tolerant of me. Man-Man and Manny assured me that wasn't the case. So, I began to wonder what the hysteria over me hurrying up to graduate was about. But Omar kept saying it was for our future and the future of our kids. Same old tired ass story.

One day though, while taking a break from studying, we were having a li'l chat, in between one of my mean spells. I remembered what the lady on the bus had said. And with less hell going on between me and Omar, what I had to do soon became clear. But instead of doing it nicely or properly, the devil got bored, so he whispered into my ears; yep, and I listened.

***

Andrea Clinton

I finally confronted Omar one afternoon, after a few days of pretending to want to talk about something. But I stopped and acted choked up to make it seem like I had something pressing on my mind. Why? Because I'd give the effect that I felt strongly about what I was holding back.

"Baby why don't you stop holding it in and say what's on your mind?"

"Okay, fine. Omar, for a person so worried about our future, and the future of our kids, why are you out there hustling where you could get knocked off or go to jail at any time? Where we gonna be then? Huh? What would happen to the kids then? They gonna go to bed crying at night like we did because their father isn't around to help them with life's trials and tribulations?!" I *really* began getting angry thinking about it. "And that's if we get to have kids! Yo black ass could get knocked off tomorrow! *Or tonight!* Yet you put all this effort into me making a better life for a so-called family, and you creating a sh—ty one for us whether on purpose or not! You tellin' ya father all my wrongs, but I bet you not tellin' him 'bout that. Not 'bout how you a big-time drug dealer are you?"

That slipped out. I don't know where the heck that one came from, but it had Satan's signature all over it. I sighed, kinda feeling good though. *Goodbye college*, I figured. *Whew!* I thought. My goal of stopping him from hustling might also wiggle me out of college if I stayed focused, and didn't go off on a rampage like how I do sometimes. I felt like General Ulysses S. Grant sending General Robert E. Lee into retreat during the Civil War. I was on to something! And Omar could see it too, but he didn't like me bringing up his father and his drug dealing. He was so swollen with anger, because he knew I had a point, a **REAL GOOD POINT**. Omar rose up out his seat and came toward me as if he were gonna grab me. But he stopped himself, turned and left out, slamming the door. But I'm not stupid. I knew I had to seal the deal *now*. You gotta know when to strike; you gotta know when to hold 'em and when to—what? Haaaa! And I was in a position to hold 'em; I'd just made a **GREAT** point. I had legs to stand on, so I struck. I grabbed my bag, stuffed it with clothes and shoes and went home to my mother's. But I was sorta pissed at myself. The point or argument I needed was there all along, but now that I had it, grrrr!!!

Later on, when he called my mother's house for me, I wouldn't come to the phone. When he came over, I wouldn't come out my room. I was pissed. I was fit to spit. And I wasn't 'bout to give him the satisfaction of meeting halfway. So I made myself scarce. One time, I locked myself in the bathroom for hours and even climbed out the window and down the fire escape.

I had to get away from him in an effort to let my point marinate in his mind. So, I went partying with Shakirah sometimes, or my girl Malika who was home from college. She had the blues too. Her man was giving her ultimatums and she needed a few nights on the town. But me, I just didn't give a damn! I wanted to cause drama.

One day, my mother finally came in my room and we talked about everything.

"Alisa, you smart. As far as school, just make him happy. And after another year or so when you're married, it'll be time for kids and that could be your excuse not to go to school."

I didn't like her advice, because that meant no fun. I'd be leaving the hot pot to marry the hot frying pan. Get the heck outta here!

Then she asked about Omar's hustling, "Are you really upset at him still hustling? Or was that just a tit for tat?"

"Honestly Ma, I think I love Omar. But I'm just the brat he made; that's why I act like that. Guess you can't spoil girls like me. But, *I don't* want him to keep on hustling. Who wants a husband who hustles? You see what happened to Daddy, no harm intended. And Omar is better than that. He usually always trying to be better. But now, he so busy trying to make me a better woman, he forgettin' about himself."

"Yeah but he trying Baby-Girl; you gotta give'em that."

"I want a man who earns his money right so that he'll be around, and we can live the good life together. Well, I don't want any old man for that reason, but I want him for that reason. But it

Andrea Clinton

seems like he's preparing for jail and sacking me with kids to tie me down 'til he comes home or something. Why else? I dunno."

That just shot outta my mouth without a lot of thought. I started to wonder if he was really preparing for that. And I realized more ideas were growing in mind.

"It's not that I want my man to stop hustling, *you know how many hustling boyfriends I'm used to having?* It's that I wanted better for Omar."

Wait! Wow! Is that how you think when you really love someone? When you care what happens to them for their own sake? That was way too mature for me, I thought. So, I quickly changed the subject.

"Sometimes I think he's trying to control or change me though Ma. It's like he got some plan in mind too."

"Girl! Listen, this is what you need to do. Get your butt on over there and tell him how you feel. He loves you and wants to marry you and so this is the best time to tell 'em."

My mother was right. *But what if he had no intentions of changing his career? What if he really didn't love me that much, but was just smooth as hell?* Those things kept creeping around in my mind.

And more confusing was my feelings for him. I thought I didn't allow myself to fall deeply in love with him, at least not more than he loved me. But then he'd do these romantic things that I guess reeled me in.

But regarding going over to him, if I went over there and pressed his back against the wall, and it turned out he didn't love me, then all of that thinking, plottin' and plannin' was for nothin'. *Yeah I wouldn't have to go to college, but then I wouldn't have him either, and I'd be left with nothing,* is what I thought. Suddenly, it all began to be just *too much*. Go or stay, go or stay? As you well know from my doings previously mentioned, I didn't go to Omar's house that night. I needed time to think about how I felt, and he needed another night without me by his side. I went to sleep.

Long story short, I went in the morning and crawled into bed with him. I told him we needed to talk. He didn't really want to. He was still angry at me for what I'd said the night that I left him, and for leaving and not talking to him, for *playing him out* as he put it. But I told him we'd have to talk sooner or later.

But he got up and walked out of the room on me, going into the bathroom. After a few minutes, he came back into the bedroom and shouted, "WHAT?"

"We need to talk Omar. I said a lot out of anger, but it was coming from my heart."

"All of a sudden?"

"No, not all of a sudden. I was feeling that way for a while, but criticized you under my breath or thought it in my head instead of talking to you about it. You tryin' to make me live right, while you live wrong, and you supposed to be Muslim, about peace."

I had to give it to him like this. I'd been acting ugly, but he needed to see he was too.

" *Well talk then!* " he said sarcastically.

"I don't understand how you want me to do the right thing for our future, but it's okay for you to continue doing the wrong thing, which jeopardizes it."

"I don't wanna talk about it," he said, reaching in his drawer to pull out a tee shirt.

"How could you say you don't wanna talk about it O'? We supposed to be getting married, aren't we?"

Omar got quiet, and I didn't know how to take that. He just turned away from me even more than he already was. So, I sat for a minute or so to give him a moment, but when he didn't say anything, I decided to leave again. I grabbed my bag and began packing it.

"That's all you know how to do isn't it? Leave! Walk out on a nigga when you don't like something, when you don't get ya way," he said pitifully.

"What am I supposed to do? You won't talk to me! Omar, I know you not stupid! You're known for being on point. And regardless of you gettin ya hustle on, you not no down-and-dirty dude. You want things, and you want a family. Why are you doin' it like this? You talkin' outta both sides of ya mouth. You not the kinda brutha who don't want nothin' in life. You ain't the type to

Andrea Clinton

pray for the world, but then f—k up in it. Why you keep stickin' with this, going against the grain of ya religion you love so much?"

He still didn't answer me, and I started feeling so low. I felt trapped in this good-person mode, vulnerable 'cause maybe he liked the b—ch in me and might wanna kick this new me to the curb. And I felt disregarded 'cause he wasn't sayin' nothin'. And on top of that, *I was believing my own bullsh—t*. I was actually feeling as if I was finally being truthful with both him and *me*. It was so confusing, and thinking back on it, it's still confusing. What the hell was wrong with me? Was I good? Bad? What? I mean, I knew I acted ugly, and I knew I'd been mean and spoiled. But what the hell was this new thing? This new experience?

"O' why you going against the grain knowing how you feel in ya insides?"

He stood there staring at his tee shirt, not saying a word. So, I was done. I turned to start walking again, and he watched me until I got close to the door and finally blurted his feelings.

"Because I don't know anything else! And I'm good at what I do. What else do I do with myself, my money, my—" He paused, shaking his head, then said, "I *got* dreams! But it's all left to chance, and too many devils hanging on me like monkeys on a tree, confusing me, stagnating me. I think I lost my self-esteem or something. And, I dunno if I can do anything else—"

Omar turned to me and started raising his voice, getting annoyed and sad, "**I been savin' up to do the right thing, but sometimes it seem like the right thing ain't made for me, or ain't gonna happen for me. It's like something written in the air or some sh—t! The only thing I know inside and out *is* the streets, and knowing that one thing, makes me happy, and it beats not knowing nothing else. Why, why would I want to feed my own people drugs, mess up their head, their life? I don't wanna do this sh—t! But if I don't have niggaz out there flingin' for me, what I'ma have? You don't think I thought about this sh—t?**" Then he turned from me, and lowered his tone, "And come on, them junkies gonna be out there copping drugs anyway."

"Omar, you smarter than that! Don't hand me that sh—t! I'm so surprised at you. You know, you won't be able to do what you do forever, and what will you be leaving behind? A wife or a widow? Kids or orphans? Or maybe we won't get that far and I'll be left with a broken heart with everybody trying to get me to move on...baby *what are you thinking?* You not stupid. No! You know how it's gonna go down O'. Come on now. *Keep it real.*"

He paused in frustration before speaking and spun away from me, in torment behind this subject. What got to him was sort of what I said, but it was a word I said that really hit home for him, *orphans*. See in the Qur'an, it speaks about a time of war when there were orphans and widows left behind. I figured this smacked him in the head and he later confirmed that for me. He didn't want to contribute to something like that, especially stemming from some crap he was into. So, he gave in.

"Aiiight, aiiight, I get you!" he shouted.

"But what you gonna do about it?"

"Just, let me think. Just chill out and let me think."

At this point I was really believing the bullsh—t I was sayin'. I didn't want him hustling because he might go to jail. College was the furthest thing from my mind, at least in that moment anyway. But I felt I hadn't driven it home for him. So, I added more drama to show him I wasn't playing.

I turned around and started to walk out again and he yelled, "All right, all right! I'll open those two stores I've been talking about."

"And?"

"And what? Come on now Alisa, baby steps! Baby steps!"

"Those damn police and the task force ain't gonna take baby steps when they kickin' the got-damn door down coming after me and the kids."

"I told you about that curse word and what you're really saying?"

"I said *got*-damn, not God, GOT, and stop changin' the subject."

"**Well what you want me to do?** I gotta get one business up and moving before I leave the other!"

Andrea Clinton

"Hire an accountant and a consultant to help walk you through starting the business until you get the hang of it. You got the dough to pay for it. And keep them legit! Do it a.s.a.p.!"

"You telling me what to do?" he wondered, looking at me, proud of my maturity, and of me being the adult for a change. He was also proud of me pushing and supporting him to do right.

I paused for a second before puttin' it all on the table. I had gotten way too excited.

"Aaaaah, yeah. If you want me to finish school and be in your life, if you want me to marry you and have kids, you gotta leave this life now! No harm intended but no good woman wants a hustler for a husband," I told him as I put my hands on my hip and raised my left eyebrow.

He just stared at me in disbelief, the woman who always dated drug dealers and had her hand out for a knot of $$$, everyday. I went into the kitchen and put some breakfast on. But I was holding my ground. Omar went and straightened up the bedroom calling me, "Ms. Billy Bad-Ass," which was awkward because he only curses when he's pissed and ready to blow.

Then it hit me. *Dammit! I said if he wants me to finish college he'd quit hustling! What if he does quit? Would I still have to keep going to school? Damn! I love him, but that much? To finish school? I knew I was gonna go over the top; go off on a rampage with all this good-girl maturity crap. Damn!* I thought.

But on the other hand, what made me get over it was being hyped on Omar stoppin' that old hustling thing. Because see, I was no dummy, **hustlin Drugs is a fool's profession.** It's temporary and unreliable money. That's why I used to date hustlers, get 'em for their money and leave 'em when they got locked up. But it's also a fool's profession because in the end, when you divide all that you've made by the years you've been out on the streets **and** in jail, it usually comes out to be minimum wage or less, and you'd have been better off working at a fast food chain. **Omar knew this.** We discussed it, but it seemed it was up to me to start saving his life like he tried so hard to save mine, even if it meant giving in to the whole college thang, for now. *Dang!* I thought.

So I took my medicine like a big girl. And Omar, seein' I was willin' to stand by my word, stood by his. In a week he found the locations for two spots. One was to be a soul food restaurant and the other was a deli next door. He got the certificate to go in and do work, paid workers to make it happen. Then he and some workers painted the stores, fixed them up, and added shelves, deli equipment and tables to the deli and pretty much the same to the restaurant, all in like two weeks. And in between, he hired managers and staff, and helped them stock supplies. In no time at all, both the deli and soul food spot were ready to go. And I knew it wouldn't be long before he was out of the street life for good. He was on a roll doing right.

But why do we black folk have to do everything so grand? On the day of the openings, he put up tents outside both places with tables and free food, plus music, face-painting, and a few vendors selling tee shirts. Hearing there was free stuff, folks came out of the woodwork. I couldn't believe my eyes. I helped on and off, but Omar knew I wasn't going nowhere near those crowds. I mostly ate, BBQ ribs, potato salad and baked beans from the soul food restaurant, plus ice cream, chips and hot sauce, and juices from the deli. All went well, and I was stuffed.

Andrea Clinton

Bo Know This, and Bo Know That, Bo Look Good, but Bo Start Crap

As the deli and the restaurant began to take off, Omar hinted to me that he stopped hustling and I believed he did. He was either at the gym working out, at his businesses working and keeping an eye on things, or checking the books at home. All this went on for over a year.

Then one day, I decided that we'd been engaged too long. But he came back at me with something different.

"Baby, you have less than a year to graduate with your associates and when you do, we'll get married. I got a double celebration planned."

He looked so sincere. But he always looked sincere, even when he did the opposite of his look. And why would I want to base my marriage on when I graduate, especially when I didn't even know if I would? Because I'd done one of the stupid things in the world. I took all the classes I was interested in first, and now I was left with maths and sciences. And I HATED those subjects. Omar thought his idea about marriage after college would make me hurry up and finish school, but what I had to do was stretch it out because there was *no way* I could have two math classes and two sciences in one semester. And I couldn't talk about it with him, because he'd think I was procrastinating, so I just did what I did; I took two classes so I could focus.

Another semester went by and when he saw I still had a few semesters to go he snapped.

"I'm starting to think you doing this crap on purpose! Fail, so we don't get married!"

I just stood there looking at him as if he'd lost his mind. First off, he never busted out yelling at me like that, and secondly, why would I go through all the trouble of studying night after night, tutoring, and so on just so I...I couldn't even entertain that notion. I just walked away.

"Alisa, Alisa!"

Of course you know, I was a bitter b—ch after that, like before when my brother jacked me up in the restaurant. Actually, I had been acting that way the WHOLE time. *Please,* even during the whole store-business thing, after that good-girl speech I gave him, I was still a mess going off about school. He was just too busy to care. I mean, I, we, had a few good times, but 65% of the time I was angry, fussing, cussing, and not looking at him nor speaking to him because he put so much pressure on me. He was always coming at me with, "If anything happens to me, with a degree you can take care of my kids..." *I was so tired of hearing that crap!* I was ready to buy a muzzle and put it on his mouth and say, "Shut up! **SHUT THE F—K UP!**"

Anyhoo, my grades were dropping. The 3.13 GPA I had was now 2.7 and still dropping due to that dang science and math business. The professors hated me because they said I was more of an English major than a Computer Programming major, 'cause I *can only read and write, and am dumb struck in math.* Whatever! And Omar would always come at me with, "Computers are the way to the future," like I wanted to hear that mess.

But I felt this hurt me and Omar's chance of happiness, so I carried on even worse if there is such a thing. I turned it up so bad, barely anyone was speaking to me. I became Hell-On-Earth. It got to a point he couldn't say anything without me going off. His patience wore thin. I screamed more. I embarrassed him in front of his family, my family, his friends, my friends. I carried on, over, and out; I was a hot mess! Then I got depressed, crying when no one was around. I didn't know what to do but to continue to act

Andrea Clinton

and react like a nutcase. I'd helped him, but I was still lost, stuck, and he didn't notice, or either he didn't care.

So, I did the ultimate, well almost ultimate. I did what use to come naturally. I gave this dude my number. He was also a student and he'd been chasing me for almost a year on campus and the fact that I had a man meant nothing. But I was so tired and ready to shuck school, knowing me failing would probably end me and Omar anyway with all his college passion. So I felt like, *whatever!* I didn't allow myself to think of the old times or the good times. I just thought about breaking out of this prison that Omar had put me in. I couldn't even go to him for help any longer; the work I was doing far surpassed his knowledge. So what the heck was I there with him for anyway? Right? Yeah, I hear what you're saying. Giving Bo, the guy from college, my mother's number wasn't right. **But screw that! You wasn't in my shoes!** You don't know the kind of pressure I was under! Don't let these tears fool you! I'm strong, I can hang, but damn! How long is a heffa' supposed to hang? I never knew anything could work a person's mind like that college physics stuff! **OH MY GOD! Are they serious? What in Hell!**

So I started seein' Bo behind Omar's back. But it was just datin', like meeting for drinks and stuff. Hell, Omar had stopped drinking long ago, and it felt good to have someone to share a drink with. We never *really* got intimate, 'cause you know I don't roll like that. A quick smooch here and there don't count.

Two months into our thing and one day this dude calls my mother's house at the wrong time. Omar and Man-Man were there talking about some business, obviously Omar wasn't out of the life. Yep, he was still hustlin' drugs, just totally off the scene now. And when the phone rang, and Bo asked for me, my brother thinking it was an old boyfriend gave the phone to Omar to tell him to stop calling. **OH BOY, WHY DID HE DO THAT**? When Omar answered the phone, he started asking Bo questions. Bo knew I had a man so he played it off and said, "Is this her brother?"

"No it's her fiancé. Where do you know Alisa from?"

"Oh my bad man, I was just calling to see how she's been. Tell her Bo said take care." You'd think it'd go as smooth as that and then it would be in the past, over, history. Or at worst case he'd tell me an old boyfriend called, I'd get scared, and then stop seeing Bo, right? Ooooooh noooooo! It couldn't go down that smooth! We're talking about me! And my stankin' ass!

My brother said when Omar left the house he was kool. Heck, he said he was kool all while he was there. But Omar must've gotten to thinking about the late nights I was coming in, although they were few, and how I was staying at my mother's house at least two nights a week now, sometimes more. Or maybe he thought about the fact that I *wasn't* coaxing him in the bedroom anymore like I usually did when he was trying to hold off fornicating. Yeah, I think that must've been the cherry on the cake.

And I guess since game peep game, he came in running game to feel the situation out, *but he already knew.*

"So Alisa," he started in, walking into the bedroom, and taking off his leather jacket. "Your side man Bo called your mother's house, spilled the beans on ya cheatin ass," he said just as smooth.

But he had that calm, crazy look in his eyes. Maaaaan, I saw my coffin, the six foot ditch they were gonna throw me in, everything but the flowers. I knew I was cold and flat-out busted, and wondered if I'd make it from the other side of the bed to the bathroom where I could lock myself in. I made the mistake of looking over at the bathroom door before I ran though, and when I started runnin', he did too and caught me. He snatched me up and shook me hard as hell. I thought I saw my head roll off my shoulders and onto the floor.

"What's going on Alisa! Hunh? **How could you cheat on me! How?"** In a squeaky voice. **After ALL I do—"** He suddenly stopped talking, but was still shaking me like crazy.

If I didn't know no better, I'd think this nigga was crying blood out his eyes 'cause he was red-hot mad, and I was afraid. But the good part of me deep down inside came out and I just couldn't make this man think I was actually cheating on him because I really wasn't. Shut up! I wasn't.

"Baby, dinner and conversation was all Bo got from me. On days when I was supposed to be in class," I said to him in a sad and scary tone and manner. Then I got bold, I dunno what the hell I was thinking. "*I'm not talking to you with you grabbing me like this.* Let me go Omar."

"OH, YOU GONNA TALK TO ME AND TELL ME WHAT'S GOING ON OR WE GONNA HAVE SOME PROBLEMS UP IN THIS B—CH TONIGHT!" he yelled, gripping my arms tighter. He squinted his eyes with BOTH eyebrows raised, shaking and jolting me between words, looking crazed.

And there it was. I had brought out the side of him I had tried so hard to resist meeting firsthand, his father. Gooot-damn! How in the world did I do the very thing I tried so hard not to do? I woke that sleeping devil, that innate quality we all knew he had in him. I knew I was dead. I knew it. *He's gonna ring my neck, stab me and shoot me; I'm dead*, I thought, as he was geared up in a crazy calm.

"Baby let me go and I'll talk to you. But don't treat me like you some crazy woman abuser. *You want me to be scared of you?*" I said trying to appeal to his conscience.

He tightened his grip, but then looked into my eyes, and shoved me down and across the bed. He pushed me so hard I rolled over backwards across the bed like I was doing a backwards tumble. I rolled across the other side of the bed and landed on the floor. I guess you say it served me right. I do too when I look back on it. But a large part of me does not because I know what he put me through. And although you say he meant me no harm, pushing me to finish school, it was still hard on me.

When I got a mental grip on what happened, and straightened out my nightgown, I leaned back on the wall on the other side of the bed, still sitting on the floor. I so called myself trying to appear terrified, but my dramatic approach came off looking silly as hell. I looked like Lucille Ball in *I Love Lucy* when she's busted in a predicament. I hoped all the theatrics made me look pitiful. Then I took some deep breaths and tried to reinforce my want for him to chill the hell out.

"I'll keep it real if you promise to chill, please."

"Bi—" he caught himself from calling me a b—ch, then he shouted with everything he was worth. "YOU BETTER PRAY I DON'T THROW YOU OUT THAT MUTHAF—KIN WINDOW! *NOW TALK!*" Then he calmed himself down a pinch—a pinch.

Maaaaan, I was scared to death. Norman Bates was live and in effect. But I had to keep my wits about me 'cause I had a flashback of his father back in the day, dragging his mother off the porch by her hair that night. Believe it or not, I didn't want that drama, just a li'l argument and then I'm sorry and then make-up goodies, you know.

To get him to relate or try to understand my point of view, I started off with, "Allah knows best," as he always said. I'd have tried anything. "I'm going to be real with you. Because I can't do this anymore. *You don't love me no more Omar.* It seems like all you want to do is pimp me; make me over, make me do what you want me to do and you don't care about how *I* feel."

"Pimp you! What kind of money dog—" he started then stopped, baffled at my words.

Omar came toward me, so I put my hands up to bring forth a grave, dramatic effect, which made him stop in his tracks. He caught himself, and started biting down on his jawbone, and that was my cue to step it up 'cause that nucka was an inhale away from lightin' my fire 'round that house.

Suddenly, between pauses, I realized a thing or two and began thinking quick on my feet. *This nucka don't know nothing, 'cause Bo ain't gonna risk a bullet to the chest.* So I relaxed. I knew I messed up, so I just made it seem like I was comin' all the way clean, "Why you think I gave him that number huh? So he can call, tonight, while you were there and you could get jealous. I knew you were gonna be there." I pulled a Cicely Tyson *and* a Bette Davis, tryin' to act my way outta that ass whoopin'. Omar just flared his nose in anger. "It was the only way I could get your attention and get you to see I can't do this college thing no more. I need a less complicated life. I need you and only you Omar, not college or Bo, just you."

Poor Omar wanted and needed to hear that. He didn't blink an eye though. I felt he was just standing there, waitin' for me to reel him in. So I just continued winning my Oscar.

"For starters, I didn't sleep with him, ever. And I've never even put myself in a place, predicament or a circumstance where something like that *could* jump off. You know I don't roll with you

Andrea Clinton

like that. I would NEVER do that to you. I might make you jealous, but I'd never do that."

I think Omar knew I didn't sleep with Bo. He should know that much about me by now. He knew I didn't even sleep with the guys I used for money, only like three out of about fifty.

"I just use to meet him at a diner for dinner or lunch during or after class. We'd talk and that's it." I wasn't lying. But it still felt awkward. "School is hard Omar. I keep telling you maybe I'm not the school type, but you not listening. You want me to do what you want me to do. I just wanted to conversate with someone who wanted to talk about something other than school and our future kids, make me feel how you use to make me feel, without all the hard work. Or be in a comfortable environment without pressure or ultimatums over my head, like, 'No marriage until you graduate.' What kind of thing is that to do to a person *you say* you love?"

He pulled his gun out of the case in his top drawer, held it, tapped it and then set it down only to pick it up again, like he was contemplating shootin' me or something. He was making me nervous. And I really got scared when he stared right at me and grunted, "A person *I say* I love? That *I say* I love Alisa?" He was gettin' wound up again. Then he dropped the gun, and stared at it on the dresser.

"Baby, I'm not going to school because I want to further my education. You *making* me go to school even when I'm having panic attacks and migraines. Where's the love in that?"

"You can't see what I'm doing Alisa? You that dumb? You can't see what I'm trying to do for us?" He paused, put his hands on his hips and turned around as if he was trying hard not to go there, to that **VERY** angry place; I'd bet it was the place his father visited when he lost his kool, as I've seen that look in Abdul-Malik back in the day. But Omar was fed up and disgustingly annoyed, as if he lost faith in me, in us. Then he turned back to me, hand on hip for a few seconds and said, "I'm tired Alisa! I'm tired!" He put his hand over his face, wiping it, and just that quick, his anger turned to anguish, like he was suffering.

He started shedding tears and yelling. Yes, he reached over and punched me, he stabbed me, he stomped me, shot me and slid me across the room with a knock out punch. He, he had at long last grown tired of my sh—t. I had finally done it, and he had finally broke down. So he continued socking it to me. But oh no, not with his hands; oh, I know what you thought when I said he punched me and shot me, but, no-no-no. No, Omar never caused me harm. No see, he wounded me with what he knew would never heal, hurtful words. He didn't have to lay a hand on me. *His words* packed a powerful enough punch, *they* cut like a knife, and then *he stomped and wounded me* with tears that pierced my heart like bullets. Yeah, he beat me all right, **he beat me at my own game:**

"You wanna know why I push so hard for you to go to school!" Omar yelled. "When my mother was in community college, she made it to her second year! All she had to do was get through one more semester. My father *worked hard out there doing anything he could to put her through school,* because it was what she wanted. She came from a poor family and she said college would buy her and her family a happy life. But somehow she allowed herself to start getting high! And then before we knew it, she was a junkie! And our whole world fell apart! No more hope for a better day. All we built went to hell—**and with her and my father fighting and arguing and the police at my door all the damn time, they took us to hell with them!**

"We had to sit up there in that house and go from eatin' roast beef and fish dinners, bean pies and peach cobbler," he said frowning even more, "to eating whatever my father could bring home **when** he wasn't too drunk, and **when** my mother didn't pick his pockets when he cashed his check! We went from living in a two-family house with televisions, living room furniture, bed sets and everything else," he became even louder, *"to being evicted on the streets, finding refuge in shelters and abandoned buildings because my mother had bit all the hands that were helping feed us!"*

Then he shouted louder and became even more bitter, scaring me completely, **"WE WENT FROM BEING A GOOD MUSLIM FAMILY THAT WOULD TAKE OFF OUR SHOES BEFORE WE WENT INTO OUR HOME, QUIET ISLAMIC HOUSEHOLD THAT SMELLED LIKE BEAUTIFUL INCENSE, MUSK AND OILS, TO CLOSING OFF A ROOM IN AN ABANDONED BUILDING, AND CALLING *THAT* HOME,**

Andrea Clinton

ROACHES, RATS AND THE WHOLE NINE. WE'D BE SO HUNGRY SOMETIMES WE WOULD FAINT, FALL OUT ANY AND EVERYWHERE, AND WAKE UP IN *EMERGENCY ROOMS!*"

He paused, but then he yelled at the top of his lungs as if he couldn't yell any louder, "AND YOU WANNA FAULT ME 'CAUSE I WANT MORE FOR MY KIDS! AND 'CAUSE *I WANTED YOU TO WANT MORE FOR YOURSELF*? He paused five seconds and then dropped his tone, "I know how that lifestyle you and Tracey lived is." Then his tone and volume flexed up and down, "You start out a gold digger, *eventually you gotta give 'em sex*, before no time you full blown prostituting and before you know it, you cover your humiliation by getting high, *and end up just like my mother, a unhealthy broke down woman* WHO LOOKS DECADES OLDER THAN WHAT SHE IS!'"

He stopped then, leaving me to think about how damn horrible of a person I was, because I already knew most of the things he was saying to me, although not all that fainting and abandoned building stuff he said he endured. But I knew of his poverty, few pieces of worn out shabby clothes, raggedy sneakers, nappy hair and dried snotty nose at times. I had seen it with my own eyes. And I knew where the gold digger stuff landed you, but, I didn't make the connection between his passion for me in college and what he was trying to avoid. *He really meant well.*

Calmly, he drilled the nail in more, only to scare me when his volume and tone went up and down, "Before I rolled up on you, you were a young, frisky gold digger, everybody knew you were. You were hittin' up drug dealers, ballers and bratty good boys with dough! So, since I had feelings for you, I tried to get you to be different, down-to-earth, to care about life and the things and people in it, instead of getting your hair and nails done at the expense of some stupid nigga who hopin' you'll give it up or want you for a trophy! I wanted you to care about your future instead of diamonds and money, and the here and now. I wanted **you** to care more about **you** because I knew until you did, you could never *really* care about me! **And I didn't want you to turn out like Geenie and Ms. Burke. Back in the 70's they ran game on men just like you and Tracey! And look, DEAD! One's head bashed in by some man's boot, and the other blasted away by some** man's shot gun 'cause they wanna run game on men for their hard earned money, and playing with their feelings!"

He paused, then, still loud and angry said, "**But, it's okay, 'cause I can't do nothin' with you!** *You too messed up in the game and I don't have the energy to keep going back and forth with you! You selfish, stubborn and you really think it's all about you, it's your world!* **You can't think outside the box!**"

What box? What in hell is he talkin' 'bout, I thought.

"Or even open up your mind to how things could be! And I don't have anymore time or energy to try and teach you about it!"

He shook his head, and as before, spoke calmly, only to end up angry and loud, "I been fighting my insides, not going toward my own religion like I'm supposed to, **JUST TO BE WITH YOU!** I kept making up excuses as to why I couldn't go to the *masjid* to hear the lectures, 'Because I gotta do this for Alisa first, take baby steps introducing her to the religion, or get Alisa on the right track first.' ***KNOWING I WAS SINNING! NOT PUTTING ALLAH FIRST!*** It's said a man should begin choosing his family before the children are born and I was trying. ***But you fight me the whole way!*** Shakin' his head in misery and loathing he said a li'l muffled, "I might not have done a lot of things right, ***but you was dead wrong.***" Then he calmed down to a very scary point, and kept looking at his gun. "You won't get no more empathy from me, ever again. *I don't care about what happens to you no more,* so don't ever come in my face again. Ever! Or else I swear by Allah I'll kill you and I'll take whatever ya brothers or ya father got for me because of it. You hear me, I swear fo' God, I'll kill you if you ever come near me again—**GET OUT MY HOUSE! Get out.**"

I sat for a second, and as his voice dwindled down from all the preaching he'd just done, *I* felt like I was in church. But I was still scared to move. Niggaz change their minds about hittin' you in an instant when you cross them. And I crossed him, *even though* I didn't sleep with the joker I stepped out on him for.

He put the gun in the back of his pants and marched out the bedroom door. I thought he left but I never heard the door close. I was afraid he might change his mind and decide to come back and shoot me but he still hadn't entered the room. Just as I was about to lean forward to peek in the living room, he came back in the bedroom, scaring me to death. I jumped, and he looked at me as if he was surprised I was afraid of him. But hell, he had a gun in his pants. He said calmly but in disgust, "Get out! Please don't tempt me." And as I started to apologize, he screeched, "**DON'T TRY ME B—CH. GO!**"

And I didn't try him either; *I ran like a fool.* I jumped up, grabbed my jeans and shirt and ran out with no shoes on. As I stepped halfway through the apartment door, he hit me with, "And *I know* how hard it is to get a degree. You didn't use to see me in New York 'cause I was picking up drugs. *I was over there getting my degree at NYU,* stupid b—ch!" Then he slammed the door behind me, and it hit me hard in the butt.

I was surprised to hear him say he had his degree; he never told me. But I knew not to hesitate with a man like him, one who's gone through what he's gone through; hell, crazy could've been just around the corner, sh——t. So, I went downstairs and threw my clothes on in the hallway before leaving his building. I remember thinking, *I should've known he wasn't in NY pickin' up drugs. He's not stupid by a long shot; that's what he has runners for.* But I didn't stand around thinking 'bout it. I got outta there while the gettin' was good; I didn't even take the BMW. One, I had left the keys back inside. And two, I knew he wouldn't let me have it, I didn't deserve it. But, *I'll worry about the pain from all this later,* I thought. Then I walked out of the building, and crossed the street at warp speed to go home. He threw my shoes out the window. I heard them suddenly soaring at me, nearly hit me too.

***

I remember sitting in my room thinking to myself, *It's been two weeks and I haven't heard from him. I am so sad and all alone, and back in my mother's apartment, full time. I did all that work getting a man who loves me more, only to take four steps backwards. I feel stupid as hell.*

Now, I'm here talking to you, a Greek Goddess stuck to a big pillar, or carved in it, whatever, I dunno. You can't even answer me nor give me advice, but all I have is you. I don't even have my clothes, my mink or jewelry from the house. They said what he didn't burn, he gave away.

And after Omar kicked me out, my mother felt so sorry she couldn't even bring herself to give honest advice. My brother Man-Man wasn't speaking to me, Manny was just calling me stupid, my father hasn't called me, and I didn't even have a clue how Omar was doing. Bo started coming by. I didn't ask him to, he just showed up. I told him I wasn't going back to college, and I guess he couldn't wait to see me with Omar out the picture.

One day, I was hangin' with Bo outside my mother's building. Omar drove up and parked across the street. As he started walking toward us, I looked over to Bo in fear. I just knew Omar was gonna jump all over him. But he walked right by us and into my building to see Man-Man or Manny. About fifteen minutes after, he left and passed us by again without even a word or a glance. He got into his Cadi and before he drove off, I walked away from Bo crying and went in the house. Bo said Omar saw me walk away crying. *He don't even love me no more,* I thought*; he ain't even got fight in him for me no more.* That hurt me to the bone. I didn't care about walking off from Bo. I just went to my room and cried my eyes out. I couldn't let anyone see me, they'd say, "You are a fool. You ran off acting stupid, not thinking of the consequences! That's what you get!" And they'd be right.

Funny thing though, can you believe I was bored one day, so I looked at my math book, and tried to answer the first row of questions. Do you know, I got them **all right**. Ain't that a b—ch! Release the pressure and—" Maybe I just worked myself up 'cause I couldn't' get my way.

This all started with all that, *get a man who loves you more* business. I did it, but it didn't make me feel any special way at all. I was loved, but where was the glitter and confetti? Wasn't there supposed to be a ticker tape parade when I got 'em? Because I totally missed the point of doing this if not. And now he's gone. Uuuuugh! What am I gonna do without him? I can't stop this crying, I'm here with this baby on the way, and no man, no husband. And I thought rehashing my story to you would help open my eyes and make me see things clearer, but you're not helping! I guess you have your own issues, being cemented to this pillar.

THE RUNDOWN

Okay, now, let me give you the rundown on later events, in the end. A few weeks after all that happened between me and Omar, I tried to call Shakirah, but evidently I'd been in my own world, as Omar put it, and for a while now because Shakirah had moved to California months before. It had seemed like that whole restaurant thing with my brother snatching me up was just a li'l while ago, but I guess not. Dang! I called her mother but she wouldn't tell me anything. I asked my brother what happened but he still wasn't talking to me. Finally Manny came into my room to talk to me. I guess he felt I had been punished enough. I asked him what happened to Shakirah and he told me.

"Ronny," he said, talkin' 'bout Man-Man's baby momma, "stormed over to the building when Man-Man wasn't home and whooped Shakirah's ass in the middle of the street. Tracey and Peaches were there. They saw it go down."

I couldn't say anything due to the guilt of not being there for Shakirah, busy acting up and dating Bo and so on.

"Yo, what was really messed up was Shakirah was pregnant."

I stared at him in shock, mouth wide open.

"Did she lose the baby?"

Andrea Clinton

"Yeah, her people said she lost the baby, and Man-Man cried the blues 'cause he loved Shakirah; he still love her. But she left Man-Man a letter telling him he wasn't sh—t and he never truly loved her in the first place and that he'll probably go back to Ronny or some sh—t so she was out. But he love Shakirah a lot. Even though it wasn't like that at first, but she had his back 24/7, unlike Ronny and her three faces, good, bad and evil."

"I'm mad at Tracey and Peaches. Why didn't they break it up and stop Ronny? F—k that!"

"Tracey was the only one out there wit' 'em at first. She said she let them fight a fair one 'cause Shakirah *was* messin' wit' Ronny's man. But then Peaches came runnin' out the buildin' yelling to Tracey that Shakirah was pregnant. And since Tracey was closer, she started trying to break it up but, couldn't, so she punched Ronny, but that rolled right off Ronny. Then somebody snatched Tracey up. Peaches got there in seconds and hit Ronny and knocked her down; then somebody pulled Peaches off Ronny. Breaking out of their hold, Peaches grabbed Shakirah and took her inside. After she got Shakirah settled, she called for an ambulance then came back out to wait for it to show up.

Manny was getting into it while telling me, like he was there instead of the fact that someone told him what happened, "While waitin' for the ambulance, Tracey came up to Peaches, but Peaches was pissed off. Peaches started arguing with Tracey, 'I don't care if she did cheat with Ronny's man, how the f—k you stand there and watch her catch a beat-down like that? Y'all sposed to be kool! And, it's our 'hood, you don't let nobody come runnin' up in it. You ain't that far gone in ya world that you don't know dat b—ch! As much as people 'round here help you cover up yo sh—t! Especially Man-Man!'

"Then Tracey came back with, '*Git out my face wit' dat tom-boy sh—t!* You know what, I ain't no young buck; I don't be out here fightin' and sh—t! And f—k that! Shakirah was f—kin' with her man, what she think? She thought she was just gonna get that off? She bought that ass whoopin'. If one of them niggaz wife come whoop my ass, leave me. If I knew he was married I bought that, gimme mine!'

" 'F—k you Tracey!' Peaches yelled back at her. 'You ain't sh—t! You and ya f—ked up example! She could lose this baby!'"

I shook my head, not believing all the things I missed, too busy caught up in my bull crap.

Manny continued, "Man-Man showed up just as the ambulance took Shakirah away. After they drove off, he turned to Tracey, but didn't argue with her about not standing up for Shakirah. Instead, he just raised his hand to hit 'er; we pulled him back though. Then he calmed down. For a while, he stopped speaking to Tracey. Wouldn't even look her in the eye, when they passed in the street. But he finally started talking to her again like a month ago, 'cause Peaches told him *she did try to break it up* and she did punch Ronny in the face when she heard Shakirah was pregnant. But Man-Man wanted to kill **EVERYBODY sis!**" Manny shouted.

"It was messed up gettin' that call from the hospital though, hearin' the baby was gone. Man-Man went over to Ronny's house and **whooped her ass!** I watched for a good two minutes before I broke that sh—t up. *F—kit!* What she expect, she killed his baby, and for what? 'Cause she jealous? Maaaan, Ronny lost him, how she got him, she cheated with him behind her man and his girl's back; karma boy. I saw her a few days ago and I threw a bottle at her."

I was sittin there while he spoke like, *Where the heck was I when the lights went out…?*

Manny then told me Ronny pressed charges and Man did a few days in jail, but she dropped them because he told her he hid some drugs in her house with her fingerprints on them and if she got him knocked off, he was going to turn state on her. He was lyin' but she fell for it. So she stopped the wicked crap and dropped the charges.

Before you go talking smack about my brother, saying he ain't sh—t, let me first tell you that after Ronny found out about Shakirah being pregnant, she broke up with Man-Man, even though he'd stopped going to see her a while before, sending Manny with $300 a week for his child. But she started tellin' people her baby wasn't my brother's, but yet she was still pushing up for child support. So Man-Man asked the judge for a blood test, and guess what? Yep, the baby wasn't his. So they finally broke up for good-good this time; no midnight quickies or anything. He was hot red mad he raised that child for those few years.

He never told Shakirah anything about Ronny's baby not being his. But Ronny assumed he told Shakirah all the crap they'd been through, and when she heard folks say they saw Shakirah in the OB/GYN's office with a li'l belly, and that she was pregnant, Ronny all of a sudden wanted to fight her for messing with her man—two years or more after the fact. Ain't nobody stupid. She wanted her to lose that baby. Ronny felt foolish in her situation with Man-Man, and that the woman he cheated on her with would prosper, forgetting the fact that they both cheated, which was why the baby wasn't his. So anyway, Manny said that was why Shakirah went to California. She wanted to get as far away as she could from Ronny who made her lose her baby, and Man-Man who I guess she also blamed. This was why he was so bitter, and especially mad with me. How he saw it was, what Ronny did wasn't too far off from being as bad as what I'd done to Omar. But he was also pissed because I had no clue about his and Shakirah's issues because I drifted into my own world. Man-Man had helped me as much as he could with Omar, but I had left him all alone and to dry on his own on the Shakirah tip.

I knew Shakirah's father lived out there in California. So, I woke up one morning, went to her father's sister house, and asked her to call Shakirah.

"I'm sorry baby," I said crying when she picked up the phone. "I stepped off into my li'l zone, and left you hanging. You know Ronny wouldn't have got that off if we was in the cut. 'Cause Ronny knows, I'd have waxed her butt for that one girl."

"Ain't nuttin' don't sweat it," she replied. "How are you and Omar? You still giving him trouble?"

"Girl, he left me, I ain't seen him for weeks. *But I miss him so much*. I cheated on him. I didn't mess around with the dude though."

"Same difference to Omar girl, you know that Alisa. You know how O' is. He's like the male version of me, he's laid back, but he ain't gonna take certain things from nobody."

"We lip-locked once or twice, me and the brutha, Bo, but I didn't feel right going *that* far. So I stopped that, and we just talked. Now, I feel like sh—t!" Then I started crying again.

"I'm sorry about everything that had happened to you and Omar, but I saw it coming, because you were **OFF THE HOOK**! Girl, you were like a tornado twirling around everybody, pulling out their hair from stress of worrying about him whoopin' ya ass one day, or fear of what was gonna come out ya mouth, with all ya mean and nasty comments to him; just driving everybody nuts! You was seriously off the chain gang out that mug, **girrrl!**"

Shakirah and I talked for almost an hour. I decided I wanted to join her out there because I had nothing to lose here. The more we talked, I just cried. She was my best friend in the world.

"Girl get out here with that crying sh—t! I got something for you too when you get out here, to cheer you up, a surprise for you, and maybe we can go party on the beach and chill-out."

After all of that, I walked, no, I ran home, packed my bags while booking my flight to Cali over the phone, and went to bed early, 6p.m. *I wanted the next morning to be here now.* I left a note for my mother, caught a cab to the airport and flew out on the 7 a.m. flight to Los Angeles.

When I got off the plane and started toward baggage, my-oh-my what a big and beautiful surprise Shakirah had for me. I started to cry. I looked up and I found a big-bellied Shakirah waiting at the entrance with her father. We were so happy to see one another and I was so happy she didn't lose that baby. We hugged for a long time, even when we stopped hugging, we started again. Then she said she had another surprise, she was having twins. I couldn't believe my ears, but that explained why she was so damn big. She looked like she was about to burst. Evidently she was pregnant for a long time before she found out because she was up there in months. She begged me not to tell anyone. Her father said she was still paranoid someone would try to kill the babies. If I hadn't cried enough before, I was surely making up for it at that point.

We went home to a very nice house. The entire neighborhood was nice, uppity. Her father worked in film in some form or fashion, but nothing real heavy she said. But that Negro was driving a Jaguar so I don't know what something heavy is in Cali, but hey, I was like, *I'll take nothing heavy if it'll get me a custom made Jaguar and a big house like his.*

We had a good ole time talking and laughing about everything. She gave me the lowdown on all the things I'd missed so busy in school and dating among other things. Like on Omar and how he was still hustling behind my back, was even in a shootout with some young boys trying to take over his set. But she said he did slow down a lot, with that incident being the only one she knew of. He sold several of his spots for $200,000 a corner. My eyes blew out of my head. He didn't hold up to his promise, and jeopardized our family, or would've been family. This didn't make me feel better about what I did, but it made me realize we were both still doing wrong, not just me. I guess you say I was still more wrong. Heck, I probably felt something was wrong deep down inside, and that's why I—well, I can't push off the blame for my actions. I was bad, rebelling to no end.

Then, scary as it was, she told me that the governor of our home state was making room in the overcrowded jails by letting out those who served 75-85% of their time and were up for parole or would soon be. She said my father, Abdul-Malik and a few others were on their way home. I immediately felt like I was going to return home to a beating with all my bad behavior. Then my father would see he's right saying us so-called pretty girls cause a lot of trouble. Not that I consider myself pretty, those were his words. She also said Abdul-Malik and Ms. Sista were going to get married again. Dang, you shoulda seen how my eyes twisted back in my head! Omar didn't tell me anything that was going on. You'd think I was away on vacation or something.

"What!"

"Yeah girl. Before I left ya brutha, Omar told Man she had been going to see Brutha Maleek, or Abdul-Malik or whatever, for almost six months. Ms. Sista went to apologize for all the wrong she did and what she put him through. He seeing her in her garments now, and living right these past years, divorced the young girl he was with and forgave Ms. Sista. He asked her to come back sometime and she did, often. Man said Omar told him that after his father learned of how their kids kept her health up and down from worry and stress, he said he wanted back in the family to straighten things out once and for all."

"Yeah 'cause who gonna go up against that big dude?" I said assuring her he is large.

Shakirah continued, "Yeah, Man-Man said he was huge, a giant. But anyway, now they getting married girl. Guess we gotta get a little hell before we get a little paradise huh?"

I just looked at her in shock, mainly because it did seem to be that way for all of us in the hood, and for decades going back before us too. First life is hell for you based on the mistakes you make, then you calm down, settle down and life looks a little bit easier or better for you; like life or God breaks ya back, tames you from being a wild horse, and then rewards you for finally submitting to his will.

With all that I was finding out, I hated college more than ever. Look at how much I missed out on. And why didn't Omar tell me any of this? I was hurt, a new wound opened up. All this was circling around me and I was wearing shades; I had no clue.

***

Shakirah's stepmother was making martinis. I never had one so I was like, "Sure I'll have one, see what all the fuss is about." I had one and it was like drinking rubbing alcohol and olive juice. I couldn't understand why it would make a difference to anyone if it was shaken and not stirred. *Nasty sh—t,* I thought. I wanted to ask her, "Do you feel special making that crap?" People have like a whole personality thing going on when they make martinis, *and it's nasty as hell.* Anyway, I got up and made myself a White Russian, and that was just right. I blew kisses in the air, kissing my hand and waving it as if I was spreading glitter, diamonds, gold after my first sip. I dunno what it's like to smoke a cigarette, but it seemed like one would've been good after the beautiful taste of that chocolaty, aaaaaah; all I could do was sigh after the first smooth sip.

But, by my third White Russian, I was barfing up everythang *and* the kitchen sink. I threw up all kinds of tan crap. I couldn't believe it. I was like what kind of vodka was that you used? Then I hoped she didn't drop no *acid* in there. I heard about folks from Cali toying with acid. Anyway, I ran to the bathroom where I continued barfing, then I sat back and I wondered. I noticed Shakirah in the doorway, wondering too. *Was I pregnant?*

I lay quiet the rest of the night, and she left me to my silence as we both lay across her big bed looking up at the stars through the skylight over our heads.

The next day, we ran and got a pregnancy test, and of course, positive. This was typical. My punishment would be that it ALL blew up in my face, leaving me a single mom. Like I said, this is so damn typical.

Shakirah's stepmother made an appointment for me to see her OB/GYN. Do you know that visit ran me $200? And all I got out of it was another test that came out positive. I couldn't believe it. Pregnant with no man. *What kinda monkey dog sh—t was this?* I wondered.

After a day of crying, I called my mother. I told her I was pregnant and she cried too, but tears of joy. She didn't have the grandbaby by Ronny anymore, even after a few years of thinking it was her grandbaby, babysitting and the whole nine. Also, she like everyone else thought Shakirah lost that baby, and so mine was the baby she was now happy about.

I stayed with Shakirah for a few months. My mother called almost every day. Then finally I went back home, mainly for my mother's and stepfather's anniversary party. I showed up the day before. We were going to the hall to decorate and all was well. Even Man-Man was speaking to me. Of course he wanted to know how Shakirah was doing, but all I could do was tell him she was fine and that she would speak to him soon. Then I hung around his new girlfriend knowing he wouldn't ask me questions about Shakirah around her.

By now, I was starting to show a little. It was the clothes I was squeezing into that revealed the pregnancy. Man said he was happy my baby was coming. But then he got sad and shed a few tears about losing his own, both on Ronny's account. It sorta killed me, not to tell him the truth, but he was a dog to Shakirah in the beginning, and for what? I mean he didn't talk foul to her or mistreat her, but he was seeing her after he settled Ronny in for the night. And Shakirah was minding her business when he came pushing up on her that night I was sweatin' Omar. And he been on her since, playing her for a fool almost half their relationship, still sneaking with her behind Ronny's back. Remembering all that got me over feeling sorry for him quick. Besides, *he'd be happy as a pig in slop soon enough with his twins*, I thought. I gotta admit though, I could also see he felt bad for how he treated Shakirah like second fiddle.

Everybody and everything seemed so unreal. Heck I was pregnant, almost three months along. But as unreal as it seemed, it was also pleasant—until Omar came walking in, with Vanessa's cousin Penny on his arm. Oh my God! Man-Man looked at me and quickly said, "Nobody knew you was coming today. Omar bought by some stuff, and I forgot to tell him to meet me outside or at home." Then he jumped in front of me, and tried to calm me down so I wouldn't hurt the baby, "Stop! Don't get mad. Calm down Alisa!"

"Don't get mad? He walking up in here with that trick, knowing I don't like her…at my mother's party, well soon to be party?" I continued to yell and go off. Omar, smug and fine as could be, just turned around and began to leave. I started walking after him and managed to catch up.

Penny, paranoid I guess, turned around and jumped in my face, "You better back the f   k up!" She shouted, busting my ear drums.

But I got bad nerves so I reacted swiftly. Before I knew it, I punched her in the face, and she stumbled off the steps of the entrance.

Catching Penny, Omar helped her get her balance. He turned back to look at me with some killer-con facial expression, while turning her toward the door to leave. He was so busy starin', giving me his killer look, he didn't even notice I was pregnant. But, I wasn't scared. I was just as angry as he was; hell, angrier. Penny? I marched back to confront my brothers.

"You can't tell me that nigga didn't know I was here," I yelled to Man-Man and Manny, "and y'all knew he was seeing her and didn't tell me!"

Manny all emotional and sensitive replied, "He didn't know Alisa, for real. Alisa calm down. Don't get the baby upset." Then he started going off in Spanish before catching himself, "*Calma te no teprocute,*" which means *stop worrying calm down.* "You could lose your baby getting all worked up. Too much of that going on around here. Mami, *calma te no teprocute.*"

After Omar and Penny left, they all sat me down trying to calm me. They told me I had to tell him I was pregnant. One of their other friends, I forget his name, ran and got me a juice from the machine while Man kept talking smack. He said he didn't think it would change anything, but at least Omar would know, and he could be helping me. But I didn't want him to. I didn't need that Negro's help. I finally got them off my back by telling them to let me think about it.

Then Manny said, "I gotta go talk to Ka'reema too, let her know you pregnant. 'Cause she was talking about whoopin' ya ass, even months later she wanna muff you up. She mad at you for hurtin' her brother, Mami. She want you more than dessert. I started to smack you around my damn self! You don't treat nobody like that when you know they love you sis. That sh—t ain't right. That nigga love you with everything he worth. I don't care how he deny it. And he got the right to still be mad at you; after everything he did for you, **you played him out!**"

"I ain't play him out. He played himself out, try ta be a player, playing me, pimpin' me to be what he wanted me to be. You can't change nobody. *And he don't look mad to me.* Look like he moved on. Typical, after I'm pregnant he can jet, get it together, but before, he put up with ALL my sh—t."

Then they both got all excited and Manny said, "What? Please! You crazy! He done been in like six fights. Almost was in a shootout!" Man cut him off as if he didn't want him to let me in on the street crap.

My aunt who was setting up in the kitchen area overheard, "Omar better not be out here acting up. He been doing so good with those stores."

I felt like my whole world was spinning around, literally, so I barfed all over the floor. Man-Man was mad because he had to clean it. Manny was smart, he grabbed me and jetted.

***

The next night was the party. I tried to stay home, but no one would let me. They kept trying to get me to go. But I didn't want to barf in the banquet hall again. It wasn't as nice as this banquet you're cemented to Goddess Athena, but it was nice for last minute. Besides, everybody would see me and probably guess I was pregnant. I didn't have anything loose fitting. At best I had a few things that fit a li'l snug, but was still cute. But my family insisted and said I could just stay for the first hour. After I got there, one hour turned to two and a half.

There were a lot of people at the party, even Ms. Sista and her clan, although she left early. My father was there too. Yeah, he was released and was now staying in a halfway house, out for the weekends or something. It was so weird seeing him outta prison after all those years, and driving a brand new Cadillac, gold with all the fixins no less. He couldn't tell I was pregnant, and I didn't mention it. I guess no one told him. Hey, I wasn't going to either.

It was surprising that I found the energy and enthusiasm to hang in there for so long, because Omar came in with some girl, and that drove me nuts because he was doin' that whole manners thing and treatin' her like a queen. I don't know why, but it never seemed like he treated me like that. I had to wonder if I was so busy being spoiled that I didn't notice or appreciate it.

Even so, after a couple hours of that, I couldn't take anymore. So, I found a pay phone and called a cab. I asked the

Andrea Clinton

hostess to tell my mother I was outta there. I was about ten feet across from Omar, and had to walk past him to get to the phone. It hurt like hell that he didn't make any advance toward me, just put his hand on his date's back as I was passing, as if he was ready to protect her from me. Of course, I had had that incident with Penny the night before, but I didn't like Penny. It's not like I was gonna attack every woman he got with. All this had me crying in the taxicab as we drove away from the party. I couldn't take it anymore.

***

I had the cab stop at the diner so I could get some banana ice cream with chocolate-covered bananas. They were notorious for this dessert, and were Omar's competition. While I was sitting there, Tracey came in looking like a million bucks, wearing and waving her jewelry all up and down her wrist, and fingers. She had fat diamonds in her ears. She even had a diamond nose ring. "So, you impregnated? I'm cuttin' up ya playerette card. You maxxed out girl. Playerettes don't get pregnant. *What was you thinkin'?*" as she looked at me like I was stupid. "Well, whatever now. Now you just another pregnant knocked up ho—a baby's momma with no baby daddy. You just a **Jack-ASS!**" as she looked disgusted.

"Whatever, shut the hell up Tracey."

"Yeah you right, whatever. Only thing you got good going for you is that Omar *will* know that's his baby, and take care of it. But you'll still be somebody baby momma, damn! **DID'N'T I TEACH YOU NOTHIN'? DID YOU LISTEN TO ANYTHING I SAID?**"

"Yeah, maybe that's the problem. *You ain't got things all worked out like you make it seem Tracey. You pencil in ya hustle as you go, and strike ya plan while you eaten' ya cornflakes b—ch.* But you ain't thorough like you make it seem. Who you foolin'? I been listenin' to you since I was a crayon pusher, and I been ya road dog since I was fifteen. I know, and nobody know better than me. *You don't know what the f—k you doin' out here!*"

"F—k you b—ch! I ain't pregnant, and don't have no kids. And I ain't left stuck in a rut wondering how the f—k I'm gonna climb out while watchin' my man with a new b—ch! Now! *Suck on that.*"

"*Whatever* b—ch. Shut the f—k up! What you up to?"

"Nothin'. Just had a hard-up dude I hit up right quick for five g's."

"*Five?*" I said knowing that was a lot for one hit.

"Yeah, a big time CEO investment banker; he gets off on watching, so he watched," as her eyes opened wider.

"You could've been raped Trace!"

"Naaa, I had my .45 in my pocketbook, right next to me. I'd have smoked him like a spliff; or like a addict on a cigarette when they run outta sh—t, hahahaaa!"

"You rolling like that now Trace?"

"Girl, the game change! You can't keep doing the same hustle using these jackasses for a grip here and a grip there. People catch on to that mess. And with AIDS out here, girl, work gets slow. **Can you imagine,** men will pay for a screw and risk AIDS, but they won't buy you diamonds and pearls to impress you enough so you want to be their woman? Ain't that a b—ch? I can make at least $1,000 in half an hour with a white male freak from Wall Street, and that's without screwin' 'em, but it's difficult to flirt with a brutha and actually get him to take me to Red Lobsters on a date for a free meal, 'cause he afraid I might be one of the young thangs who got AIDS?"

"Trace, ya ever think it could be ya' reputation has caught up with you? That you a flimflammer? *Ya think?* I mean come on, even my uncle who only visited here for two weeks from Texas wouldn't even give you five minutes a year ago, and he is the biggest, nastiest country corn out there."

"Whatever. That's why *I'm making that money*, which is what **you** shoulda been doing instead of trying to **fall in love.** That crap is for the birds, love birds."

Andrea Clinton

"My aunt told me years ago Trace that the gold digger stuff works in stages. She said before you know it you'll be tricking 'cause ya game gets old and tired, and your mind and body gets worn out. And then before you know it, you get a pimp for protection. She said if not, you end up dead somewhere, 'cause the game is like that. And that ain't including getting high to wash away the dead feeling you get from selling ya soul for money."

"Yeah, that's what they say," she replied as she slouched down at our table, having a care-less attitude. "But like Kizzy say in Roots, 'Massa can take my body, but he'll never take my soul—

Then she changed the subject real quick, and went into her stare updating me on others who were like us, all about the benjamins. "*Varina* was killed last week. A man stabbed her up. She was dating him for like a year, and he was buying her big-time stuff, and then going back to his wife and kids. But he tested positive for full blown AIDS, thought is was just a bad cold, and said she gave it to him, and killed her, *in their favorite hotel room.* But get this, they later checked her body and she didn't even have it," she paused and then, "Nessy was killed two months ago.

"And, aaah," as she took a deep breath, "Dude she was using realized she was runnin' game, and that she had four other men like him. He followed her around and found out from a few of them that she was making all of them think she was their girlfriend. He strangled her. But she stabbed him so the joker was caught. He didn't get much time though, 'cause one of the boyfriends was one of the mayor's officials, and he helped him with a good lawyer and stuff; *they got him off.* They know Nessy probably had some friends who knew her dirt with them all, but they don't know that friend was me. So I was able to put the pieces together from what she told me, I saw in the court room and found out from others. You know half the city work up in county."

"Damn! I didn't hear about either of them. Damn!"

"She taught me airthang I know 'bout these here streets; Ness was my mentor, ya know, and they killed her. *That kills me, stifles me*," Tracey grunted and almost shed tears but held them in with every fiber of her being.

"That's how I'd feel if someone ever called me and told me some nigga took you out Trace. I ain't gone lie. You was wrong teaching me all that sh—t, and especially at the young age I was. I realized it long ago, even when I still followed you. But a part of me would die if you die. Take what you got and make good on it Trace, please baby."

Changing the subject with a motive, "So I guess you didn't hear they found a man floatin' in Weequahic Park either."

"Naaa. Was it in the paper? What happened?"

"*He tried to get his stuff back from me.* I dated him for a few weeks. He gave me about, aaaah, $22,000 in credit cards, a few diamond rings and a mink coat. Then when I pulled the, *you lied to me, you're married* scam, and tried to scat, he got pissed, after a week of thinking about it. Took him that long to catch on to what hit him. He came and tried to get all the stuff back. He smacked me and started acting crazy. So, I lit that muthaf—ka up. Shot 'em three times," she told me, pulling out a cigarette. "I told that nigga I liked westerns. He didn't believe me. Girl, after what happened to Nessy, I was like, 'I ain't takin' no chance wit' these niggaz out here, white, black or otherwise. I used to hear 'bout dudes killin' a sista 'cause they got played, but, Nessy and a few other sistas we know from the hood, that was too close to home for me. I couldn't take chances with that man."

"Tracey? You crazy? Oh my God, what are you doing out in them streets girl!'"

"Girl please," she said lighting her cigarette. "That muthaf—ka tried to strangle me, talkin' 'bout I played him. I don't care what scam I run, if you married, keep ya ass home. You gonna come out here and play in these here streets and then wanna have a temper tantrum, 'cause game met game? *Girl please!* F—k 'em."

"Who helped you dump the body?"

She just looked at me and sat back while she inhaled her cigarette, constantly looking at me as if she was saying, 'read my mind.' What a look she gave; gruesome; scary; dark; *cold.*

"Never mind. I got a feeling I don't wanna know." I believe 'til this day it was either Man-Man, Manny, or Omar. Why else would she have spoke to me like that with her eyes, except to say so. So many times she helped the three of them. She saved them from jail a few times keeping her ear to the grind, and they'd give her a few grand for it, to show good faith. Knowing she'd need a favor some day, she'd often give a grand back. I just know it was one of them; some street talk just goes without saying.

We got to talking and she said she'd drive me home. But hell, she made my stomach hurt. I didn't know if I wanted any parts of her. But, I paid the cab driver who was waiting and sent him on his way.

I don't know why, but I wanted to go past Ms. Sista's first and tell her I was pregnant if she didn't see it herself. I talked Tracey into taking me. Now, I don't know what made me wanna go over there. What the hell did I do that for?

I saw Ms. Sista leave the party early, so I knew she'd be home by now. When I got there, we sat in her living room, talking. Ms. Sista told me how disappointed she was in me and Omar. She felt he had turned his back on his faith for me and that's why it wasn't going to work for him, and she thought I was just being a b—ch, although she didn't say it. I was happy that she blamed us both and that all the weight didn't fall on me. But I wish she would've told me how much of a vile mood Ka'reema was in regarding me, 'cause Manny exaggerates sometimes.

When Omar's sister showed up, she put her bag down and barely even noticed me at first. "Hey Ma," she said as she kept walking toward the kitchen. I figured, okay, she's mad but not crazy. Maaaaaaan, next thing I know, that girl came flying out the kitchen, back in the room like a bull on crack, yelling like she lost her mind, "I know this b—ch didn't walk up in here like it's all good! You don't know I been looking for you?"

She charged at me, and Ms. Sista grabbed her and tried to hold her back. But Ka'reema was too strong for her. She shot past Ms. Sista and punched me dead in my face. She was there before I knew what hit me. I fell on the magazine table on the side of the couch. I felt so humiliated I could've killed that ho. She's like a freakin' beast in the ring. I jumped up and started swinging back, and a little more than nicked her face as she lunged at me, trying to duck my right hook. It surprised both of us that I made it that close. But hell, that just pissed her off more.

"Oh you fightin' back? You tough Alisa?" She went into a serious tomboy boxing stance, with her mother calling out to her.

Then she threw a death kick and hit me in my neck, *What the f—k,* I thought. I started choking and, yes, I over exaggerated it to feed her anger, with hopes she would calm the hell down. But she hit me with a Foreman uppercut. I went up a li'l, almost in the air, and then doooooown. I was punch-drunk. Finally, I began throwing up, and that seemed to chill her out a bit. Now she was just talkin' smack about all her brother did for me, and how all he did was show me love, blah, blah, blah.

I was so physically and spiritually hurt and filled with anguish that when I finished throwing up, I struggled to stand. When I did, I threw another punch, then another. I missed her as she stepped back. I dunno if the barfing made her sympathetic or if she wondered if I might be pregnant, or saw my stomach. But she didn't hit me anymore, just stared at me suddenly with much less anger.

Ms. Sista yelled, "Ka'reema stop! You gonna make me sick too! My blood pressure!"

Ka'reema backed up, looking at her mother, then turned to me, "You lucky my mother here! Get the hell out my house before I change my mind." Then she backed up, but stood at a close enough distance so she could lunge at me again if she wanted, if I said something.

So I hurried toward the door because if anybody could make you lose your baby, it was that ho. She wasn't just a woman, she was a jungle-ite, a he-she, a female Luke Cage from the comics, and maybe even a medium size Bigfoot. Those weren't human hits I took daggonit!

When I went outside, I found Manny talking to Tracey. He forgot to tell Ka'reema I was pregnant, I figured that. I doubted that she would endanger her niece or nephew on purpose. But she gotta live with the fact that she did it for the rest of her life now.

When I came out, mad, crying, with a purple neck and cheekbone, he was like, "What the hell happened?"

"That b—ch in there!" I yelled.

Half-excited, he yelled, "Damn! I forgot to tell her. Let me see your face?" As I was pitifully almost falling down the stairs, he came and helped me. Then he and Tracey got mad as they looked at my bruises.

Then Ka'reema came outside yelling at Tracey, "And I should whoop ya ass for bringing her over here!"

Tracey threw her hands up as a cop out, "I don't want no bullets flying 'round here K'." She winked at her to let her know she wouldn't fight her fair. "Go 'head wit' that sh—t! But you f—ked up for doing that to her! That's grimy as hell."

Manny turned to Ka'reema while helping me, putting my arm around his neck and screaming, "Why the hell you hit my sister stupid ass?! She pregnant with ya brother's baby! Ya niece or nephew!"

Ka'reema was about to yell out all kinds of whatevers but she paused. Then she yelled, "So what! I didn't know! Sue me! But f—k that b—ch!"

We all knew the trouble she was in when Omar found out. Tracey just pulled her cigarette in deep, staring at Ka'reemah looking like she was wondering if she should burn her, and I don't mean with the cigarette. Manny continued helping me.

I was hot mad; I just lost it. At this point, I didn't care if Ka'reema whooped my ass. I was by the garbage can near the front steps and so I pulled out a 40 oz. bottle of beer and threw it at her. It missed and broke on the wall.

"F—k you b—ch! You ain't sh—t!" I yelled at her.

Maaaaaaan, she flew down those stairs like a bat out of hell! I reached into the garbage and grabbed another bottle swinging it at her and cracking her in her damn head. The bottle barely busted open though, and Manny pushed it out my hand, blocking me from her.

I was sick of her though. And what could she do that she hadn't already done? Manny stepped up to hold Ka'reema back, grabbing her left arm, as she's a lefty. But that heffa' hooked me with her right, nicking my chin. What kind of grabbing was Manny doing for her to get that off? He knows she's like a bull when she gets mad! And what kind of person would still fight after learning I was pregnant? I never understood that about some women. I fell back and almost stumbled into the fence, four feet away. Tracey caught me and pulled me out the gate.

"Come on before I have to shoot this b—ch and deal with Omar later."

Manny pushed Ka'reema down on the ground, hard. I heard her elbow knock on the cement when she fell, and she was grabbing it in pain. He almost started kicking her, but stopped himself and went to help me. I grabbed my stomach. I felt like Shakirah now, feeling that this chick was trying to hurt my baby. If I had a gun, I think I'd have shot her, 'cause I started looking at Tracey's purse hard.

Ka'reema jumped up and tried to come after Manny, but not too much 'cause she was still in pain. But Ms. Sista had just come outside. She hurried down the stairs and grabbed her daughter. Manny starting yelling, "Ma, she pregnant! Alisa is pregnant. Ka'reema gonna mess around and make my sista lose her baby! Why she going out like that! Please, take her in the house. I'm not gonna keep holding her back Ma."

Turning to me, Ms. Sista asked, "Did she hit you in the stomach?"

"No! I'm good. I just wanna go home. I'm good."

Ms. Sista getting sick with worry fell back, but gripped the porch railing and sat on the bottom porch step. Ka'reema becoming afraid of her mother's high blood pressure snapped out of her anger and tended to Ms. Sista. Manny put me in the car, and told Tracey to take me home. After we left, he and Ka'reema took Ms. Sista to the hospital. As much as he wanted to step off from K'areema, he didn't want to see no harm come to Ms. Sista.

But I heard after they took Ms. Sista back to be seen in the hospital, he took Ka'reema outside and jacked her up, smacked her, and shook the crap out of her. What is it with men and shaking? Don't they know that is still hitting? Anyway, she knowing she was dead wrong didn't fight back, which was rare for Ka'reema. She must *really, really* like Manny.

When I got home it was around 12:30 a.m. My face was hurting badly. I was so upset and didn't feel I deserved that, whether she knew I was pregnant or not. I kept thinkin' about what Ms. Sista said in her living room, before **Atilla the Hun** came busting in actin' all barbaric. She said that me and Omar's relationship was doomed from the start because he being Muslim didn't go about it the right way, Islamically. She said she warned Omar about this often, but he wouldn't listen, like he was in a trance or under a spell.

After I got a bag of ice and put it on my face, I called Shakirah and told her what had happened. Then I got out the Qur'an Omar had given me in the past and investigated some of the things I heard him talk about that I never read up on. I didn't know what else to do with myself. I read until I fell asleep.

About 2:30 in the morning, not long after my mother and stepfather came home, there was a rapping at the apartment door. I'd just started waking up when they came in. My mother opened the door and saw Omar standing in the hallway.

"Hey Ma. I just wanted to see Alisa and apologize to both of you for Ka'reema fighting her. She said she didn't know Alisa was pregnant, even though that's no excuse. And I wanted to ask about the baby. Nobody even told me, *I don't think that was right.*"

My mother was mind-boggled by what he was saying as she'd just come in from the party and had no clue what he was going on about. Moms came in my room all nervous to check on me. "Alisa, Alisa! What happened to you?"

I sat up in bed as she turned on the light. My mother saw all my bruises and damn near screamed my head off, "What the hell happened? Ka'reema did this to you? Why did she do this?"

But I just ignored her acting all frantic and crazy.

"Omar is in the living room. He came to see you. I can't believe this sh—t! Where were you? Why, I just don't get it!"

"I don't wanna see him lookin' like this. Tell him he got what he wanted; I got my ass whooped. He should feel better now. He probably told her to do it."

Omar hearing this raised his voice speaking to me, "Alisa I would never do that. You should know I wouldn't do that to you."

"Stoppit Alisa! He just found out," my mother said. "He knows about the baby and came to apologize. Go on, go." She tapped me on the butt helped me up and walked me out with her hands on my shoulders, my body was sore as hell.

As I headed toward the living room, she ran past me to the kitchen to get ice and hydrogen peroxide. In the living room, the light was on what seemed like full blast, so Omar saw his sister's work long before I was seven feet away from him. He looked me in the face and turned his head, shakin' it in anguish and disappointment at what Ka'reema did. Tears immediately built in his eyes; he was so hurt he couldn't even bite down on his jawbone. He almost looked weakened at first.

"I'm sorry," he said, putting his hand over his face in grief.

My mother yelled from the kitchen to my stepfather, "Babe, did you see Alisa's face?"

"I thought I heard him say something about fighting or—" He stopped short as he came into the living room and saw my face. "Oh my God! Ka'reema did that? You see this sh—t Omar? Look at her!" He was almost drunk. "A black and blue face and a pregnant belly? What's wrong with that picture Omar? That sh—t ain't right!" He said as he began walkin' back to his room angered.

"Yeah, that's what he said. He said his sister Ka'reema did it. But he feels bad babe, ain't his fault," my mother told him.

He turned toward Omar, "Do ya sista know this girl here pregnant? Is she crazy!" To Omar's silence, my stepfather just turned and walked back to his room in disgust, shakin' his head.

Omar, still looking away said in a low voice again, "I'm sorry; I really am sorry. And I'll deal with her tonight." His nose flared in anger at Ka'reema putting him in this situation. "She shouldn't have done that to you, pregnant or not; it wasn't her place, nobodies."

"Not too long ago, you wanted to though, remember? At your apartment? When you kept stopping yourself. You even picked up your 9mm gun. I guess you wanted to bust a cap in my—" He cut me off.

"I'd never cause you any harm. I moved my gun because I saw you were scared and looking over where you knew I kept it. I didn't want you to get no ideas, so I moved it."

We stood in silence. I was happy to hear that. It was one of the things on my mind. Back then, during our big fight, I thought he contemplated killing me; you had to see his fury to know what I'm talking about. As Omar stood before me, he took a deep, humiliating breath, with his eyes watered, as if he wanted to just

Andrea Clinton

break down and cry but decided to try to remain strong. But he couldn't bring himself to look at me anymore, so he stared off to one side or another, trying to focus. So, I stared at him, to read his body language and peep his emotions. He was done with me.

"So, you pregnant?" he finally asked.

"That's what they tell me," I said being sarcastic.

I turned my head away from him as he was now looking at me. I couldn't bear looking at him. I was so angry with him and his whole family.

"Yeah, I can see it. Why didn't you tell me? I had the right to know."

"I had the right to know you were still hustling drugs, but you kept that one to yourself didn't you? But then, you had to. How else would I have been the only grimy one in the relationship if everyone knew *you* were still doing wrong?"

"I, aaah, I apologize for any wrong I've done you. It was never my intention," he said very bland.

I guess he was trying to be diplomatic, but he should've done more than be so bland. He should've begged me back; held me until I stopped being stubborn and we made up! He knows how I am!

"Apology accepted. Too bad I wasn't given the opportunity to offer the same type of apology for all I've done. But then, I wore out my welcome didn't I? That's why you kicked me to the curb."

He tilted his head and took a deep breath in annoyance of me bringing it up, especially since it was apparent I was pregnant the night he shoved me across the bed and broke up with me.

"Look, I'll make it easy on you," I said after a moment. "I know it can't feel too good seeing what your sister did to me and your baby, so, I'm going to bed. Now you can go do you with ya lady friends, Mr. Muslim Man." I turned and started walking away.

"What are you gonna do?" he spit out of his mouth, as if I really was just *that* grimy in his eyes. Like I was one of them girls who'd get an abortion so a baby won't slow my role.

I turned back around and looked at him in disbelief. *He couldn't think I would get rid of my baby, could he?* I thought. Being offended, I began walking away again. I put up my hands as if that were the last straw with him.

"I'm sorry. I'm not trying to disrespect you," he said. "I just wanna know; I wanna hear it myself. I don't want nobody relaying nothing to me about *my* baby."

I stopped and looked back with my eyes squinted in anger, "Omar, you think only you Muslims have morals and principles?"

He looked like he felt helpless and stuck in this situation, and wished he chose his words more wisely. "No. I didn't say that. I just wanted to get some idea," veins popping out of his forehead. "Some idea of what you wanted to do. *That's all.* Just wanna make sure we're on the same page."

I went off like I lost my mind; pregnancy had me forget I was afraid of how crazed he could get, "You know what I want to do! You just wanna be hateful just like ya sista 'cause you mad at me 'cause I did you wrong! Like you was so innocent the whole time and I was the devil incarnate."

"I don't want to be hateful." He started chewing down on his jawbone. I felt he *hated* me being pregnant with us having all that stuff going on between us, and him dating different women, doing his player thing again. I was offended that we—me and the baby—weren't desirable, especially after seeing us there, needy for love and his attention. So I doubled back on my words and **gut-punched** the sh—t outta him. Damn real, a woman scorned!

"Don't make that disgusted face at me. You don't have to worry. I won't ruin your plans out here in these streets and with the ladies. I plan on getting an abortion first thing tomorrow morning, then go back to doing my gold digger thing. Why should Tracey get all the money out here?" I said, while raising my eyebrows and smirking at him in a rude girl demeanor.

My mother who was listening in on us burst out of the kitchen and into the living room. She passed him and grabbed me, shushing me as I grew angrier and loud at his silence.

"So you don't have to worry about this horrible sinful *baby of the bed* as y'all call it! Coming in here looking down on me and talking to me like, 'Let me see what Ms. Sinful Bad-ass, Can't-Get-Right is gonna do wrong now!' You ain't betta' than me! And Omar you ain't foolin' nobody with all that you fell weak when you was with me bullsh—t. Don't gimme that cop-out stuff y'all

Andrea Clinton

be talkin'! *YOU SLEPT WITH ME NIGGA! Each day, each night, each month, each year* and that's a long time to be making a mistake, falling weak! You know what you did. *You ain't foolin' me!* You's a sinful muthaf—ka just like me! **JUST LIKE ME! JUST-LIKE-ME!** You ain't no betta' than me **NIGGA!** You ain't no betta' than me! *Remember that!*

He just stood there, tears rolling down his eyes, anger boiling. He looked as if he was filled with mixed emotions, tryin' to read if I was sayin' that out of anger or speakin' how I felt about him, the baby, everything. He knew I could get grimy when payin' a joker back for crossin' me and he just crossed me, asking me was I gonna get an abortion. And he knew I wasn't above gut punchin' a nigga when they're down, *by all means.* So he stood there lookin' as if he just caused his baby's death; it was killin' him.

"Alisa please!" my mother butted in. "Be quiet. Don't disturb the baby more than it's already been. She just mad Omar. Please, let her cool down." She was trying to get him to leave, and not keep this going.

"Ain't gonna be no baby Omar!" I kept ripping into him. "'Cause that's how I roll, **right Gee!** *Right Omar?!* **RIGHT NIGGA!"** I bellowed with all I had, with my mother holding me back.

He snapped; Omar reached in his pocket, took out a knot of money and threw it hard at the floor in front of me. He turned to walk out the door. Then looking back, said calmly, although angrily, "Since you decided, here, I'll spring for the abortion and then some." And with that, he stormed out, went to his car and after a minute or so, he sped off.

I swear I could've shot his ass. It didn't make no difference to him if I kept the baby or not. As I lay on my bed crying, with my mother rubbing my back, I felt it was like Ms. Sista said, "All this stuff is happening with you two because you did things your way, instead of God's way." She said nothing good would ever become of us, and it never did. After I saw and heard Ms. Sista say that in my mind, I thought, *When will this hurt be over with? It's like an ongoing punishment out this mug.* Was I that bad?

I spent the whole night tossing and turning, sad 'cause it was clear me and Omar was over. But most of all I was wondering,

Should I keep this baby? Be like every other girl, left with kids, somebody's baby-mamma? For what? I knew what would happen if I did that, I knew. Eventually, welfare, having way less than half the things I was used to, loneliness, and mad responsibilities. I didn't know what to do. I needed to decide.

If I got an abortion, at least then I could pick up where I left off dating for dough, self-preservation. 'Cause things are changed now. *I wasn't thinkin' about choices before. I was keepin' my baby.* But I didn't know how Omar felt. But now, after what he said, I know, the baby was a burden. He picked that fight on purpose. He doesn't want any ties to me. But, I—I can't imagine killin' me and Omar's baby; that's *too* wicked. But then, that baby mamma stuff, **UUUUUGH!!!** And I'm way too selfish. And there's a woman in New York who will do an abortion up to six months of pregnancy. Malika, Sherry, KC and half the rich girls go to her. It's safe with antibiotics, herbs. And hey, *Tracey made five g's?* We could watch each other's back for that. **Uuuh!** Decision made, I had a life to live. So, the next business morning KC gave me the secretary's number and I made the earliest appointment for the abortion, which was months away, *actually,* a day or so after *this party.* But at the time, I couldn't stick around 'til the abortion so I left Man-Man and Manny a note saying, "Maybe you'll get a niece or nephew the next go-round." I left my mother a note saying, "Ssshhh," and she knew what that meant. *Don't tell anyone, I'm still pregnant.* Then I boarded the next flight back to California. I stayed with Shakirah until I was almost five months pregnant. When I put on my li'l nightgown, you could see my stomach cupping with a li'l basketball look.

I kept in touch with my mother who was prayin' I didn't get an abortion. She was so afraid she didn't tell anyone back home I was still pregnant. She just made them think another one bit the dust. *I hadn't even told her my decision,* and to get me to keep it she was overly nice about everything. But, I'm stubborn, once my mind is made up—and, my mind is already made up of what I'm going to do so, she could stop.

Finally, Shakirah, having just had the twins, a boy and a girl, decided it was time to tell Man-Man. We took the train back home,

Andrea Clinton

as I couldn't fly, so the family could see the twins. She decided to tell Man-Man a week before we came back, and although he forgave her somewhat for leaving with his babies and not letting him know she was still pregnant, he had no words for me. After all, I was supposed to be his sister and I didn't tell him.

But what did I care? He was the one having double dates with Omar and other women. Please! Tracey had given me the 411 on everythang. What he did was two-faced in itself, so what allegiance did I owe him?

Anyway, we got back in town and took a taxi van home. I stayed outta view while a few close friends and family were all over Shakirah and her babies. My mother set up tables in the yard, and cooked a lot of food—fried chicken, BBQ chicken, yams, macaroni and cheese, collard greens, cornbread, peach cobbler, banana puddin' and all that junk. I stayed in my damn room, didn't wanna see anyone. Everyone thought my mother finally shipped me off to Georgia after my abortion; that's the rumor that was going around. But I stayed in my room and kept my door locked.

Shakirah was kind though, even with having all that spotlight on her and the twins. Most would've been in their own world. But she kept coming in the room to check on me, "Alisa you straight?" But one of those times, Shakirah came in and bought Peaches and Tracey. She was worried as she hadn't checked on me for two hours. And they were determined to follow her to see what she was up to, at least that's what they told me later on. When they arrived in my room, after screamin' and huggin' me, Tracey kneeled on the foot of my bed, sat back and they gave me the 411.

Then, "So what's up pimp? You good?" Tracey said to me being sarcastic. But then she hugged me so tight it hurt my head. She came in smiling with them gold and diamond teeth, diamond nose ring and her diamond rings, necklace and tennis bracelets on looking like a gypsy, earrings all up both ears now.

"Yeah I'm kool," as I leaned against the headboard.

"You really not feeling ya family huh?" Peaches said.

"Nope. They always tryin' to get funky, or blowing my stuff up worse than everybody else's. So, I'm thinking about going back to California."

Kneeling on the foot of the bed again, "Girl no! Chill out. I got you," Tracey said. "Have the baby. Let Moms babysit while we get that playerette-pimpin' money; get our mack goin' on again."

"Tracey shut the hell up!" Me and Peaches said, as we all laughed. Peaches sat between me and Trace on the edge of the bed.

"This girl done really hung up her pimp *AND* player hat," Tracey said putting her hands on her hip staring at me like she was shocked. "You not gettin' ya grub on no more Alisa? **You going from scrimps and steak,** *back to pork and beans and hot dogs?* Gonna feed that baby puree beans in a bottle?" She raised her eyebrows trying to talk me into my old ways.

"Anyway," Peaches intervened, "ya family say something to you about the baby?"

"No, they don't know nothin' and I wanna keep it that way," as I looked at her and Tracey asking them to keep quiet.

"Oh, okay. I got you," Peaches assured me she wouldn't say a word.

"I dunno, I might tell." Tracey butted in. "Unless you give me $200. **Extortion ho, pay up!**"

I just looked at her shaking my head and smiling.

Tracey's suspicious ass looked at me, moved in closer, then started, "Oh snap, you still runnin' game ain't you nigga? You don't want them to tell Omar 'cause you want him to think you got an abortion, play on his guilt! Aaahaa-haa! You crazy!" She went for a high five. "I feel you dog. I got you too. *U'm ain't gon' say nuffin,*" she said being silly, speakin' even more ghetto than usual.

"Tracey shut up! She ain't runnin' game on Omar. You always think somebody trying to run game!" Peaches said as she screwed up her face at a smiling Tracey who knew I didn't tell Omar I'm still pregnant. Then Peaches looked at me. "Oh snap," she said seeing me staring at Tracey with a semi-smirk on my face. "*You really runnin' game on Omar?* Oh my God, that man gonna kill you one day! Yo Alisa, you ain't learn yet playin' them games. Yo Tracey done turned this girl out! Yo, **you Tracey's ho!** I can't believe you didn't tell Omar you still pregnant; you ain't learned yet? Tracey really turned you out."

Andrea Clinton

"Like a 50-cent crack ho, **haaaaa**!" Tracey said. "And you knew I knew b—ch. Yo, game know game. Can't tell me I don't know. And girl, them niggaz deserve it. He runnin' round here with all them hos, actin' like him and Alisa didn't mean nothin'. Who he foolin'? Get'em girl! Rrrruuuuuuf! Ssssick'em, haahaaa. Continue gut-punchin' that ass! *POW!* **Oh she my peoples!**"

Turning to Shakirah, Peaches said, "She gonna get Alisa killed!"

Shakirah started looking through one of her bags. "You better hope that *pow* don't fire back, literally," Shakirah said.

Peaches shook her head agreeing with Shakirah, ashamed that I was still playing games. Shakirah had nerves saying anything. Hell, she just did the same to my brother, hiding her pregnancy. I sat quiet, and Peaches looked ashamed of all of us

"Anyway, back to your family. So they giving you grief?"

"Yeah Peaches, I'm tryin' to avoid them. I'm gettin' a hotel room; be away from everybody. Have my mother come spend the night with me so we could just talk and she could spoil me."

"Sounds good, as long as I can sleep in ya room, while you there. That is when I'm not home with my mother," Shakirah said. "Wait let me go get your food now before I forget again."

"Oh," Peaches said, "I'm coming to your mother's birthday party too. I just bought my outfit. And ya cousin Shorty, although he's six feet," we laughed, "pushed up on me so we'll see what's up at the party. It's gonna be in your yard right? I'm puttin' it on; I got a red sleeveless outfit, **BOW!**"

"**With ya manish ass!**" Tracey said making us all laugh.

I forgot all about that party, I thought, *Dang! I was so busy trying to dodge people here.*

"Well I got a *cute, tight, sleeveless, short, skimpy* dress I'm wearing," Tracey said with excitement, grossing Peaches out.

"Yeah, I bought this baaaad dress, navy, satin, with matching shoes by this young black designer called Ikeema, in Newark," Shakirah said. "It ran me $300, and the shoes are fly as hell so I hope they have that deck built in the yard in time so we can get our dance on."

"Shakirah, how could you not remind me? Dang I forgot!"

"Ho *you told me!* You hear this girl?" as she turned to Peaches and Tracey.

"Dang, now I'm depressed all over again," I said.

It was as if I didn't say anything. Everyone just kept talking and laughing as if it were my problem that I didn't prepare ahead how us women usually do, or if I had nothing to wear, forgot, or whatever. But, after all the laughin' and jokin' on one another, they stayed for about an hour, and we laughed and were being silly about everything and nothing at all. It was nice though, seeing my peoples again. I missed them and was hurt at how I was so bogged down with school and Bo on the side, in my own world that I forgot about them. And after a while, after being around them, laughing like we were, I began to miss my man. And then being woke didn't seem like much fun anymore. So I went to sleep.

After the cookout, I talked my mother into coming with me to a hotel. So we got a room right outside of town. She was acting paranoid like Shakirah, worried something would happen to my baby, so she was down with me staying away from the rest of the folks. My moms spent two days with me without going home at all. My stepfather even came and sat with us for a few hours each day. He was worried about me too. Neither of them told Man-Man or Manny I was still pregnant, and my stepfather said their believing I had an abortion influenced Omar to believe it. But what got me was that the rumor going around, that I had an abortion and was shipped to Georgia, conflicted with the *fact* that I was in Cali, and my brother's knew I was in Cali, but they believed the Georgia rumor; people are stupid.

Anyway, Shakirah called me at the hotel and told me that she and Man-Man wanted to move the party, make it a big bash at this big expensive hall, well Man-Man was paying, she was planning it.

"How she hooked up our party, huh, we gonna make her birthday party fly, off the hook!"

But I was like, "In two days?" I'm like, it's sorta late to change a li'l backyard dinner to a banquet hall bash. But they were determined because she threw them *a nice baby shower with all the food and music*, and he definitely had the dough to make it happen, so he did.

Andrea Clinton

Here @ *The Party*.

Are you all caught up Goddess Athena? Well those are all the events that took place, which led to me up here alone, at my mother's birthday party. There are a lot of people here, even Ms. Sista and her clan. And I resolved myself to the fact that Omar would most likely show up at some point with some woman.

When I was downstairs, before Penny drove up and got in my face, I stayed away from Ka'reema, who I couldn't believe they'd allowed to come. I avoided Brother Abdul-Malik like lung cancer 'cause I know that's what he probably thinks I was to his son, suckin' out all his oxygen. And I avoided Ms. Sista, although it pained me not to talk to her. But after an hour or so, she made her way over to me. I turned around to see who was tapping me from behind. I looked into her eyes, dropped my head in shame and I began shedding tears. She reached out to me, to give me a hug. Of course I leaned forward so she couldn't see my belly. She hugged me tight, but I sheltered my belly with my big Fendi bag. I'd learned how to do that so no one was the wiser. She felt for me in my *lonely without him state*; because she related to my mischievous ways, she always did feel for me.

"My son got a woman just like his momma, troublesome." She paused, looking and smiling at me. "It's the curse of the pretty woman that we act like that. People always telling us how pretty we are, so we think the world is our oyster; bunch of saps we are. Omar, he couldn't help but go after you. It's in a man's nature to be attracted to women who are like their mothers, *and sometimes grandmothers.* How you gonna climb out of this mess, and get ya man back? That's what you need to be asking yourself," she said.

"Ms. Sista, too much has happened. He won't forgive me for all I did, and I won't forgive him for gettin' over me, trading me in for other women, and so many, like changing pants."

"I *dunno about all that.* But you know like I know, you'll get ya man back. You see how me and Brother Abdul-Malik are back together, after what, 12 years, maybe more, I dunno. You know what it do to a relationship to overcome a bad experience? To learn and prosper from it? Girrrrl, make a young man into a man, and a young woman grown. 'Cause you feel like you been through something, and you have."

"Ms. Sista, you know all that is over my head right now."

"Making up isn't for everybody. But, it's darn sure for y'all. You both look lost or like something's missing without each other, like you have nothing to look forward to. You both look like the walking dead. All sad, and *you look pale.* It'd be a shame for y'all to let it go; a shame."

We spoke for a few minutes more and she was happy to know I was doing fine. She made a li'l more mention of Omar, but not much.

"Omar hasn't been the same. He went through a spell of these tantrums and acting up out here in the streets. He felt like you snatched the rug from under him, made him forsake his lord, only to cheat on him. But for the last couple of months he's been calming down and going to the *masjid,* making his prayers five times a day and attending classes there. May Allah guide him, *amin.* He's been visiting his father daily at the halfway house, taking him to the *masjid* and other stuff. He's been doing good. He finally sees not marrying you, he bought a lot on himself and he knows that it probably cursed y'all situation, 'cause you put the things in this life first, not God, ALLAH. But it's made him a better Muslim," she said, proud he learned from his mistakes.

I just nodded and shed more tears. "I guess him messing around with me slowed him down from what he was trying to get back to huh? I guess now he knows I'm no-good for him, too un-Islamic," as I shed a few tears.

"I dunno what he thinks sweetie. Allah knows best. But I think he learned a few lessons of his own. Hopefully you did too."

"Yeah, but what good are they to me now?" I asked, as I began to turn away.

She felt bad for my sorrow and invited me over to her house. I told her I would call her and maybe we could go out somewhere. I was really not in the mood for that house nor the people in it, namely Ka'reema or Omar, who could possibly pop over just when I was there, and Lord knows how that might turn out.

Ms. Sista and I parted ways. I immediately went and sat in the corner with Shakirah and Peaches, so I could continue hiding my business.

I had a small glass of apple juice, mainly because I thought people would think it was a glass of Hennessy and would assume I *really did* have the abortion, and they did. So, I sat there, sipping on my glass of apple juice, fake Henny, and I just looked at everyone dancing, and mingled with my girls every now and again. I was glad all my friends and family were up dancing and enjoying the expensive festivities Man-Man and Manny paid for. Manny couldn't let Man-Man pay for the party alone, since he too was her son.

Manny of course came over and kissed me on the forehead. We spoke, he let me know he knew I was pregnant, but he didn't tell Man-Man, 'cause Man would've just ran and told Omar. And he promised not to tell Ka'reema, which set my mind at ease. Then we dropped the subject and watched everyone dance. They played some song and Manny jumped up and started dancing with some girl. Ka'reema got angry, but, I think after that issue with me, he had her in check 'cause she chilled out, all the way out.

I felt my mother looking at me, so I turned to her, and she put her finger up signaling she'd be over to me in a minute, when she finished talking to my aunt Tina. So, I just sat there thinking to myself. Finally I couldn't take it anymore. I wanted to be just as happy and giddy as everyone else, especially the love-birds Man-Man and Shakirah. I had always thought that by the time I was pregnant, I would be happily married. I had high hopes for me and

Omar, and I never knew it 'til now. I just took too much for granted. And I still had feelings of love for him, and those feelings were strong, even after everything that happened. I know I love him, but I began to ponder, *am I in love with him though?* Could I be *in love with him*, **really** *in love*? Being *in love* and loving or feeling for a person are two different things. I never thought about it to this degree. But I am; I'm *in love* with him, and I have been all along. Just too arrogant and selfish to see, and now it's too late.

Older girls always said not to let yourself fall in love at a young age. Tracey taught me to *never* allow it. So, I never allowed it, nor asked myself, *are you in love with him?* My head was in too many places anyway, with school and my father in my life now. And what good is it to realize I'm in love with him now? Why now? I realize it at a time when I can do nothing about it. It was as if Satan had taken me by the collar, pushed me to behave badly, and when he was done having his fun, and making me mess up my life, he kicked me to the curb.

I'd followed my Great-Grandma's instruction; yep, I did adamantly. *I found a man who loved me more than I loved him.* But what came after that, no one prepared me for. Was I supposed to merely stay with him? Show him love so long as he continued loving me more? Was I supposed to give him my heart and true love once I knew he loved me more? And what would happen if he stopped loving me? It was just too much to think about, and there were no answers. *How do you die and leave a person with something of significance like that, knowing the effect and importance of advice from the deathbed? How do you die and leave the most crucial part out? How? That's just evil!* **Evil!**

Finally my mother came over to me. She said the faces I was making 'cause I was all caught up and confused in what I was thinking about, was gettin' to her. She hugged me and asked me to tell her what was on my mind. I didn't want to talk, so she pulled me into a small coatroom off to the side. She tried to dance it out of me, holding my hands, trying to get me to groove with her in the two step. But, I was feeling my woe too strong for all that. So I just began shedding tears, heavily, and with the most humiliating and helpless face a daughter could wear, and standing there pregnant, my mother felt my pain.

"When I was young," I told her as I began to shed tears, "Great-Grandma said to me when she was dying to always get a man who loves you more than you love him. I did, I had Omar. But, when I arrived, when I knew he loved me more than I loved him, I didn't know what was next. So, being young and all about what I was about, I mistreated him, and, I, I took him for granted. I acted spoiled, rotten, and I didn't care. I think a part of me thought what she was saying is that not only would he treat me like a queen, but he'd always be there for me, no matter what. I thought I had time to get right, and be a better fiancée. I thought he'd never let me go. But he did; *he dumped me,*" as I cried harder. My mother pulled me into her and I cried so, so hard.

"Poor baby. *You just think too much Alisa.* The philosophy is that a man takes a woman who's in love with him for granted, especially if they figure *you really* love them. Once you got a man who loves you more than you love him, he'd treat you like a queen, and while you thinking straight, 'cause you not the one bent over in stupid love, you can nurture that relationship to being what makes you both happy. You only needed to relax and enjoy the ride baby, and in return for him making you his queen, you just had to treat him like a king. That was all."

Talking about feeling stupid. I felt like a real jackass, and the penalty, the price of my stupidity was the man I love.

My mother just hugged me until I told her to go join her party. She went to the bathroom and got me a wet paper towel, and that's when **Ms. It** walked in. Talk about having bad timing, Penny came strutting in like she was gonna show me up in front of my own family. I saw her and just lost it; I believe she of all people saw my belly and decided she was gonna be the bell of the ball. As I was dashing out after Penny, fussin', Shakirah and Peaches saw and rushed out first, you already know how that went, with me, us backing her up outside and almost knocking her chin off.

Up here, on the balcony, I could've stood all night looking up at the stars, but, I saw what looked like Omar's Cadillac. Maybe it was, maybe it wasn't; so many people drive them Cadillac's nowadays. But the last thing I wanted was for anyone to see me, and disturb the beautiful quiet and the scenery I was experiencing.

So now I'm over here on the lounger, in the here and now, lonely and all alone, with my pants' loosened, a leg on each side of this lounger improperly opened but comfortable with this big belly. I'm leaning back with my hands behind me, holding me up while I dig in the scene, and enjoy this beautiful night air. The night sky is a dark room with still fireflies through and through. This is a comfortable night. It's a good night.

As my Grandma says oh Goddess Athena, "No need to fret. Just think it over, and weigh in." Well, I've thought my story over, and regarding me and Omar, I've weighed in, and as sad as it is to say, I realize now, we really are over, and *it is what it is...*

The End.

Andrea Clinton

Epilogue

I guess that's the host I hear coming to tell me I'm not supposed to be up here. But they're going to have to call security because my stomach feels relaxed now with my pants open. Don't know how much longer I can wear them fastened.

"I was about to give up looking for you—I thought you left.

Oh my God, that sounds like, what, Omar. It is him, Athena. Look at him walking to the balcony, staring up at the sky like everything is kool. Let me sit up and fix my clothes before he looks down and sees my belly.

"No, sorry to disappoint. I'm still here."

Aaiiight, my clothes are fixed. He won't be able to tell I'm pregnant.

Why's he staring at the floor? What's he getting up the gumption to hit me with?

"I forgive you for going out with that guy."

"Gee, that's what I've been waiting all this time to hear."

I can't resist Athena. I dunno why I gotta hit him up with sarcasm. I think it's my nerves; I'm gettin' nervous. *Why?* Because that's him, OMAR. Okay, okay, calm down, calm down. I know, ain't he cute? I hope he don't see me looking at you and think I'm crazy. You think he know I'm talking to you in my mind? What? *You want me to break the silence and admit I was wrong?* **Oh my God!** I dunno. Okay, stop rushing me. Dag-gonnit! Okay!

Ummmppp, he beat me to the punch. Next pause, I'll say I was wrong.

"Okay. I aaaaaah, Alisa, I did some wrong. I wasn't hearing you about school. I just wanted what I wanted. I can't say maybe you aren't cut out for college, I know better. I even came to the conclusion that maybe, which I'm sorry I didn't think of at the time, but maybe you should've changed your major to something *you* were interested in, something more enjoyable to you. Instead of listening to me say computers are the way to the future."

"Should've, could've, would've."

Goddess, I'm sorry, nothing kosher is coming to mind for me to say. I'm afraid; I don't know if he's gonna walk out *anyway*. He could have a woman downstairs and I'll really look like a fool giving in. Plus, *he expects me to act like a butthole*, so this ain't far fetched. Okay, let me tune back in to what he's saying. Wait a minute, he's silent again. Okay here's my chance.

Nope, too slow again.

"Alisa, baby, I know you ain't got nothin' left for *me*, but I'm really trying here."

"*Trying what?* What are you trying Omar?"

Goddess, that's it, I can't be nice. For what? We're done remember. Please, he don't love me no more, he just has a huge conscience about what *he* did wrong. Okay, okay, I'll try; gimme a minute.

"All right Alisa. I see where we are. We're just, done, over. Fine, I get it. And we can't even be civil."

Athena, he's walking toward the door. I just can't do right by him. If God gives me one more chance—

"Like I said Alisa, I forgive you for cheating on me with that guy, whether you slept with him or not, and I don't believe you did, but I don't know if I will ever forgive you for killing my baby. May Allah have mercy on your soul for it, *amin*."

"May he have mercy on yours for accusing and assuming I'm so wicked, cruel and selfish, I could kill my baby." Yeah Athena, I'm leaning back, gonna rub my stomach too so he can see my pregnant belly. Show him he don't know me like he think; and

I'm not that wicked; I basically dropped the abortion thought after I made the appointment. When I calmed down, so did the notion.

Look at Omar, taking three steps back and staring down at my stomach. His face is tight. "What? Aaaaaay, yooooooo-man. You said—your brothers said you did it."

"I was mad at all of you. Nobody would give me no understanding. So I kept it to myself."

Athena, he's so in shock, he's startin' to shed tears. Why do I do this to him, always?

"Yo, you said you were getting an abortion."

He's more humble now than he was before. I feel so sorry for him crying. I feel double-bad now. Will he please stop shedding tears Athena, aaaah.

"I'm sorry. I shouldn't have let you believe that. But I felt so all alone, abandoned. And it seemed like as soon as you got rid of me, the world was yours: women, two stores doing good, people admiring your player status again. But I could never kill my baby."

Look at him in shock over my belly. He wanna smile, blush, cry; he's so handsome.

"You looked so small, with no stomach when you were downstairs. Wait you were drinking?"

He's looking over at my glass of apple juice, my fake Henny. Oh my goodness, he's disgusted. "Why you drinking with my baby?" He's lifting my glass ready to start an argument. I don't know how this is gonna play out.

I'll take the high road Athena. "It's juice. You just don't have no faith in me at all do you? Not even any hope that I know *some* good do you? Damn. Maybe *I am* the devil incarnate."

"No, you just bad sometimes and you get a kick outta being like that. Can I touch it? I won't for long. I don't wanna make you feel uncomfortable."

"Go ahead, I'm fine. It's your baby, touch it."

It feels good having him here with me, talking about the baby. I'm almost overjoyed. But I gotta be careful, some woman can still pop up here talkin' 'bout, "Are you ready yet baby?" or something like that. If I mess around and get excited, I'll get my feelings hurt. I know you think I'm paranoid, but I don't like surprises.

He's rubbing my stomach gently, still in shock.

"Wow; aaaaaaw man. *I'm glad you didn't kill my baby.*"

He's starting to look a little sad.

"And I'm so sorry you thought I ever could be down with that, with what we meant to each other, *even with my bad ways.* I may not have done the college thing right, but look how I was reading the Qur'an, even when you weren't there, asking you questions and stuff. I thought those things stood for something."

"We just didn't do things how they were supposed to be done, so it all went foul. And I just didn't know what to think. You changed so darn much. I felt like I couldn't pray enough for you, or for us. It started seeming like trying to help you, and change you to be better than them hood-rat gold diggers you use to run with was killing you, shredding ya spirit. I didn't want to think you were that bad a person. But you were acting crazier and crazier. I could never figure your feelings or emotions, or what you would or wouldn't do or say next. And after that dude...."

That Bo thing must still bother him, 'cause he's pausing, dropping his head. It's time I speak up and soothe his hurt feelings.

"I'm sorry I stepped out of bounds on you with another man. I was just tryin' to act out. I never thought it would've gotten to you like it did, to kick me out and get rid of me forever. I thought when and if you found out, we'd get past it. *Well, I really thought you'd just give me my way and let me quit school since that's where I met him.* I didn't know you'd bring us to an end, especially when you know how I like playing my games sometimes."

"I don't play when it comes to another man, and I told you that many times Alisa; a hard head makes a soft—"

"Truc, you got that. I just let my stress from school overtake me. But I never cheated on you, EVER! I mean *I know it doesn't mean anything now,* but I'd never do that to you. I'm not two-faced like that. What was mine was yours, and yours alone; everything."

"It does mean something now. You still mean something to me; can't seem to live right without you. My heart hurts when I see your pictures, or some of your things."

"O' you wasn't thinking about me until you found out I was pregnant. You were too busy with ya two stores, chillin' with

Andrea Clinton

Penny and that heffa' I saw you with at my mother's anniversary party."

"I knew you wouldn't give me credit and think about the fact that I'm smart enough to realize I only have those two stores because of YOU, so you must've loved me to some degree to push so hard for me to go for it. And I figured you'd never think that you caring that much about me is what would make me NOT hate you. It showed me that you really did love me as much as I loved you, because you were serious about me not going to jail. You put all your rebellious ways to the side to look out for *me*, in a way nobody ever really did. You used my feelings for you to put my back up against the wall, and make me do right, and I did. But I knew you'd feel too sorry for yourself to see I'd think about all of that."

"But you didn't do right. You still continued to have runners out there hustling."

"I had something important I had to deal with, that I couldn't just up and walk away from."

"Even if it would've landed you in jail? You lied to me Omar."

"I had to do it. I had to do what I did."

"No. I think you just didn't care what happened to the relationship anymore."

"*No!* Baby, I can't tell you *everything*. I really, REALLY had to do something for a good friend. I had to."

"No, *you had to secure your future family.* And what friend would you put before your family? *Where was the love for me?*"

Omar's probably looking away 'cause he don't wanna lie, but he can't tell me the truth. He's not answering me. What's he hiding? Oh I think I know who.

"Omar, who? Who were you—*Man-Man?* Aaaan-huh. Helping him do what?"

"Baby, you know I can't—"

"*After what you allowed us to go through, maaaaan, you better tell me!*"

"Aww man. Look here."

Look at him, taking a deep breath and thinking it over, "promise you'll take it to the grave? You can't go talking."

"To the grave; I promise."

"Something went **bad**, and if Man-Man didn't have this money, it was either him or your father. *You follow me?* Either one gettin' taken out by the powers that be would've killed Man-Man, and that's my boy, true friend, my brother like no other. I had to have his back. And you know Manny and *his* temper, so he couldn't be a help; he doesn't even know 'til this day about any of this. So, it had to be me to help Man-Man. It was only right; he was there for me almost all of my life; from the time we were in that picture ya mother has of us at three years old where Man broke his potato chip and gave me half, on up 'til now *baby*. He's **always** been a brother to me, and I couldn't leave him hanging for **nobody**; he good people. That aside, you should know better than to ever think I wasn't thinking about you, or our life together."

"But you were so cold when you came to the house to see me, even after you saw my black and blue marks that your sister gave me. You didn't come and grab me or hug me or anything. It was like you didn't love me no more, and like you weren't thinking about me any more."

"I almost died when I saw your face. My knees buckled, *I couldn't believe it*. I wanted to wear that black eye for you. If she wasn't my sister, I might've taken her life; I was so pissed. *And I was always thinking about you*, praying and everything—I just figured too much had happened for anything I could've done to make a difference. I cried like a little girl when I left your mother's apartment. I wanted to hug you so **bad**, girl, you will NEVER know what was in my heart that night. I wanted the whole problem to go away and have my baby come back home. And it took everything I was worth not to wreck out! Even though I did act up later. But I swear I wanted to hold you. But so much fury and confusion was in me, damn there thought I was gonna pass out. But, I wanted to hug you so much it hurt, I really did."

"*Then why didn't you?*"

"Because, **you bad Alisa**. And I was hurting too bad on the inside, and I knew *you* were. I couldn't think right. And with all the talk about what Ka'reema did to you and how you could probably lose the baby because of it, I was scared. And then you wasn't making it no better, mouthing off, talking about getting an abor—*I can't even say it.*"

"And Penny? You always wanted her or somethin'?"

"*Come on now baby; you gonna pick me apart?* Penny threw herself my way that day, the night before your parents' anniversary party. She wouldn't step off, so I let her come there with me to see if you still had feelings. I saw you a li'l while before I came in, when they bought you there, when you were walking in the door. I didn't see your stomach then though. But I got mad when I saw you did still love me, because I wondered how you could do what you did with that brutha, knowing you had strong feelings for me."

"Stupid I guess. And, I wasn't thinking about feelings and love. Just face it, you spoiled me. You should've listened to your first mind when you said you were going to tell me 'no' sometimes, even if for no reason so I didn't become *that* spoiled monster you hate in women, but you didn't. You were down with *everything.* You gave me unconditional, way-way too early, and I guess I didn't know what to do with it, took it for granted. If Bo would've been a female, I'd have still gone to lunch with 'em, something to do to get away from school. But, was I *that* bad, honestly?"

Was that good enough Goddess? Am I on point with him yet? *Wink or something.*

"You were horrible. *I thought you were possessed*; I thought a demon crawled up in you and set up shop; embarrassing me in front of friends and family, cursing me out like we were niggaz in the streets, you even put ya hands on me a few times. Had me seconds from physical abuse; *Allah forgive me.* I mean, I, more than anyone knew you were pulling your hair out over school, but, sometimes, you were just **ridiculous**. But, I was trying to bear with you, since I was the one putting the stress on your back about college. But you just took it too far Alisa."

"Well, I'm sorry. I'm very sorry. And I pray to God, or as you say, Allah, us breaking up was punishment enough. I'm also glad I don't come between you and Islam anymore. Being a proper Muslim is going to help you be an even better man than you already were. I realized with us being apart, you are a very good man, aside from the street activity. I think being a proper Muslim will help you live more peaceful; that's what you wanted anyway. That's what you always wanted; glad you finally got it."

"Wasn't easy getting where I am; had it out with my father because I acted up so horribly in the streets after we broke up. He said he'd kill me before he let me turn out like him, let a woman get me off my *deen,* religion. He bust me in the head a few times to prove it too; he even pulled a gun on me saying he'd end my life before he let a woman end my life. He said, '**Ain't gone be no instant replay with my kids life!**' But that's a story for another time. He just hated to see me suffer and he knew my pain. He went over the top with the gun though, but, I guess I pushed him."

"Yeah, I heard about your shoot outs you were in. I can imagine how much he hates and blames me for what you were doing. But you good now, so it's all good for you and ya father, everybody."

"Yeah, *Alhamdulillah,* praise due to Allah. It will be good for the baby too. I just needed to snap out of it, calm down."

"Yeah, but as for me, I think I'm a whole other type of job and responsibility, too much for you to try and handle again. You don't need someone like me for a girlfriend; I can't get right."

"Slow down, you act like I asked you to be my lady again. There *you* go assuming. Hahahaha ahahahaaaa."

Look at him, cracking that joke on me and laughing; I'm playing if off half-smiling. I don't mean to shed tears, but the thought that he's breaking it to me nicely is making me sad, making tears fall from my eyes. But, he's just that kind of man to spare my feelings by telling me he ain't interested in a round two, through a joke.

"I hear you. I'm not mad at you. I can see why you don't want me no more."

Wow, even more tears beginning to fall from the thought of him putting me on knock-off.

"No—no I don't want you for my girlfriend anymore, never, ever again. That part of us is **dead**. **Dead** to the world. I've matured. I've moved on in my *deen*, meaning *my religion*, and I've outgrown a lot of things, and fortunately, a lot of bad habits. I know it's only been months, but, Allah has a way of teaching you.

Andrea Clinton

He says He will have you submitting to His will either willing, or unwillingly. But either way, *you will submit*. He brought me unwillingly because all I wanted to do was be there for you, with you; not putting Him and His will first. So, no, I'm not interested in you being my girlfriend anymore; I won't anger Allah Again."

"Okay, okay, I get it. And, I understand. You don't wanna bring hell in ya life twice."

"But, I do still have feelings for you. I still love you."

Athena! I'm trying to stop shedding tears, but I can't. Why is he sticking this dagger in my heart and so deep? I know I was wrong, *but I'm sorry. I swear*, I don't know how I'm going to get through this night. I want to go to sleep! *It's finally over for good*. I always thought it might be a tiny bit of hope, *maybe*. But he's like his father now. He's not gonna sin like that no more, and he's not gonna have my troubled *you-know-what* back in his life. I can see it; he doesn't trust that I matured just like he did. I don't blame him. *I got issues*. But I did mature. I know what I had, and I see what I have now, nothing. What better lesson to learn than how your bullsh—t can end you up lonely and alone?

"I know you still have feelings for me Omar, I guess. And, aaah, I love you too. But I guess I've grown up also. I'm willing to accept and deal with the punishment for my actions. *No beef.* You deserve someone who's caring, and mature enough to show it on a regular, under pressure or not. Not a spoiled, selfish ghetto princess like I was. I'm glad you want better for yourself Islamically and otherwise. I believe what we went through taught me to chill the hell out and grow up too. I don't have the same needs or wants as before. No stilettos, diamonds, well *I still like diamonds, let me not get carried away*, but you know what I mean; I just want a healthy baby. Imagine me not thinking of myself first any more. Huh, I think the baby is the cause of that though. Don't worry about me, nor my tears. I didn't really think you'd want me for your girl with what you're into now."

"Alisa, I'm not trying to hurt you, stop crying baby. Come on, listen, I am saying, I can never be your boyfriend again. I can't go through that with you again. It's against what I believe in, and fighting what I believe in ends me up hurt; and as much as I love you, I just can't do it again. Islam won't allow for me to have a girlfriend. Not now, not ever; it is what it is. So, I can't go there, I gotta live right. I don't think either of us can last in a round two of how we were living, do you? *I didn't think so.* And, I aaah, I guess, to avoid that, I instead want *you to be my wife.* There's a place in my heart and the only woman who can fill that place is you."

"*Your wife?*"

"Yeah, my wife. *Vacation over baby.* I need you back home."

I'm trying to stop blushing Athena, and being so happy. Because I'm happy, but, I've lost all faith in myself. *I'd just mess up in some way*, I can feel it.

"It won't work Omar. I'm too spoiled and messed up in the head. And I'm not good for you or your religion. I'm too messed up in my ways. I'll just bring you down, make you mess up again."

"No, *you won't.* I wouldn't let you, and you never had me messing up to begin with. If you recall, I was messing myself up, living foul before we started kickin' it, hustling, guns. But just like I was messing up, I've been fixing up. No way will my child come into this world with me out there in them streets, or both parents screwed up in the head, arguing through the house, police at the door, or fighting in the streets. And I don't want the baby to be born without us at least trying to make it work, especially when we *still in love*; what sense does that make Alisa. You denied it to yourself, *I know you*, but I **know** you in love with me too; I knew when you fell in love. Stop fighting it; stop fighting me."

I can't help but giggle at what he's saying. I'm proud of him, hoping what he got will rub off on me—maturity and religion. Guess he'll keep on until I give in; listen to him.

"We'll just have to have a good understanding, and I have to do everything Islamically. It's the only chance I have of not hustling. It keeps me balanced, and it will keep us balanced too. I'm not gonna force you, you know that, but I gotta do what I gotta do, or I'm doomed."

"I dunno. Too scared I'm gonna mess up and you'll leave me for good. Then I gotta go through that hurt and pain all over again. You don't know the hell I suffered at my own hand Omar."

Andrea Clinton

268 | Life Knows No Bounds

"If I wasn't trying to be on this deen correctly, I'd caress your face and kiss you softly, telling you, *'I got you,'* and **I've always had your back**. But since I am trying to live right, baby you just gonna have to let my words have the same sentiment. **I'm never leaving you again**, death will have to do us part, 'cause I'm in it to win it. And leaving don't make me feel no better. Breaking up makes me feel worse, lonely and all alone."

My goodness Athena, he is killing me right now. Lonely and all alone? Them my words. **He missed me tooooo.**

"Alisa look, as long as you don't take me for granted, and stop taking my kindness toward you for weakness, Allah, God willing, we'll be fine."

"And my spoiledness, you know that's going to take time, and you gotta stop laying the world at my feet. I like it too much. I mean I've grown, but I still like stuff, it's gonna take time."

"Understand, I love giving you the things you desire; I'm a man, a real man, and being able to give your lady nice things makes any man, *feel like a man.* Just dig ya-self, and don't make it all about you. I just want to do for you and my son what needs to be done, so we can make it in life and have nice things you know."

"Oh, it's a boy is it?"

"That's right it's a boy. I told you I'm a man.

"Whatever."

He got us both smiling.

"Stop changing the subject, we talking about marriage. On the real tip, we're gonna both end up trying to be with *somebody sooner or later* Alisa. I want it to be you, I need it to be you."

"Omar, before I answer I got something to get off my chest."

I'm pausing 'cause I feel I shouldn't share this with him, like maybe I should keep some things to myself. I already told him he spoil me too much, shootin' myself in the foot. But I guess you say this will show me how much I love him, huh? Well, here goes.

"My Great-Grandma once told me, on her deathbed, 'Get a man who loves you more than you love him.' She meant so I never have to worry about him being a tyrant. So he would love me so much he'd give me the world, and I could give him love and everything in return. She was basically saying to assure he'll love me too much to hurt me. But I didn't get everything she was saying, and it led me to other ideas, most of them confusing and wrong. Being young, silly, and practically raised by Tracey and her crew, I thought she meant for some ill reason, like to gain. Then I wondered if she meant so he would never leave me. I guess I'm saying, I rode on the coattail of what she said, throughout our relationship. I messed up, and just wanted you to know more of what was driving me when I was acting so crazy and out of my mind."

"I dunno, since I'm the man, how to address that. I mean what she actually meant don't sound bad at all. But I do know this Alisa, you need to love while you have a love. Boyfriends come and go, but real love only pops up every now and then. Just marry me, so the three of us can be a family like we were supposed to be *anyway.* We past due Baby-Girl. And we gotta make up for lost time. Marry me Alisa–"

"*Aiiighht,* I wanted to marry you anyway. I'll marry you."

"You better. Acting ghetto with that, 'Aiiighht.'"

We're both finding ourselves taking a breath of silence that's filled with relief.

"Alisa, I gotta tell you girl. I been losing my mind out here without you."

Oh man, I'm reaching out to touch him but he's sitting back so I cant touch him? We gotta get married **soon**; *this will never work.*

"No, no, no. No touching. I told you I'm doing *everything* right, Islamically. Allah don't have to punish me twice to get me to listen. I'm going to go call the *masjid* and see about getting things set up so we can get married. After we're married, you can come home and touch me all you want. But until then, back up fresh girl."

I miss his handsome smile, he's a sweetheart with his handsome self.

"But sweetie, you—you just touched my stomach."

"It was a reaction, I was in shock. Plus I was touching the baby, not you."

How is he laughing like he really believes that? He got me laughing too, but I'm laughing because I'm happy. I got my baby

Andrea Clinton

back. And I **ain't** ever lettin' this handsome chocolate bar go nowhere, no more.

"Omar, okay, it's been real, but can we leave and go get some ice cream from the restaurant? The baby wants ice cream."

"Okay baby, come on. I'll call the masjid from the deli."

Oooooh, the first time he's helping me up while I'm pregnant. Does that touching count?

"O', big wedding? Small? Soon? After the baby?"

And what a lovely ring Athena? Did you hear us both sing out, "Soon." Our souls miss one another and neither of us can live with the waves of absent affection between us.

We're finally in the place we both needed to be; we're together. And this time we're on the path to doing things right. We're leaving out now, but I promise we'll be back to celebrate our reception. I'll catch you up on everything, *I promise*, wink-wink.

P.S. Don't think 'cause it's all good between Omar and me, it's gonna stay all good. Haven't you learned *anything* about me yet? Ha-haaaaaaaaaaa!

"By the way Omar, you never told me you had a degree."

"Yeah, *masha'Allah*; God's will."

"A degree in what? Do tell."

"A bachelor's in engineering."

"What type of engineering?"

"Come on girl; think about it, I was a drug dealer. What type of engineering do you think?"

"Beats me. I don't know that stuff."

"Chemical Engineering, hahahaha. You still slow."

"I'm not slow, man shut up, and stop laughing at me. And why didn't you tell me?"

"Come on baby, you know I stay on the low, ssshhhh."

"Yeah but you kept that on the low for *a few years*; yeah okay, *I got ya low Omar*."

"*I bet you do*; I bet you do. Ssssswwwwh."

ON THE FLIP SIDE

Look at her. Aaaw man, I never thought she could get prettier. And I can't believe I'm back in it with Alisa again; *Oh Allah,* w*hat in the world have I gotten myself back into?*

To Be or Not To Be
Continued...
Let Me *Find* The Ways

Andrea Clinton